REVOLUTION

THE JACK RANDALL THRILLERS
BOOK 8

RANDALL WOOD

TENSION BOOKWORKS

For information contact:

Tension Bookworks

248 Nokomis Ave. Venice, FL 34285

www.tensionbookworks.com

Tension Bookworks and the portrayal of the screw are registered trademarks of Tension Bookworks.

Jacket and Cover design by Derek Murphy

Book design by Matty Dalrymple

Cataloging-in-Publication Data is on file at the Library of Congress

Wood, Randall, 1968-

Revolution / Randall Wood – 1st ed.

ISBN-13: 978-1-938825-66-8 (Ebook)

ISBN-13: 978-1-938825-64-4 (Paperback)

ISBN-13: 978-1-938825-65-1 (Large Print)

ISBN-13: 978-1-938825-39-2 (Hardcover)

ISBN-13: 978-1-938825-29-3 (Audio)

2024122701

WARNING!

This book ends in a cliffhanger!

The story of The Twelve Shepherds was originally released as a serial novel and was published in several separate episodes. Due to the readers' requests, it has now been re-published in novel form. The resulting manuscript was too large to fit into one novel and as a result the Shepherds saga will now encompass six novels.

This book, *REVOLUTION*, is part four of The Twelve Shepherds saga, and also book eight of the Jack Randall series.

The author and the publisher apologize for any confusion.

rev•o•lu•tion

a sudden, radical, or complete change

a fundamental change in political organization,
especially the overthrow or renunciation of one
government or ruler and the substitution of
another by the governed
activity or movement designed to effect
fundamental changes in the socioeconomic
situation

a fundamental change in the way of thinking
about or visualizing something: a change of
paradigm

1

———

"No one can prevent hurricanes, but prosperous communities are much better able to withstand them than poor ones."

—*Robert Zubrin*

S quirrel gazed into the building through the broken storefront window. This one had become that way courtesy of a metal sign that had been flung across the street by the wind. The sign now lay inside, covered in a layer of broken glass and rainwater. *Department 229, Used Furniture* it read in bold red letters. Links of chain trailed across the floor after it. As he stepped inside, the odd shapes of couches and chairs and stacked mattresses broke up his view of the interior. His feet crunched on the broken glass, and he scraped the tiny fragments off the bottom of his Jordans before walking on the concrete floor. An old mirror caught his reflection, and he flinched before realizing what it was.

He reflexively looked behind him for witnesses. It was how he got his name. Not that he liked it, but he had to admit he had earned it. He was always on edge, indecisive, flinching at the slightest threat. Never sitting still, always in motion. Like a squirrel.

As soon as the storm had passed, he had fled the house. His mother had wanted him to check on the neighbors, but he had other ideas. When the power had gone out, he'd started planning. But he was limited by geography. That and income. He didn't have a car, so he was forced to confine his looting to the area he lived in. He'd quickly ruled out houses—in this neighborhood that meant getting shot. He had started with the few remaining businesses on this block. So far, he'd not come up with much. A few dollars from a desk in the back of the laundromat, and a handful of jewelry at the consignment shop. The liquor store was already being emptied, and when he arrived the owners had just shown up with shotguns. The others had fled, and he had as well, moving on to easier prey.

There had to be an office or something in this place; he just had to find it. Creeping farther into the back, he left behind the faint light coming in through the broken window. He ran into a table, and it screeched as he moved it across the floor. He knocked over a chair and lamp, and he stopped to rub his shin where they had connected.

The wind howled through the broken glass, and a painting fell from the wall with a crash behind him. He cried out and leaped away, dragging his plastic shopping bag of loot behind him and toppling more clutter.

Catching his breath from the scare, he sat down on an overstuffed couch. He should have brought his friend Coby with him. Coby was fat and dumb, but he wasn't afraid of everything. Together, they had powered their way through similar situations before. But Coby's mother wouldn't let him out, so Squirrel was on his own. He planted his hands to push himself up and was almost on his feet when the couch next to him flew apart with a geyser of stuffing.

The blast of the shotgun overpowered the raging wind for only a second, but it was all Squirrel needed to hear. He found himself face down on the cold tile but scrambled to his feet and was running. Any thoughts of looting were driven from his mind.

He rounded a chair just as it too burst apart.

"Run, motherfucker!" A yell went out behind him, followed by another blast.

Squirrel forgot about the crooked path through the furniture and ran over the tops of them as fast as his twelve-year-old legs could push him. Gasping for breath and with ringing ears, he sought only to escape.

The shotgun roared again, and he dove for the floor between two couches, only to be coated with stuffing and bits of cheap leather.

"Run, little boy. Run!"

Squirrel ran, faster now toward the front, desperate to escape the laughing man behind him. He flung himself through the broken window just as the one next to it exploded outward. He landed on the sidewalk. Shards rained down, cutting his face and back. Several pieces were shoved into his hands as he pushed himself up and off the wet concrete to run down the road. The glass in the soles of his Jordans slipped on the wet concrete, and he slid headfirst into the puddled street. He ignored it and jumped up again, rounding the corner with tears in his eyes and fear pounding in his heart. Behind him, he heard the man roaring with laughter.

In front of the furniture store stood Sanford Brown. The smoking shotgun was clamped in his fist as he doubled over with laughter at the sight of the fleeing boy. The laughter was maniacal and showed no sign of stopping. Eventually the wind brought some rain, and the laughter died to a chuckle. He looked across the street to find his boss standing in the doorway with a large handgun in his fist.

He did not look happy.

"What?" Sanford spread his arms, proclaiming innocence.

"You gonna bring every cop in town!"

Sanford gestured around with the shotgun.

"Ain't none of them gonna call nobody! I was just having some fun!"

"Well, have your fun over here and do it quiet!" The man turned and went back inside.

SAMUEL JACKSON STORMED BACK into the building and waved the gun at his second-in-command.

"Dumbass is out there shooting at kids!"

"Kids?"

"Some kid poking through the warehouse across the street. As if I don't have enough problems! We got power yet? What the hell is taking so long?"

Samuel Jackson was not a tall man, built more like a fireplug. Short and wide and low to the ground. A heavy frame wrapped in heavy muscle. His large bald head and thick neck helped to solidify the description. A product of the streets, he had been labeled with many nicknames based on his appearance while coming up, but none of them were lobbed in his direction anymore. Not since he had become the head of drug operations in Miami. Anyone who did so quickly found themselves breathing in ocean water. His scarred hand now used the .357 as a pointer, and despite its large frame it looked tiny in the man's grasp.

"I want some more people here, too. You get ahold of anybody?"

"Power's out and so are the cell towers. Sat phone's working. The second generator don't want to start for some reason. I got the first wired to the lights and the refrigerator. That's about all it'll handle. If the second one decides to start, I'll hook up the air."

"Mother—" Jackson stopped himself. He'd been trying hard not to use the word since the actor he shared a name with had gotten so famous for it. Wasn't his fault, he was older; his momma had named him that first.

Jackson stopped and wiped the sweat off his head for the hundredth time since he'd woken up that morning in a pool of it. The air conditioning had been off since early the previous day, and the combination of the wind, rain, heat, and humidity had made sleep next to impossible. On top of that, his place was damaged. Not his beachside mansion—that was flooded beyond all hope—but his strip club, where he spent his time and did business. He wanted to send someone to find another generator, but he had nobody to send. His crew was now made up of three people, with another one hopefully on the way. When, he didn't know, since the conversation had been cut off by the cell phone service dying. The whole damn town was coming apart.

A damn hurricane. Not his first one—he'd survived Andrew when he was a kid and a couple smaller ones since, but he wasn't supplying drugs for half the east coast back then.

Things were different now: he had a business to run.

"Who we got?"

"Still just you and me. Sanford and the kid out front. If Dom makes it here, that's five."

Jackson nodded at his second. He had always been his second. Wallace was his name, and he had never acquired another. A detail man. They had been together since high school. At first running pot and working the playgrounds and football games. Then branching out into the neighborhoods. Jackson was wise enough to see that territory was money and he spent his profits on muscle and hardware until he owned half the town. A major war with his rival the year before had given him a majority stake. With that over, he'd worked at branching out, becoming a major supplier for the east coast traffickers. He now ran an empire—one with cops, judges, politicians, and Coast Guard officers on the payroll. All managed from his bar in lower Miami. The same bar he now stood sweating in, while outside Nature showed her strength. For once in many years, he was powerless, both literally and figuratively.

He paced the room twice before walking to the door again. Here the breeze offered some relief from the heat. Sanford and a young kid named

Kobe sat outside on bar stools they had pulled from inside, standing guard under the tattered awning to keep out of the rain. Sanford cradled the shotgun in his arm and was busy wiping it down, while the kid had a pistol tucked under one leg to keep it both out of sight and dry.

"They come back?"

Sanford snorted. "Hell no. They workin' the street a couple blocks down, headin' south."

Looters. Dumb ones. They had worked their way down the street, breaking into the surrounding businesses before being driven away by a blast from Sanford's shotgun early that morning. Evidently, it had been enough for them to remember who owned the bar, and they were now giving it a wide berth. Except for the kid Sanford had just scared off, they had not returned.

Jackson eyeballed the two. The man with the shotgun was his best muscle. A big man who enjoyed getting bigger. He now sported a tank top two sizes too small, soaked in sweat and rain, and a pair of wraparound sunglasses. Like Jackson, he was a product of the streets and had been in his employment off and on between prison stays for many years. What skin wasn't covered in tattoos was covered in scars. Usually the sight of him alone was enough to extract the desired result.

Nevertheless, Jackson had learned to use Sanford very selectively, as the man's temperament was one of thinly controlled anger. That, and he had a taste for young flesh, something Jackson frowned upon, but was willing to overlook to get the results he needed. So far Sanford had proven to be very reliable in that regard.

The other man was little more than a kid. Kobe something. Jackson didn't know his last name and didn't really care to. A street kid and self-imposed orphan, he had somehow worked his way into Jackson's organization simply by showing up every day. Odd jobs became regular ones until he was not so much an accepted member, but more like a familiar piece of furniture. He did as he was told and never spoke unless addressed. Otherwise he faded into the background until needed. Where he lived and what he did were not in Jackson's memory, but he had been checked out by Sanford and deemed useful. What he lacked in intelligence he made up for in work ethic. Even today, with the hurricane not even fully gone, he had simply appeared out of the damage and looting and reported for work. Jackson had nodded approval before sending him outside with Sanford to counter the looters.

Jackson scanned the streets. The storm had

done some serious damage. Power lines were down and crisscrossing the streets. Windows were broken. The higher ones by the storm, the lower ones by the looters, but it was hard to tell the difference. A sign for a pawn shop three blocks away was now resting on a car parked across the street. The three palm trees in sight were stripped of their fronds. The rain still fell, occasionally pushed horizontally by the gusting wind. It would take weeks to clean up, and since their neighborhood was not rich and white, they wouldn't start here for some time. Jackson estimated he'd be without air conditioning for at least a month. Sirens sounded in the distance, and he automatically turned his head in their direction, but all he saw was a fat woman with a shopping cart crossing the street a block away. The cart was full of liquor bottles lifted from a nearby store.

"Nothing else to do," Jackson mumbled before looking beyond her. There was nobody else in sight.

"Any sign of Dom?"

"Nope. No cell service back up yet, either. He said he's coming in," Sanford replied with a shrug. Dom would show up when he showed up it said.

Jackson cursed and pitched his cigarette into the street before turning and stalking back inside.

He stopped to eyeball Sanford and pointed to the shotgun.

"Keep that thing quiet."

"You got it, boss."

Sanford watched his boss spin around to the sound of the satellite phone ringing. He watched him go before turning his gaze to Kobe. The boy was silent as usual, but his eyes were watching the end of the shotgun as it tracked back and forth across his chest with every stroke of the oil rag.

"Thing only works by making noise," Sanford told him before smiling that evil grin of his. Kobe put on his best tough-guy face and nodded in agreement before turning his gaze back to the street.

Like the men he now worked for, Kobe was a product of the streets. Born to a crackhead mother who turned tricks out of their small apartment, he had no idea who his father was. In and out of his grandmother's care most of his younger life, and back and forth to his mother's during brief periods of her being clean, he'd learned early on to fend for himself. After failing the eighth grade twice, he'd given up on school all together. Despite the years of education, Kobe could barely read and write. When a signature was called for, he man-aged two capital letters followed by an illegible scribble. He'd been arrested three times in his short life, for petty theft and burglary. Claiming hunger as his motive, he'd been let off easy all three times. He'd received probation and appointments with the social services office, which he always managed to forget.

Two of his friends had died from drugs. One from an overdose right in front of him, and the other shot through the head when he had tried to rob a fifteen-year-old dealer. Kobe had learned to stay away and, other than the occasional beer to fit in with the older kids, had, against all odds, stayed clean.

He divided his time between his mother's apartment, the nearby "jungles" where the homeless resided, and abandoned buildings when the weather was bad. He showered at the mission or the nearby "Sally," Salvation Army, when he needed it, and sat through droning sermons at the nearby church if breakfast was included. When the traffic at his mother's place got too high, he would find cars to steal and live out of. Temporary housing, as he liked to call it.

When burglary of houses and businesses had proven to be too dangerous, he'd turned to cars. There, he had found his niche. First using them for housing before taking their stereos and GPS units and then learning to hot-wire the older models and taking the whole car. He sold the stereos to fences and the cars to chop shops, and the income was enough to keep him off the streets. One of the chop shops had hired him on occasion to deliver a car they had "remodeled," and Kobe had found himself working for Samuel Jackson's outfit. Once there, he had hung around until they gave him a job.

Now here he was, sitting outside a strip club in the middle of a hurricane, watching a madman clean his shotgun.

Jackson stormed inside to find the phone ringing. Wallace answered it and then held it out for him.

"Bennie in New York," he whispered as Jackson took it.

"Yeah?"

"Where's my stuff?"

"Been a little busy here."

"With what?"

"Turn on the TV, man. It was a hurricane! What you want from me? I don't control the damn weather!"

"I want product. You said you could deliver, so deliver."

"I *have* product. There's just nothin' moving. Airport's shut down. I got no boats. Cops got the highways all closed. If it wasn't for this fancy-ass phone I wouldn't even be talkin' to yo fat ass!"

"I don't give a shit about your storm. If you want your money, get me my product by Friday, or I'll go somewhere else."

Jackson opened his mouth to protest but the phone was already emitting the warble of a severed satellite connection. He fought the urge to throw it across the room, but reined himself in. It was his only connection to the world right now. He needed it. Without a word, he turned and stomped across the room, tossing the phone to his second-in-command as he did so.

"The man ain't happy," Wallace observed.

"Asshole don't even watch TV long enough to know there's a damn storm outside!"

He paced the floor and frowned at the sound of the wind. It was a symbiotic relationship he had with the east coast mobsters. He was taking in about a million a week profit, four million a month, all in cash that had to be laundered. Big stacks of money that had to be turned into legitimate income that he could then invest or hide off-shore. It was a problem that most would love to have, but still a problem.

With his Columbian connections importing him raw product directly he gained an edge. The Mexican gangs took a cut for their services, and by not going through them he had used that advantage and become not just the major supplier here in Miami, but the source of product for several outfits on the upper east coast. The discount he got from the Columbians helped offset what he charged on the other. In return for product at a cheaper price, the outfits gave him access to their money laundering operations. Something Jackson seemed to be in ever greater need of. He needed to keep the supply going or his customers would simply take their needs elsewhere. It was simple business, something that Jackson understood very well.

Drugs. It was a business like no other, and few understood it as well as he did. Through a combination of common sense, a superior IQ, and an ability to turn any situation to his advantage, Jackson had risen to the top. Adaptability. It was what had gotten him here more than anything. Today presented a unique problem, but it was far from being his first.

Most of his problems were caused by the

people who worked for him. Some took a liking to the product they dealt with. Some got too greedy or liked to show off their wealth to the wrong people. Some talked themselves into thinking they were more important than they were. These people became dangerous to Jackson's business. When someone fell into this category, the answer was swift and decisive. They simply disappeared.

His other problems were mostly about territory. He had fought those wars coming up, and the threat of a rival operation was no longer at the top of the list. Now his territory battles were of the internal nature. Dealer A wanting more territory and was willing to battle with Dealer B to get it. Like a father with squabbling children, Jackson handed down discipline harshly, and his dealers soon learned to stay in bounds.

But since the drug business was cash only, he also had to be ever watchful for cheaters and thieves. Despite his ruthless reputation, every few months one would try—the last one's burned and mutilated body had been found on the corner where he had worked. The coroner had said whoever had done it had used a welding torch and started at the man's feet. The lesson had not gone unnoticed. Most on the streets and in the force had shrugged it off. It had just been Samuel

Jackson taking care of business, something they had come to expect. But then some on the force had known it was coming before it happened.

Jackson understood that the cheaters, the thieves, the internal issues, and even the mobsters he dealt with, were all less of a threat compared to the police. From the locals and all the way up to the DEA and FBI they were his number one problem. To counter that threat, Jackson had invested heavily in bribes. He found cops and agents and politicians that he could buy, and he gladly spent the cash. He now had people at every level, from the locals here in south Miami to the offices in Washington DC. He often knew of any operations against him before they even got started. He had people everywhere.

Yet, here he was today. With a flooded beachside home. A bar with no power. A crew he could count on one hand, and nothing to reach the outside world with but a damn satellite phone.

"Whatcha wanna do, J?" Wallace asked.

Jackson pulled out his pack of cigarettes and mentally counted its contents. He may have to ration what he had left, but not right now. He lit up another and took a strong drag before answering.

"How much we got in the crib?"

"Fifty."

"Fifty? You're sure?"

"Fifty," Wallace repeated.

"We got to get it north, something better than this morning's idea."

"How?"

"I don't know, mutha! But if we don't, those assholes will go west coast on us, and we'll have to go to war again to get back on top. So how about you think of something?"

"Okay, okay. Boats are all out?"

"Every one of 'em. Even if they weren't, ain't nobody going out in that storm. Suicide. And I'm sure as hell not risking fifty keys on a boat right now. What's it doing, anyway?"

"Weather chick says it's gonna cross the state and either head north into Alabama or Mississippi from there, or it could stall out in the Gulf before it turns around and heads north-east again."

"Damn. We gotta hurry."

"What you thinking?"

Jackson wiped the sweat from his bald head again and walked behind the bar. He poured a shot of whisky, neat, as if he had a choice, while he gave it some thought.

Downstairs in the back of the walk-in cooler were fifty kilos of uncut cocaine earmarked for his contacts up north. DC. Baltimore. Newark. New

York. He had to get them there—and soon. But there were no planes flying. No boats leaving. And this damn storm, which was supposed to have tracked well south of them, was now turning around to screw them a second time. He had to get the fifty kilos north, now. A simple A to B problem.

"I see only one option."

2

———————

In September of 1989, Hurricane Hugo, a Category 5 storm, caused $7 billion in damages and killed 50 people.

Tyler Turner examined the damage outside his house through the cracked window in the front door. At first glance the car looked okay. The one palm tree in the yard had been stripped bare during the night and then laid flat on the ground next to the Chevy, missing it by inches. Taking in the view of the surrounding homes, he saw enough space to drive through the yard to his neighbor's driveway to reach the street.

"What you waiting for?" he asked himself before pulling his hoodie up over his head and venturing out.

He pulled some stray fronds from the hood of the car and a plastic bag from where it had become snagged on the wiper blade. Releasing the bag to the wind, he watched as it was rapidly carried aloft and sucked away to the west. The winds were still strong, mostly steady now, but still gusting enough to bend the trees. Debris made its way down the street, mostly trash from the nearby yards, as that was the kind of neighborhood he lived in. He eyeballed the ditch in front of his house. Full of brown water with ripples on the surface. It would take weeks to drain. The mosquitos would be fierce for days.

Putting it all aside, he pulled the rear door open and threw his bag in. The wind tried to slam his hand inside, but he stopped it by planting his body in front of it. Pulling a cell phone from his coat, he shoved that inside as well before letting the door slam and opening the driver's door. The seat was wet on the passenger side, but he ignored it. The quality of the window seal was the last thing on his mind this morning.

He inserted the key and held his breath before turning it. The motor ground and made an effort before stalling. He stopped. Was it going to start? Everything was wet. The battery. The wires. Everything. The hurricane had made sure of it. But he didn't have a backup. So he tried again, this time letting it go for a few rounds. The engine caught and he carefully fed it gas to keep it going. After a minute, he let up and the car settled into a smooth idle. He adjusted the seat and turned on the wipers.

The view out the front windshield was of the tiny row house he had occupied for the past eleven months. A Florida home they called it. Probably built sometime in the early '70s. A concrete block structure with a stucco exterior. A semi-flat roof sheathed in metal. Ancient crank-out windows, which had been broken and replaced many times, sat behind metal bars that had been added when the neighborhood started to decline. A one-car carport had been added to one side and now held all manner of used appliances and car parts and other trash. It seemed to be a requirement on this street, and he was amazed it was all still there.

Other than adding a new deadbolt and some hidden cameras, he had done nothing in the way of repairs or improvements since landing there. Still, the little house had survived the latest hurricane. Just one of many in its past, so he had to give it some respect for that. Battered and broken, it still stood. It was a survivor, like him.

Dropping the car in gear, he turned away. He might not see the house again, but if he did, he might have to put some time into fixing a few things. Not sure why—he didn't even own it—but he felt he owed it somehow. He took some small amount of comfort knowing that if he did come back, the little house would be waiting for him.

He idled the car through the tall grass, out his neighbor's driveway and into the street without getting stuck in the flooded yard. Forced to weave around fallen trees, downed wires, and rolling trashcans he eventually made it to a major road.

Cars were on the streets, but not many. Some people out and about looking at the damage. A few were wearing orange vests and hardhats. They were gazing up at the power lines and speaking into radios. He steered away from them. Progress was slow due to the debris everywhere. All the stoplights were out, and he was forced to wait for hesitant drivers moving across intersections. The freeway was closed, blocked off by heavy barrels and a cop with a radio, so he was forced to the secondary roads. He glanced at the dash clock and cursed. He was going to be late. But then the person he was meeting was also driving through this mess as well. They would both just get there when they got there.

Luckily, the GPS still worked, and he used it to find his way north as best he could. The city looked eerie in the strange light, the concrete holding a green tint like the sky possessed right now. Some of the buildings seemed to glow in the stabs of sunlight that would briefly break through the marching cloud cover. Their surfaces had been power washed by the storm and were now free of their dirty coats of dust. It distracted him enough that he almost missed the building he was traveling to.

The strip mall parking lot was empty, but he wasn't surprised. It was made up of the usual collection of tax offices, Chinese take-out, beauty parlors and laundromats, but there was nothing here anyone needed today, that was for sure. Not to mention the early hour. He circled the building once and then parked facing the street. He was alone. Getting out, he stretched and yawned. The storm had robbed him of both sleep and coffee.

Scanning the area and seeing no activity, he walked to the tax office and let himself in. He tested the lights and was surprised to find that the place had power.

"Should have spent the night here," he mumbled before turning the light off and making his way to the back room by the light of the window. He went past two empty offices and a storage room, before finding the back door inside a small conference room. He unlocked it and then took a piece of sheet magnet covered in blue tape off the door. Opening it just wide enough to see out the back, he slapped the magnet on the door and closed it. Finding a chair, he pulled the .45 from his belt and set it on the table before leaning back to wait.

He'd almost dozed off when he heard a car outside. The wind almost hid the sound of the person's arrival. The footsteps were also muted, but not the knock. Twice. And twice again.

"Come on in," he yelled as he set the gun down.

The white man was tall and thin. Dressed in a pair of jeans, T-shirt, and a windbreaker. A pair of hunting boots were on his feet, and they were wet, the same as his salt-and-pepper hair, which was plastered on his head. Evidently, it was raining much harder in the direction he had come from. The clothes were rumpled, and he needed a shave. In his left hand, he held two paper bags sporting grease stains. In the other, he held a cardboard carrier with two steaming cups in it. He set them down without any greeting. They were long past that.

His name was Special Agent Lyle Smith, and he was with the Drug Enforcement Agency. They had known each other for over a year, ever since Smith had recruited him from his department back in Michigan. It was not the first time they'd had a meeting in this office, but it had been two weeks since the last one.

"Please tell me that's fresh coffee."

"The diner next to the station is still up and running. They've been keeping us supplied all night. You hungry?"

"Starving. I lost power soon as it hit. Nothing in the house but a cold can of soup and some melting frozen food."

"What kind of soup?"

"Tomato."

"Sounds tasty."

Smith tossed him a bag, and they both ate in silence for a few minutes.

"You look tired," Smith remarked.

"So do you," Tyler answered before stuffing another breakfast sandwich in his mouth.

Smith smiled at the blunt answer. It was just like the man.

Deputy Tyler Turner of Detroit sat in the office chair dressed in street clothes: faded jeans, a T-shirt with Jay Z on the front and a black do-rag. The earring and gold chains were new, as were his posture and his walk. A man of Dominican descent, he was a third-generation cop on loan to the DEA from the Detroit gang unit and had been working undercover for Smith for the last eleven months. "A little undercover work that would be great for his future career," they'd told him. It was a half-lie that they both knew but never acknowledged out loud. Smith almost regretted it, but it was too late now to do anything. The man was in too deep.

"How's it looking?"

Turner chewed and swallowed. "Good. I'm next to the man himself. Jackson's making money like he's printing it. I did the drops the other night and—"

Smith cut him off. "Hold on." He reached in his jacket and pulled out the recorder. Uncoiling the charger, he plugged it in the usual outlet and hit the record button. Turner sipped his coffee.

Smith dictated his name and the date and who he was meeting with into the machine before playing it back to be sure it was working. He set it on the table between them, next to Turner's gun, and motioned for him to continue. Unknown to Smith, Turner's recorder was already running in his pocket.

"What's so damn important it couldn't wait?"

"Got a call this morning, right before I called you and then the cell service went out. Jackson is hurtin' for people. His crew is scattered, or out of contact because of the storm. He was behind on deliveries *before* the storm hit. He's gotta be desperate to move some product now. Wallace told me to come in as soon as possible and to pack a bag."

"So, that just might mean you're gonna be staying there for a while."

"I'm not so sure. I think I might be taking a trip."

"You think he's going to *drive* the stuff up?"

"What other options are there? Airports are closed. Coast Guard has the ports all locked down. Only an idiot would take a boat out in that weather. I wouldn't get on one now even if they weren't. Besides, he'd never risk the product like that."

"I don't know," Lyle stalled.

"This is too good! If I can get in that car, I can connect Jackson with everyone he's dealing with. DC for sure. But I counted fifty kilos in the cooler last Tuesday and nothin' has gone out, man. Nothin'! DC won't get all that. Fifty is too much, even for them. I bet it goes to at least two other outfits, maybe even three or four. This is our chance to bust the whole chain."

"You'd be on your own. No backup or way to track you. I don't like it."

"We'll never get another chance like this!"

Lyle eyeballed the man in front of him. The new tattoo on his arm was a reminder. Tyler had gotten it to cover up a Marine Corps tattoo from years ago just so he could do undercover work. The man's devotion to the job was without question, but it was his aggressiveness that worried Lyle. Of all the undercover operators he had worked with, Tyler was the hardest to deal with. Always wanting more. Attack. It was drilled into him by the Corps, and as his handler Lyle constantly worried about him overreaching. One slipup and Tyler would simply disappear. Tossed off the back of one of the three boats Jackson used, never to be seen again.

But he had to admit, Tyler was smart. Tough

and bold, as well. He was also a natural actor. All of these traits had served to get him close to Samuel Jackson in a matter of only ten months.

"If he tells me to do it and I don't," Tyler said, "we're done."

"We can go to the grand jury with what we have already," Smith stalled again.

"We could have done that a month ago, and that still only gets us Jackson. If I go on this delivery, we get the whole network."

Smith racked his brain for options but couldn't find any. He desperately wanted to run this by his boss, but there was no time. And there was nobody else to consult with. They were the only two men who knew who Tyler Turner even was and what he was doing.

"Lemme think for a minute. First tell me about your time." He waved to the recorder.

Turner covered the last two weeks of his job from memory. Smith took notes as fast as Turner talked. Names, addresses, quantities of drugs delivered, descriptions, estimated amounts of cash. The money involved was big. Turner was estimating an average of 80k in cash from thirteen different drop-off points. Daily. And that was just the trade here in Miami. Jackson was also supplying the entire upper east coast. What Turner was learning was some of the best intelligence Smith had ever gathered. On top of this, the man knew what it took to build a case and was careful to separate what he knew to be fact from his own opinions. He spoke for twenty minutes without stopping, and Lyle didn't interrupt. He then went over everything twice, asking a number of questions. After an hour, the lights flickered, reminding them.

"I need to go, man. Jackson's waiting. What's it gonna be?"

"I don't like it," he said.

Turner had been waiting for that. He had planned his argument on the way over, and he now played it.

"Think about it. Jackson's supplying the east coast right now. That means the New York, Boston and Jersey outfits are probably washing his money for him. If I go on this trip, I can connect Jackson to all of them. But that's not even the best part."

Smith knew he was being baited, but he took it anyway.

"And what's that?"

"We make all the connections, but we sit on them. We don't move on the east coast until we're ready."

"Why would we do that?"

"'Cause as soon as Jackson goes down, they'll need another source of product. Most likely it'll come from the west coast ..." He let the statement trail off on purpose.

Smith refused to go there. Turner just gave him his poker face before pushing it.

"You just gonna sit there and tell me you don't have another nigga-on-a-string out west just like me? C'mon, man!"

Smith ignored the barb and sipped his coffee. It had gone cold, so he pushed it aside.

"I don't. But I'm sure somebody does."

"Well, all right then."

"No. There's no 'all right then.' You and I are too low to make that decision." Smith pointed at his charge and scolded him, "Don't go off thinking like a cowboy on this. Not how it works. You know how long cowboys last: eight seconds."

"Look. I'm tight with the man and getting tighter, but I'm not involved in anything around the long-range deliveries. I'm not in the inner cir-cle. Jackson keeps that all compartmented. I never see the stuff come in and I never see it go out. I'm just in the local stuff. Sure, I hear talk about the boats and the cars and even a train once, but nothing else. This is our chance to pull the whole thing down, including the cops and politicians on the take. Then, when the east coast outfits switch to the west coast, you've got even more. Opportunity is knocking."

Smith toyed with the recorder. Turner stuffed the last of his sandwich in his mouth and chewed hard, watching the man think.

"All right, go. But keep your phone on you!"

"I'll call when I can, dad." He was already up and moving toward the door. Lyle groaned and watched him go. But not before issuing a final word.

"Damn it, Tyler. You get dead and I swear I'll piss on your grave."

The man cackled. "I got this, man. Gimme seven more days and we're done. We'll get a beer and see a Pistons game." The man walked away before Lyle could reply.

Lyle had opened his mouth to call him back, but clamped it shut instead. Tyler was right; they'd never get another chance like this. He still had a bad feeling as he watched him feel his way down the dark hallway to the front door. He waited until the door slammed shut behind him before getting up and unplugging the charger. He wound it around his fingers as he walked to the front of the office. He was just in time to see Tyler's car leave the lot. If Tyler kept his cell phone on him, one that had been modified to maintain GPS location without showing it on the screen, he could still find him.

But that meant little if the man was dead when Smith did.

3

59.2 million. Population, as of July 1, 2015, of the 185 coastline counties stretching from Maine to Texas.

Sydney watched as the pile of paper she had abandoned on the table jumped into the air a few inches and landed several more inches away from its takeoff point.

Two more of those and it's on the floor, she thought.

She had no plans of trying to stop it. Her hands

were firmly planted on the armrests, and she had already tightened her seatbelt to the point it was making her legs numb. In an effort to fight off the growing nausea, she turned her head to look out the window. The plane was descending rapidly. Into what, she couldn't tell. The sky was an odd grey-green color behind a thick layer of rain. They were passing through the tail end of hurricane Nancy, a category four storm that had already battered Miami and, to a lesser extent, Jupiter, their current destination.

A rattle of paper drew her attention back inside, and she saw Jack flipping through a stack of documents in the seat across from her. If the bouncing plane and sickening downdrafts had any effect on him, he didn't show it. Other than turning on the overhead light when they entered the clouds, he had done nothing to even acknowledge the rough ride. It irritated her.

"You enjoying this?"

He looked up. "What?"

"This storm! You enjoying it? Why do I let myself get talked into these things? 'The storm will be gone by the time we get there,' you said! Does it look like sunny Florida outside to you?"

She bit off the accusation as the plane took another sudden drop. Her stomach threatened to leave via her throat, but she managed to keep its contents down until the plane regained somewhat normal flight.

Jack glanced out the window at the storm and then back to her.

"It's a storm, Syd. Nothing we can do about it, so why worry?"

"I—"

Before she could say more, the overhead speaker crackled, and the calm voice of the pilot filled their ears.

"Land in about ten minutes," he informed them, not a trace of strain in his delivery. The man was as calm as a Hindu cow. It did nothing but infuriate her more.

"Why?" she repeated her question.

"We need a break in this case, Syd. The Shepherds just took out another one. Why would we not check it out?"

"I thought ... I thought we were trying to stay ahead of them? Let the locals work the scenes and leave us to focus on the big picture. What happened to that?"

Jack frowned but had to agree with her. The Twelve Shepherds case was a monster. A vigilante group that had operated in over a dozen states so far, taking out those they felt had escaped justice.

The press had had them on the front page almost every day for the last eight months. The Shepherds had targeted six people before killing a federal judge who had been taking bribes. That made it a federal case. The FBI had taken over, and Jack had been assigned to lead the investigation. So far, he had failed.

A few days ago, he and his team had captured a member of the group, but before he could be fully interrogated, the man had been sprung from captivity by his colleagues and escaped, putting the investigation back to square one and Jack in the cross hairs of several politicians. He had been leaving California and on his way back to DC when the Shepherds had struck again. This time in Florida. Jack had taken the opportunity to buy himself some time. He split the team, sending most of them back to DC, while he and Sydney diverted to Florida to see what they could learn from the latest target. Jack was hoping the side trip would bear some fruit, as he needed some ammunition to face the political beasts he'd be squaring off against in DC. The hurricane passing through the area had not really factored much into his decision. His plan was to land, check out the crime scene while the plane flew to Georgia for some routine maintenance, then return to pick them up before flying on to DC. The scheduled maintenance was a convenient excuse. It would buy him three days at most. At least that had been the timetable he had told his boss.

"We are. I just ... I need some time, Syd. There are people back home that are not happy. Especially when they see this."

He held up a copy of the *New York Times*. The headline read: Occupy Movement Storms the Offices of Goldman Sachs.

Sydney swallowed and immediately regretted it. Her stomach was doing flips now. A moment later, she felt the plane level out a bit and the ride smoothed some.

"You ... you think they're related?"

"I don't know what to think," he replied. "But I wouldn't count it out. They may be directly related, or one is just encouraging the other. Or it's a combination of both. I need time to think, and I just don't have enough."

Another round of turbulence strained their seatbelts and was punctuated by the sound of the gear coming down. The plane began to fishtail as the pilot fought the wind to line them up on the approaching runway. Sydney leaned into the aisle in an effort to see out the cockpit windows but saw nothing but a wall of water and clouds.

"Robert will get us on the ground fine," Jack reassured her.

"If he doesn't ... I'm puking on him first," she answered before grabbing the armrest again.

"First?"

"Don't laugh, you're second."

Jack laughed anyway, his first in several days, before going back to the paperwork and leaving her alone with her stomach. While he had been scanning the papers, his thoughts had been elsewhere. They needed a break in the case, something he could use to make up for the escaped Shepherd and the negative headlines.

What that break might be he had no idea. He hoped to find it in Florida, because it certainly wasn't in the pile of paper he had in his hand.

He tucked the papers under his leg and turned off the cabin lights, so they wouldn't reflect off the cockpit windows. Outside, the rain streaked across the Plexiglas and the light changed every few seconds as the clouds raced by. They broke out of the clouds only a few seconds before the gear hit and, true to the pilot's word, the plane survived to land in one piece.

Sydney calmed her stomach and pried her hands loose from the chair before unbuckling and gathering the papers from the floor.

"This better be worth it, Jack."
Jack didn't reply, but he had to agree.

AN HOUR LATER, Jack stood in the doorway of a small house, staring at the taped outline of the victim on the floor. His coat blew up a bit and he grabbed it before it could brush against the frame. Every surface around him was covered in a thin layer of volcanic ash left over from the forensics team. The door and frame were intact; no sign that someone had forced it. It had been opened voluntarily from the inside.

Glancing behind him, he stepped back two paces and held out his hand, his finger extended. He pumped an imaginary round into the outline and then lowered his hand with a frown, before looking across the room to the couch. A small card with a number on it told him where the envelope had landed. It was a clear shot.

"No mud inside? No footprints?"

His question was directed at Sydney on the other side of the room. She was examining a stack of pictures taken of the body before it had been removed. The question was loud since the wind was still blowing pretty hard.

"Doesn't look like it. Just rainwater and dog prints. Whoever did this got no farther than the door."

"No need to," Jack muttered.

"What?"

"Nothing."

Jack walked back to the driveway and let the crime scene workers flow around him. The ride here from the airport had been long and full of detours around flooded areas. All of them due to the hurricane that was still leaving the area. A storm the killer had made good use of, it looked like.

"Why did he open the door?"

"Sir?"

A passing tech had heard Jack talking to himself. He waved her off with a smile and shake of his head before walking to the sidewalk and gaining some space. The humidity and wind were still high, and Jack was sweating under his coat now. But he was already short of clean clothes, and with the sky promising more rain, he kept it on. There were no laundry facilities on the plane.

"Who opens the door in a hurricane? Who would you even expect to see out in a hurricane?"

The question stuck. In normal weather, the possibilities were endless, but in weather this severe, the person knocking had to look like they belonged there.

He watched the parade of people moving about the scene. A cop? Or perhaps someone dressed as one? A neighbor needing help? Not likely. The man was a recluse, for obvious reasons, and none of the neighbors had even spoken to him outside of the occasional "hello" on the sidewalk. No one had reported any visitors or strange vehicles. A fireman or volunteer checking on people? Maybe, but they did that before and after the storm, not while it was in full swing.

"Any ideas?"

Jack turned to find the local detective assigned to the case on the sidewalk with him.

"Not really. How we doing?"

"Canvass is through. We went a block in both directions. One neighbor claims she saw a car leaving the house across the street around the estimated time of death. It's been vacant for six months. The garage door was open on arrival, so we checked it out. Nothing. There's a ton of prints everywhere, but you'd expect them with the house being for sale. No traces of anyone being inside other than what you would expect from normal traffic. Doors and windows are all intact. The locks are all good. The agent says she hasn't shown the house in a few weeks, but other agents have. We're tracking them down from the cards they left behind. Everybody else was hunkered down and watching the storm on TV. Nobody heard a thing either, but with that wind I'm not surprised. The convenience store at the end of the street has cameras that catch the intersection. A few cars and a FEMA truck, but the cameras are aimed at the parking lot and not really angled to catch plates out in the street. The distance was too great anyway, plus the lens was pretty fogged up with rain. We can try to enhance it, but I'm not optimistic.

"The one round we have is a 9mm. It passed through his head and into the tile and concrete, so it's distorted to hell and back. Looks like a boot print on the door, a partial due to the rain, but that might be what put him on the floor. A little residue, but not point-blank. Your guy just stepped up and put one in his head. Death was instant. Not even that much of a mess. If the dog hadn't tracked it around, it would have been a very tidy crime scene."

Jack shot him a look.

"Sorry. Just pointing out that your shooter was good. He left nothing behind that he didn't want to leave. The storm erased everything else."

"Not the first time I've heard that," Jack told him.

"Yeah, I imagine so." The detective didn't envy the Bureau man; it was already looking like a dead-end case. He didn't bring up the victim—they both had no problem seeing why he had caught the Shepherds' attention. Even the most hardened criminals despised child molesters.

"What color was the car?"

The man flipped through his notes.

"White."

Before Jack could follow up, Sydney emerged from the house and stripped off her booties before spotting them and walking over.

"Anything?"

She shook her head. "No. He didn't have any security cameras installed. No alarm system. FPL says the power was possibly out at the time. If so, it was dark as hell when it happened. What do you want to do?"

Jack stuck his hands in his pockets and fumed. It had been a long shot, but they couldn't not come. His attention went to the end of the block where the police had set up a barrier. A woman with a microphone to her lips was talking into a camera. He and Sydney were in the background.

"Let's get out of here. I'll make a decision after I see all the video. I still have a few questions."

Sydney suspected Jack was stalling, but kept her mouth shut. Leaving Florida meant facing his boss and the rest of the politicians back in DC, and she knew how much Jack hated that.

"I'll get the car."

DEACON LOOKED UP JUST in time to see the reporter speaking. She had palm trees blowing in the wind behind her, and the banner at the bottom of the page read LIVE FROM JUPITER, FLORIDA, so he grabbed the remote and turned the volume up.

"—claimed by the Twelve Shepherds today. Sean Travis, a man who faced a long list of child sexual assault charges, was gunned down in the doorway of his Jupiter home, sometime during the night. Whoever the shooter was, it appears it used the cover of the passing hurricane to carry out its deed. Authorities are so far withholding comment, but we are told a press conference will be scheduled for later this afternoon. Sources outside the sheriff's office report that the FBI has taken over the case and are currently on scene."

"What?"

Deacon tuned the woman out and examined the view over her shoulder. The cameraman cooperated and zoomed in on the house and its perimeter of yellow crime-scene tape, just as the familiar pair of Jack Randall and Sydney Lewis appeared. They walked away from the house and conferred for a moment, before noticing the cameras and departing. Deacon stabbed the mute button with a finger, before yelling at his secretary.

"Margaret?"

Her voice came not from the doorway, but from the intercom. Her way of scolding him for not using it.

"Yes, sir?"

"Get me, Jack."

"Isn't he on his way here now, sir?"

"Evidently not."

He picked up the remote again, but the face of his chief investigator was no longer on the screen.

"What the hell, Jack?" he muttered.

"Dom's here."

Jackson looked up from his warm drink and massive plate full of shrimp. Everything in the cooler was thawing, so they had decided to eat well while they could. He swallowed his mouthful, waved the man forward, and pointed to the empty seat in front of him. Wallace took his usual seat off to one side.

"Where you been?"

Tyler, known to these men as Dominic, walked forward with his new shuffle-walk and sat as instructed. He eyeballed the heaping plate of seafood and answered the man's question.

"All over, boss. Trees blocking the roads everywhere. Cops got the freeway shut down. Powerlines everywhere. People lootin'. Some nigga tried to jack me; had to wave him off with my .45. It's crazy out there. I must have used every damn road in the city just getting here."

Jackson considered the answer before accepting it as truth. Bad as it was outside, the man had still made it here. That said something.

"You made the D&Ps two days ago, right?" He was referring to the drop-offs and pick-ups. Business jargon for crack dealers wasn't that much different from real business.

"Yeah. Me and Teddy."

"Where's the car you used?"

"In the warehouse. Something missin', it wasn't me, J. The count was good, I—"

"Ain't like that." Jackson cut him off and indicated he should have some shrimp. "Eat up, they just going to start stinkin' up the place soon. Tell me about the car." Despite being full of eggs and sausage, Tyler did as he had been told.

"From the dealer. We s'pose to exchange it on Monday for a new one."

Jackson nodded; it was what he had hoped for. A former customer who had gotten in over his head was the owner of a BMW dealership. To pay off his debt, he supplied cars to Jackson's delivery men when they dropped off product and picked up the payments. They rotated the cars every three days.

"Four door? Big trunk?"

"Yeah, a nice one, too. A seven-something model, I think."

"Good. I need you to go get it."

"'K. What we doin'?"

"You four gonna take a little trip. Deliver some product up north."

"You four?" Wallace piped up from the other table.

Jackson turned to his second. "Yeah, you four. You see anybody else here?"

"Why can't he go get Teddy?"

"Teddy's a kid. I need some cool heads to make this happen."

"I can try to find him," Dom popped in, "but he's just got paid, so he be drunk as hell till tomorrow or next."

"I need *you* to go," Jackson repeated, ignoring Dom and pointing at his second.

"But—"

"No time for that. You going, you the only one who knows where to go anyway."

Wallace bit his tongue and stewed. The job was beneath him, but he didn't see a way out.

Jackson turned back to Dom and caught him with a mouthful of shrimp. He glared while he slugged it down and wiped his mouth on his sleeve.

"Go get the car. Make sure it's clean. Empty the trunk and fill up the tank, then bring it back here."

Without a word, Dom left. As soon as he was out of sight, Wallace rose and took his seat.

"Don't stick me in a car with that asshole, J. I swear I'll kill the mutha."

Jackson knew it wasn't Dom he was speaking of, but Sanford. Wallace called him Sanford and Son, after the old TV show. There had been bad blood between the two from day one. Wallace thought Sanford was too dangerous, too unpredictable, to be so close to the top man. That someday one of his screw-ups was going to bite them all in the ass, and he let Jackson know it every chance he got. Jackson, however, recognized the need for having a man like Sanford around. His presence alone kept his workers from thinking too much, from entertaining thoughts that caused problems for Jackson. He was a constant reminder of what they would face if they ever put those thoughts into action. Something that Wallace did not project. While being second to Jackson, and trusted to keep the books, which gave him only a certain degree of power in itself, it was not the same as that of Sanford's. When the dealer's body had hit the sidewalk, everyone knew who had manned the torch, and it wasn't Wallace.

"I got no choice here. You the only one who has the names and the places in your head. Who am I gonna give that to? Kobe? Shit, I may as well just tell the feds myself! He might last a whole five minutes in one of their little rooms. Has to be you. You'll be in charge. Let Dom drive; he knows how to do it with a trunk load of product. Put the other two in back and keep 'em quiet. You just four brothers from the Sunshine State going home after a hurricane. Make your drops, ditch the car at the airport, and fly home. That's it."

Wallace frowned at the mission and played his last card.

"What then? You got three who know too much."

Jackson checked the door behind him before answering that. As usual, he was ahead of his second.

"Dom is proving to be a good soldier. If he does good on this, he can join the delivery crew. Sanford doesn't have the ambition, but we'll keep an eye on him anyway, but I doubt he'll even remember the address or even the name of the town by the time you come back. We can always get another Kobe. Maybe take care of that before you head back. Up to you."

Wallace considered the plan and then considered his options for changing it. Maybe he could take care of his Sanford problem on this trip as well. He'd have to watch for an opportunity.

"All right. We taking all fifty? Four stops?"

"DC. Baltimore. Jersey. New York. Boston is good for another week. I'll come up with something for them by the time you get back."

Wallace reached for a shrimp and then tossed it back in the pile. They were starting to get warm already.

"Road trip. With shitheads," he exclaimed, his disgust showing.

"You coulda been an accountant."

"Not enough pussy," he countered.

They both laughed and gazed at the empty stage in front of them, it was more like none-at-all today. The shiny brass pole, which normally had a half-naked girl twisting her body around it, now looked out of place. Hopefully, the power would be back on soon, and with it the music would start, and the girls and the traffic they attracted would return with them. Until then, it would be just Jackson.

"When do we leave?"

"Soon as Dom gets back with the car."

"Well, I better get my toothbrush." He levered himself up and made his way to the back of the bar. They both kept a bag packed and ready in an office closet, but it would be the first time he had used it.

4

———————

In August of 2011, Hurricane Irene, a Category 1 storm, caused $2.3 billion in damages and killed 34 people.

The National Weather Service now reports Hurricane Nancy is back to Category Four strength with winds reaching 130 miles per hour. The eye is currently forty nautical miles south by southwest of Ft. Myers, moving north-west at this time at thirty miles per hour, but expected to turn sharply *north within the next four hours. Residents along the west coast of Florida are urged to evacuate, as the eastern wall of the storm will be tracking right along the coast. Specifically, the cities of Ft. Myers, Cape Coral, Port Charlotte, Northport, Venice, Sarasota, Bradenton, and the entire Tampa Bay area, including St. Petersburg, Clearwater and Tarpon Springs. Again, if you are a resident of those cities, particularly the barrier island communities, you are urged to evacuate to the east. This is a major storm that will result in high winds and massive flooding. Expected storm surge will be augmented by high tide within the next few hours. All counties along the coast are now under a flood warning. This storm may also produce multiple tornados at any time with little warning.*

Our computer models now predict the storm will travel north and then east as this cold front and the jet stream push down from the north. The spaghetti models now take it north-east making landfall somewhere north of Clearwater and crossing through Gainesville and eventually Jacksonville before once again being shoved out over the Atlantic. The storm may weaken slightly with the combination of high-level wind shear and being over land, but our model tells us this weakening will be slight, perhaps only enough to drop Nancy to a Category Three.

To repeat: The National Weather Service now re-

ports Hurricane Nancy is back to Category Four strength with winds reaching 130 miles per hour ...

THE CAR WAS RIGHT where Tyler had left it, and the keys were in the usual spot. Aside from a coat of dust, it appeared to have survived the storm unscathed. The battered Chevy fit in the spot next to it, and he was relieved to see that the gas caps were across from each other. Rooting around in a nearby cabinet, he located the siphoning pump. Each vehicle had about half a tank left. The pump was manual. He had some work to do.

Feeding the tubes down their respective holes required no thought and Tyler soon had the gas flowing. The mindless task practically required his mind to wander, and he was soon grappling with his decision to go on this trip.

He had no second thoughts about Jackson and his people—they were dangerous and deserved what was coming to them, and he thought it was worth the effort he was putting forth to make that happen. He had tried to keep his own personal thoughts away from the job, knowing that as soon as you developed an ax to grind in this business, it was the beginning of the end. He had seen other cops do it, each of them getting caught up in the enormity of the job they had, the discovery that they were just barely keeping up. It made them want to stretch the rules a bit, or even take more chances, in order to get a little farther ahead, to show that their work had made a difference. Tyler knew that even if they were successful and took down Jackson and his men, a new Jackson would move in and fill the void in a matter of days. But that would be the next guy's problem.

So why had he fought for more time? Was he already past the stage he was trying to avoid? This trip meant he would meet more unsavory people —several if his suspicions were correct. His chances of not coming back increased with every meeting, yet he had asked for it anyway. Was he one of those cops now? A crusader, they called them.

Or was he trying to be the hero? He didn't want that—the idea embarrassed him actually. Was it just the challenge? A test of himself? That wasn't as bad, maybe. Like a soldier who had yet to go to battle, he both longed for it and feared it at the same time. The nagging question of whether he was up to the task, with only one way to find out. Tyler had seen war already, and plenty of action on the streets of Detroit, so he already knew the answer to that question.

His thoughts were interrupted by gas splashing out of the BMW. Tyler cursed and jumped back in time to save his shoes, but the fluid dripped down the side of the BMW, creating a clean trail through the dust which labeled his actions to any careful observer.

He cursed himself. "Damn! Pay attention."

He reeled in the hoses and then listened hard to the noise from outside. The wind was howling less, and he could now hear the rattle of rain on the warehouse roof. Good, it would erase his mistake. He tossed the pump back into the cabinet he had gotten it from and popped the trunk. A couple of empty cardboard boxes. He tossed them aside and measured the space with his eye. It looked big enough to hold fifty keys. He scrounged a packing blanket and a bottle of bleach from the cabinet and deposited them inside before opening the garage door. He was outside, and the rain was blasting the dust off the car a second later, while he watched the door come down behind him, slowly blocking the view of his Chevy. Like the house, he would probably never see it again.

His thoughts returned to the trip and his fight to go on it. Was it the thrill? He couldn't deny that there was a certain amount of adventure in doing undercover work. While there was no denying that it was exciting, doing it every day both burned you out and made you want to puke at times. Was he an adrenaline junkie, or maybe just stupid? Was he smart by asking that question of himself?

Like Jackson, Tyler had divided the people he dealt with into two groups: smart and stupid. To survive in the drug trade, it helped to be stupid, he reasoned, just be a worker-bee and not aspire to anything beyond. The other end of the spectrum required a capable mind, one that weighed the risks and rewards of the profession with a brutal honesty that most lacked. Samuel Jackson had a frickin' PhD in crime. It was why he was on top. It was the ones that fell into the middle that had the problems. They thought too much, or not enough, depending on your point of view, and it usually resulted in their unpleasant and abrupt end.

Was he, Tyler Turner, ex-soldier and now undercover cop, smart enough to bring down Samuel Jackson? Or would his lungs be full of warm Gulf Stream water by this time next week?

He pushed the thought aside and adjusted the .45 in his belt before turning the corner and heading back to the club. Like a soldier yet to be battle tested, there was only one way to find out.

"So, your question is why did he open the door?"

Jack answered, "Yeah. I mean, if it was a Girl Scout or something and the sun was shining, I wouldn't even ask. But this was during a full-blown hurricane, and I don't see a guy like him just opening the door for some stranger on his front porch. It doesn't fit."

"A neighbor?"

"The detective says they were all buttoned up. And the guy wasn't the friendly neighbor type. Only one of them knew his name."

Sydney squirmed in the seat and put some thought into it while they drove back to the police station. Outside, people were cleaning up from the storm. A power company truck had half the road blocked, and Jack had to wait for traffic before moving around it.

"A disguise? A cop maybe? Or a powerline worker?"

"That's what I'm thinking."

"I'll dig into it when we get to the station. What are you doing?"

"I want to see more camera footage. This town has a lot of choke points. Bridges. Freeway intersections. There couldn't be that many cars out at the time. I'll be watching some film for a bit."

"Okay. I'd hurry if I were you."

"Why's that?"

"Tech at the scene told me they had to hurry because the storm might be coming back."

"Coming back?"

"Yeah. It's out over the gulf and might get pushed back at us by this big cold front moving down from the north. Not a big chance, but still."

Jack shook his head at the news. "Even the weather is screwing me."

Sydney almost said they shouldn't have come but held her tongue. Jack had his reasons. Hopefully he would tell her them when he was ready.

"You all got a piece?"

Jackson had them all gathered in the bar. Their bags lay on the stage and had been consolidated to save space. They each nodded. Tyler had already inventoried that himself. Sanford had his shotgun in his hand and an automatic tucked into his belt. Kobe had what looked like a well-used Glock in his belt while Wallace had a .357 Python in a shoulder holster. Tyler had his .45 automatic and wondered if it was enough. He'd always carried a .380 tucked into an ankle holster when on the job back in Detroit, but nobody did that here and it would label him as a cop. He'd moved the baseball bat he kept on the floor of his car into the BMW. He assumed he'd be driving but wasn't sure.

Jackson was laying down the law. Wallace was in charge, as expected, but Tyler had watched Sanford take the news and had not liked what he had seen. The man's nostrils had flared briefly, but otherwise he'd remained stone faced. Wallace had watched him as well, and Tyler could tell he didn't like what he had seen either. Nothing either of them could do about it, so they waited.

"Stay on the interstate. Don't speed. I lose fifty keys to a speeding ticket you will not survive prison! They know you coming, so just do what you do and get the hell out. Somebody tries to renegotiate, you tell them to call me. You call me before and after every drop."

Tyler had heard it all before. It was what he did. Every week. Him driving with an Uzi under his seat. A second man sat in the back with bags of dope between his legs and a second Uzi in his hands. Behind them would be another car with three other men, all of them armed to the teeth.

He drove the speed limit and obeyed every

traffic law. Never sped up to make a yellow light and never took the same route twice. The night ended with a phone call, which produced an address, at which he would find Wallace, who would count everything twice before deciding the amount matched what they should have. Only then would Tyler let himself relax. He'd been tested once. His shrug and blunt "Count it again" had been met with a sneer. They let him sweat for twenty minutes, which he had spent game-planning how to kill the three men between him and the door, before Wallace told him he could go. Evidently, his show of bravado had been enough to give him a pass.

Now he was with three people who didn't know the drill, and for a much longer trip. How was he going to deal with that? Usually, he got over the fear a few hours after going home to his little row house. Had a drink. Watched a movie. Did some push-ups. Whatever it took. He'd had to give up the drinking before it owned him. Now he'd have no outlet; he'd have to be "on" for the next several days. To escape, he'd have to shoot each one and then walk away. Which one would be first? He imagined that would sort itself out.

Jackson's tone brought him back around. He'd

given them the stick, now it was time for the carrot.

"You all get this done and there'll be a nice bonus waiting for you when you get back."

Bonus? What would that be? Jackson's usual bonuses came in the form of cash or some time with one of the dancers, or both. Tyler had been on the receiving end of one of those bonuses once. She was there for two reasons: one she was good at, the other not so much. Tyler had caught her looking around his place a little too much. He'd let her, knowing the information would get back to Jackson and not cause him any issues. He couldn't turn her away without raising suspicion, so had let the girl do her job. Since he wasn't sure where her visit and their activities fell in his job description, he had chosen to not inform Agent Smith.

The drugs were already boxed up. Weighed and taped and packaged like fine china. The outsides of the boxes read like amateur movers. Kenny's bedroom. Mary's clothes. Kitchen stuff. Anybody looking would assume they were just fleeing the storm. Unless they were doing their looking with a dog. To counter that, Dom had left the cap off the bottle of bleach in the trunk, the fumes would be fierce after a few miles of shaking. Even then it may not be enough to beat a dog.

They would have to make a decision before that happened.

Jackson watched as they carried the boxes out and deposited them in the trunk. The streets were empty. Tyler added the two suitcases before covering the whole thing with the shipping blanket and then slammed the lid against the light rain.

"That trunk leak?"

Wallace answered that one. "The car's brand new, J. I'll call you when we get to DC."

"You'll call me every two hours."

Wallace sighed. "All right."

"WHAT DO you mean you can't come back?" Jack was on the phone with his pilot and not liking what the man had to say.

"I'm sorry, Mr. Randall, but the plane's still down. We got a warning light on approach, and after we landed the mechanic looked it over. The nose gear has a down gripe. The plane can't fly again until it's fixed."

"And how long for that?"

"The parts come in on Tuesday."

"The parts ... Tuesday! Can you get a loaner from the charter company?"

"Sir, I don't think it will matter either way. You've heard about the storm turning around? They're closing airports all over Florida and southern Georgia. We might be able to take off, but I doubt we'd get there in time. I'm looking at the latest weather report, and I don't think anybody is going to be flying anytime soon. The airlines are cancelling flights into the region already. Once the planes that are there now are gone, there'll be nothing left."

"Crap. How long will they be closed?"

"There's no telling, sir. Once the storm has moved through, they'll give us an estimate, but until then it's anybody's guess."

"Robert, you're a bundle of good news, you know that?"

Robert forced a sympathy laugh. He remembered warning Jack about the storm when they flew in, but it was not the time to remind him. His boss was very easy to work for most of the time, but he seemed pretty agitated ever since he had picked him up in California.

"Sir, not my place but, the Coast Guard maybe? Or the military?"

"Take too long to set up. Besides, their mission takes priority over taxiing me around. What I got you for."

"Yes, sir."

"I'll find a way but get the plane back up as soon as you can. Tell the mechanic I don't mind the overtime."

"Will do, sir."

"See you when this is over." Jack hung up and walked back to the FOB waiting area. Outside the windows the tarmac was oddly empty. Most of the planes had fled the storm already. He found Sydney sitting in a leather easy chair reading a *Robb Report*. The TV on the wall showed a radar image of the storm in multiple colors. A lot of it was red.

"Any luck?" he asked her.

"The girl at the desk says there's nobody heading north. One plane going to Denver, that's it."

"Denver? That's about ... seven hours, maybe more if they have to divert around the storm. Then another eight to DC, that's if we can even get a ticket."

"I take it the plane is still down?"

"Waiting for parts now. Pilot says they're closing everything around us anyway."

"So, what do you want to do?"

Jack had watched a weather report and was no longer stalling. In his bag was a hard drive of several traffic camera video logs. More were being sent to the Hoover building. He'd also received a motivating call from Larry advising him to get home as soon as possible. He was now back to his normal self, and sitting still was not in his nature.

"Let's go see what kind of car we can rent."

Sydney raised an eyebrow but said nothing. She just gathered up her things and followed Jack.

As they passed the counter Sydney raised the magazine and smiled at the girl behind the counter.

"Can I steal this?" she asked.

The girl smiled. "No problem. Enjoy your trip?" She offered a sympathetic face.

Sydney made her "I give up" face and followed Jack. He was already several paces ahead. She hurried to catch up.

5

3,700. The number of miles of coastline from Maine to Texas.

At first, they had been quieted by the storm damage, each of them gaping out the windows at the destruction as Tyler weaved them through the network of roads trying to get north. Power lines, roadblocks, trees, and once an entire roof off of a nearby home, all blocked the road. Tyler cursed and consulted the GPS for detours around it all. So far, Wallace had not questioned him.

But now the damage was lessening, and Tyler noticed the police presence dropping with it. He struck out west toward a major road and found the freeway entrance blocked but unguarded. He squeezed the car between two barrels, took the ramp and soon had the car up to just under the speed limit. The scenery became less interesting, and the occupants of the back seat began to get bored.

"What you gonna do with your piece, Kobe?" Sanford demanded.

"What you mean?"

"Your pussy, man! You even *know* what to do with it?"

"*Shiiiit*, I knock that stuff out," Kobe replied.

Sanford thought that was hilarious and laughed, shaking the seat in front of him holding Wallace. It was a subtle challenge that Wallace chose to ignore.

"How about you, Dom? You pick yours out yet?"

"After this trip I'm sure I could use some," was his neutral reply. He kept his eyes on the road and changed lanes to pass a power company truck.

Getting no bite from Dom, Sanford moved on to Wallace. "How about you, fearless leader, you got your piece reserved?" He shook the seat again. "I don't want to steal anything from the boss."

"You pick whatever one you want; I got my own."

"Whatever I want? Why thank you," Sanford replied with exaggerated manners. "I'll leave Sheila for my man Kobe here and think about my choice while we travel."

"Don't stick your junk in Sheila, Kobe," Tyler told him. "Yo shit will just rot off."

"Now why you wanna do that?" Sanford asked. "I just having some fun with my little man here."

"We ain't on this trip for fun," Wallace said. "Now why don't you quit running your mouth and watch for cops instead?"

"Watch for cops, watch for cops. Yes, sir. I am watchin'." Sanford nodded before sitting back and glaring at the back of Wallace's head.

Tyler glanced in the mirror to see the look on Kobe's face. The bravado was still there on the surface, but he had unconsciously shifted away from Sanford. The tension rose a notch but luckily Sanford chose to sit back and hum a tune only he could hear while he looked out the window. Wallace tolerated it for about one minute before reaching for the radio. He thumbed through the stations until he found a weather report.

"*Hurricane Nancy has now stalled over the Gulf of Mexico and is regaining the strength it lost when traversing southern Florida. The front moving down from the north has gained speed and our models now predict it will drive the storm on a north-easterly course when it arrives. This path will take the now Category Three storm across northern Florida and back out over the Atlantic. By that time, high-level winds will have taken effect and will begin to shear off the top of the clouds, greatly reducing the storm's energy. It should then move up the coast, losing even more strength as it travels.*

"*The National Weather Service has now issued a hurricane warning for all of northern Florida and parts of southern Georgia and South Carolina. We expect torrential rain and flooding, as well as coastal erosion due to the storm surge. The cities of Gainesville, Jacksonville and Savannah have all been placed on alert. If you are a resident of these areas, we urge you to take shelter inland and avoid areas of flooding. This storm is not to be taken lightly. We here at News 8 will, of course, be monitoring the situation and issuing updates as they come in. Stay tuned for—*"

Wallace cut the woman off and turned to Dom.

"How long to Jacksonville?"

"At this speed? I'd say four hours, but with all those people getting out of Dodge? We could hit some serious traffic."

"That storm's comin' back?" Kobe asked.

"Shut up," Wallace told him. "Can we get ahead of this bitch or not?"

Tyler shrugged. "Maybe."

"Maybe? That all you got?"

"What you want from me? I ain't no weatherman! We get north of Jacksonville then yeah, we ahead of it. It'll pass behind us and we home free up the coast, sounds like. You in charge; what you want to do?"

Wallace stewed in his seat. Damn storm was screwing everything up. First it screwed him by putting him in this car with these assholes, now it was coming back to screw him a second time. He knew one thing: he couldn't turn around and go back. Jackson would have his ass.

"Beat the storm," he said.

"You sure?"

"What I said, ain't it?"

"All right, I hear you."

Wallace turned around to find Kobe worried and Sanford smiling.

"You got a problem with that?"

"Me?" Sanford asked. "No problem here ... boss."

Kobe wisely shook his head. Wallace turned back around and contemplated the semitrailer swaying from side to side in front of them.

"Speed it up some."

Tyler knew better, but he chose to follow directions this time. He now kept pace with the surrounding traffic before pushing buttons on the GPS.

"Just over four hours to Jacksonville," he read aloud.

Wallace simply grunted and pulled out his cell phone. After a minute, he set it down.

"No service," he informed them. "I'll use the sat phone when we get gas."

DEPUTY KYLE WARNER stood on the side of Homeland's main thoroughfare and waved his flashlight at the cars creeping by. It was something he had been doing for the past few days while they worked on fixing the bridge over the river and into Georgia. The traffic had been mostly local at first, with the occasional family from out of town passing through on the annual vacation. Taking the rural route—obviously the driver's idea. Most cars held a smiling dad at the wheel while a bored wife and kids shared the seats next to them. Now the storm was coming, and the traffic had increased with people fleeing the coastline and avoiding the highway. Kyle just waved them on, it didn't change the job any, except for the damn rain.

His six-foot frame was wrapped in layers, mostly against his will. A workout shirt kept the sweat off his skin and also served as a layer of protection from the bullet-proof vest he wore over it. While thinner than the armor he had worn in Iraq, it was still thick and stiff and always managed to rub him the wrong way no matter what position he was in. Over this, he wore a black department sweater, which also itched, but kept the wind from chilling him. The slicker kept his sidearm dry, but other than that, it just served to keep the sweat in and the rain out, to a point. The wide-brimmed hat he wore over his military haircut kept the rain off his face, but it also sent it down the back of his collar every few minutes. He ignored it, having tolerated worse on many occasions.

Kyle turned back to the line of cars and saw several more had joined them. They inched forward at every opportunity, and he had to wave one down in order to keep it from blocking the intersection. The road was a boulevard for eight blocks before meeting the bridge, and the crossings matched the nearby streets. Why the cars couldn't keep from blocking the intersections, he couldn't figure out. The drainage ditch served to keep most of them on the pavement, but every once in a while, the tracks of a four-wheel drive truck would be found in the morning. Kids and their toys. He been one of them not too long ago.

He shrugged his shoulders against the yellow department rain slicker in an attempt to tighten the collar against his neck, but it was so heavy it failed to move. He was forced to use his hands to adjust it and that resulted in more rain traveling down his arms to soak the sweater he had on over his vest. Despite their length, the rain had worked its way inside his boots, too, and he felt the telltale heat of blisters forming. The boots were old and broken in, leftovers from his days in the army, and he'd had to work hard with the shoe polish to make them presentable enough for his new job as the village of Homeland's only deputy. His father had vetoed the boots twice before finally giving them a pass. Kyle looked down at them now and observed that they were nowhere near the shape they had been in before the storm, but then he no longer needed his father's approval.

Connor was the sheriff now and Kyle turned his head to spot him through the rain. A high school friend, Connor was a few years older than Kyle, but they had played sports together growing up, and there was both respect and familiarity to help them deal with their sudden promotions. Kyle shielded his eyes against the rain to look for his new boss and could barely make him out a hundred yards away waving traffic over the now single-lane bridge, his yellow slicker making him glow in the semi-darkness of the storm. A "target indicator" Kyle had called it, and Connor had reminded Kyle that he wasn't in the army anymore. Cops that couldn't be seen tended to be hit by cars with distracted drivers at the wheel, and Kyle had learned there was no shortage of them.

Which was why he was currently standing out in the middle of the road with a hurricane coming right at him. Drivers would enter town, find the line of cars waiting, and then turn off the main road and wander around town in a futile attempt to find another bridge over the river, as if the metropolis of Homeland, population 910, needed more than one. They eventually found their way back to the main road and got back in line. Kyle was here to prevent the wandering and get these people out of their town as fast as possible.

But it was boring work. Worse than guard duty. So his mind wandered and usually fell on his current situation. He turned to face back south and couldn't help seeing the general store a few blocks back. A woman on a ladder was placing boards over the windows, the blows of her hammer traveling to him on the gusting wind.

It was all her fault.

———

"TIME TO FILL UP," Tyler informed them.

"Fill up? You got half of a tank!" Sanford spouted off from the backseat.

"You wanna run from the cops on an empty tank? We fill up at half. Always," Tyler shot back before mumbling, "Tell me how to do my job."

"What?" Sanford spit.

Sanford was testing him and Tyler had to let him know he wasn't going to be. He locked him in his gaze in the rearview and let him have it.

"I said don't tell me how to do my job, nigga, I—"

"Both of you knock it off!" Wallace yelled. He spun to find Sanford seething in the back with his pistol in his hands. "Put that away before some-body sees you with it. All we need is some trucker with a cell phone calling it in!"

"Mutha can't keep his mouth shut—" Tyler started.

"I said leave it!" He turned back to Tyler. "Drive the damn car!"

Tyler shut his mouth and drove, but not before exchanging a look with Sanford in the mirror. Sanford returned it by poking him in the head with the gun before hiding it under the seat. He smirked and eyeballed Kobe before slapping him on the back of the head and gazing out the window. Kobe flinched but said nothing.

"Just a few friends out for a drive!" Sanford said before laughing.

Wallace chose to ignore him this time and gazed out the window on his side. Tyler checked the rearview and was relieved to see nobody behind them close enough to see the gun being waved around.

This dumbass is going to get us all caught or killed, he thought. He glanced at Wallace, but he was stone faced. Maybe if Tyler got him alone, he could broach the subject of ditching Sanford somewhere before he screwed this whole thing up. He shot a look in the rearview at Kobe. The boy was up against his door as far as he could go, shooting nervous glances at Sanford every few seconds. Tyler didn't envy him. The boy was in a tight jail cell, with a crazy person holding a gun for a roommate and he was just getting to know him.

Tyler gave him the guy-nod in the mirror, and the boy returned it. It loosened him up a bit, knowing he was not alone. Sanford had stuck his head against the glass and closed his eyes. Good.

He turned back to the GPS and worked the buttons.

"We'll get gas up here in Melbourne."

Wallace grunted for a reply. Tyler changed lanes and drove on.

6

In September of 2008, Hurricane Ike, a Category 4 storm, caused $29 billion in damages and killed 103 people.

"Bang! Bang! Bang!" Jerri yelled over the wind.

She got three thumps for an answer from inside before smiling and driving in the last nail. The wind blew her straight blond hair into her eyes as she descended the ladder, and she had to feel her way down the last few rungs. The wind was getting worse, but at least she was all boarded up now. Like most in her little town, she had plywood already precut to fit every window. Most of it saved from previous storms. A few houses in town were worthy of the fancier plastic, but most couldn't afford to spend the money. This was old Florida. Tile roofs and swimming pools were not too abundant here. Homeland was just across the bridge from Georgia, in the middle of the Okefenokee, and barely survived by pulling cypress trees from the swamp and grinding them into mulch. Mostly for the homes with tile roofs and swimming pools found on the coast.

Looking up the street, she saw a line of cars slowly making their way through town heading for the bridge. The repairs to the "old lady," as they called it, were still ongoing and traffic had been down to one lane for the last week. Between that and the area's reputation for writing speeding tickets, traffic had slowed way down. But it was all they had to support the town. Mulch and tickets. Jerri didn't approve, but she didn't blame them either.

She dug the leftover nails out of the pocket of her hoodie before they started poking holes and rounded the side of the building. The door was only half covered, and through the top half she could see Aaron's worried face. He waved vigorously and then resumed the rocking that kept him calm. A hand would flail on occasion, but mostly he just showed signs of being excited. It wasn't his first storm, but this one promised to be bigger, and Jerri was worried about how he would handle it. Last time they had treated it like something fun, an inside-the-house party. It had worked, to a point. She was hoping she wouldn't have to sedate the boy, but if it came to that she was prepared.

She deposited the hammer and nails in a metal footlocker they kept outside the door and walked to the edge of the road to get a better look at the storm to the west. The sky was turning from grey to green. She had seen that before. The rain would be coming down in buckets. Maybe even some hail. She could already hear trees cracking and popping in the nearby neighborhoods. Squinting into the wind, she could barely see the sheriff's car at the end of the road in front of the bridge, and Kyle about halfway back from that. A Georgia highway patrolman was on the other side, and they worked the radios to let twenty or so cars pass at a time. She'd been told it was boring work, but there was nobody else to do it. The local volunteer fire chief had had to supervise most of the storm preparation.

"Get her done, Jerr?"

Jerri turned to see Frank walking towards her. The wind was so loud she had not heard him drive up. She accepted his peck on the cheek and a quick hug before answering.

"Put the last board up just now. How's the school?"

"Ready as it's gonna get. I'd say we got about a couple hundred there, maybe a bit more. Plus all the dogs."

"Probably a hundred of them there, too, right? It'll be puppy season soon."

"There's room for more, you know."

"No, too many people in a strange place. Aaron doesn't do well in situations like that. We'll just hunker down here."

"How's he doing?"

Jerri turned and found Aaron watching them from the doorway. The boy still didn't fully approve of Frank, especially with his mother gone. Frank had tried to connect with him a few times but wasn't sure if he was making progress or not. They had a mutual love of root beer, but other than that were still searching for common ground. He tried a wave but got nothing in return.

"His mom will be back when her deployment is over, then they're going to park her at Naval Air Station Jacksonville for her next tour. She'll be home every night. It'll be good for him."

"I could stay," he offered for the hundredth time.

"No. Who would take care of Belvedere?"

"Puh, Belvedere will probably sleep through this. I'm more worried about the house than I am about a ten-year-old basset hound."

"You get the roof done?"

"No, but the paper is down tight. Should hold. It'd be done by now if I had a little help."

They both looked down the street at the deputy directing traffic. If the young man had noticed them, he didn't let on. Just waving his flashlight and answering the occasional driver's question, he seemed to not even notice the couple. Jerri raised her arm to wave but then thought better of it. Not yet.

"Kyle will come around, Frank. Give him time."

"I'm old, Jerri. I don't have that much time left."

"If you're old, what does that make me?"

"Semi-old?"

"Thinks he's funny, does he?"

"I try. Where you gonna be after this, the clinic?"

"Depends on Aaron. If there are wounded, I'll do what I can."

"All right." He sighed heavily before giving her a hug. The wind rattled the sheet metal over their heads and pine needles showered them from the nearby trees.

"Getting worse. Sure you'll be all right?"

"This old building's seen worse. She'll keep us safe," Jerri answered. "Besides, I got all the stuff I could possibly need right here. You better get a move on." Jerri gave him a quick kiss and then moved off toward the door.

Frank looked the place over. It was the town's hub. A combination general store, coffee shop and gas station with a deli in the back sitting one block off the main drag. Just about everyone in town was there a few times a week. The store was the eyes and ears of the community, and Jerri knew every inhabitant by first name. Many since they were kids, and she had helped to bring them into the world as a nurse working at the clinic. Her husband had run the store for years before his second heart attack had proven fatal. Now there was just her, their daughter away in the Navy, and her grandson. They all lived in the back of the store in a nice three-bedroom apartment and, since everyone came to them, they hardly ever left.

He turned and spotted the deputy looking his way before quickly turning away. Frank frowned. Maybe not everyone—there was one who refused to come there anymore. And for that Frank blamed himself.

He pulled his hat down tighter against the wind and walked back to the car, which like him was retired from the police force. Aaron watched and Jerri waved from the door as he pulled away. Frank avoided his son and took a side road to get to his place.

No reason to push the issue today. There were other things going on.

"He's gonna get us busted. Bringing him on this trip was a mistake, man—he can't hold it together."

"Jackson said he was going," Wallace replied. "I tried, but the man insisted."

They were standing outside the gas station bathroom having a quick conversation while Kobe pumped gas and Sanford went inside. Tyler was making his case but not getting anywhere.

"I think we should ditch him. Leave him at the next gas station and let him find his way home on his own, before he fucks this whole thing up."

Wallace frowned at that. He'd catch hell from Jackson if they did that. He'd survive it, but at what cost? And that was only if everything went well on the delivery end. As much as he hated him, he knew Sanford's presence would keep most from entertaining ideas of getting all fifty keys for themselves. His muscle, attitude, and crazy persona worked well for that.

"Look, man, we only going as far as New York. After that, you can ditch us and find your own way back if you want. I may do the same. I need you to be cool till then. He's crazy, but we might need that before we're done here, you hear me?"

Tyler spit on the ground and shook his head to show his disgust. He knew what the man was saying wasn't far from the truth, but like himself, he had no choice.

"Just keep him off my ass while I'm driving, okay? I swear, he waves that gun around again, I'll leave him lying on the side of the road. Problem solved."

"You just drive. I'll worry about Sanford."

"All right, dog. We better move; this storm gonna catch us if we don't."

They rounded the corner to find Kobe

standing at the pumps looking nervous. They quickly saw why. Sanford had parked himself in the driver's seat with the door closed.

Tyler walked up and Sanford ignored him, staring straight ahead and drumming his fingers on the wheel.

"What's this? I'm driving."

"Figured you could use a break. I'll take it for a while," Sanford answered without looking at him or Wallace. He snorted hard and continued drumming his fingers.

Tyler looked at Kobe who tapped the side of his nose before looking away. What the hell? Was Sanford high?

"What the fuck, man? Git yo ass in the back!"

"You get in the back! I got this!"

"Don't even—"

He was cut off by Wallace rapping on the roof. Tyler shot him a look and Wallace jerked his head toward the other patrons of the station. Several were now watching the two men shouting at one another. They were attracting too much attention.

"Let him drive."

"But—"

"Let's go. Now."

Tyler reluctantly got in the back with Kobe, while Wallace took his usual place in front. Sanford cackled as he dropped the car in gear and pulled out. A block later, they hit the freeway on-ramp.

"Now we'll make some damn progress. Slow ass mutha can't—" He was cut off by Wallace's gun being buried in his ribs.

"You pull that shit again, we'll leave you here. Forever. You got me?"

Sanford's face collapsed. He had pushed it too far. He'd also underestimated Wallace.

"All right, all right, iz cool. I hear you."

Wallace kept the gun there for another half-minute to drive the point home before stowing it under his leg.

"Drive. Under the speed limit. The next stop, you switch with Dom and that's the last I want to hear about it. Everybody got me?"

They all muttered to the affirmative.

Tyler watched Wallace's face out of the corner of his eye. Maybe the man hadn't gone soft just yet. There was still some of that street toughness under the layers of fat. The accountant had balls. Or did he? Tyler saw a small twitch in the corner of his mouth. Was this an act? Maybe. He guessed they would all find out soon enough if it worked or not.

The car slewed to the right as the wind gusted

higher. Sanford worked the wheel to keep them in their lane. The semis were having a hard time. They passed one flipped on its side in the median, its empty trailer split open and flapping in the wind. A large wrecker was parked on the edge with its lights flashing. Traffic slowed to gawk.

"Shit's getting real," Tyler observed.

Wallace nodded and reached for the radio. They needed an update.

Tyler listened as he tried station after station. He noticed more cars entering the highway with every on ramp. People were getting the hell out of the way of the storm. He exchanged a look with Kobe.

"Ever been in a storm like this?"

"No. Just yesterday."

Tyler nodded. The kid was more relaxed now that he shared the back seat with Tyler. "We'll be on the other side soon," Tyler assured him. "It'll pass behind us."

Before the kid could answer, another gust hit them, and they swerved with the other cars. Sanford cursed the wind and held the wheel with both hands.

Wallace found a station with an update, and they all listened closely. The storm had changed course, moving slightly north of the previously projected path. That meant the eye would pass to the north of Jacksonville.

"Shit," Wallace cursed. "Damn thing's trying to head us off."

"We get above J-ville, we should cut to the north and let it pass us," Tyler said.

"How's that?"

"It's moving north-east, we move north-west. Soon as it's out over the ocean, we can cut back."

"So let's do it now," Sanford said.

"We do it now, we cut right into it. We gotta get above J-ville first, above the path it's taking."

"How long?" Wallace asked.

Tyler shrugged. "Depends. With the wind and the traffic. All these people buggin' out? We take the 295 west, we might be fine."

"West? You just said that's right into the storm!" Sanford said.

"Well, east is right into the ocean, dumbass! Hand me the GPS."

Sanford was no longer in the mood to argue. He peeled the GPS off the window and handed it back to Tyler without taking his eyes off the road. Tyler punched buttons and started looking for ways around Jacksonville, but options were few. Jacksonville, by area, was one of the largest cities in the United States. An urban sprawl that encompassed countless rivers and inlets and, as a result, highways and bridges crisscrossed the town in every direction. Navigating the mess was never easy, doubly hard in these conditions. If they had left an hour earlier, they would have been past all this already, but it was too late for that.

"Okay, we take the 295 around the city if we can. If traffic gets bad, we get off on 23 and cut up though this secondary road and just keep heading north-west until we're clear of the storm."

Wallace nodded, not letting on that he was lousy with directions. Tyler punched buttons and then handed him the GPS. Wallace passed it to Sanford who managed to remount it without letting the car be blown off the road. He examined the map on the tiny screen and then took in the numbers on the border of the tiny screen.

"When's the storm supposed to be here?"

"It's gonna be tight. It's probably okay to speed up now—cops ain't gonna be passing out tickets in this shit."

Wallace nodded at that, as well. He was already regretting letting Sanford drive; this was clearly Dom's game.

"Do it."

Sanford changed lanes and they were soon passing cars. Another truck was in the ditch, on the other side this time. Two state troopers and an ambulance were in attendance. They didn't even look up as they sped by.

A CHEVY IMPALA.

It was all they had left, and the manager at the counter had not looked too thrilled to be renting it to him after Jack told them it was going to DC. That mood had changed when the manager found out the car wasn't coming back. If it got damaged, they could do the paperwork on their end. And from the sound of what he'd been hearing on the news, the car was heading right into the storm. He was going to caution them until he saw Jack's FBI credentials when he produced his wallet to pay. Between that and the Black American Express card, the manager had forgotten about the whole thing. Jack signed the papers without looking at them and hurried outside. The roof did little to shelter them from the rain traveling sideways on the wind, and they dumped their bags in the back seat without checking out the car. As soon as Jack had the seat and mirrors adjusted, he'd floored it out the gate.

Now they were passing cars at well over the

speed limit in the left lane, but Jack was more worried about the storm and not making it to DC as he had promised Deacon, than he was about speeding tickets. Sydney just braced herself and snugged her belt tighter. Jack noticed and slowed down a notch, but not much.

"You figure that thing out?" He pointed with his chin at the center console.

"What?"

"The GPS."

"I could try, but I'm a little busy bracing for impact."

"Sorry. It just looks tight. We need to get to Georgia as quick as we can, or this thing's gonna nail us."

She started punching buttons, feeling her way through the device. A warning popped up and told her not to operate the GPS while driving. She wondered why was it any different than a radio? Whatever. She clicked OK and moved on. She put in the address of the Hoover building on the awkward keyboard and the device displayed the word "Calculating" before offering a map of the east coast of Florida. A red line that followed I-95 was now highlighted. The corner readout produced an arrival time.

"Says we'll be there in twelve hours," she reported.

"Yeah, right. Not at this speed."

"You're doing seventy?"

"That's the speed limit, but everyone's doing it. I imagine traffic usually does at least ten over that. It'll get slower when we get near Jacksonville. Does that thing have an alternate route function or a detour button?"

"Hell, Jack, I don't know. What's wrong with the route it's giving us? Says it's the fastest."

"Just want to know our options."

"A nice hotel is an option. One made of bricks? You know, huff and puff and all?"

"You're funny. Humor me, please?"

"All right." She punched more buttons and did her best to ignore the wind trying to shove the car off the road.

The rain increased, and Jack thumbed the wipers to their highest setting. They were past their needed replacement time, but so far were keeping up with the rain. The tires, not so much. They had hydroplaned once, and Sydney had been sure they were off the road, but somehow Jack had kept the car straight. She pushed it all aside and concentrated on the device in front of her. She thought she had found it when the screen suddenly froze.

"Searching for Satellite Signal," she read out loud.

"Damn. Takes some serious rain to do that. Give it a minute."

Sydney sat back in her seat and glared at the storm ahead of them while she waited. The sky had that awful green color that promised more to come. Like it was saving the best for later and just letting them know. A series of billboards appeared, and she couldn't help reading the names of the hotels on them out loud as they passed.

"All right, all right. I get it. But you can explain to the boss why we didn't make it. Oh, and to Debra, too," was Jack's answer.

She frowned at both proposals.

"Just don't kill us, please. I'd hate to die in a rental car."

"I'll try my best."

7

60.1 million. The number of housing units, as of July 1, 2014, of the coastal states stretching from Maine to Texas. An estimated 44.9 percent of the nation's housing units are located in these states.

S heriff Connor Clancy stood at the edge of the bridge connecting his town with the state of Georgia. The view was one that he had never seen before. While the water ran from west to east on its way to the ocean, it now appeared to move sideways across the narrow chasm. Driven by the wind alone, the water was now breaking in small waves on the far shore. While he knew, and understood, what was happening, the image still defied logic.

The bridge creaked and groaned with another gust, and he watched the reaction of the pale-faced woman in the front passenger seat of an SUV as her husband navigated them slowly across. Connor didn't blame her; the Old Lady was making noise like he'd never heard before. But the engineer had assured him the bridge was safe. Despite missing half of its steel planking, it was more than able to handle the weight of a single lane of traffic.

But he'd never mentioned the bank, and now Connor watched as another chunk of Georgia clay broke loose and tumbled into the water to leave a brief orange stain before disappearing. The concrete post was more exposed with every wave it seemed. Connor was no structural engineer, but common sense told him this was not good.

His radio squawked and some words poured through, but he couldn't get it to his ear in time to hear it.

"Repeat for me, Tommy?" He'd been saying that a lot today.

The trooper on the other side of the bridge repeated his question. "How's it looking now?"

"Worse. That wave action is cutting into the bank even more now. She's really complaining about it too. A couple of those temporary steel plates are jumping up and down. Not sure how much longer we should keep her open."

Connor watched as his colleague walked to the edge of the bridge on his side, the radio held against his head. They were only fifty yards apart, but he could barely see him. It was like looking into a mirror.

"I can't see it for shit from here. Your call, Connor. I'll back you up either way."

Before Connor could key the mic to reply, the bridge groaned under another gust causing the metal plates to rattle to the point he could feel it through his feet. He reflexively took a step back and looked to the bank to find even more of the concrete footing exposed. He knew they were driven deep, but how much more of this could they stand?

"I don't like it. If it gets much worse, I'm pulling the plug. I'm gonna call the state boys and tell them to close the exit. Soon as the last cars cross, we can shut her down."

"Sounds like a plan. I'll do the same on my side, even though there's nobody heading your way. Let me know when you're out of cars."

"Will do."

"ALMOST THERE," Jack informed her.

Sydney had frowned at the choice but had had to agree. 295 had practically been at a standstill, and Jack had raged against it for miles until they had gotten off on 23 headed north-west. Their improved speed had lasted only a few short miles before slowing down again. They had crept along at forty miles an hour for the last thirty minutes and now were at a start-stop pace for the last two on entering Canton. Jack had been creeping the car over onto the shoulder to get a look ahead but had been defeated by the driving rain and other cars doing the same thing. They now had the turn in sight, but so did everybody else.

"Looks like you have a lot of fellow crazy people," Sydney observed.

Jack took the rebuke silently. He was working the problem. The traffic in front of them was turning right, heading back east toward the high-way. They obviously thought that, since it would meet the interstate above Jacksonville, traffic would be better once they got there. Jack wasn't so sure. 301 was only two lanes and they were both clogged. He doubted it would be any better after they got to the interstate. I-95 through Georgia was three lanes, but as soon as it hit South Carolina it dropped to two, with very few exits. Jack didn't want to bypass one bottleneck just to get caught in a second bigger one. A car six spaces in front of him turned left. A BMW. He saw the glow of a GPS on the dash before it disappeared into the rain.

"Where is he going?" he muttered. Sydney didn't hear him and continued to look out her window at the storm. Jack consulted the GPS, punching buttons and examining the tiny screen for options.

"Let's go more north."

Sydney heard that. She turned and gave him a look that labeled him as past crazy.

"You're serious?"

"Look, if we stay in this traffic we'll get stuck in it for hours. If we turn here, we can jump north for a bit and then cut back over later." His finger traced the path on the screen.

"That's north-*west*, not north. You'd be heading *toward* the storm. Are you trying to kill us?"

"Only for a little bit. But if we sit here, it'll catch us for sure."

Sydney rolled her eyes and turned away from him to examine the storm and the traffic. What were all of these people thinking? Go home! Inside! Why are you out driving around? They couldn't all be trapped in their cars with madmen at the wheel like she was, could they? The car next to them pulled up even and she saw the driver rocking out to whatever he had playing on the radio. It was as if he drove in this stuff every day. The young girl sitting next to him wasn't so calm: she stared outside at the storm with wide eyes and pursed lips, clearly scared. Sydney watched them until it was their turn to pull ahead.

"When we get back to the Hoover building, I'm locking myself in my dungeon office until I run out of paperwork. Then I'm going to do somebody else's until I'm ready to come out."

"So is that a vote in favor of my plan?"

She threw up her hands in a gesture of futility.

"Why not?"

Jack smiled and hit the turn signal.

"YOU SURE THIS IS RIGHT?" Sanford asked.

Tyler had the GPS in his hand again and was giving him directions from the back seat. He'd been talking Wallace through its operation for the past few miles but had been unable to see what he was inputting. He'd finally handed it back to Tyler, but there was no time for him to see what Wallace had done.

"Traffic on 95 is practically stopped. We gotta go around it. Just keep going. We'll cross the bridge up here in Homeland and then turn back east a bit. We'll cut back to 95 when we get to Jessup."

They were now on a two-lane back road with trees close on both sides. Muddy logging trails led off to the left and right at regular intervals, but houses were few. They passed a mulching operation with stacks of trees piled high around a large mill. Piles of mulch in several colors were separated by low concrete walls. The car took on layer of debris as they traveled by. The wipers were now set on high and barely keeping up. There was standing water everywhere they looked. Sanford was weaving around fallen branches and other debris and only heard half of what Tyler was saying.

"What's the name of this damn town again?"

"Homeland."

"Then what?"

"Just cross the bridge and keep going north."

Sanford leaned forward in an unconscious attempt to see better.

"Damn!" He swerved just as another tree branch impacted the road in front of them. Several limbs snapped off and were sent skidding down the road in front of them by the wind.

"Watch them wires!" Wallace pointed.

Sanford swerved around them before they passed a fire station on the right. One of the bay doors was open, and the engine was inside with the lights running. As they passed, they heard the siren sound, and Kobe turned and watched as the engine pulled out behind them and headed back the way they had come.

"They going the other way," he reported.

Sanford glanced in the rearview to see it himself but quickly turned back to the road. They entered the edge of town a few miles later.

"Look at this shit," Sanford commented. "Redneck central. Bunch of crackers in their shacks out here in the swamp."

Tyler watched out the window and had to admit that Sanford was right. The houses were all old and mostly wood or painted concrete block.

Many showed signs of neglect and previous storm damage which had never been erased. It got slightly better the more they traveled, but the town reminded him of several he had seen before. A place where whatever major employer had left long ago, leaving behind an empty town full of despair. Almost every home was boarded up. The ones that weren't were obviously empty and had been for some time. A speed limit sign whipped back and forth and threatened to remove itself from the ground to become a missile. Tyler watched it, waiting for it to launch, until they were past.

The car slowed as they entered the town proper. Storefronts greeted them with plywood covering the windows. A shuttered fast-food outlet. A few people were still pounding nails, but most had fled indoors. A cop decked out in rain gear was waving traffic forward with a flashlight. They all held their breath as they passed. The cop ignored them and watched the traffic coming at him. They drove on a few more yards before hitting a line of waiting cars.

"Ahh, shit! Look at this!"

Traffic ahead was a line of brake lights. Tyler could just make out the superstructure of the bridge in the grey gloom ahead. The line of cars was backed up to a sign telling them the road was down to one lane ahead for bridge repairs. A police car with its lights flashing could be seen up ahead. A patrolman with a yellow slicker and a Smokey Bear hat wrapped in plastic walked around with a big flashlight.

Sanford saw him too. He snaked his handgun from under the seat and wedged it between the center console and the seat next to it. Wallace saw it.

"Be cool, man."

The car rolled to a stop behind the one in front.

"I'm cool ... I'm cool."

They waited.

SHERIFF CLANCY STOPPED the cars and walked out onto the bridge in order to see the far bank. The rain and wind had increased to the point that he couldn't see it without doing so and he wanted to know what was happening.

To his shock, a full two feet more of the concrete pillar was now exposed, and the water was rapidly eating away at what remained. The bridge groaned and this time he felt a vibration travel though its steel skeleton and up through his legs.

"This is over," he voiced out loud.

He ran back to the front of the bridge and waved the cars back. A driver rolled down his window to protest but was drowned out by the rain. Connor grabbed the barricade and pulled it across the entrance before the car and its upset driver could make an attempt to cross.

"Bridge is closed!" he yelled before jumping in his car and pulling it across the entrance. By moving it, he also gave the traffic a place to turn around. They could now do a U-turn and travel back down the boulevard to his deputy two blocks back.

He tossed the hand-held down in favor of the car's radio.

"Kyle? It's Connor."

No answer.

"Kyle! You hear me?"

"Repeat, whoever's calling?"

"Kyle, it's Connor. I've just closed the bridge. Tell those cars waiting that the freeway is closed, too, and then tell them how to get to the school. They'll have to shelter there. No exceptions! Don't let them go to the highway!"

"All right, I got it. Can the school handle all these people?"

"They'll have to. Get 'em moving."

"I'm on it."

Connor switched frequencies and tried Tommy, but after repeated tries he got no answer. He gazed out his side window to see a barrier up on the other side as well and no sign of Tommy's car. The heavy steel plates making up the temporary deck of the bridge rattled up and down and he estimated three inches of daylight visible when they did. Dislodged bolts skipped across them and over the edge. Connor gazed past it in time to see brake lights in the distance. Tommy was heading home.

"Guess he got the massage already." He switched frequencies again and tried to reach the fire chief.

"Mark, Connor. You up?"

"I'm here, Connor. They closed the freeway. Not that it matters, you won't be getting any more traffic."

"Not that it matters?"

"You know that big cottonwood just north of my station? Well, it's across the road now. Take us a whole day to clear it. The boys and I are going to hunker down in the station. I'm afraid you and Kyle are on your own till this is over."

"All right. I closed the bridge already. The supports are getting washed out and the deck is loose. We're directing traffic to the school. Check in when you can, all right?"

"Okay, Connor. The troopers are moving out toward 10, I'm going to—"

A burst of static threatened to pop Connor's eardrum. He reached out and adjusted the radio before trying Mark back. All he got was static.

"Tower's down," he told himself. He tossed the mic aside in disgust and levered the door open, launching himself back into the storm. The wind slammed it as soon as he let go, and he walked to the nearest car. The driver cracked his window.

"Turn around and follow the signs to the school! The bridge is closed and so is the highway! You'll have to take shelter there!"

"What about—"

Connor ignored him and moved on to the next car. There was no need to explain any further, especially to a guy dumb enough to be driving out in this storm in the first place. He waved him around, and while doing so he saw Kyle doing the same two blocks away. The car he just spoke to swung around in a U-turn. He tapped on the window of the next car, which didn't seem to want to follow.

JACK ROLLED his window down at the deputy's approach. The button took it all the way down automatically and Jack got a blast of wind and rain in his face before the young man blocked most of it with his body.

"Sorry, folks. The sheriff has just closed the bridge. It's under repair and the winds make it too dangerous to cross. I'm going to need you to turn around."

"And head back into the storm?" Sydney asked.

"The State troopers have closed the freeway as well. I'm afraid you'll have to shelter here with us. The school is five blocks back and about a mile east. It's a new building on high ground and we have plenty of room for y'all. Okay?"

Jack saw no other choice. Their gamble had not paid off. So, they'd spend the night with the locals. It was only time lost and not worth the risk.

"If you say so, officer. I guess we don't have much of a choice."

"Not with Mother Nature." The deputy grinned and actually tipped his hat at Sydney, flicking rain off the brim and onto Jack. He ignored it and rolled the window up. Gazing ahead, he saw the young deputy move on to the next car and rap on the window.

"Good ol' country boy," Jack commented.

"Feeling old, are you?" she asked.

"A little, maybe. What were you doing at that age?"

"Pulling mangled people out of wrecked cars. You?"

"Jumping out of planes and getting shot at."

"Well, maybe country boy here is smarter than both of us?"

"Probably," Jack admitted.

He counted the cars ahead of him and then measured the distance to the next break in the boulevard. Four cars, maybe five. There were already some that had turned around at the front of the bridge and were feeling their way back the way they had come. He watched their brake lights in the mirror as they followed the signs to the school.

The deputy finished with the car in front of them and moved on to the next. Jack drummed his fingers on the wheel and listened to the rain pound the roof. The wipers could barely keep up now, and he was treated to a stop-motion like film of the deputy, his yellow slicker a blob of color in the horizontal downpour, walking toward the next car as the rain came and went.

"Let's go, Barney," he urged him on.

"His name was Barney? How do you know that?"

"No. I'm kidding. Small town deputy? Barney Fife? Get it?"

She gave him a blank look.

"Don Knots?"

"I have no idea what you're talking about."

Jack sighed and returned his gaze out the windshield.

"Gawd, maybe I am that old."

"Just be cool," Wallace said. "Hear the man out and don't give him any shit." He shared a look with Tyler in the back and then eyeballed Kobe. The boy was still nervous, and he had one hand under his leg gripping his Glock.

"Get your hand out where the man can see it, dumbass. Shit like that makes 'em nervous. Why you kids get shot all the time."

"If these damn cars would move, I could get us out of here!" Sanford hissed.

"No, don't run," Tyler countered. "He's just

gonna tell us to turn around or something. Be cool."

"Don't tell me what to do, mutha!"

Wallace snapped his fingers—something he could do loudly—and it cut them both off. "Both of you quit it. The man just wants to talk, so be cool and talk."

Sanford swallowed the rebuke and watched the deputy get closer. His hand snaked down and pulled the handgun up higher in the seat crack. Wallace was about to push it back down when the deputy arrived at their window. He tapped twice with his flashlight.

8

In October of 2005, Hurricane Wilma, a Category 3 storm, caused $21 billion in damages and killed 22 people.

Jerri made a final check of the doors and windows and found them all holding. It was unusually dark inside with them all boarded up. A little claustrophobic. Hopefully that wouldn't be a problem. Her grandson wasn't one to venture outside too much, but he did enjoy looking out the windows. Hopefully, she could keep his attention focused somewhere else.

She glanced back out into the main room to see Aaron working on the puzzle she had given him. It was a new one. Over 1500 pieces. It should last him about an hour and a half. Hopefully enough for the worst of the storm to pass. The boy rocked back and forth and rubbed his head as he arranged the pieces, his arms and hands in constant motion. He hadn't spoken in a few days but was showing signs of wanting to. Mostly when he wanted something, or to laugh—she loved to hear him laugh.

Autism. She had exhausted herself reading everything she could on the subject. Her nurse's brain sifted through the research available and discarded the pseudoscience that surrounded it. All in an effort to figure out her grandson's miraculous brain and how it worked.

That his brain was special was without doubt. Aaron could do amazing things. High functioning, they called it. Her daughter's nickname for her son was Sponge, because he absorbed everything put in front of him. She would tease him with it and make him laugh. A book lasted a couple of hours. A puzzle about the same, if it were big enough.

Math was just another fun thing to do. Drawing. He could draw all day and sometimes produced things that nobody could understand until they asked him. For an answer, he would usually show them the book he had gotten it from. It would be up to them to figure it out from there.

Once, he had made a large cone out of a piece of scrap cardboard. He wrote "the universe" down its side and carried it around for a day or two, holding it up to things. When Jerri had asked him about it, he had brought her a book with the picture of a man in a wheelchair on the front. She found the diagram on page twenty-nine. It was Stephen Hawking describing how the universe expanded. Jerri had tried to read the book but had gotten hopelessly lost in the first few chapters.

How he did it, she didn't know, but he did. Now, if only he would come back. Return to the little boy he once had been, before he had crawled into his shell. Jerri's research told her that time would fix a lot of Aaron's issues, but she was tired of waiting.

"*Comment est le puzzle*, Aaron?" she asked him in French.

Aaron made a "good" gesture without taking his eyes off the table. She saw that the pieces were all arranged into separate groups. Not by color, but by shape. Number of tabs vs number of blanks. Edges here. Corners there. As usual, he was starting with the first row and working his way down, as if he were writing the puzzle rather than just putting it together. She checked the floor for dropped pieces. A dropped or missing piece could bring on a fit, and although that had been happening less and less, she wished to avoid one while the storm raged.

But the floor was clear, and Aaron was content for now. She left him alone and walked to the kitchen. Lifting the phone from its cradle, she was not surprised to hear a busy signal. The lines always went down here. People just didn't want to trim their own trees after spending a day of doing so at work. So, the lines came down often when there were storms. She replaced the phone and wondered how Frank and Belvedere were doing. They were only eight blocks away, but it seemed like miles when there was a storm. If only Aaron wasn't afraid of the dog, they could both be here with her and Aaron, and maybe the boy would finally let Frank in.

Her thoughts turned to Kyle, out there in the storm doing his job with only Connor to help him now. He was still hurt, and she understood that. Better than she hoped he would ever know. Like most, he had searched for an outlet, something to direct his pain at, and had found it in her. She didn't blame him; she had done the same thing. All she could do now was hope that he came around. But there was nothing she could do to make that happen. It would have to come from Kyle, and then only when he was truly ready. But like Frank had said, time was getting short.

The sheet metal roof over the gas pumps gave off a deep hum as the wind pushed it sideways. She followed the noise to the last board she had put up. This one from the inside and containing a narrow viewing slit. Frank had cut it for her, after she had commented about not being able to see what was happening outside during the last storm. Now she felt like a prisoner in solitary confinement, peeping out at the world though her tiny window.

The wind had found some purchase on the edge of the sheet metal and was now working it up and down in rapid four-inch increments. The rattle was loud and promised to get only louder. By her experienced eye, the sheet metal would probably hold. At least until the wind shifted. She'd have to check it again after that and hope it didn't end the day embedded in somebody's house.

A different pounding sounded from inside the house, and she quickly turned away from the storm and back inside.

Entering the kitchen, she found Aaron slapping the table and his head in rapid succession.

"Aaron, honey, what is it!" She tapped the hand slapping himself and he stopped, but the pounding on the table continued.

"What? Tell me?"

Aaron stopped long enough to point at the table. The puzzle was on row eleven and for some reason had come to halt. He pointed at the end of the row and pounded the table again.

There were a thousand pieces left to go. But Jerri knew better. If Aaron said the piece was missing, it was missing. She got down and examined the floor. Nothing. She picked up the box and shook it. Still nothing. She opened it and checked the gaps between the two lids. It wasn't there. Where else? Did it come that way!? If so, it would be hell for the boy. *He had to finish.* He had to. He pounded the table again harder, and she reached out to stop him before he hurt himself.

And there it was. Stuck to his forearm. He had leaned on it, and it had stuck. He couldn't see it.

"Aaron look. Aaron look. Aaron look." She repeated it until he looked at her and she pointed.

First at his arm and then at the same spot on hers. Aaron put it together quickly, feeling his arm until he found the missing piece. It immediately went in its place.

"Silly boy." She forced a laugh, and he laughed with her before picking up the next piece as if nothing had happened. She watched him for the next two rows and mentally counted the new puzzles she had bought. Other people stocked up on food and water when a hurricane was coming. She stocked up on puzzles.

She heard several sharp sounds coming from outside, but they stopped and didn't repeat, so she ignored them in favor of watching her grandson and his magic brain. Across from her was an empty chair and she again found herself wishing Frank was with them. She wondered again how he and Belvedere were doing.

KYLE STEPPED FORWARD to speak with the next carload of people. How hard was it to understand that the bridge was closed? He had explained it to the man several times. *Yes, it's closed. For you, too. The bridge doesn't care if you're the vice president of whatever company and neither do I. No, you can't go across after everybody else leaves. You will turn around and go to the school like I told you or I will arrest your dumb ass.* He tried to put it aside as he tapped on the window of the next car.

"Hello, gentlemen."

"Officer." Sanford nodded. "What's going on?"

"I'm afraid the bridge is closed. I'll need you to turn around and follow the signs to the school. You can take shelter there until this blows over."

Sanford exchanged a look with Wallace, who said, "For how long?"

"Long as it takes, I'm afraid. The freeway's been closed as well. I'm sorry, but there's no other choice."

"That's not going to work for us," Sanford said. "What other roads are there?"

Crap, not another one like he'd just met? Kyle leaned farther in to get a better look at the men. They were obviously not hearing what he was telling them.

"Sir, I don't think you're hearing me. This is a major hurricane. You need to take shelter. The roads are all closed. Now, I need you to turn around and make your way to the school. Understand?"

Sanford turned to Wallace. Kyle took the chance to shine his light into the back seat. He found the stone face of Tyler Turner and the scared face of Kobe staring back at him. Kobe shifted nervously in his seat. He was sitting funny. The light came down and he saw the butt of the gun poking out from behind his leg.

"Nobody move!"

Kyle stepped back and went for his gun, but his hand got caught in the yellow rain slicker and held him up for a split second.

It was all Sanford needed.

As soon as the deputy had shouted, Sanford went for his gun. He beat the deputy by a fraction of a second. The first round hit him square in the left chest, spinning him around and knocking him off his feet. The next round got him just below the vest. Kyle's own round pierced the side of the car as he went down.

"Son of a bitch!" Wallace yelled. "Let's go!"

Sanford ignored him and put the car in park. Opening his door, he took two steps and glared down at the young man flopping in pain in the puddle. He stepped over him, put a foot on the hand holding the gun, and took aim, waiting for the man to look up at him.

"Leave him! Let's go!"

JACK'S BRAIN had labeled the sound as a gunshot immediately, and he didn't have to look far to see the source. The body of the deputy had not even hit the ground before his own gun was in his hand and he was opening the door. Sydney was only a second behind him.

"Gun!" his training made him shout.

He leveled the Browning through the gap between the door and the A-post of the rental car and centered the sights on the blurred shape of the man standing over the deputy. The rain soaked him, and the wind robbed him of a clear view of what was happening. He centered the tritium sights on the outline of the car door and squeezed off a shot.

THE WINDOW next to Sanford shattered, making him flinch. Two more shots rang out from his left, and he quickly ducked back into the car.

"Go, you shithead!" Wallace screamed at him. "Go!"

Tyler grabbed Kobe by the neck and shoved him down on the floor as Sanford dropped the car in gear and hit the gas. The BMW responded and jumped forward to impact the car in front of them and he swore.

"Move!"

Slamming the car in reverse, he backed up. A second round struck the car, and another shattered its way through the back and front windows, missing Wallace's head by an inch. Sanford slewed around the car in front of them and, with steam pouring from under the hood, threw the car into a U-turn across the grass divider. The wet ground threatened to stop the car, but Sanford gunned his way through it, jumping back onto the wet pavement with the rear end fishtailing from side to side. They ricocheted off a telephone pole and then straightened out. More shots rang out, and Kobe yelled from the back seat as they passed the shooter. Wallace pumped rounds out the rear window as they raced away.

"Who's shooting?" Sanford yelled.

"I don't know; just get us out of here!"

Sanford leaned forward in an effort to see through the steam and rain covering the shattered windshield. He swerved around the car in front of them just as another round impacted the front. The engine whined in protest and Sanford lost power.

Sanford looked down at the gauges to see them

climbing into the red. The car was dying. He looked up just in time. Smoke joined the steam pouring from under hood.

"Look out!"

The car had drifted right while he was examining the dash and was now heading straight for the side of a building. Sanford yanked the wheel left, only to discover he had lost power steering. Before he could get another hand on the wheel, the car hydroplaned in the flooded street, jumped the curb and smashed into the brick wall.

The rain drummed down hard on the roof, covering Tyler's cursing.

JACK'S first round missed his target, and the man turned and dove back into the car. The rain cleared for a second, and Jack saw a gun's silhouette in the passenger's hand. He leveled the Browning at it and squeezed off another two rounds before his eyes filled with rain again.

"I can't see!" he yelled to Sydney. He got no reply.

His eye caught her moving forward on her side using the car in front of them for cover. The occupants had ducked down out of sight. Jack mopped the rain and hair off his face and looked up in time to see the car slamming into the one in front of it. The gun was still being waved around by the passenger, but Jack held his fire and struggled to see beyond them out of fear of hitting the people behind them. The car backed up and then pulled out, barely missing the legs of the deputy lying in the road and then crossed the grass median, throwing up mud and grass in a double arc behind it. Sydney sprinted forward to the next car and planted her arms across the hood before squeezing off a round. Jack fired once before the door got in his way and then repositioned, firing again through the open window. The car fishtailed violently, and he tried to follow it. His own gun sights were barely visible through the rain and wind. The sound of his rounds piercing the skin of the car were his only indication that he had hit anything. The door defeated him again as the car moved farther, and Jack extracted himself from its cover and moved to the side of the road. Checking behind him to make sure he was not entering Sydney's line of fire, he saw that she had abandoned the idea and was running toward the deputy.

Cars were now moving all around him in a desperate attempt to flee the area. Jack stepped farther into the median to escape their charge. He spotted the car in question now over a block away, smoke billowing from the front, and was about to give chase when it swerved into a building and came to a crashing halt. It rolled slowly back into the road. Jack took off after it.

"GET THE HELL OUT!"

Wallace pounded Sanford on the arm and woke him up before looking into the back seat. He found Kobe on the floor, breathing hard and staring back at him with wild eyes, any bravado he'd had before now gone. Dom lay on the seat over him, his hands clutching his chest as blood poured out between them.

"Aw, damn!" He shoved Sanford. "Get another car!"

Sanford pulled himself from the car on unsteady legs. A stream of blood trickled down his face and was washed away in the rain. He gazed about like a drunk and tried to orient himself as to where he was. A car sped past him, the driver staring at him with panicked eyes while his wife and kids cowered down in their seats.

"Stop that car, you idiot!" Wallace yelled.

Sanford glanced at the gun in his hand as if

noticing it for the first time. A car. They needed a car. His fogged mind put it together and he raised his head to look for another one. There were several, but they were all running in the other direction. Nothing was coming his way.

"There aren't any!" he yelled and then laughed. It was funny. Why, he didn't know. He touched his head where it was starting to swell and came away with blood. Damn. He turned to see Dom being pulled from the car by Kobe. Wallace was struggling to open the trunk; he dropped the slippery keys in the puddle and then frantically searched for them. Kobe dragged Dom away toward the buildings. Where were they going?

He was about to order them to come back when a bullet shattered the remaining glass in the back window. By reflex he spun and fired back. At what, he didn't know. There was nothing but a wall of rain in front of him.

Wallace forgot about his search for the keys and sprinted away toward Kobe and Dominic, firing wildly behind him as he did so.

"Run!"

Sanford's brain came fully awake, and for once he followed Wallace's order. They were both quickly around the corner and out of sight of whoever was shooting at them.

Wallace stopped long enough to scan the area. Everything was boarded up. There were no cars in sight—not that he could see very far. They had to get off the street. He pointed with his gun at the space between two buildings and nobody questioned him. They all moved out of sight as fast as they could.

9

51.5%. The percentage of U.S. homes that have a prepared emergency evacuation kit.

Jack crossed the median and dodged fleeing cars in a desperate attempt to keep the men in sight. He had seen them emerge and had counted four of them. One fumbled with the trunk lid for several seconds before Jack had a somewhat clear shot. If he'd hit anything, he couldn't tell; he was shooting at shapes behind a wall of water and wind. Regardless, his rounds had an effect. The four men abandoned their efforts to open the trunk and fled to the west, around the corner and out of sight.

Jack increased his speed, forcing himself to not hug the walls of the buildings, but still ready to dive into the cover of a recessed entrance if needed. Sprinting forward in spurts, he covered the ground to the corner without drawing any fire. Dropping to his knees, he stuck his head out for less than a second.

Nothing. He stood up and did it again.

The street was empty. They were gone.

"Four against one, Jack," he told himself.

To go any farther would be stupid. He eye-balled the car. It was finished. The steam from the crumpled radiator had stopped, its contents now puddling on the wet pavement beneath it, but the smoke still came. He had hit something with fluid in it, and it was now burning off on the hot engine block. Satisfied that the car was going nowhere, he turned back the way he had come.

The street was empty. Every car had fled into the side streets and disappeared. It was somehow eerily quiet. With no cars present, the only sound was the wind and the rain.

He heard a shout through the rain from the direction of the bridge. A man's voice. He repeated whatever he had said louder, and Jack heard Sydney scream back over the storm.

Jack ran.

WALLACE GOT out in front of the small group as they ducked between two houses. Every window and door in sight was boarded up tight and not one vehicle was to be seen. He stopped in a driveway and spun in a circle, looking for options, while Kobe and Dom shuffled up. Dom was holding his chest and blood could be seen staining his shirt. Wallace ignored it as Sanford caught up to them.

"We need a car!"

"So, take one!" he shouted back.

Wallace eyeballed the windows of the nearest house. A sticker caught his eye. "This home protected by Smith & Wesson." The picture was the view down the barrel of a large gun. Wallace believed it. They were in the swamp, one full of redneck crackers. He knew the type and imagined a dozen guns in every house. It would take them a few minutes to get through the plywood, and before they were halfway, he was sure bullets would be punching holes in it from inside. They had to find something else.

Looking down the street, he spotted the elevated roof of a gas station. Two blocks. Maybe three?

"Follow me!"

He set off between the houses and the others struggled to follow. The rain erased any sign of their passing, and they were soon out of sight in the gloom.

JERRI EXAMINED the roof of the garage with her flashlight as best she could, and was relieved to not see any signs of water getting in. The last storm had found some purchase on the corner of the building, and the shingles had come off one by one until there were enough of them gone to expose the tar paper seam underneath. Luckily, the storm had passed before the damage had gotten too great. Still, the water had made it inside and she had been worried for a few hours. Now the roof was new. She just wondered if they had used enough nails.

The big bay doors rattled with a strong gust,

and she moved the light to shine on each of them as well. Shut and locked and with a metal brace providing added rigidity, she was not as worried here. But they sure did make a racket. If one of them blew off somehow, it would not necessarily endanger her or Aaron, but Frank's vintage Mustang would certainly take a beating. He'd been restoring it here in his spare time, and it still had several years to go at the pace he was advancing. Not that she cared. She liked to talk and hand him tools while he tinkered with it. Sometimes she wondered if he was going slow on purpose, but then quickly decided that she didn't care. She liked the little car. It had some memories attached to it, ones that they both shared.

Pushing the thoughts aside, she reentered the store and then the house.

"Bang bang!"

Aaron was yelling! Her happiness was short-lived, though. She hurried forward and searched for the reason. His tone was not one of distress or anger. He was yelling back at noise from outside. It was something she had taught him before it was time to nail up the boards. Something banging on the house would surely set him off, so she had made it a game. She would yell and wait for his tapping answer before wielding the hammer. That way Aaron would know it was just her. She walked closer to him, still at work on the puzzle.

"Who's banging, Aaron?" she asked.

Aaron pointed toward the store she had just come through. "Bang bang," he repeated before adding two more puzzle pieces.

Jerri listened hard but heard nothing. Her hearing was not what it had once been, and this wasn't the first time that Aaron had called her attention to something she had not heard herself.

"Outside?"

Aaron pointed again. "Bang bang."

She followed the pointing finger and retraced her steps through the dark aisles. On the way, she made a mental note to check the generator again to make sure it was in standby mode. If the power went out, the unit would come on automatically and power the row of coolers along the back wall, saving her as much inventory as possible, she hoped. She wondered if she would have to commit insurance fraud again. The last storm had knocked out power and the generator had kept pace. But the people of her town did not all have generators. Nor did they have a lot of money. Jerri had given away everything she could and then claimed it all as a loss a few days later when the insurance man had finally arrived. Nobody in town had said a word, and the insurance man had signed off on it without question. It wasn't a lot of money, really, but she had felt a little guilty just the same.

She walked down the aisle as best she could in the dim light, keeping to the middle so as not to knock anything off the shelves and trying to save the flashlight's batteries. Reaching the door, she peered out the narrow slit. The wind and rain were getting worse, and the sky was much darker. There were no cars to be seen at the end of the street and certainly nobody out walking. She wondered if Connor and Kyle were still out in the storm.

The corner of the roof over the gas pumps was still being worked over by the wind and would occasionally bang down rather hard. She estimated the range of motion to now be double what it had been earlier. There was still some time before it would be separated, but not much. All she could do was hope that the storm passed before that happened. She hated the thought of the sheet metal being torn away to fly through the green sky and end up embedded in somebody's house nearby.

"Bang bang," she whispered. It was probably what Aaron was hearing. She was about to turn away when her view was blocked by something else. She flinched and drew away as a man's face filled the opening. A large black man. She had never seen him before. He was examining her in a way that made her nervous and she saw a trickle of blood run down the side of his face. He smiled at her, but not in a friendly way.

"Open the door!" he ordered.

She hesitated. A large handgun entered the frame and was pointed at her.

"Open the door! Now!" His face told her it was the last time it would be a request.

She slowly reached out and turned the lock.

10

In September of 2005, Hurricane Rita, a Category 5 storm, caused $12 billion in damages and killed 7 people.

Sheriff Clancy had just stepped out of the last car's way when something tugged at his sleeve. He looked down to see a small hole in his yellow slicker. A sharp crack reached his ears.

"What the ...?"

He stuck a finger in the hole, trying to figure it out when more cracks reached his ears. With a start, he realized he was being shot at.

Ducking down, he searched for cover. The only thing available were the cars around him, and they were soon speeding away in any direction they could find. He glanced back at his own cruiser a half a block away and quickly dismissed the idea.

"Where?" he asked himself.

The sound had come from the direction of Kyle, but he couldn't see anything except moving shapes through the thick rain.

More cracks sounded, prodding him into action. Pulling his sidearm, he ran to get behind the retreating car in front of him. He kept pace with it as best as his extra weight would allow and gained a block before the car turned away down a side street. He moved on without its reassuring steel bulk in front of him and soon saw the shape of someone lying in the road. Another shape appeared, this one with a gun, and knelt over him. A woman. Her long black hair trailed behind her in the fierce wind. The yellow slicker told him it was Kyle on the ground, but he had no idea who the woman was. He crept forward and saw her yelling at his deputy. He circled left to get behind her, keeping his gun centered on her shape as best he could.

More cracks sounded from farther down the street.

"What the hell is going on?"

Getting no answer from the storm, he launched his bulk across the street and got himself behind the woman without her seeing him. The gun felt slippery in his hand, and he made a futile attempt to wipe it dry on his pants before creeping forward. The woman was now tugging at Kyle's clothes, but he couldn't see what else.

With another deep breath, he moved forward, his finger on the trigger and centered on the woman's back. She had a gun in her hand! Kyle was struggling to move on the ground beneath her, and Connor almost pulled the trigger, stopping only when he realized the round would pass through her and hit Kyle as well. He moved to the right, but before he could get a clear shot, she set the gun down in the puddle of water and blood and cocked her hand back.

FRANK WALKED around the house with a flashlight of his own, for the eighth time in the last hour. Doing so required him to step over his basset hound. The dog had chosen to lie in the doorway again. Outside, the storm raged, rattling the boards covering the windows and scraping tree branches across the roof, but Belvedere was unfazed. He had seemed a bit lost earlier when he was unable to find a spot of sun to lie in and had finally given up and chosen the doorway. Something he did so as not to miss Frank leaving. From there, the dog could see both the front and back doors. It was a strategic move that the dog had figured out years ago. Belvedere now watched him with one eye while he was again stepped over.

"Not to worry, old man. We're not going anywhere for a while."

Belvedere offered one thump of his tail in acknowledgement before closing his eyes and trying to return to his normally scheduled mid-afternoon nap.

Frank smirked at the dog's easy-going attitude. He wished he could feel the same.

He returned to the kitchen and tried to improve the reception of the TV by giving it a whack on the side. It cleared up for a few seconds before blanketing the broadcast in a light layer of static again. He frowned at the picture but held off on further TV discipline.

Not that it mattered. He could still make out the colors and lines of the broadcast enough to see what was happening. The storm was coming right at them. They were on its north-east side, the worst spot to be in. The wind and rain would be at its highest here and maybe even strengthen a bit as it met the warm waters of the Gulf Stream for the second time. Its speed of travel was the only good thing about it. It was moving back out to sea quickly. Hopefully it would move on without too much damage.

The map switched to a shot of a foolish reporter standing on a boardwalk in Jacksonville. Why they did this was beyond Frank's understanding. Did they really think people would not believe that the storm was there unless they actually stood out in it and showed them? He watched the man scream into the microphone while trying to remain standing and waited for a flying stop sign to come along and lop his head right off. It didn't, though, so Frank quickly lost interest. It's a storm. It's going to rain. The wind will blow. How many different ways were they going to find to repeat it? It was the reason he hardly ever turned the volume up.

Leaving the TV where it was, he rose to make another circuit of the house. He stopped at the mantel over the fireplace and listened as the wind blew a low drone across the top of the chimney. He played the flashlight around inside the pit but only saw a small trace of water. The house was doing okay.

The pictures on the mantel caught his eye, and he paused to give them some scrutiny. There were several of Kyle. His high school graduation shot. Another from basic training. One of him and his mother, Kyle kneeling next to her wheelchair so he could get both their faces in the shot. Her hand resting on his arm. Another of the three of them. Her, much skinnier, wearing a brave smile and one of the head covers that Jerri had found for her. Kyle's graduation picture from the Police Academy with both him and Frank in uniform. Another of Kyle and him standing next to a Homeland police cruiser. It was less than a year old. It was the last one they had taken together.

The wind picked up and pulled his thoughts away from the pictures. Frank moved to the front door and put his eye up to the hole he had drilled in the board. The yard was still occupied by the dumpster half full of old shingles. He'd tied a tarp over it to keep them from being sucked out and

thrown across the street and it seemed to be holding. He was examining water levels out in the
street in front of the house when the lights flickered and died.

"Crap. There's three days of steaks for dinner,
Belvedere."

Frank had made enough ice to keep the meat
in the freezer good for that long in the likely event
they lost power. Now he'd have to cook what he
had or throw it away. The grill had enough gas,
he'd made sure of it. They would eat well, minus
cold beer, until the power came back on. The dog
offered a single thump of his tail in approval.

"Don't get too excited."

He reached out and touched the yellow slicker
hanging on the coat rack next to the door. In his
bedroom closet was his hat, now wrapped in plastic, on the shelf over his uniforms. On a hook inside the door was his Sam Browne belt complete
with a Colt Python .357 older than he was. He had
carried it his entire career and had only fired it
twice. Once to kill a gator that refused to leave a
woman's back yard after chasing her inside, and
once to change the mind of a poacher who was
thinking about running from him. Two shots in
over twenty years. It was something Frank was
rather proud of.

Now the gear just reminded him of where he should be: out there with Connor and Kyle. Facing the storm and protecting the people. Not in here alone with a dog who didn't even feel the need to acknowledge that there was a storm. He should be out there. He turned the flashlight off.

Or with Jerri. But he couldn't do that either. Not until Kyle came around. And Frank was still at a loss as to how or when that was going to happen. Time, Jerri had told him, give him time. But how much time was there?

The wind howled again and this time a larger branch hit the roof. Belvedere opened an eye for a moment, but that was all. Frank turned the flashlight back on and went to investigate.

THE RAIN LET UP JUST ENOUGH for Jack to see Sydney kneeling over the downed deputy. The man was thrashing around, clearly in pain and screaming. Sydney was struggling to hold him still and avoid his kicking feet while yelling to him over the rain. Jack checked behind him for any movement but saw nothing but storm. The cars which had been waiting in line had fled into the side streets, and windows in the nearby houses were all covered in plywood. A fresh deluge of rain ended any further observation, and Jack ducked his head into the wind and ran back toward Sydney, the Browning held tight in his wet hands.

A new voice brought his head up, and he saw the yellow clad form of the sheriff standing behind Sydney with his gun drawn. The wind howled louder and took away the words, but they were clearly unfriendly.

Jack broke into a sprint.

"Hold still!"

Sydney was trying desperately to help the deputy, but he was thrashing around so much she couldn't get through to him. The puddle they now both lay in was rapidly turning red, telling her she didn't have much time. She finally set her weapon down in the puddle and used her free hand to slap him hard across the face.

The deputy's eyes snapped open, and he stared at her in disbelief.

"Look at me! Stop moving! You'll make it worse!"

Kyle's eyes focused on her long enough to tell her he was back. She reached for his collar and was about to rip the sweater open when a shout from behind her stopped her cold.

"Freeze! Police!"

A booted foot reached out and kicked her 9mm out of the puddle and into the grass. Sydney sat up and raised her arms.

"I'm—"

"Don't move!"

"I'm trying to—"

"Get off him! Now!"

Sydney didn't know who was behind her. She looked down to see the eyes of the deputy slowly closing.

"He was shot! We need to move him!"

"Just ... just get away from him!"

Sydney raised her head only to see a black shape coming at them through the rain. The downpour let up for a moment and she saw who it was.

"Jack! Wait!"

JERRI THREW the lock and then rapidly retreated as the man shouldered the door open. His wild eyes scanned the interior, and he walked in a few feet before pointing the gun at her again while he scanned the room.

"Stay right there!"

He turned back toward the door as Jerri stared down the barrel of the gun.

"Get in here!" the man yelled without taking his eyes off her. She silently prayed for Aaron to hide, as three more men appeared in the doorway. One of them was held up by his companion and struggled to the counter. Blood stained his hand and shirt where he held it over his chest. The companion was a boy, late teens at best. The last man inside was big, and he shut the door firmly behind them before examining the street outside through the tiny viewing port. He locked the door and spun around, aiming a giant revolver at the first man.

"You stupid muthafucka! I told you to be cool! What the hell was that!"

"He made us, man. What was I supposed to do? Just do what he said?"

Wallace kept the gun aimed at the man's face and considered pulling the trigger, but as much of a fool as Sanford was, Wallace needed him right now. Soon as they were out of this mess, he vowed to blow his damn head off, but right now he had other priorities. He waved the gun at Jerri and the door beyond her.

"Check out the back. No shooting! Someone will hear."

Sanford wisely kept his mouth shut and did as he had been told. Jerri shot a nervous glance at his departing back.

Wallace watched her before eyeballing Tyler and his bleeding chest. He turned his attention to Jerri.

"Anybody else here?"

"N-no."

He walked forward and aimed the gun at her point-blank.

"You sure?"

"DROP THE GUN!" Clancy screamed over the wind.

Jack kept coming, not hearing a word.

"Jack, stop!" Sydney screamed.

Connor shifted his aim to Jack, just as Sydney's cry pierced the storm. Jack skidded to a halt ten yards away.

"Drop it!"

"I'm FBI!"

"I said drop it! Do it now!"

Jack dropped the Browning in the grass and raised his hands.

"We're FBI!" Sydney said.

Connor hesitated.

"My badge is in the car!" She pointed.

"Don't move!"

"Officer!" Jack yelled.

Connor shifted his gaze and point of aim back and forth, unsure of what to do. The car next to him was full of bullet holes, but these two were still here?

Jack tried again. "Officer!"

Connor centered his gun on Jack's chest. "Don't move!"

"Jack ..." Sydney called.

"Stay there, Syd!"

Jack raised his hands higher and slowly turned around. Connor's finger tightened on the trigger. What was this man doing?

"Don't move!"

The man kept turning.

———

SANFORD STORMED through the house and quickly scanned each room from behind his gun. A small living room with a kitchenette led to three bedrooms and a bathroom. In the dim light he found it hard to see, but after a quick check he decided the rooms were empty. Every door and window was covered in plywood. He returned to the store and stuck his head in the garage to see the cars and machinery, examined a second boarded-up door, and then retreated to the store.

"Looks clear," he reported.

Wallace was looking out the viewport again. He turned and nodded before walking around the store. He spotted the phone on the wall and lifted the receiver long enough to determine there was no dial tone. The phone was then ripped off the wall and flung away down an aisle.

Dom groaned.

"What's up with you?" Sanford asked him.

"I'm shot, you dumbass."

"No shit?"

"You find a car?" Wallace asked, stopping the conversation.

"In the garage." He pointed with the gun in his hand.

"Keys?"

"Ask her."

Wallace fixed his gaze on Jerri, who was looking at Dom.

"Hey! Princess! Where are the keys to the car?"

"In the garage. On the hook by the door, but the car won't start—there's no engine in it."

"No engine? Where's yo car?"

"With a friend. It's in her barn while she's at the shelter."

"How far?"

"A few miles. Your friend needs a doctor."

"Yeah, well, I need a car first, lady. You got nothin' else?"

Jerri just shook her head, afraid the answer was going to enrage the man.

"What about the product, man?" Sanford interjected. "We gotta go get it!"

"With what? Damn car's full of bullet holes thanks to your dumb ass! Now shut up and let me think!"

Dom let out another groan, and Kobe shot Wallace a worried look.

"Just don't stand there, stupid. Get him some bandages or something!" Wallace spun around and pointed the gun at Jerri. "You got some stuff here somewhere, don't ya? It's a damn store, isn't it?"

"Yes, over there." She pointed.

Wallace pointed to Kobe. "He don't know anything. Get him something!" he ordered her.

Jerri swallowed and forced herself to leave the corner she had been in. The big man with the tattoos followed her as she traveled down the aisles.

Alcohol. Tampons. Some tape. An ACE bandage. Some kitchen gloves. A pair of scissors. She gathered the items and fought hard to not look in the direction of the house while doing so.

Where was Aaron? She fought hard not to look toward the back. Obviously, he was hiding, but for how long?

They came to the front, and the big man stopped his pacing long enough to let them pass. He muttered under his breath and cursed between looks through the viewport and more pacing.

Jerri averted her gaze and approached the two men at the counter. The men eyed her suspiciously.

She put on her best nurse's smile and set the items on the counter next to them before unpacking the gloves and putting them on.

"Let me see?"

The man nodded and pulled his hand away. She raised the bloody shirt to see an entrance wound just under his right collar bone. She peeled the shirt up higher, cut it away with the scissors and examined his back.

"No exit wound. The bullet is still inside." She unpacked a few tampons and placed them in Kobe's hand before guiding it to Dom's chest, covering the wound with it. "Put pressure on it."

The boy nodded and did so. Dom winced before giving him a nod that he was okay.

"Can you breathe all right?" She placed her hands on his chest "Take a deep breath for me."

Dom nodded again with clenched teeth and did as she told him to before asking a question.

"It hurts. You know about this stuff?"

"I was a nurse for many years."

Dom took the information without commenting.

"Where else does it hurt?" She probed his belly. He didn't wince or pull away. She frowned and checked his pulse.

"He gonna be okay?" Kobe asked.

"I don't know. What was he shot with?"

Kobe looked to Dom who nodded.

"Pistol, I think. Some white dude blazing away at us. It came right through the car door and got him." Kobe's eyes widened as he realized the bullet would have hit him if Dom hadn't pushed him down.

Dom shook his head at the explanation and added, "It was the first guy. He shot me through the door."

"Whatever," the boy said. "You still shot."

"I'll be right back," Jerri told him. She turned and walked toward the apartment.

"Whoa, lady! Where you think you're going?" Sanford yelled.

Jerri froze and tried to ignore the big gun the man was waving at her. She took a breath and with her voice calm, she answered him.

"I'm a nurse. I have some equipment in my room. I need to get it."

Sanford looked at Wallace who shrugged. "Let her. Kobe, you go with her."

He waved the problem away and returned to looking out the hole in the plywood. Sanford waved his gun at her before moving aside. Kobe followed her toward the back, his own gun now in his hand.

Sanford watched them go until they disappeared through the door. He then traded looks with Dom. Dom grit his teeth and held his stare until Sanford smiled at him before returning to the front of the store.

11

54.3%. The percentage of U.S. homes that have an emergency water supply.

E d swiveled around long enough to pick up the papers again. It was two pages. An editorial. Hardly enough to fill half a column. But then *The Gettysburg Address* was only 272 words. Martin Luther King's *I have a dream* speech came in at 1,667. The Declaration of Independence was a one-page document. It wasn't the length; it was what it said. He shook the pages before reading it one more time.

Jack kept his hands raised and slowly kept turning, bracing himself for the coming round. The sheriff was wild-eyed, the gun shaking in his hands. That, and he had given up on listening. Jack was doing the only thing he could to hopefully snap him out of it.

He stopped when he was fully facing the other way and waited while the wind blasted him full in the face with rain.

CONNOR'S FINGER tightened on the trigger as the man kept turning. Was he going to run? Was this woman with him? He was about to yell at him again to get down when the man's back appeared in full view. The letters FBI were emblazoned across it in one-foot-high letters. Connor's mind clicked and he realized his finger was on the trigger and the barrel was trembling.

He aimed the gun at the ground and took a deep breath. He looked at the woman on the ground kneeling over Kyle. Her hands were in the air and blood was being washed away. The puddle they both were in was now red.

"We're FBI," she told him in a calm voice. This time he heard her.

"What the hell is going on?"

"I'M NOT A NURSE ANYMORE, but I was years ago. I still have my bag of equipment back here, somewhere. This place is such a mess. Been meaning to clean it but never seem to find the time."

Jerri kept up the meaningless talk as she led Kobe back into the apartment. She was trying to warn Aaron that she was coming and was not alone. She knew her bag was in the closet and prayed that Aaron had not chosen it for his hiding place. This kid following her was hard to read. He looked straight off the street. The gun in his hand was not something new to him, though. He handled it as if it was in his hand more often than not. But he was young, and his baby face could not hide his fear and confusion.

"You know what a blood pressure cuff is?" she asked him over her shoulder.

"A what?"

"That thing the doctor puts on your arm and squeezes it with?"

"Oh, yeah, I seen that."

"Look in that bottom drawer for one." She pointed to her dresser on the opposite side of the room.

The boy stopped and eyeballed the room first. It was a big bedroom with a bathroom. He could see through the open door next to the closet she was heading for. Seeing no other exits, he decided this woman wasn't going anywhere and did as she had instructed. Jerri saw this and walked around the bed toward the closet, pausing once to kick some of Aaron's clothes under the bed and out of sight.

Jerri smiled for a brief second when she heard the drawer screech open. It had worked. The boy was down on one knee and probing through the clothes she had stuffed in there. She held her breath and cracked the door to the closet open.

Empty.

Her relief was quickly replaced by a shock of fear. It traveled through her as she realized that there was only one other place Aaron could be. He was under the bed, less than a foot away from the boy with the gun. It jolted her into action.

"Never mind, I found it!" she called.

She snatched the dusty medical bag off the floor and her stethoscope off the back of the door as fast as she could and spun around to find the boy getting to his feet. He retrieved his gun from the nightstand and waved her back into the store with it.

Jerri traveled back around the bed and tried a new tactic. "What's your friend's name?" she whispered.

Kobe glanced toward the store before whispering back, "Dom. Dominic."

"And yours?"

"Kobe."

"He's hurt bad, Kobe," she told him. "He needs a doctor."

Kobe frowned at that. "Ain't gonna happen, lady."

"Okay, okay." Jerri searched for something else to say. "I'll do my best for him, but unless we get him to one, I don't know ..."

That got Kobe angry. "Just fix him!" He waved her forward with the gun again.

"All right. Okay."

Thinking quickly, Jerri dropped her stethoscope and then turned around to retrieve it. The boy stood over her but backed up to let her reach it. Jerri used the ruse to look between his legs and under the bed.

Aaron stared back at her with wild eyes. He had both hands clamped over his mouth and tears streamed from his eyes. The bottled-up fear looked ready to burst forth at any second.

"All right. Okay," Jerri repeated. Aaron immediately calmed a fraction and nodded back to her. It was both a question and a statement they often used together. Jerri managed a tiny nod of reassurance before getting back to her feet.

"Let's go, lady!"

Jerri steeled her face and walked back toward the store. They passed the half-finished puzzle on the table, and Jerri worried that it might give them a clue to the boy's presence. Aaron was safe for now, but how long could the boy hold it together?

Outside, the wind surged and the rattling noise of something metal skidded across the roof. The house groaned as it fought the onslaught. Jerri and Kobe both looked up at the roof as the storm picked up strength.

"All right. Okay," she repeated before walking back to her patient.

THEY HAD to scream introductions over the wind.

"A car in front of us! They opened up on him when he told them to move. The guy got out and was about to finish him, but I got a shot off and they ran for it!" Jack tried to explain over the sound of the wind and rain. "They crashed down the road a block and then took off on foot!"

Connor was only half listening as he watched Sydney strip the shirt off Kyle and then work on the vest. Her hands kept slipping off the straps due to the rain. The puddle they were both in was only getting redder.

"We need an ambulance!" she yelled.

Jack looked over his shoulder for a moment. He was keeping an eye out for anyone approaching.

"Closest one is back by the highway, but they're cut off by some trees that are down!" Connor told her.

"You have a hospital!?"

"A hosp— No, just a clinic! But the doc is only there on Tuesday!"

Sydney raked her wet hair out of her face and gave up on the straps. She needed her trauma scissors. *But then what, Syd? You're in a frickin' puddle in the middle of a hurricane!*

"We've got to move him!"

"But—"

"Get him in the car! Now!"

Sydney had a command voice of her own when she needed it, and the two men holstered their weapons long enough to grab Kyle and shove him in the back seat of the car.

"You drive!" she ordered Connor. He obediently got into the front seat with Jack, who now had the Browning back in his fist. The doors slammed shut and the young sheriff dropped the car in gear.

"How far?" Sydney demanded, her voice only slightly less loud.

"A dozen blocks, maybe. But it's just a clinic. They don't have much."

"Anything's better than here. Let's go!"

Sydney wiped her hands on the cloth seats in an effort to dry them enough to work on the straps again. She attacked them and managed to rip a fingernail off, which produced a round of cursing. She was about to try again when the butt of a knife was thrust in her face. Her eyes popped when she took it in. It was a combat knife, a Fairburn-Sykes dagger. Its black seven-inch stiletto blade was designed to inflict maximum damage. Where the hell had Jack been keeping that? He held it out without a word or

explanation and kept his eyes on the street behind them.

"Jesus, Jack," was her only comment. The
blade went through the nylon like it was butter,
and she handed it back before prying the vest off
the man's chest.

"How bad?" Jack asked. She glanced up to see
him no longer watching their back. The storm had
reduced visibility to a matter of yards anyway.

"Dunno yet." She ripped his shirt open and
probed the man's chest after using her sleeve to
wipe away the blood in an effort to find the
wound. Eventually, she found a small hole in the
abdomen. She plugged it with her thumb and the
bleeding stopped. The man groaned with the
sudden increase in pain.

"One in the belly," she reported. "Just missed
the vest. Must have caught it when he was turning
or falling."

"He gonna be okay?" Connor asked while he
fought the storm and the steering wheel.

Syd shared a look with Jack, who shook his
head slightly. *Better to lie for now*, his look said.

"No way to know yet," she told him. "We almost there?"

"Couple blocks."

Connor was guiding the car by memory more

than by the view out the windshield. Jack was already hopelessly lost. The rain was like a cloud of fog all around them and the young sheriff was using the centerline of the road to keep them on track. Their top speed was about ten miles per hour.

"What's his name?"

"Kyle. He's ... he's my best friend."

Sydney looked at the pale face of the young man. He looked too young to be wearing a badge and a gun.

"Hang on, Kyle," she whispered.

The rain pounding on the roof was her only answer.

TYLER LAY on the countertop next to the cash register and tried to slow his breathing. It was getting harder. He looked down at the stack of tampons he held over the entry wound. They were saturated. His hand was now glued to them with his own blood, and he knew that if he pulled it away all the clotting would come with it. It was bad.

He'd seen wounds like this before while in the Marine Corps. If the corpsman got to you in time, and they had good commo and extraction, you had a good chance of making it. But that was in the Corps. All he had now was a retired nurse and three assholes, two of which he was sure would be just fine with him dying. On top of that, they were all stuck together in a damn convenience store inside a hurricane. If he was going to make it through this, he would have to do something drastic before he got too weak to do so.

He raised his head enough to see them. Wallace was pacing in front of the front door with the little viewing port. Sanford was wandering around the store and smoking a cigarette from a pack he had helped himself to from the rack. Every once in a while, he would shoot Tyler a look that read, *Why are you not dead yet?* There would be no help coming from either of them, he knew that.

What about Kobe? The boy was a follower. He'd latch onto whomever was in charge, or whomever was left alive. That, and he had just saved the boy's miserable life. He'd seen it on his face when they were speaking with the woman.

He gazed at the two men again. If I can put these two down, Kobe will do whatever I tell him, Tyler thought. It may be my only option.

First, he'd have to tell the woman he was a cop. But how to do that? Maybe if he told her she could get Kobe out of the room long enough for him to take down Sanford and Wallace. Only then would this woman be safe and his chances of seeing a doctor in time would improve.

His own gun was stuck in his belt in the middle of his back under his shirt. To get it, he'd need both hands. One to push himself up and the other to retrieve it. Could he do it and be fast enough to take them both out? Sanford was the biggest danger. The man never stood still. Even now he was wandering around the aisles, whether he was burning off nervous energy or just too high, Tyler couldn't tell. The pistol never left his hand. Wallace had stuck his gun back in its holster, but Sanford kept his clamped tight in his hand while he worked on the cigarette with the other. Maybe if he put it away. Tyler could wait for Wallace to look out the door again, and with his back to him Tyler could take him out first and then target Sanford. They would both have to be close together though, and not behind the aisles. It was a long shot, but he had to do something—and soon.

A shot of pain hit him, and he let out an involuntary groan. Sanford looked over with disgust. Evidently, Tyler was not dying quickly enough for him. He returned the look only to get a cocky grin followed by a puff of smoke blown in his direction.

The wind howled louder, and the building groaned. Wallace turned back to the door just as Jerri appeared with Kobe behind her. She was carrying a bag with a caduceus embroidered on the side and had a pink stethoscope around her neck. Tyler had a brief moment of hope, but it quickly faded at the sight of Kobe following her with a gun in his hand.

Whoever this woman was, she and Tyler were now partners—she just didn't know it yet. He almost hated to tell her.

12

In August of 2005, Hurricane Katrina, a Category 3 storm, caused $108 billion in damages and killed 1,833 people.

The clinic appeared out of the wall of rain, and Connor parked as close to the door as he could. The roof had little overhang and no gutters, so the rain poured off it in a steady deluge that flooded the small parking lot. Sydney looked up from her patient when the car stopped and took in the building and the sign.

"A vet's office?"

"The vet's office was next door," Connor explained. "It's been closed for a year. The clinic is right next to it. The red door."

Jack sized up the gap. There was no way to get inside without the storm beating them up. He spun around and faced Sydney.

"We'll get him. You get the door."

She nodded before eyeballing the distance to the door. "Let's go."

They all bailed out at once, and the storm slammed the two upwind doors shut. Sydney had to force it back open and hold it long enough for Jack to grab Kyle around his chest. Blood flowed freely again, and Jack ignored it as it soaked his shirt. Connor gathered up Kyle's legs, and they struggled through the rain to the front door.

Sydney tried the knob, but as expected it was locked. She drew her sidearm to change that, but Jack stopped her.

"No! Somebody might hear! Just boot it!"

Sydney nodded and holstered her H&K before backing up and then planting a solid kick to the door right next to the lock. It gave a bit under the impact but refused to open.

"Again!"

Sydney slammed her foot into the door again, this time rewarded with the sound of splintering wood. But still the door held.

"C'mon, Syd! Let's go!"

She reared back again, and this time put all her weight behind the kick. The door slammed open with a shower of splintered wood, and she lost her balance, tumbling inside before she could catch herself. She rolled over in time to see Jack and Connor enter with Kyle. She jumped up and slammed the door shut behind them. They laid Kyle on the floor in the small waiting room, and Jack snatched up a chair to wedge the door shut. The wind pounded against it in protest and the chair vibrated in response, but it held.

Sydney limped to the next door and pulled it open as Jack hit the lights. Thankfully, they still worked, and she was treated to a series of doors off a short hallway. An office followed by a series of exam rooms. Most of them empty and covered in dust. The two larger ones appeared to be still in use, so she picked one and yelled to the men behind her.

"Bring him in here!"

She yanked fresh paper across the bed and laid it flat as they arrived. She flung the one chair out into the hall and then started looking through the drawers.

"What do we do?" Jack asked.

"Get his clothes off—all of them. Dry him off and get him warm."

Sydney slammed the drawers of the small chest looking for equipment, anything she could use to stop the bleeding. She instead found cotton balls and tongue depressors. Boxes of medication samples and Band-Aids. Reflex hammers and tape. All of it worthless to her, right now.

"What the hell! This is my mother's frickin' medicine cabinet! Where's the real stuff?"

"Maybe in the hallway?" Jack called out. "There's got to be a supply room somewhere!" He was cutting Kyle's pants off with the dagger while Connor stripped off the coat.

Sydney followed the suggestion and raced out into the hallway. She found a door with a lock on it and an opaque glass window. This time she didn't hesitate. Drawing her gun, she smashed the glass open and reached in to work the lock. The door slammed open, and she crunched the glass beneath her boots. Shelf after shelf of supplies greeted her, as well as some items on wheels in the back of the room.

"Jackpot."

She began yanking items off the shelves. Bags of fluid. Bandages. Kerlix. Iodine. ACE bandages. IV supplies. She found a plastic bin and loaded it to capacity. She took note of some equipment parked in the back under protective covers but dismissed it. She didn't have time right now.

"Get the bleeding stopped first," she told herself.

She returned to the exam room to find Jack holding pressure on the entrance wound and Connor covering Kyle with a blanket from under the bed. The floor and side of the bed were already sticky with blood, and she noticed that Jack's shirt was as well. Later. She had other things to fix first.

Yanking a box of latex gloves off the wall, she slipped a pair on and grabbed the Kerlix first.

"Let me in there, Jack."

Jack stepped aside and Sydney began stuffing Kerlix into the small wound as fast as she could. The bleeding slowed until it became a trickle. Sydney followed this with two layers of 4x4 dressings and then slapped a sheet of plastic over the whole thing before taping it down on all sides.

"Anything I can—?"

She cut Jack off. "I need that ACE bandage. Connor, you hold him up and we'll wrap it around him. It's a pressure bandage—it has to be tight!"

She planted another stack of 4x4s over the previous pile and then placed the stretchy fabric over
it. Connor sat Kyle up, and she and Jack wound
the bandage around his abdomen from belt to
lower chest several times. Sydney pulled it as tight
as she could before clamping it off.

"I need a stethoscope ... and a B/P cuff."

The two men jumped. Jack found a cuff on a
hook in the hall next to a scale, and Connor found
a scope sitting on the desk in the office. They col-
lided in the hallway in their haste to return.

Sydney held up a finger for silence, as she tried
to listen over the sound of the storm pounding the
roof with rain. Her face clouded and she tried
again in various spots.

"It's so noisy that I can't tell. He may be quiet
on the left." She wrapped the B/P cuff around his
arm on the opposite side of the wound, grabbed
his wrist and pumped the bulb.

"What does that mean?" Connor asked when
she stopped.

Sydney threw the scope around her neck with
a practiced motion. "The round may have
bounced around and hit a lung. There's no exit
wound. That means it could be almost anywhere
inside before it stopped. I can't tell. His pressure is
okay—not great, but okay."

"What else can we do?" Jack asked.

"I need ..." Her mind raced, struggling to pull up checklists she used to know by heart. "I need a pulse-ox monitor. Or any monitor, really. Let's look around."

"Pulse ox ...?" Connor asked.

"It's that little thing they clamp on your finger when you're in the hospital."

"Got it. Seen it on TV." He raced off to search for one.

"I'll stay with him. You know what I need, right?" Sydney asked Jack as she pumped up the cuff again.

"I'm on it. You okay?"

"Yes, I'm fine. Just go!"

Jack went. He heard Connor slamming drawers in the room across the hall, so he ventured down to the next. It was a copy of the first and he found nothing. Moving on, he looked in every drawer and shelf he came to but still found nothing like what Sydney needed. The door at the end of the hall was locked and made of heavy wood. He bypassed it for the moment. A smaller door revealed itself to be a broom closet. On the top shelf were a variety of cleaning products and a cardboard box. It read *Lifepack* on the side.

He pulled it down and opened the top in a

shower of dust. Inside was a machine made of faded plastic, its once white color now a pale yellow. On its front were two black handle-looking things. If it was what Sydney had sent him for, it was a much older model. He scooped it up and carried it back to the exam room.

"Is this what you wanted?"

She looked in the box and her eyes widened.

"Wow. That's older than me. Let's plug it in and see if it still works."

She found an outlet and carefully plugged in the device. Instead of sparks, she got a welcoming yellow light.

"Boys, we may be in business."

———

JERRI LISTENED to his lungs again, with Tyler watching her face. She frowned before noticing him and then told him the truth.

"You have a pneumothorax."

"Wass dat?" Kobe asked.

"A hole in his chest cavity," she told him. "His lung is collapsing. Clear off the counter."

Kobe balked at the order, but after a look from Tyler, Kobe did as she'd asked. He pulled down a display of candy and then knocked the rest to the floor. They swung Tyler's feet up and laid him on the hard surface.

"Better?" she asked her patient. She stripped off her jacket and wadded it up before placing it under his head.

"Yeah ... a little."

"You need a chest tube."

"You say so."

Jerri looked at Kobe but quickly dismissed him. He was obviously not the one in charge.

"Excuse me?"

Wallace spun around. "What?"

"I—I need some things. In the store. Can I?"

Wallace waved the gun at the shelves. "Watch her, Kobe."

Jerri pushed off the counter and walked the isles with Kobe following. She gathered tape, more tampons, and a small box of diapers. Racking her brain for what to use, she grabbed a box of straws before deciding they were too big for what she needed.

"Smaller," she mumbled.

"Smaller what?" Kobe asked.

"Smaller straws. I need smaller straws."

Kobe looked at the ones in her hand.

"So, get a juice box," he said.

Jerri stopped and blinked. The answer was

right in the next aisle. How did she not think of that? She went around the end to the cooler and grabbed some juice boxes. Cherry flavored—Aaron liked apple.

Returning to Tyler, she saw that he was breathing faster already. She had to hurry. Dropping her items on the counter, she moved around to the other side and rooted in the items Kobe had pushed off onto the floor.

The spindle. She found it on the floor in the pile of candy he had pushed over. It had about an inch of receipts piled up on it, and she stripped them off and tossed them aside. She eyeballed the stainless-steel spike before turning around and selecting a bottle of grain alcohol off a shelf. She twisted the bottle open and dropped the spindle inside to soak.

She had a decision to make. Needle decompression with the spindle and straw, or a full-blown chest tube? The storm shook the building again and made her decision for her. Whatever she did, it would have to work for hours.

Clearing more space, she reached into the medical bag. Although she had not seen or done a chest tube in years, the mechanics of it were coming back to her. It was simple, really. A tube into the chest cavity hooked up to a suction device, which drained air and blood away so the lung could inflate and do its job. A plumbing problem, one that any first-year doctor or paramedic could do.

Except that they would have the right equipment and others to help them. Jerri was on her own and had a gun to her head. Her hands were sweating inside the gloves.

She had one IV bag and one bottle of sterile water. Two IV sets. She needed more. She needed some bigger tubing, something to act as the actual chest tube. But what? Maybe out in the garage? In the kitchen? Her mind walked the building in search of supplies.

The fish tank! They had gotten it for Aaron's birthday, but it'd not been set up yet. There was tubing for the filter in the box.

Ignoring the teenager with the gun trailing her, she found the box under the counter. The tubing was just the right size. She pulled it free of its packaging and turned to Kobe.

"I need a bowl from the kitchen. A big one." She used her mother's voice and waited. The boy couldn't meet her gaze and moved off.

Rummaging in the drawer under the cash register she found the paper punch. Squeezing the tube to fit inside its jaws, she snipped several holes in the last couple of inches and then used the scissors to cut the end into a beveled tip. By the time she was done, Kobe was back with a large steel bowl.

"Perfect." She set the bowl down on the counter and then tossed in the tubing, scissors, a couple of the straws, and a small pocketknife from her pocket. Kobe flinched at the sight of the knife but said nothing when it went in the bowl. His eyes widened a bit when she proceeded to pour an entire bottle of grain alcohol over the contents, filling the bowl to the rim.

Her patient let out a groan and grabbed at his chest.

"You okay?"

"Can't ... breathe."

"Hold on. I'm working on it," she told him.

After grabbing the sterile water bottle, she dumped it out in the soda fountain and returned the lid to it. Snaking the end of the tubing out from the bowl, she traced its outline of the top and then attacked it with the knife, carving out as tight a hole as she could.

She pointed over Kobe's head. "Silicone. There's some in aisle two."

He moved quicker this time, and Jerri exchanged a look with Tyler before resuming her work. Cutting more holes and separating the filter from the reservoir of the IV tubing, she reassembled the components into the picture she had in her head. The IV bag was inverted, and she carefully adjusted the tubes so the long one was underwater and the short was aligned to allow air to escape. When she was satisfied, she sealed it all in place.

"Clamp. I need a clamp."

She walked a few feet to a display of potato chips and pulled a set of clips off the holder. Testing the spring, she hoped it would be strong enough to squeeze the tubing shut. She measured off two feet of tubing and clamped it before cutting it cleanly a few inches down. Thankfully, the straw was a tight fit, so she used it to reconnect the two pieces by sliding it inside both ends and then pressing them together. It all went back in the bowl to soak.

She turned to Tyler. He was struggling.

"It's going to hurt. Are you ready?"

Short of air, he could only nod.

"Lay flat for me."

He did and she palpated his ribs until she found the spot she wanted between the fifth and sixth rib. She put a gloved finger on the spot and doused the area with Betadine. He flinched when the cold liquid hit his skin.

"Something ... to bite on."

Kobe grabbed a pad of sticky notes and stuck them in Tyler's mouth. Tyler bit down hard and nodded.

"Hold his shoulders," Jerri told Kobe, who hesitated.

"Put the damn gun down and hold his shoulders!"

She reached into the bowl and pulled out the knife. Holding it over Tyler's ribs, she glared at Kobe until he did as she had told him. He tucked the gun into his pants and put his hands on Tyler's shoulders, pushing him down on the cold Formica.

Jerri stuck the knife in before she lost her nerve and cut a half-inch incision deep into the space she had marked with her finger. Tyler flinched but held himself down. When she was deep enough, she stuck a finger in the hole and reached for the scissors. Inserting them, she used them to spread the hole wider until she could see. A little deeper.

A stream of blood suddenly flowed from the wound, coating her hand and dripping on the floor. She dropped the scissors and reached for the tubing, shoving it into the hole vacated by her finger and advancing it until the perforated tip was well inside. Tyler squirmed and Kobe leaned on him harder until she stopped advancing it. With one hand firmly holding it, she took a deep breath and unclamped the tubing.

Blood filled the tube and advanced to the empty bottle. A couple of inches filled the container before air bubbles appeared. It was working. She let out the breath she was holding and examined her patient's face.

"Okay?"

He spit out the sticky notes and clenched his teeth before speaking.

"Hurts, but ... I can breathe."

"Good. Hold still, we're not done yet."

A few minutes later Jerri had the tube sealed against his ribs and held in place with a few stiches and some tape. She didn't like it, but it was the best she could do with what she had. She took some small comfort in the fact that the more she worked the more slowly he breathed.

She finished and stripped off the bloody gloves before using the stethoscope. Better. Not great, but the lung was working again and moving air. It was all she could hope for.

"It's working," she told him.

"*Dieu aide moi,*" Tyler whispered.

"*Je ne suis pas lui, mais je vais essayer,*" Jerri replied.

"You speak?" he asked.

"I learned in high school. Even went to Paris once."

"I'm from the Dominican Republic. It's a bit different."

"Yes," she agreed before glancing toward the front of the store. "Do they?"

He smiled at the question. "They barely speak English."

"I see, I—"

"I need you to listen closely. I have something I need to tell you."

"Yes?"

"I'm a police officer. I'm not one of them. I'm undercover."

Jerri's eyes became saucers.

"My name is Tyler Turner," the man whispered. "I'm DEA. These men are drug traffickers. You must believe me."

"I ... I do. But what can—"

They were cut off by a yell from the men in front.

13

82.0% The percentage of occupied housing units that have enough nonperishable emergency food to sustain everyone for three days.

Beeping.

Sydney half listened to it as she cleaned Kyle's arms with alcohol. She had found some IV supplies. Most of them were expired, but she didn't really care right now. She had two bags of saline and one bag of Ringers. Both would serve to keep Kyle's blood pressure up, but only for so long. The saline would eventually leach back out of his blood vessels, and unless they had stopped the bleeding by then, Kyle would be worse off than before. The Ringers was better for this, but she wanted to save it for last. What she needed was some Hespan, but that was a pipe dream. She'd have to make do with expired saline and hope for the best.

Her biggest fear was an internal bleed that wouldn't stop. If the chest cavity was punctured, the blood could pool in the space normally occupied by the lungs, and since she couldn't hear a damn thing, it would be bad before she knew about it.

She applied the tourniquet and watched the veins on Kyle's arm pop up. She selected the best one and deftly inserted the needle. The flash of blood rewarded her marksmanship, and she advanced the catheter over the needle before withdrawing it and connecting the tubing. She pulled the tourniquet and watched the site for infiltration. Seeing none and getting a nice steady flow of drops in the chamber, she taped everything in place and removed the gloves. She'd give him

200cc's and drop it down to a maintenance drip. And then see how his blood pressure changed.

"Riding a bike," she muttered, before getting up and checking the monitor.

The monitor was a Lifepack 10. A model that had been phased out years ago. It was the machine she had learned on. The fact that this one even worked was a credit to the company. Back then, these monitors had been bullet proof, and made to work in any environment, no matter how wet, dry, cold, hot, or bloody. The only bad things she remembered were the cords that were too short and the awful battery life. That was not a concern today since they had no batteries. The monitor was plugged into the wall and unless they lost power, it would probably keep working. Right now, it was providing an EKG on its tiny green screen with a corresponding beep for every heartbeat. It allowed her to monitor her patient without having to constantly watch him. But she still worried about its age. The monitor could die at any second, and she may not notice in time if it did.

"How we doing, Syd?"

Sydney sighed. "Better. Not much, though. He needs a surgeon."

She spun on the small stool to see both Jack

and Connor dressed in button-down shirts. Clean and white and crisp.

"New wardrobe?"

"The doc likes to keep a few shirts in his office. T-shirts, too." He tossed her one.

Sydney caught it.

"You ever wonder why he might do that?"

The two men exchanged a look. "He's a rural doc—travels from clinic to clinic. Figured he keeps them handy so he doesn't have to pack them with him."

"Maybe," she allowed. "Or it could be because his shirts get bled on and puked on a lot. Just sayin'."

They both frowned and examined their shirts. Despite the possibility, they were better than the wet and blood-soaked items they had exchanged them for.

Connor walked to the bedside and looked down at Kyle. His color was better, but that was about it.

"How's he doing?"

"I honestly don't know. I'm giving him fluids to maintain his blood pressure, but if he's bleeding internally ... there's no telling. We just have to get him through the storm. Where's the nearest hospital with a helicopter?"

"Jacksonville."

"Soon as the storm clears, we call them or get a ground unit in here somehow."

"Before that," Jack said, "we have to find the guys who did this."

Connor nodded at Kyle and then at Jack.

"How do we do that?"

"I'd like to even the playing field. There's four of them. Only three of us and we have to stay with Kyle here. Is there anybody else in town with some law enforcement experience? Or maybe some soldiers who still know what they're doing?"

"No other soldiers that I know of, besides Kyle here. Oh, everybody here's armed. This town is redneck as hell if you haven't noticed already, but none of these boys has ever been up against anything more dangerous than a gator or a hog." He paused for a long moment and looked at Kyle before going on. Jack and Sydney exchanged a puzzled look.

"There is one person who can help us."

JERRI'S EYES widened as her patient mumbled in French. Wallace questioned her from the door.

"What's he sayin'?"

"Stuff about home. A beach somewhere. It's the pain," she offered, hoping he was naïve enough to believe her.

Kobe watched as Tyler faded off to sleep.

"What now? He gonna be okay?"

"I guess that depends on your friends there. I need to talk to them."

"Just stay here," the boy told her. The gun was out, and his false front was back. "Yo, boss! Lady wants to talk."

Jerri patted Tyler's leg before Wallace turned and walked over.

"What?"

"Your friend here is in a bad way. His lung collapsed. I managed to get it inflated, but it's only temporary. He needs blood—and a surgeon."

"You got one here?"

"No, Jacksonville is the closest, and—"

"Shit, lady!" Sanford cut in. "Ain't nobody going to Jacksonville! Not out in this storm!" He laughed and then helped himself to a beer from the cooler before sitting back down.

"He's gonna have to tough it out for a bit," Wallace told her. He eyeballed Tyler's still form lying on the counter and the blood coating the floor.

"He alive now?" he asked.

"Yes."

"Keep him that way."

Jerri fumed as he walked away. She watched him pause at a display of maps and then select one of northern Florida and southern Georgia. He and the big one with the tattoos spread it out and started looking for a way out of town. She listened for a bit before Kobe interrupted her.

"Why ain't he awake?" he asked.

She examined Tyler. He wasn't asleep. He was listening.

"The body shuts down in order to heal itself."

Kobe watched Tyler's chest rise and fall for a bit before walking away. He selected a candy bar from the pile on the floor and ripped it open with his teeth. She watched him as he wandered around.

The boy was scared and trying hard not to show it. Jerri had no idea what had happened to bring them here, but she knew these men were very dangerous. The leader seemed to be calm, but the other two made her very nervous, especially the big tattooed man. She watched him as the two spoke, his mannerisms spoke of one who was under the influence of something. That, combined with his temperament, made her want to flee.

But could she? There was a back door in the

garage she could get through very quickly. But how to do it and take Aaron, too? And what of this man lying on the counter in front of her? Could she abandon him here, knowing what he had just told her?

Her eyes wandered toward the back of the building. How long could Aaron hold it together? Could he stay under the bed until these men left? What if he was discovered?

The thought of that and what might happen afterward painted pictures in her mind she didn't want, and she quickly pushed them aside. She distracted herself by checking the chest tube and listening to Tyler's lungs again.

Maybe this man lying before her was the answer? Maybe he knew what to do?

As if to answer her, his eyes cracked and then snapped open. He glanced around before meeting her gaze and holding it for a moment. He offered the faintest of smiles and an encouraging wink before adopting his unconscious façade again.

I'm working on it, the look told her.

THE NATIONAL WEATHER SERVICE *now reports Hurricane Nancy is maintaining its Category Four strength with winds reaching 130 miles per hour. The eye is currently twenty nautical miles northeast of Gainesville, moving north-west at twenty-five miles per hour. The storm is expected to maintain this path for the next four hours and reenter the Atlantic north of Jacksonville. Residents along the upper east coast of Florida and Georgia are urged to evacuate if they have not already done so. Specifically, the cities of St. Augustine and Jacksonville and up the coast to Amelia Island, Jekyll Island, Kings Bay, and Brunswick. Again, if you are a resident of these cities, particularly the barrier island communities, you are urged to evacuate. This is a major storm that will result in high winds and massive flooding. Expected storm surge will be augmented by high tide within the next few hours. All counties along the coast are now under a flash flood warning. This storm may also produce multiple tornados at any time with little warning.*

Our computer models now predict the storm will travel north and then east as this cold front and the jet stream push down from the north. The spaghetti models now take it north-east, making its way up the coast of Georgia and the Carolinas, before once again being shoved out over the Atlantic. The storm may weaken slightly with the combination of high-level wind shear and being over land, but our model tells us this weakening will be slight, perhaps only enough to drop Nancy to a Category Three.

To repeat, the National Weather Service now reports Hurricane Nancy is back to Category Four strength with winds reaching 130 miles per hour ...

JACK PICKED himself up off the wet concrete and leaned into the wind hard, using the shelter of the car to cut the rain and wind that had thrown him off his feet. The deputy's rain gear kept most of the rain out, but Jack was already soaked underneath it, so it didn't really matter. He grasped the car's door handle and forced the door open, wedging his body between it and the interior, slowly working himself inside before letting the wind slam it shut behind him. He paused long enough to catch his breath, and the windows quickly fogged. He cracked a window just enough to rectify that, and it whistled back at him in protest.

He looked outside at the storm and cursed. It was getting worse. There were more tree branches in the road and more debris being flung through the air. Shingles made erratic paths across the sky, resembling bats with broken wings. A couple skipped off the hood of the car and left marks in the paint. Jack frowned at the damage. Between that, the bullet holes, and the blood-soaked back seat, he doubted he was going to get his deposit back. He started the car up, turning on the high beams. The lights barely penetrated the wall of water in front of him.

He glanced behind him at the clinic. Its few windows were boarded up, and the direction of the wind was from the side where the closed veterinarian's office was. As a result, it was somewhat protected. At least until the eye passed and the wind changed direction. When that happened, the clinic would get its full force from the north. On that wall was a single-door garage, the contents of which Jack had not thought to ask about. Either way, the three of them should be safe until he got back—from the storm anyway. Connor had wanted to come with him, but Jack had overruled him, arguing that Sydney couldn't take care of Kyle and defend herself and him at the same time. That, and there was the possibility of Kyle getting worse. If that happened, Syd would need a second set of hands. The two reasons, coupled with Jack's badge, were enough to convince the young sheriff to stay.

None of this changed the fact that there were four armed men out there somewhere, and while

Jack wanted nothing more than to hunker down and wait out the storm, he couldn't let the men shoot any more people. The eye of the storm was coming. It would provide a short period of calm, enough to let the men out of whatever hole they had crawled into. They would be desperate to escape and desperate men with guns did damage. Jack had to find them before the eye came if he hoped to prevent that damage.

But first, he needed some help.

Dropping the car in gear, he wrestled it around in a U-turn and entered the street the sheriff had described.

Jack repeated the instructions out loud to himself. "Four blocks down and one block left. The house with the dumpster in front. Frank."

He kept the car in the middle of the road and crept forward. The wind rocked it, but the car stayed in contact with the concrete. He navigated around three tree branches and one set of patio furniture before reaching the intersection. Turning left, he found a row of houses close together and this helped lessen the wind some.

The reflective tape on the side of the dumpster glowed in the headlights, and Jack pulled the car up next to it as close as he could, using it to block the wind. He left it running and shoved the door open with his foot before bailing out and moving bent at the waist up to the porch.

The porch kept the majority of the rain at bay, so Jack was able to wipe the water from his face before sizing up the door. Like the windows on both sides, it was covered in plywood with a small hole cut in the middle. Jack looked down to make sure his badge was showing and pounded on the wood.

He heard a dog bark from inside. He pounded again.

He was rewarded with the sight of a human eye filling the hole. He held up his badge for the man to see, and the eye got wider.

"Step back!" he heard a man yell.

Jack did and a second later a hammer impacted the other side of the wood. The plywood jumped out a fraction. The pounding continued. When the gap was wide enough, Jack grabbed the edge and pulled. The hammer was replaced with a few strong kicks and the gap widened enough for Jack to see inside.

He was met by a large man holding a large handgun. Jack's face fell and he raised his hands.

"Show me that badge again!" The barrel of the gun pointed to the badge on his chest. Jack snaked a hand down and held up the shield. The man squinted at it for a moment, and finally the gun fell to his waist.

"What the hell is going on?"

It was the second time in the last hour this scenario had happened. Jack was starting to think it was standard procedure here in this little town.

"I was just passing through! There was a problem at the bridge. One of your deputies was shot! I need your help!"

"Get inside!" Frank held the door open, and Jack snaked in. He slammed it behind him and Frank threw the deadbolt before he turned to find Jack face to face with Belvedere. The dog let out a growl while simultaneously wagging his tail.

Frank addressed the dog first. "You can't do both, you dummy. Go lay down."

The dog took one last sniff at Jack before following directions and returning to his spot in the doorway. He circled twice before lying down where he could see everything.

"Don't worry about him, he's all talk," Frank said before sticking out a hand and examining Jack's face. "Frank Warner. You're Agent Jack Randall?"

Jack shook the offered hand. "Yes. Have we met?"

Frank smiled at that. "No, but we get TV out here in the swamp. In color, even."

"Sorry."

"Tell me what happened?"

"My partner and I were waiting in line at the bridge when they closed it. One of your deputies, Kyle, walked up to the car in front of us, I assume to tell them to turn around. Anyway, something happened and next thing we know the driver gets off a shot at Kyle and puts him on the ground. Before it could go further, my partner and I got a few shots off at them. They ran for it and crashed their car a few blocks away and then took off on foot."

"How bad is Kyle?"

"He's stable right now. My partner's a former paramedic and she's taking care of him at the clinic. I left her with Connor Clancy, and he gave me directions here. I'm worried about what these guys might do. Connor said you were once the sheriff here? Can you help me find them?"

Frank was standing in front of him with a hard look on his face. He seemed lost in thought.

"Frank?"

"What? Yeah, yeah. Let me grab a few things. That all you have?" He pointed to the Browning in Jack's armpit.

"Yeah. I've got three magazines. 9mm."

Frank pointed. "In that closet, there's a 12-gauge. Shells are on the shelf above it. Let me get suited up. I'll be right back."

With that, he walked away toward the back of the house and Jack made his way to the closet. He found the gun leaning against the corner. A Remington 870 that had seen a few years. Jack grabbed the box of shells off the shelf and carried them to the couch. He cycled the action, and shells fell to the floor. He inspected the chamber and took a glance down the barrel before reloading the gun and cradling it in his arms. The shells went in his pockets. He looked up to see Belvedere watching his every move.

"Sorry to interrupt your nap there, big guy," Jack told him.

The basset hound snorted and dropped his head to the floor. Jack took that as clearance to look around. He walked to the fireplace and saw a row of pictures. Frank in uniform in front of a patrol car. He and a happy woman at a scenic overlook that Jack guessed was the Blue Ridge Mountains. The next one shocked him and he leaned in to confirm what he was seeing. It was a picture of the young deputy, Kyle. He was kneeling next to a wheelchair occupied by the elderly lady.

She wore a headscarf and looked much thinner than in the previous picture.

Cancer. Jack frowned and stepped back. He looked around the room and noticed an urn with the woman's name on it. She had passed just over a year ago. Kyle was Frank's son—why hadn't he said anything?

The sound of Frank's approach prompted Jack to move away from the pictures. If Frank didn't want to mention it, then Jack would respect that. Besides, they had other things to worry about right now.

Frank reentered the room dressed for the weather. Heavy waterproof boots were on his feet and a pair of Gore-Tex hunting overalls covered his legs and chest over a wool sweater. He tossed a similar pair to Jack.

"Try 'em on. You'll get hypothermia if you don't stay dry, even in this temperature."

Jack set the shotgun down and sized up the garments. The pants were a no-go, but the sweater would work. He put it on and immediately felt warmer. Frank had strapped the handgun, a large .357, to his body with a Sam Browne belt, and donned a department rain slicker over it. He reached in the pocket and pulled out a box of 9mm shells. He tossed them to Jack.

"They're old, but not too old. Should work fine."

Jack quickly replaced the rounds he had fired earlier and slammed the magazine back home in the Browning.

"Ready as we're going to get. Where do we start?"

"Not sure," Jack replied. "There's four of them. They were in a BMW, and I got off a few rounds as they pulled away. Evidently, I got lucky and hit something necessary and they drove into a building after a couple of blocks. It was raining so hard I could hardly see, but I may have hit one of them. They were bailing out of the car when I caught up to 'em. After we exchanged a few rounds, they decided to run and disappeared into the houses. Four to one wasn't something I thought I should take on, and around that time my partner started screaming for me. I got back to her just in time to convince Clancy not to shoot her. After that, we did nothing but take care of Kyle."

Jack stopped and waited for Frank to ask about Kyle again, but he didn't. Instead, Frank's mind was working the problem.

"If it were me, I'd be finding another car as fast as I could and bailing out of town."

"Connor says there's a big tree down across the

road. Evidently, your fire guys called him and let him know about it just before the communications tower went down. The bridge is out in the other direction. Either way, they'd need a car first, and everybody seems to have theirs locked up. I'm thinking they found a place to hunker down for a bit. But the eye is coming."

"You think they'll try to grab a car and make a run for it when it gets here?"

"What I would do." Jack shrugged.

Frank thought that over before nodding in agreement. "Yeah, that makes sense."

"You know the town. I don't," Jack said. "I don't know where to look."

"There's not much town to look through. The school is where almost everybody is, but that's a few miles away. Lucky. We built it on the highest land in the area. I can't see them going there; they must be somewhere close. Let's go look around. What you driving?"

"A rented Impala," Jack informed him with a grimace.

Frank snorted. "I guess we'll take mine. It's my old cruiser. I bought it at the police auction, and it's still got the spotlight on the A-post." He added with a grin, "I was the only bidder."

"All right. I'll follow you." Jack was relieved. He

wasn't sure how Frank would take the sight of Kyle's blood coating the back seat.

Frank grabbed a hammer, and he and Jack forced their way back out onto the front porch. They paused long enough to pound the sheet of plywood back up while Belvedere barked in protest from inside and then ducked around the side of the house to the garage. Inside, they found Frank's old cruiser, a Ford Crown Victoria. Still police blue but stripped of its insignia and sporting plain black rims. It still screamed "police car" at any distance. Frank started it up, and the big V-8 answered with a confident rumble that spoke of power to spare. Jack settled into the passenger side and secured the shotgun in the rack in the middle of the dash, itself a leftover of its days on the force. Jack was surprised to see a radio installed. It was a civilian model but no doubt programmed to monitor the police and fire frequencies. The Plexiglas divider separating the front from the back was also still in place. Some cops never really retired. He held his tongue.

"Let's start at this car they were driving. Where is it?"

"Back on the main road," Jack answered, "a few blocks short of the bridge."

Frank turned right and led them into the storm. Jack was lost before they had gone one block.

14

In September of 2004, Hurricane Ivan, a Category 4 storm, caused $18 billion in damages and killed 92 people.

Mark Dawson sat in the La-Z-Boy his crew had parked in the middle bay of the fire station and watched the wind and rain beat on the windows of the large overhead door. The safety bracing creaked and groaned with every gust, and some water was making its way in and around the edges. Mark had thought it best to place a guard on it in the event it started to fail. His boys had responded by moving the chair out of the day room and parking it between the two big red trucks. He'd frowned at first, but now admitted it was a good idea. He had another hour before it was Steve's turn, but he found he was enjoying the view of the storm.

Might have to drag a second chair out here, he thought.

There were only four of them, all volunteers, here at the station instead of with their families at the school. So, he cut them some slack. They were trapped inside by the storm and that was bad enough. He was debating whether to have them venture out and work on the tree when the eye came but had decided to play that by ear. The cottonwood was huge, and their chainsaws were only so big. They had them for cutting holes in roofs and walls, not for commercial logging. Two of his men were pros with a chainsaw, though. They ran them all day at their day jobs, which was the only reason Mark was tempted to have them attack the tree. He didn't like being cut off from the town, especially since they had lost communication. The logical thing to do was to wait until he could get hold of the local logging company and have them send out one of their huge skidders to shove the tree off the road. Then they could cut on it whenever they got around to it. Either way, the storm would most likely make that decision for him.

Another gust threatened to implode the doors, and they creaked and rubbed against the big inner tubes they had sandwiched between them and the front of the trucks. It was an old trick, but it worked. He and Steve had held the inner tube to the front of the trucks, and Rich had creeped them forward until they made contact with the door. Now the wind would have to move the truck if it wanted to blow the door in. Crude but effective. Mark had more confidence in the inner tubes and trucks than he did the extra bracing on the door, but it was all they had.

The door to the crew quarters opened and Rich wandered out to stand next to him. He took in the rain beating on the glass and frowned.

"It's getting worse. The eye should be here in about an hour or so. How're the doors handling it?"

"Okay, so far. How you know when the eye's coming?"

"Steve keeps trying the radio and caught a bit of a report. I had to leave; the constant static was driving me nuts. Isn't it obvious what's happening? I mean, it's gonna rain hard and blow hard for the next day or so. There, I just gave you a full and accurate weather report all by myself."

Mark had a short laugh. "True enough. I'm sure he's just passing the time. What are you guys doing?"

"Rob was reading a book, probably sleeping by now. I was watching a movie."

"Which one?"

"Perfect Storm."

Mark laughed again. "Appropriate. Wait. Didn't they all die in that?"

"Yup."

They both fell silent for a moment and watched it rain.

"What the hell!?" Rich walked to the window and planted his hands on both sides of his head in an effort to see better. "You see that?"

"What?" Mark asked. He didn't want to get up, the chair was comfortable.

"There's somebody out there!"

That got Mark's attention. He worked the footrest lever and got to his feet to join Rich at the window.

"Where?"

"Across the road. To the right."

Mark saw the bobbing head of a hooded man walking as best he could in the ditch across the road. The ditch was deep and full of water, but it offered the only shelter from the wind. The man's head was down and aimed toward the ground as he fought his way forward.

"Shit. He doesn't even see us. Watch your ears."

"What?"

Mark ignored him and jumped up in the nearest truck. Rich saw him don his earmuffs and quickly stuffed both fingers in his ears.

WAAAAAAAA!

The sound of the air horn shook the doors and the fluids in Rich's body. He ignored both and gazed outside to see the man's head come up and stare towards them. He began gesturing wildly behind him and the two men soon saw two more figures climb out of the ditch and head toward them. A woman and what appeared to be a small girl. The smaller one lost her footing and clung to the larger one.

"Let 'em in!" Mark yelled.

They both ran to the regular door and tore at the hurricane shutters. By the time they got them down, the three were outside and crouched against the door.

"Careful it don't yank your arm off," Mark advised before grabbing the door with Rich and bracing his feet. Rich threw the lock and Mark let it crack open.

The wind grabbed the door and flung it wide, dragging the two firemen with it. They held on and yelled for the people to get inside. The man dragged the woman and child toward them and then shoved them both through the door. They collapsed on the tile floor and struggled to catch their breath. Rich and Mark wrestled the door shut and locked it.

Steve emerged from around the corner. "What the hell?"

"Don't just stand there. Help 'em up!"

They each grabbed a person and got them to their feet. It looked to be a husband and wife and their preteen daughter.

"Are you okay?"

The father nodded, his teeth were chattering. "Th-thanks. Our car went off the road and into the water. We couldn't stay inside. I remembered seeing the station on our way into town, so we tried to find you."

Mark stared at the man, shocked by his stupidity. Rich was also dumbfounded.

"What the hell were you out driving around in a damn hurricane for?"

"They were shooting at us!" the little girl chimed in.

"What?"

"I ... I can explain."

Steve's medic eyes were evaluating the trio and seeing signs of hypothermia. He cut into the conversation before it went any further.

"Let's get them warm and dry first, Chief."

The men were all friends, on the job or not. Steve only called him Chief if it was important. He quickly saw what Steve was seeing and got himself back on track.

"Yeah, all right. Rich, go find them some dry clothes and a few blankets. Let's get them in the day room." He guided the man and his family inside after his men. He exchanged a look with Steve.

Somebody was shooting at them?

Steve just shrugged. He had no idea either.

I'm sure as hell going to find out, though, Mark thought.

WALLACE FINISHED his business and flushed the toilet, half-expecting storm water to come gushing out the second he did so. Everything else seemed to be underwater in this damn town. His neck was sore from looking out the little peephole, and he didn't like what he was seeing. The storm was going full force and there was nothing he could do to stop it. They had to get the coke and get the hell out of here.

He kicked the door open and walked into the bedroom to find Sanford waiting for him.

"Told you to wait up front."

"Ain't nobody going anywhere, not out in that shit. Besides, I gotta piss too."

"So piss." Wallace moved to walk past him, but Sanford put a hand on his chest.

"You best back that shit up," Wallace told him.

Sanford dropped the hand and whispered, "Ain't like that. What we gonna do here?" He looked to the front to make sure they were alone.

"You think I'm jacking off in there or something? What you think I'm thinking about?"

"All right, so what's the plan?"

"Ain't nothing moving till this damn storm quits. When it does, we gotta be ready. We send Kobe out to get us a new car and then use them tools I saw in the garage to break into the trunk of the Beemer and get the product back. Then we get the fuck out of this hole and back on the road."

"Yeah, okay. I figured that much. But we got more problems than that."

"If he can't travel, we leave him here." Wallace shrugged.

"He'll talk."

"The hell he will. He talks and he'll get a shank his first day in jail. He knows that."

"All right, then. What about her? Huh? What's gonna stop her?"

Wallace looked away. "I ain't got that far yet."

Sanford puffed his chest out. "I have."

Wallace had an idea what Sanford's plan was already. "And what's that?"

"We use her to make sure we get out of here. Once we're clear, we don't need 'em anymore."

"Them?"

"Her and Dom. Both of 'em are just loose ends. Jackson don't like loose ends. Soon as we clear this town, I say we find a quiet spot and leave 'em. Permanent like."

Wallace thought it over. It was simple. Brutal. But that's how life worked sometimes.

"All right, but not until I say so. For now, we keep her busy taking care of Dom. The center of this storm s'pose to come and I think it calms down when that happens. If Kobe can get us a car before then, we make a run for the coke and then blow. After that, I'll decide on your plan."

Sanford nodded. For once, Wallace was agreeing with him. He turned and walked to the small bathroom. Wallace let him go and returned up front.

Under the bed, Aaron clamped both hands over his mouth. The words he had just heard threatened to overcome him. He loosened them enough to whisper the words to himself.

"All right, okay. All right, okay. All right, okay."

The toilet flushed again.

WALLACE WALKED BACK through the store, not even slowing to look at Dom. He didn't want to meet his eyes, for fear the man would see the thoughts in his head. He moved straight to the peephole and took a good look before calling out.

"Kobe. C'mere."

Kobe shot a worried look at Dom, who gave him a nod of encouragement. "Get something big," Dom told him.

Kobe nodded back and shared a look with Jerri before leaving them both and walking up front.

"Need you to go find us a car."

"In that shit?"

"Yeah, in that shit. Nobody else gonna be out there, you can have your pick."

Kobe hesitated and Wallace turned away from the peephole and fixed his eyes on him.

"You got a problem with that? What? You scared of a little storm?"

Kobe puffed up. "Naw, man. I ain't scared."

"Then grab some tools and get on it."

Kobe turned toward the garage entrance and shot a look at Dom before disappearing inside. He returned with a crowbar and some other tools which he'd stuffed in his pockets.

"Don't get some dinky-ass little car. I want something big enough to hold all of us." Wallace waved his gun to indicate both Dom and Jerri. "You got it?"

Kobe nodded and put on his best brave face. Wallace ignored his fear and shoved him towards the door.

"You ain't back soon, we leaving without you." He threw the lock and grabbed the handle with both hands before pushing it open. The wind howled and seemed to suck the boy out and into its grip. Wallace slammed the door behind him and threw the lock before stooping down to peer out.

"Ha ha! Go, little man, go!"

THE WIPERS WERE SET at their highest rate, but they made little difference against the onslaught of rain. Jack struggled to see down the side streets for any sign of the men they were after, but the limited visibility and constant motion of the foliage was too hard for him to filter. He determined that they would have to be within half a block or closer to see anybody dumb or desperate enough to be out in this weather. Maybe farther, if they had their lights on. He had cautioned Frank against using theirs, and he had quickly agreed. It cut their speed only slightly. The flooded streets were doing that already, and Jack gazed down at the wave they were making as they passed through another waterlogged intersection.

"Which way?" Frank asked.

Jack leaned forward and examined the road in front of them, only to realize it was the boulevard leading to the bridge. He spotted its steel frame in the gloom off to his right, then turned and located the building he had used for cover.

"It has to be to the left somewhere."

Frank pulled the car across the divider and

wrestled it through the wind to aim in the right direction. A block later, the BMW appeared out of the gloom.

"There it is."

"Florida plates. Are they from a dealer?"

Jack looked and saw the word at the top of the license plate. Despite his age, Frank had good eyes.

"They are. I wonder if there are papers inside."

"Does it matter right now?"

Jack frowned at that. The older man was right. The car was totaled and wouldn't be going anywhere without a tow truck. Whatever was inside could wait.

"Something to keep in mind for later. How about we circle out from here? Expand a block with every lap?"

"Sounds like a plan."

Frank eyeballed the car one last time, before passing and turning at the next intersection. His thoughts were with Jerri and Aaron at the store. Only a few blocks away, it was boarded up tight. They should see it on the second or third lap.

"I can't see a damn thing. Let's use the lights."

Frank turned on the spotlight on his side and played its beam across a house. The doors and windows were boarded up and the faint glow of a light from inside showed between the cracks. It looked undisturbed. Jack plugged in a portable handheld light Frank had produced from under the seat and used it on the other side of the street. They checked for broken wood or windows, signs of forced entry. Cars that were not in their garages. Anything.

"What if they broke in the back door?" Frank asked.

"No way to tell without going out in the storm. Let's just see what we can see this way first. If we come up empty, we can go back and start looking for that."

Frank shone the light on the back of the house butting up to the one in front of him. He could make out the back door and one window. They were still boarded up, but there was one that was out of his view still. He realized their chances of finding these guys were pretty slim, but they couldn't not look. Maybe if they were seen? It might change their minds about doing something stupid. He flipped the headlights on. Since they were deploying the spotlights, it now seemed foolish not to have them on.

"There's a van sitting out," Jack said.

"That's Jay. He builds furniture in the garage now. Lost his job at the warehouse when they moved out. He doesn't have a choice but to park it outside. It's a piece of shit he uses to haul what he builds around. Surprised he didn't park it out where it'd get the most damage. It's probably worth more in insurance than it is Blue Book."

"Anybody else you know that would leave their car out?"

Frank thought about it. "Only one I can think of is the Tindall's. Brian tried deep fryin' a turkey last Thanksgiving and burned his garage to the ground. His brother's got a barn outside of town, though, so I imagine he put his truck in there for the storm. He's a few blocks west. Worth checking out, though. There's a few others, most of them have no engine in 'em, but you wouldn't know it from the road."

Jack grunted for a reply and pulled his light from the van to play it across the next house.

15

An unnamed hurricane that struck Florida and South Texas in 1919 killed over 500 people on ships at sea.

Kobe watched the car slide slowly down the street from his hiding place behind the thick hedge. He'd only gotten a couple of blocks before spotting the van in the driveway of the small house. He'd been about to get closer when the car and its two spotlights appeared. Cops. Nobody else used spotlights like that.

The rain pelted him, and he shivered in the wind. He was soaked to the skin before he'd gone twenty feet, and now the wind was sucking his body heat away. He stuffed his hands in his armpits and his teeth chattered as he cursed the slow-moving vehicle.

It was closer now. He could make out the shapes of two men in the front seat. The car wasn't even a police car, just an old Crown Victoria that used to be one. Who the men inside were, he didn't know and really didn't care. All he wanted was to get the van and get out of this little town.

His thoughts turned to Dominic. The guy had saved his ass. Kobe wasn't the smartest kid in the world, but he could see where the bullets had passed through the car. If Dom hadn't put him on the floor, he'd of caught every one of them. The one that was inside Dom should have been his, and he knew it. He wasn't sure what Wallace and Sanford were planning, but he'd already decided to get himself and Dom away from them at the first opportunity. If this lady they had found could help with that, she'd have to come, too. How, he had no idea. Thinking long-term was something he rarely did, but the situation he was in now was forcing it, and he was discovering that he was not very good at it. He needed Dom. Dom would know what to do. If Dom died, he'd be all alone against Sanford, and that frightened him more than anything.

But first they needed a car. Without transportation, they had no options. The van looked like a piece of crap. But its age told him he could start it within a few seconds of getting inside, which was all that mattered. He checked to see that the screwdriver was still in his pocket as the cop car traveled on. He let the two men and their spotlights get another block away before standing up and running across the street.

He ducked down behind the van and let it shelter him from the wind for a bit before looking through the window. He checked the house first. There were people inside. He could see light through the cracks between the plywood covering the windows, and it blinked at him as people walked past. The side door to the house was only a few feet away and looked to be a solid wood door with a storm door over it. No plywood. That wasn't good.

He eyeballed the interior of the van. Two seats only, a driver and passenger. The rest was empty and held what looked like a few blankets and some scraps of wood. A healthy coat of sawdust covered the dash and floor. The ashtray held a million butts. No keys in the ignition or on the center console either. His luck was holding.

A gust of wind rocked the van, and a falling branch impacted its roof before skidding off and barely missed his head. He ducked down in case there were more.

The house was too close. He'd make some noise getting in and there was no way to prevent it. If he were doing this back in Miami, he would pass this up without even thinking about it and find a better option. It was a recipe for getting shot.

But he had no other options. Hopefully, the wind would cover the noise. If he could get inside without them hearing him, he would have time to work on the ignition. Once the van was started, it was his. He'd be out on the street and gone before they could get outside.

He pulled the shim from his belt and got ready to circle the van. The wind would be full in his face as soon as he rounded the corner, and the rain would make him practically blind. But most of the job of shimming a door was by feel, anyway.

He paused to warm his hands again before setting out.

JAY SQUEEZED MORE oil onto the shaving brush before dabbing it across the frame of the automatic. While his wife was pacing her way around the house, checking the windows and roof for leaks, he was using the weather-induced jail time to clean his guns. So far, he had cleaned the .45 his grandfather had left him, and the rifle he was ready to use next month when he and his buddies went after hogs across the bridge in Georgia. The shotgun he kept in the hallway closet would be next. It was sitting next to him on the couch waiting.

His wife stalked past him again with a frown. She didn't like that her mother's coffee table was being used for this chore, or the fact that he was even doing this in the house, but Jay had assured her that the ammo for the guns was in the bedroom and not on the table, so she had let it slide this time. He couldn't get to the garage right now, could he?

"You get gun oil on that couch, you'll be making me a new one," she warned.

"Yeah, yeah. How's the house doing?"

"Maybe if you'd look yourself, you'd know," she shot back before stalking away.

Jay sighed. His wife feared everything. Snakes. Frogs. Bridges. Strangers. Lately, it was stuff in the food and the trails in the sky left by the airplanes. Crazy shit she'd read off the internet. He regretted getting the computer now, but he needed it to sell the furniture he made out back. Before the storm had knocked out the internet connection, she'd been reading horror stories about hurricanes ripping the roofs off of houses and sucking the people out to their deaths. He'd tried to tell her what hurricane straps were and how many he had installed, but she didn't want to hear it. So, she had been on roof patrol for the last ten hours, stalking laps around the house with a flashlight and taking her fear out on him with every pass.

A gust rattled the plywood on the window behind him and he paused to see if the noise continued. Should he maybe go out and check how things were holding up? He had a quick exit. The year before he had been out scrounging wood at an estate sale and found a solid oak door that was the exact same dimensions of their rotting side door. He'd swapped the heavy oak for the cheaper one and replaced the frame, as well. She had bitched about it not having a window, but he'd promised to install one when he could. So far, it had yet to happen. But it was one less hole in the house to board up when the storms came. That was something.

LESS THAN TEN feet away from where Jay was cleaning his guns, Kobe slid the shim down the crack between the rotting rubber seal of the door and the window. He used both hands to maneuver it around and on the second try felt it grab. A quick yank was rewarded with the lock popping up. He smiled and slid the shim back into his belt.

He took the handle in both hands and leaned his body into the door. He didn't want the wind to grab it and slam it open. The latch disengaged, and he eased the crack wider. The wind caught the gap, so the best he could do was a controlled open-ing. The door's hinges creaked loudly as he al-lowed himself to be pushed back.

JAY'S HEAD came up from the shotgun he had just broken down. He knew that sound. Metal on metal. It was familiar, but out of context. He stood up and cocked an ear, waiting for the noise to repeat.

KOBE SLID onto the plastic seat and pulled out the screwdriver. The wind rocked the van again, and he braced himself by planting a foot against the open door. His foot was wet and slid twice across the vinyl surface of the door, before he managed to wedge it against the arm rest and hold it there. He didn't want the door moving around and making more noise, or slamming shut on his leg. He had work to do.

He wedged the screwdriver into the crack in the plastic cowling of the steering column and applied pressure. The molded plastic quickly cracked and parted, so he reset the tool and pried again. A second crack split the cover enough for him to pry it into two pieces, remove it, and toss it aside. He next knocked the ignition switch apart until the mechanism was bare.

Before he could insert the screwdriver again, a gust of wind rocked the van and his foot came dislodged. The door swung half shut before being slammed back open again, and the hinge screamed loudly in protest. Kobe cursed and reached out to grab it. Fighting the wind, he managed to slam it shut.

"SON OF A BITCH!" Jay knew the sound now. It was his van! Someone was trying to take advantage of the storm and steal his van!

Cheryl came running into the room to find him rapidly assembling the shotgun.

"What is it?"

"Somebody's stealing my van!" he replied before standing up and fumbling with the shells in his pocket. Cheryl retreated as he racked a shell into the chamber, and he added another before stuffing his feet into boots.

"You going out there?"

Jay shook his head in amazement. "Yeah! Can't do much from in here!"

"But the storm!" she countered.

"It's not gonna suck me away. Stay in here!" He pushed past her and made for the door.

Kobe mouthed a string of curses as he tried to maneuver the screwdriver with his cold and shaking hands. He had just planted it home and was turning it when the door to the house burst open. Luckily, the wind tried to slam it back shut and Kobe caught sight of the shotgun now stuck in the crack. It prompted him to move faster.

The van started on the first crank and Kobe revved the engine once, before slamming it into reverse. He didn't bother checking the mirrors; he just ducked down and floored it.

He was halfway to the street when the windshield shattered.

Jay couldn't believe it. First the wind had smashed his hand in the door, and then, when he forced it back open, he found a teenage kid in the front seat of his van. Who steals cars in a hurricane? The question was still in his head when he brought the shotgun up and fired.

Jack's head jerked around at the sound. He and Frank had cracked the windows of the cruiser to help keep the windows from fogging up. He had clearly heard a gunshot.

"Shotgun maybe?" Frank asked.

"Back the way we came?"

"I think so. Hard to tell." Frank spun the car into a U-turn.

***

KOBE TOOK the van all the way across the street, and it jumped the opposite curb before he could stop it. Slamming it in Drive he floored the accelerator again, spinning the tires in the saturated turf before finding purchase on the curb and shooting back out into the street. The man from the house was now running down his driveway and taking aim again. Kobe aimed the van down the road and ducked down. The blast impacted the rear of the van with a loud thump, followed by the whistle of wind through the new holes. He steered around a fallen limb in the road and the next shot went wide. He took the next turn on two wheels and the man disappeared behind the wall of water.

"MOTHER ... FUCKER." Jay stood in the middle of the road and cursed the rain where his van had just disappeared. He was suddenly fully aware of the storm. He was soaked. His jeans guided the rain into his boots, which he hadn't had time to tie, and the wind plastered his wet hair to his face and threatened to knock him over. The shotgun steamed as the water ran down the barrel, and his next thought was that he'd have to clean and oil it again.

What the hell was that all about? Why would someone want his crappy van bad enough to go out in a hurricane to steal it? Stupid.

He'd have to call Sheriff Clancy when the storm was over. Would he even believe him? He could barely believe it himself. First, he'd have to calm down his wife. That would be a few hours of work right there.

He turned and headed back to the house. Cheryl was probably losing it. He wasn't looking forward to the next several hours.

SANFORD SMILED to himself as he sat on the toilet. Wallace was so stupid. How the hell he had gotten so high up in Jackson's organization was something he never understood. So what if the two of them went way back? This was *business*. There was no room for the weak. It's why Jackson had sent him, Sanford was sure of it. Jackson needed someone strong to make sure Wallace got the damn job done! Sure, he'd said Wallace was in charge, but Sanford didn't believe that was what Jackson really wanted; it was just for show, something for Dom and Kobe to hear. Sanford was reading between the lines, and the lines said he was the guy running this show. Sure, he'd let Wallace think he was the man, but when the shit got real, Sanford would take over and there was no way Wallace would fight him. If he did, well Sanford would just take care of that when the time came.

Sanford finished his business and flushed before moving to the medicine cabinet. He scanned the interior and, when he didn't find what he wanted, moved to the small drawers.

It was in the bottom drawer. He pulled the hand mirror out and set it on the edge of the sink before reaching inside his shirt for the vial hanging around his neck. He tapped a pair of lines out onto the mirror and used a credit card to cut and spread them. He already had a rolled twenty in his pocket and used that to snort the cocaine into both nostrils. He dabbed the remaining bits up with a damp finger and rubbed his gums before tossing the mirror into the trash.

Leaning on the sink with both hands, he enjoyed the rush. A smile pasted itself on his face, and a rap beat entered his head. He bounced to the rhythm only he could hear and grinned at himself in the mirror. His time was coming! If his plan worked out, he'd be the number two man when he got back to Miami. Even if he got back all by himself.

The beat went on, and he found his eyes roaming the small space. Towels. Knickknacks on the back of the toilet. Lady's shampoo in the corners of the shower. A toothbrush holder.

He stopped.

The toothbrush holder. It was full. Two regular brushes and one smaller one. It was a Star Wars toothbrush, one with little pictures of Yoda on it. Sanford picked it up and examined it closer. It was well used.

"That lying bitch!"

———

"The pain?"

"It's there," Tyler replied. "But I can manage."

Jerri checked the chest tube from the floor all the way back to the point it entered his chest. It was working, but it was just a temporary measure at best. The man was obviously in pain and trying to hide it. She eyeballed the bare skin in front of her and was surprised to not see it covered in tattoos like his companions. The man seemed to have only one and it looked fresh. She took out a fresh dressing and a roll of tape to recover the area. She stiffened slightly when Wallace returned from the bathroom. She'd been listening for any sound of them finding Aaron, but so far nothing. The little boy was holding himself together.

"Sit back. This is going to hurt a bit," she warned him. "Stay on your side."

Tyler nodded and watched Wallace until he was back at the front door. He switched to French and whispered.

"Listen. I have a gun. It's in my belt under my shirt. If the boy isn't back soon and the two of them are close, I'll do my best to kill them both. You understand?"

Jerri's face switched to one of horror. "No, no you can't start shooting in here."

Wallace raised his head and glanced in their direction. Jerri recovered and made a show of checking Tyler's pulse. Wallace dismissed them both and turned away to get himself a drink from the cooler.

"Just get on the floor, and I—"

"No, you don't understand. I'm not the only one here."

Tyler's face clouded. What was she talking about? He was about to ask when there was shouting from the back.

Jerri dropped the bandage and ran.

SANFORD KICKED the bathroom door open and examined the room.

"Where are you!" he called.

He grabbed the closet door and threw it open. Nothing. He kicked a pile of laundry in the corner, scattering it across the room.

"I know you're here!" he yelled louder.

He opened and slammed the closet door.

"You best come out!"

He grabbed the edge of the bed and flipped it in the air. The mattress and box spring crashed against the wall.

A scream rang out, high pitched and piercing. Aaron, recoiling in fear, lay on the floor with the tattooed giant standing over him. Sanford reached down and grabbed a fistful of Aaron's clothes, yanking him to his feet.

"I got you, you little shit! Think you can hide from me!" Blood poured from Sanford's nostrils and his pinpoint eyes promised pain.

Aaron opened his mouth and screamed again.

KOBE WAS LOST. Every damn street looked the same now, and all of them were flooded. He had creeped the van through two deep puddles out of fear of either stalling the engine or driving into an unseen ditch. He could barely see the road in front of him and the square shape of the van seemed to invite the attention of the wind. On the last turn, it had threatened to overturn, so he had cut his speed and tried to keep better track of where he was going and where he had already been.

The van was getting sluggish, too. He looked at the rear windows and saw that the van was listing to the left. Was the rear tire flat? The holes the shotgun had punched in the side were near the rear wheel well. Maybe some of the shot had found the rubber. Since the van was empty and the wheel wasn't a drive wheel, he could keep going. They'd have to change it before they left town, though.

He returned his gaze out the front windshield and tried to see through the spider web pattern the shotgun had created. His headlights were reflecting off a stop sign and lighting up every crack in the glass, so he turned them off and was surprised that he could see better. Stupid to have them on anyway, with those cops out looking around. He checked his mirrors for any telltale sign of the spotlights and discovered that the driver's side lacked one. Still, he saw nothing.

Left, or right? He didn't know. Between the rain and the hasty exit he had made while fleeing the shotgun, he was totally lost. He took his foot off the brake and went left, just as the rain increased.

A drop of water snaked its way down his back and set off an involuntary shiver. Even his underwear was wet under his jeans. He shook his head hard to clear the water from his face, and when that didn't work, he tried wiping it away with his already soaked shirtsleeve. A sharp pain made him pull away, and he examined his sleeve after returning his hand to the wheel.

Blood. There was blood on his sleeve. His head was bleeding! He probed carefully with his hand

and felt two tender spots, which stained his hand crimson. He wiped it on his pants.

Was he shot? Or was it from the glass, maybe? Either way, it scared him. He needed to find the gas station and that lady. She could fix him up. The face of his own mother flashed in his head for a second and he shoved it aside.

The road ended in a T-intersection. Taking a guess, he turned right and headed straight into the wind. Was it changing direction, or was it just him?

16

In August of 2004, Hurricane Frances, a Category 2 storm, caused $10 billion in damages and killed 8 people.

S ydney cycled the blood pressure cuff again and frowned at the result.

"That bad?" Connor asked.

"He's not better, despite the fluids," she explained, letting some of her frustration out in the process. "He's got a bleed, and I don't know where."

"So, what can we do?"

Sydney sighed and rose from the stool. Replacing the stethoscope around her neck, she paced in the small room. Connor glanced out the crack in the plywood at the storm and then back.

"He needs a surgeon."

"You said that. I don't see that happening any time soon. There's nothing else?"

She'd already game-planned everything she could. Kyle was wearing dog tags, a leftover habit no doubt of his army days. But they had his blood type on them, O-negative, and she'd already determined that neither of them were compatible donors. The thought of doing a direct transfusion, like she had done for the young Marine in Africa a while back, had entered her mind, but without a donor it was impossible.

"The only other thing we can do is buy time until we can get him to a surgeon, and for that I need blood. Whole blood. PBCs. Plasma. Hell, I'll take anything. Either that, or I need somebody who's O-neg and try a direct transfusion. Otherwise, he's going to bleed out."

She stopped pacing and looked at the young sheriff. She was complaining out loud and shouldn't be. It was bad enough the young deputy was going to die; his friend didn't need the whole how and why spelled out to him. Especially when they couldn't do anything about it. She was about to apologize when she saw his face.

"What's wrong?"

"Say that again. About the blood."

"What? You mean a direct tranfu—"

"No. The kinds of blood. What were they?"

"Whole blood. PBCs, plasma—"

"PBCs! What's that?"

"It stands for Packed Red Blood Cells. It's ... it's like condensed blood. They spin out all the other stuff and just leave the red blood cells. Why?"

Connor got to his feet and faced her. "The fire department ambulance. It has it."

"What do you mean?"

"I ... sometimes I have to make supply runs for them. They can't do it themselves or we're without coverage, so either me or Kyle run into Jacksonville and grab a bag of drugs and a cooler full of stuff and bring it to them. The cooler is a new thing, and I ... I looked inside once and—"

"You saw a bag labeled PBCs," she finished. "Where's the station?"

"It's twelve miles away! Between here and Jacksonville! We share it with two other towns. But the tower is down. I can't even talk to them. It doesn't matter, anyway, they can't get to us."

Connor fell into the chair and buried his face in his hands.

"Can you get to them?"

"There's a tree down across the road. The chief told me right before we lost the tower. A big ass cottonwood. Thing's gotta be six feet across. It'll take a year to saw it in half."

"You have to go."

Connor looked up at her. "What? How? I don't even have my cruiser!"

"Then go get it!"

"In that storm!?"

"Screw the storm! You have to get the blood and the medic and bring them back here!"

"I ... how?"

"I don't care!"

Connor stared at her, his mouth hanging open.

"Look at him!" she ordered. "Look at your friend."

Connor did so and saw his best friend lying on the bed. Pale and hooked up to wires and tubes. The blood on the floor had dried into the sticky puddle.

Sydney grabbed a handful of his collar.

"Connor. You are going to get dressed, and you

are going out in that storm. You are going to get your car and drive it as far as you can. Then you are going to run, walk, crawl—I don't care—until you reach that firehouse and get Kyle the blood he needs. And you're going to do it right now!"

Connor started nodding before meeting her face and nodding harder.

"Okay. Okay. I'm going." He threw himself to his feet and reached for his rain gear. "Wait. What about you? You'll be all alone."

Sydney pulled her H&K from its nylon holster and held it up. "I'm a big girl, Connor. I can take care of myself. Besides, nobody even knows I'm here. Now get going."

"Yeah. Yeah, okay. I'm going." He donned the heavy rain gear and grabbed his hat before reconsidering and tossing it aside. Sydney followed him to the door where they exchanged a silent look. She gave him her best nod of encouragement, before he forced the door open and threw himself into the storm.

Sydney stood in the puddle left behind and watched as the yellow rain slicker became a blur and then faded from sight all together. It was maybe a half mile to his car. Once inside, he should be safe. She told herself it was worth the risk.

She was about to brace the door to give it more strength but decided to leave it the way it was. What if he got hurt and had to return? She might be too busy to let him in.

She returned to her patient.

"Just you and me now, Kyle," she told him. "Don't you leave me too."

The only answer she got was the howling wind.

She wondered what Jack was doing.

"WAIT! BACK UP!"

Frank did as he was told and stopped them in the middle of the intersection. Jack was gazing intently down the side street, but all Frank could see was a wall of water.

"Brake lights, I think. I don't see them now."

"Should we follow?"

Jack took a breath and let it out slow. Had he really seen them? Or had it been another mirage created by the storm? They had seen lights twice they thought to be cars, but they had always turned out to be houses when they got closer. But these lights, these lights were red.

"Yeah, let's go see. Let's keep the spots off, too."

Franks grappled with the wheel, and they headed off after Jack's lights. Frank kept the car at an even speed and checked the houses as they passed. Going faster was just too dangerous.

"You ever been in a storm like this?" he asked the agent.

"No. A couple bad nor'easters. I have a place in Delaware that got tore up a bit by Sandy, but nothing like this. You?"

"This is my third, not counting a few near misses. First when I was six, scared the shit out of me. Lost the roof of my house to Charley in 2004. Took my fishing boat and sank it out in the swamp. Friend of mine ran across it a few weeks after and we managed to pull it up in one piece. It was over three miles away from where I kept it. Amazing what these things can do."

"You ever out in one though, like this?"

"Nope. This is my first. Guess I'm getting more stupid in my retirement."

They scanned the side streets at the next intersection.

"Which way we headed?" Jack asked.

"This road? It heads east and then dead ends at the river. Why?"

"Let's say it was them I saw. Why would they be

going this way? Wouldn't they be trying to get across the bridge or back to the highway?"

"You'd think so. Unless they have a reason to stay, or they're just lost."

Reason to stay? Jack thought that one over and remembered the man trying to get into the trunk of the car before they ran.

"Let's go back to the car they were driving."

"Why would they go back there? It's totaled."

"I'm not sure yet. But there's something we need to check out."

"O ... kay."

WALLACE EMERGED from the cooler with a beer clenched in his fist, only to see Jerri bolt for the back of the building. Sanford was yelling and someone was screaming.

"Hey! Hey! Where the hell you going!"

He drew his gun and moved to head her off, but she beat him by a few feet and sprinted through the small living room and into the bedroom.

They both found Sanford holding and shaking a small boy by the shirt with his feet off the ground. The boy was screaming as fast as he could suck in air, while Sanford shouted curses into his face from a few inches away. Blood spewed from his nose, and he sent it flying in the boy's face as he yelled.

"Answer me, you little shit!"

Jerri moved in to stop him, but Sanford planted a boot in her stomach, and she crumpled to the floor.

"Lying bitch!"

"Put him down!" Wallace yelled.

"She been lying this whole time! Little fucker was under the bed! I got you now!" He shook the boy again and the boy screamed louder.

Jerri caught her breath and crawled forward.

"Let him go! He can't speak! Don't hurt him, he's just a little boy!"

"What you mean he can't speak? He yelling, ain't he!" Sanford shook him again and Aaron screamed louder. He covered his ears and wailed.

Wallace stepped forward and shoved Jerri back down. Sanford was high and enraged. There was only one thing he was going to listen to.

"Put him down!" he ordered.

Sanford didn't hear him. "Little mutha gonna—"

BOOM!

Wallace's gun fired a foot from his ear. The

sound was deafening in the small room and cut through his enraged mind. He froze and looked at the man, the smoking barrel now only inches away from his face. Aaron, too, was shocked into silence.

Wallace cocked the gun and let Sanford get a good look down the barrel.

"Put him down ... before I put you down," Wallace told him.

Aaron dropped to the ground and immediately ran for Jerri who scooped him up and began whispering in his ear.

"All right, okay. All right, okay. All right, okay."

The boy buried his face in her chest, and she covered his ears. It was the only thing that worked sometimes. She looked up to see the two men facing off. One of them frozen and with a gun in his face, the man holding it seemed to be begging for a reason to use it.

Wallace backed off and reached down to gather up Sanford's piece from the carpet. Sanford watched and his muscles twitched.

"Leave."

It was directed at Jerri, and she wasted no time. Picking Aaron up, she moved him out of the room. She stopped in the living room and looked around. What could she do? Seeing the puzzle, she parked Aaron in front of it.

"Need to finish," she said, and held her breath.

The boy picked his head up and examined the room before seeing the puzzle. He slowly disengaged and reached out for a piece. She watched as his shaky hands struggled to put it in place. It was followed by another and another and soon he had adopted the steady rocking motion and was using both hands. She pulled his headphones from the clutter on the TV and slipped them on his head. He didn't acknowledge them. Good. They would shut out most of the noise. Only then did she settle back and listen for what was happening in the next room. As she listened, she gazed out the door and saw Tyler lying on the countertop. He had a hand behind his back and a look of pain on his face. She motioned him back and he followed her lead.

"All right, okay."

"What the hell you good for?" Wallace asked Sanford, the gun still aimed at his head. "You got that shit up your nose. Bleeding all over the damn place." He held out his other hand. "Gimme it."

Sanford wiped his nose on his arm and left a bloody streak. He gazed at it as if he had just discovered it. His breathing finally slowed to the point he could think and speak.

"Bitch lied to us. Pissed me off."

"Gimme the stuff."

Sanford reached inside his shirt and yanked on the chain holding the vial. It parted easily and he tossed it to Wallace, who held it up and examined the contents.

"That much since we left makes me wonder."

"Wonder what?" Sanford spit.

"If you in control or not."

Sanford reached out and grabbed the sheet hanging off the upturned mattress and held it to his nose.

"I got this."

Wallace kept the gun aimed at him while he debated the veracity of the answer. Sanford forced himself to calm down. He took a few deep breaths and pinched his nose shut with the sheet. Wallace backed up another step and watched him.

"I'll hold this shit for a bit, *and* your piece. Motherfucker, you even look at me wrong, I drop you and leave your ass here! You hear me, boy?"

Sanford had misjudged Wallace. He saw that now. The man still had some street in him. His answer would determine whether or not any more of his blood would be on this sheet today.

"I hear you, man. I'm good."

Wallace stared him down and Sanford wisely looked away.

"You're on the door until I change my mind. You move from it, and I take that as a sign you comin' for me, and I end you. You got it?"

Sanford wisely said nothing. He simply nodded once.

"Go." Wallace waved him out with the gun.

Sanford ripped a section of sheet away and took it with him as he stalked out. Wallace watched his every move until he was past and then followed at a distance. They passed Jerri and the boy without comment, and Sanford continued on to the front door while Wallace watched from the doorway. He exchanged a look with Tyler and gestured for him to watch the big man. Tyler nodded in understanding.

Wallace turned back into the room and found Jerri on the floor between him and the boy. Aaron was rocking and putting puzzle pieces in place almost as fast as his hands could move. Wallace waved the gun at him, and she flinched.

"You got any more surprises in here?" he asked.

"N-no. I'm sorry. He's just a boy. My grandson. He's just scared."

Wallace ignored her crying and examined Aaron at the table. He was rocking and humming and no longer acknowledging his presence.

"What's wrong with him?"

"Nothing. He's just autistic."

"What? Like a retard or something?"

"No. It's different. He's just ... special." Jerri knew it wasn't the time to educate the man on the difference.

"Special, huh? Well, you keep his special ass in here and out of my way. You hear?"

"I-I will. What about your friend?"

Wallace spun around and looked at Tyler, stretched out on the counter and connected to the tubes. He looked around the room they were in. There was a pile of folded laundry and some pillows on the couch next to him. From there, anyone sitting could see through the door all the way to the front, where Sanford now sat on a stool gazing out the viewport.

He pointed to the couch with one of the two pistols he now held. "Move his ass in here."

"It's not good to move him. He could—"

"I wasn't asking no question, lady! Move his ass in here!"

"All right."

She got to her feet and checked Aaron, but he was engrossed in the puzzle, so she moved past Wallace and out to the counter.

"You okay?" Tyler asked.

She nodded. "He wants me to move you to the couch. Can you do it?"

"Do I have a choice?"

"I'll clamp the tubing first. Hold on."

Jerri moved behind the counter and pulled down a display of bag clips. Using two she clamped off the chest tube as best she could, before carefully placing each bottle into a plastic grocery bag. She tied another bag around the handle of the first, so she could carry it as close to the ground as possible. She checked it twice before facing Tyler.

"You ready?"

He replied through clenched teeth. "Yeah."

Jerri knelt and he threw his arm over her shoulder.

"Don't forget my gun," he whispered in French.

"Let's go."

Tyler rotated himself on the counter until his legs could fall off the side, and Jerri helped him sit up. He let out a small cry between clenched teeth before lowering himself to the tile floor. Jerri snaked a shoulder under his arm and helped him stand. The pain shot through him and his legs buckled, but he rallied and stood again.

"A little help?" Jerri voiced toward Wallace.

Sanford turned his head, but Wallace shook his head no. He turned back to the peephole after shooting another grin at Tyler. Wallace frowned at Tyler's bloody shirt. He didn't want blood all over himself, too, but still came forward to take his other arm.

"Thanks, boss."

They made the twelve steps to the room, and Tyler was lowered to the couch. Wallace backed off to a spot where he could see everybody at once, including Sanford, who was still working on his bloody nose.

Jerri positioned Tyler semi-reclined and slightly turned on his wounded side. She un-clamped the tubing and was relieved to see it still flowing. She just hoped that the activity had not disturbed any clotting that had taken place, or even worse, reopened any wounds. Her patient continued to take deeper breaths, fighting the spike in pain, but eventually they tapered off.

"Okay?"

"Yeah. Just hurts. I'll live."

Wallace cut them off.

"Where's yo piece?"

"Back in the car, I think," Tyler lied.

To their relief, Wallace didn't question that. He handed Tyler Sanford's gun.

"You see that dumbass from here?" he asked just loud enough to be heard.

Tyler gazed through the open doorway and found he could see Sanford, sitting on his stool as ordered, straight down the right aisle of the store.

"Yeah, man. I can see him."

"Fucker moves off that seat without my say so, you put his ass down. Got it?"

"Yeah, but why not—?"

Wallace dropped his voice so only Tyler could hear him. "Later. We still might need him."

That was all the explanation Tyler got before Wallace walked out. He watched the big man as he pulled a chair from the kitchen table and planted it in front of the door to the garage. From there, Wallace could see both Sanford and Tyler through the door. He sat down with his gun in one hand, and the drink he had dropped in the other. Tyler turned away to exchange a look with Jerri.

"That guy is smarter than he looks. Be careful," Tyler whispered.

Jerri rubbed her stomach where Sanford's foot had impacted. It was tender all the way across. She kept her face neutral as she palpated, sure that her pain was nothing compared to his.

"He's not the one I'm worried about so much."

They both looked at the giant man sitting at the front door. Now stripped to his T-shirt, the blood and tattoos stood out under the bright fluorescent lights. As if feeling their gaze, he turned and exchanged looks with Tyler. Tyler responded by waving the man's own gun at him. Sanford's eyes narrowed, but after a glance at Wallace he returned to gazing out the peephole.

17

In October of 2012 Hurricane Sandy produced hurricane-force winds covering a 175-mile distance from her center, and tropical storm-force winds extending beyond a 500-mile radius.

"Who are you?"

Sydney's head came up off her chest and she swiveled it around to the door before realizing the voice had come from inside the room. Kyle was awake and looking at her.

"My name's Sydney. How do you feel?"

"You're the lady from the car. At the bridge."

"That's right. Do you remember what happened?"

Kyle took a couple of breaths and gazed around before reaching for his belly. Sydney shot out an arm and stopped him before he could yank on the bandage.

"Is this the clinic?" he said.

"Yes. Your friend Connor and I brought you here. Lay still. You've been shot."

Kyle put his head down and the memory came flooding back.

"Four of them? In a nice BMW. Dealer plates. The kid in the back had a gun under his leg. I was going for mine and the guy in front pulled one. I tried to—he shot me?"

"Yes. I was in the car two places behind. My partner and I returned fire, and they took off."

"Your partner? Who are you, again?"

"My name's Sydney Lewis. I'm an FBI agent. We were passing through, trying to get through town, and got caught by the storm."

"The storm," Kyle repeated before listening for a moment. "It sounds worse."

"It is. Only about half over. We seem to be safe here. This building is brick and seems pretty solid."

Kyle attempted a shrug, and the pain shot through him.

"My gut."

"You'll want to sit as still as possible. The bullet is still in there."

"It is? No exit wound?"

"No. You a medic?"

"Like a corpsman, you mean? No, just a Marine."

Sydney stood and wrapped the blood pressure cuff around his arm again. He watched her and then examined the IV bag hanging from the ceiling. He knew enough not to speak until she was done.

"Your pressure is up a bit. That's good."

Kyle fingered the oxygen tubing in his nose.

"Thanks. Anybody else hurt?"

"Just you, on our end," she replied. "Jack thinks either you or he might have hit one of them when they ran."

"Jack?"

"My partner. Agent Jack Randall."

"Sorry. I'm a little slow."

"That's okay."

"So where is he now?"

"Connor gave him directions to the house of the previous sheriff. Frank somebody? And then they were going to go looking for the guys who shot you. The bridge is down, and a tree is blocking the other way out, so he thought they better find them before something worse happens. I sent Connor to the firehouse to get me some more fluids and bring the medic here. The radio tower is down and there's a big tree in the road between us, but he went anyway."

Kyle nodded at the news before voicing a name.

"Frank Warner."

"He didn't give a last name. Said he was sheriff less than a year ago, you know him?"

"Yeah ... he's my dad."

KOBE WRESTLED the van around another corner and set off back the way he had come. Was every street in this town a dead end? He had to find the store. He was worried about running out of gas. The gauge said only an eighth of a tank remained, but it hadn't moved since he had started driving, so he was starting to wonder if the gauge even worked. The tire was shaking the van more as well and he knew the rim and concrete would slowly shred it until it left the van entirely. If that happened, he might have to stop and change it. Storm or no storm, if he showed up with a van that they couldn't drive, Wallace would just send him right back out for something else. He'd been looking for another vehicle while he tried to find his way back to the store but had yet to see any. Did this piece of crap even have a spare?

He took another turn, and the street looked familiar. He recognized a tree, one with a freshly broken limb that hung in the road. He had passed it not long after leaving the store. He was close. He slowed down and examined the view more carefully.

The defoggers were not keeping up, and his breath was clouding the shattered windshield. He cracked a window to help. The wind immediately filled the van with noise, and he winced as it assaulted his ears. It was bad, but not as bad as when he had been out in it. The breeze sent a shiver through his wet body, and he was reaching for the heater controls when a sound cut through the din.

Metal. Someone or something banging on metal. Or maybe just metal banging on metal? With a jolt he realized what it was. The roof! The roof over the gas pumps at the store. The storm had been working on it when he left, and the sound was like that of a drum as it flapped the metal panels up and down against the frame. He was close.

He cracked the window farther and ignored the rain as he listened closer. It was ahead of him, and maybe to the left. He increased his speed and made it to the next intersection before listening again. The banging was louder here. He turned, and a half a block later the store appeared out of the gloom. He pulled the van in as close to the door as he could.

"WHAT THE HELL IS THIS?" Sanford asked.

"What you see?" Wallace asked.

"Kobe's back."

"Well, let his ass in."

Sanford threw the locks holding the door shut against the wind and used both hands to control it as the wind forced it open. Kobe dove through the opening and then stood, dripping a puddle under his feet.

Wallace looked the boy up and down before asking, "What the hell happened to you?"

Kobe reached up and wiped the blood from his head. The two wounds had bled the whole time he was driving, and he was too ignorant to know that it was his own fault for not letting them clot off.

"Some cracker with a shotgun went off on me."

Wallace grabbed his head and looked him over.

"You'll live. What you find us?"

"Damn! What the hell happened to the windshield?" Sanford called out from his perch at the peephole.

"There ain't nothin' out there, boss. Only thing I could find was this old van. I shimmed the door and popped the column no problem. And then cracker head come out of the house and started blasting at me. I gunned it out of there. He put one through the windshield and another in the back end, but I got away. Storm's so bad I couldn't see shit. Had to drive around a bit before I could find this damn place again."

He stopped talking and shivered, his teeth chattering. Wallace took in the blood and the wet clothes before holding out his hand. Kobe dropped the screwdriver in it.

A noise behind them caused them to turn and they both saw Jerri standing in the door listening. Behind her they could see Dom, his head up and

Sanford's gun wrapped in his fist. He had it aimed in the general direction of Sanford, who was still looking out the window.

"Whus goin' on?" Kobe asked.

"Nothing for you to worry about. Tell me about this van."

Kobe described the van and its lack of gas, shattered windshield, and flat tire before Wallace stopped him. Blood was trickling down his forehead again.

"Go see the lady and get your head fixed, then find some dry clothes."

The boy walked away, and Wallace turned to find Sanford had spun on his stool and was staring down Dom. Wallace snapped his fingers to get his attention.

"What's it look like?"

"Like he said, it's a piece of shit. Windshield's shattered. Left rear tire is blown. It's got room for all of us, though."

Wallace made a face and thought it through. "Gas ain't a problem, we'll fill it before we go. The windshield will just look like storm damage. Gotta change that tire, though."

"Even then, it's still a piece of shit," Sanford countered. "Might get us to the next town, then what?"

"Then Kobe gets us something else, or we buy something. I don't care, long as we get the product north."

Sanford glanced past Wallace. Dom was no longer watching them. He was watching Kobe while Jerri patched up his head.

"And then what?" he whispered. "He don't look too ready for travel. And that kid? Fucker might start screaming again anytime. You got a plan for that yet?"

"I'm working on it."

Sanford looked away and back. He had a plan, but he kept his mouth shut.

"So, what do we do now?"

"You go out and see if we can change that tire. Gas it up while you're out there. I'll think about our problem."

Sanford frowned, but didn't protest. Wallace spun the screwdriver around his fingers before handing it over. He pointed at the door with the gun.

"Get moving."

———

JERRI CLUCKED as she examined Kobe's head.

"Yeah." He shrugged like it was no big deal, putting on a show for Dom.

"Well, you're lucky it's glass and not buckshot. It could have gone right through your little skull. Hold still." She picked out the glass and the blood flowed. She gathered it in another maxi-pad and applied pressure.

Dom shifted a bit and winced at the pain. Kobe caught his eye, and Dom gave him a confident nod before closing his eyes.

"He okay?" Kobe whispered.

Jerri glanced at Tyler and, seeing his eyes closed, made a decision.

"No, Kobe, he's not okay. If your friend doesn't get to a hospital soon, he's going to bleed to death."

"You save him."

"I'm not a surgeon. I—"

"Don't gimme no bullshit, lady. You know this stuff. You save him."

Jerri stopped and fixed him in her gaze. He was a child, scared and putting on a show, but he had a gun tucked in his belt, so she had to measure him first. What she saw was an act, so she responded in kind, looking him straight in the eye.

"Don't you talk to me that way. I'm trying to save his miserable life. And yours, too."

Kobe backed down and looked away. She looked under the bandage.

"Cut's too deep. You need stitches. Sit down in that chair and hold this." She planted his hand on the bandage and pressed until he held it there himself. He watched Aaron working the puzzle. The boy had ignored the new arrival.

"Who dat?"

"That's my grandson. He was hiding under the bed. He's autistic and doesn't talk, so don't bother trying. You leave him alone, and he'll be quiet."

Kobe didn't know what autistic was, so he let it go. He began untying his shoes and stripping off his wet socks. Jerri dug in the medical bag and found the suture kit. She laid it out on the small coffee table and then tipped the lampshade up. Kobe eyeballed the needles as she selected a curved one and threaded it.

She moved in and tilted his head into the light.

"You ain't got some of that ... stuff? You know—"

"Numbing agent? So it doesn't hurt?"

"Yeah." He glanced at Dom, who appeared to be asleep.

"No, Kobe. It's a convenience store, not a hospital. Thought you were a tough guy?"

Kobe made a face. "Fine."

"Hold still."

She placed her first stitch, and, to his credit, Kobe only flinched once. Jerri glanced in Aaron's direction. He had slipped the headphones off without her noticing. *How long ago did he do that?* she wondered. He showed no signs of listening to their conversation. He just hummed a bit with the rocking and worked the puzzle. She had another one standing by for when he finished that one.

Jerri's mind raced. She had only spoken with Tyler twice, and even then, it had been brief out of fear they'd be caught. They needed to separate themselves from the two men in the front of the store somehow. Tyler had told her about the cocaine, and she had no doubt that it was priority number one for them. Tyler had hoped to take the two men out before Kobe returned, but the opportunity had not appeared. Now they had Aaron to consider, and Kobe had returned. Kobe was a wild card, one they could hopefully use until they had other options. But how? Tyler was already weak and getting weaker. She was going to have to find a way out of this herself, for all three of them.

"So, what did you find out there?"

Kobe shrugged. "This old blue van. It's crap, but it runs. Full of sawdust and wood and shit."

"Uh-huh." She immediately knew whose it was. Jay's van was infamous. There had been pools betting on when it would finally die. The van had outlasted two prior pools already. "So, what are you planning to do with it?"

"I dunno. Get the hell out of here, I guess. We can all fit in it and still have room left for the—" He cut himself off. Jerri pretended not to hear.

"What about Dominic here? He saved your life, I take it? If you try and take him with you, he'll die."

"He ain't gonna die."

Jerri stopped suturing and faced him. "You sure about that, are you? Are you a doctor? Did you go to medical school?"

"No."

"Well I did, and you're wrong. You better find a way for us to get him to the clinic. If we were there, I'd have some real equipment—maybe enough to really help him."

Kobe fell silent and Jerri resumed suturing. She glanced at Tyler and saw him open one eye for a moment. He was listening.

"Where's this clinic?" Kobe asked.

"Not far. Maybe a mile. There's a van there, too. I might have the keys here."

Kobe's eyes opened wide at that.

"You had a van all this time?"

"Keep your voice down," Jerri hissed. "You expected me to help them? Really?"

"Lady. You don't know who these guys are."

"Maybe not, but I know this: If you don't get us to that clinic, your friend here isn't going to make it. Get us there, and you can take the van and leave us behind. By the time the storm is gone, you can be three states away. Think about it. Now, hold still, I'm almost done."

Kobe held still and Jerri finished the job between glances at Tyler. His eyes were closed now, and his breathing was deep and regular. She couldn't tell how much he had heard. She also watched Kobe's face as he turned the information over in his feeble mind. Would he do what she needed? Maybe he needed some encouragement. She stopped what she was doing and walked over to Tyler. She made a big show out of checking his pulse and the tubes. Kobe followed her with his eyes, and she made sure he got a good look at the blood pooling in the bottles.

She looked back at Kobe and shook her head. "Whatever you're going to do, you need to do it soon."

Kobe nodded and glanced over his shoulder. Wallace was seated on the stool and watching outside. Sanford was out in the storm.

"Where's the keys?" he whispered.

18

In August of 2004, Hurricane Charley, a Category 4 storm, caused $15 billion in damages and killed 15 people.

Connor flattened his body against the wall of the house and let the wind hold him up for a moment. He was exhausted. He'd managed only three blocks with at least another six or eight to go. He'd either fallen or been blown off his feet a dozen times already and had taken a flying tree limb to the chest that put him down for a few minutes while he choked on inhaled rain.

He squinted into the deluge and checked the sky. Was it lighter to the west? He couldn't tell, and he gave up looking in favor of lowering his head to keep the rain out of his mouth. He sucked in ragged breaths and willed his aching legs to go on. Every part of him hurt. From his feet rubbed raw by the damp socks and leather, to his fingers, cold and cramping as their heat was sucked away by the storm. But he had to go on; Kyle needed him to.

A cloud of loose shingles slammed into the side of the house he was up against, and he took that as a warning of more to come. Pushing off, he made a dash for the next house, this time cutting across the yard and traveling down the leeward side. There was a fence, but it was a short one, so he rolled himself over it to land face down in the soggy grass. The wind blew his slicker up over his head and he found himself out of the wind and rain for the first time since he had left the clinic. He used the time to catch his breath and let his face fall to the soft grass.

This is good, he told himself. *I just need a minute*

here. I'll go in just a minute. The ground felt like Velcro, holding him down. The grass was so soft. *Just one minute.*

No. *NO!* He had to keep moving. He pushed himself up and spun around. The wind pushed the slicker back down and he ran on, pausing only at the corner of the house to pick his next path.

There. The Jacob's house. Around that and across the Anderson's backyard to the Murphy's. After that, he could wade the ditch and get behind the downtown buildings until he got close enough to go around them and get to his cruiser.

His cruiser! Holy shit, did he even have the keys? He frisked himself and found them in his pocket. *Idiot! Now you check?*

He laughed. Only it wasn't funny. But it was. Wait until he told Kyle. He'd laugh, too.

"Later," he told himself. "Time to go."

He pushed off into the storm again. Tree branches flew at him as he crossed the narrow lane, and he dodged them as he made for the opening between the two homes. He wondered if Mrs. Anderson was watching out her window. If she was, she'd be telling him what he was doing wrong. Maybe when this was over.

He ducked his head and moved on.

"WHAT DO THE JORDANIANS THINK?" the Director asked.

Unlike Jack, the Director of the FBI was on a plane. This one had departed Tel Aviv several hours ago, and after a stop in Germany to pick up a few people, it had taken off again for the long flight back to DC. He and his staff were tired. It had been a stressful week.

Unlike his predecessors the Director was not a career lawman. He made his mark as a lawyer, one that had taken on some of the most ruthless dictators in the world. Whether you were an African tribal leader trying to exterminate a rival clan, or a third-world arms dealer aiding in the genocide that leader was pursuing, you did not want the attention of the man and his backers. Several times the UN had followed the Director's guidance and now he was both feared as a worthy adversary or respected as a valued ally. His reputation, now combined with his position with the FBI, gave him the influence needed to pursue the goals that were previously handled by the Department of State. Diplomacy had given way to law enforcement, and as much as the diplomates grumbled, they couldn't deny the results he was getting.

"They'll stay out of it, as long as the Palestinians do."

"And the chances of that?"

"Good, I think."

"What if the next ISIS attack involves a Palestinian?" an aide asked.

"What if it involves a Jordanian?" he shot back.

The Director sat back and rubbed his left arm. The ache had begun about an hour ago, and he had chalked it up to the firm mattress of the embassy. He was looking forward to his own bed, it had been several weeks since he had used it. A glance out the window showed him the green coast of Iceland passing below. Soon, they would be over the north Atlantic again and see nothing but blue until they reached Canada. The ache in his arm grew sharper, and he rubbed it harder. Was it getting hot in here? He reached up for the overhead air nozzle, but the pain jumped up another notch with the movement. His forehead started to sweat.

"Sir?"

He lowered his gaze and found his secretary looking at him, her face clouded in concern. He attempted a smile to ease her worry, but the pain chose that moment to climb higher. Now it was in his chest, he clutched at it.

"Sir!"

The aides stopped their banter and looked to her.

"Are you all right, sir?"

The Director opened his mouth to reply, but his vision tunneled, and he pitched forward, his seatbelt catching him before he could hit the carpet.

"Sir!"

The aides, all jumped at once and caught the man. One of them released his seatbelt, and they lowered him to the floor. The man clutched at his chest with both hands and began to breath rapidly.

"He's having a heart attack! Tell the pilots!"

The aide took one more look at his boss before bolting to the cockpit. The two pilots were relaxing in their seats as the autopilot took them over the ocean. They had little to do for the next several hours. The arrival of the aide changed that.

"The Director's having a heart attack! Get us on the ground!"

"Okay."

Like all good pilots, this one already knew the nearest division runway which could handle the jet. Luckily, it was military and even owned by the Air Force. He cancelled the autopilot and dialed in the new heading, while the co-pilot changed frequencies.

Keflavik was one of the most isolated bases in the northern hemisphere. A combination air force, navel, and civilian airfield, it occupied a shelf of flat volcanic earth on the western edge of the island nation.

"Keflavik control, November six-one-six-romeo-kilo."

"Keflavik control, Romeo-kilo."

"Keflavik control, November six-one-six-romeo-kilo inbound DCA is declaring a medical emergency. Requesting clearance to first available runway."

"Keflavik control, roger your medical emergency, Romeo-kilo, come right bearing two-eight-four. Contact tower on one-one-two-point-eighty."

"Copy bearing two-eight-four."

"Romeo-Kilo. Traffic at your three o'clock. A C-5 outbound, should pass well under you."

"Roger, Keflavik. We're looking." The co-pilot dialed in the tower frequency and gave the pilot a thumbs up, before looking outside for the giant cargo aircraft. It appeared below them like a breaching whale, and after confirming they were well clear of its path, he focused again on their approach.

"Keflavik tower, Romeo-Kilo up on one-one-twelve."

"Roger, Romeo-Kilo. You have cleared priority for runway eleven. Heading one-zero-six, how copy?"

"Copy one-zero-six. We have it in sight."

"Copy Romeo-Kilo. Please state your emergency and souls on board."

"Twelve. Two-zero souls on board. One of my passengers is having a heart attack tower. Romeo-Kilo."

"Copy, Romeo-Kilo. We have medical en route."

The pilot acknowledged the information with a double click of the mic, before he and the co-pilot dove into the landing checklist. The plane came down at a rapid rate, and they both paused at different points to work their jaws and equalize the pressure in their ears. The pilot pulled the aircraft out of the dive, with just enough time for the gear to deploy, before setting the G-5 down with a chirp on the runway. Without waiting for instruction, he took the first presented taxiway and angled for the flashing lights of an ambulance parked on the apron. He brought the plane to a stop and shut the engines down, before addressing his co-pilot.

"You got this?"

"I got it." the man assured him.

Leaving his co-pilot to take care of the aircraft, he unbuckled and moved aft. He found the door being lowered by the crew, and the passengers gathered around a man on the floor.

"Who is it?"

"The Director!"

"Damn," was all he managed, before a pair of paramedics climbed the steps and shoved him aside.

"There it is."

Frank pointed through the windshield at the dark shape of the BMW up on the sidewalk against the brick building.

"Gary won't be happy about the brickwork, but he's had that thing for sale for over a year now. What now?"

Jack was examining the streets around them. He didn't want to get shot while checking the car out. Visibility was only thirty yards at best, but he thought he saw a little more light to the west. The eye of the storm, maybe? If so, it could be both a blessing and a curse. It would help them see better while they looked for wherever the shooters were holed up, but it also might prompt them to come out and try to find another car and possibly shoot someone else to get it.

If it was the eye, it would only last for a few minutes. Most people thought the eye of a hurricane was calm. That description was only partially accurate. It was calm compared to the remainder of the storm. They could still count on some serious wind, and only a brief break from the rain.

"One of them tried to get in the trunk before they took off," Jack said. "I'm wondering why."

"While you were shooting at them?"

"Yeah."

Frank examined the car again. It sat over the curb, surrounded by a puddle several inches deep. The front was crumpled, and one side had all its length dented. All the doors still hung open, and he could see a few holes punched through a rear door as well as two in the front fender. The front and rear windows were also shot out.

"Looks like a hell of a battle."

"I was shooting at a shape behind the rain," Jack replied. "I got lucky."

Frank's eyes were telling him otherwise, but he kept that observation to himself as he examined the streets past the car.

"Looks clear my way," he said.

"Mine too. Let's see what we can find out."

Jack left the car and approached the wreck with his gun out, examining every direction as he walked up to the trunk. Frank paused only long enough to fetch a crowbar from the trunk of his cruiser before joining him. Jack took the bar, and they walked into the puddle. He wedged it into the crack under the lock and braced his feet. Frank moved left to give him some room.

"Wait a minute."

Jack had been about to apply all his weight to the bar when Frank's call stopped him short. He turned to find him dragging his foot in the puddle. He bent over and rooted around with his hand before coming up with a set of keys. They had a BMW fob on them and a tag. Franks held it up to what little light they had and read it.

"Some dealer in Miami," he yelled over the wind before holding them out to Jack. "I'm shocked!"

Jack smiled at the man's sarcasm and selected the first key. Frank grabbed Jack's jacket to hold him in place while he fumbled with the lock. The trunk opened.

The smell of bleach filled the air for half a second before being swept away by the wind. Jack examined the interior. Suitcases. He picked one up and found a blanket underneath it. He tossed it aside and then removed another before lifting it. Boxes, all of them quickly being soaked by the storm. The first one read *Kitchen* on the side. He popped it open.

"Either somebody's baking a lot of cakes," Frank yelled, "or that's not flour!"

Jack dug his hand deep into the box and felt more of the same. It was obviously cocaine. He counted with his fingers and did the math. Fifteen kilos. There were four boxes. He popped the tops off them too. The last one wasn't quite as full.

"About fifty keys, give or take!"

"A shit-load!" Frank said. "What do you want to do with it? Can't leave it here!"

Jack looked at Frank's cruiser. "How much room you got in the trunk?"

Frank smiled. "Enough!"

A few minutes later, they had the cocaine transferred over. Jack carefully replaced the suitcases inside and even dropped the keys back in the puddle where Frank had found them, before climbing back in the passenger side.

Frank offered him a towel. Jack didn't bother to ask where he had gotten it. Frank's cruiser appeared to be the MacGyver of police cars: it had everything. He rubbed his head dry before returning it.

"I take it we're not going to keep looking for them?" Frank asked.

"No, I think we'll let them come to us."

"That's what I thought. I know just the spot."

Frank spun the wheel and fought the wind as they crossed the boulevard and turned behind the buildings across from the wrecked car. Frank slowed to a stop between two of them, and they had a direct view of the BMW from less than a block away.

"How's this?"

Jack frowned and considered it. He could see the car and maybe twenty feet on either side of it. He wouldn't be able to see them coming, but neither would they see the two of them waiting. With Frank at the wheel they could be around the corner and right on top of them in a matter of seconds.

He looked in every other direction. The alley stretched off to the south for a block, and Jack could see the next intersection where the road curved. On the other side was a ditch full of water. Behind them was the cross street and more alleyway. It was as good as they were going to get.

"All right. I guess we wait."

Frank settled in and adjusted his mirrors so he could watch behind them, while Jack twisted in his seat to get an easier look at the car. The storm beat on the car with loose debris, and the metal roof of the building they were up against sounded like a snare drum. Through the crack, they could see the sky to the west.

"Looks like it's getting a little lighter," Jack commented.

THE NATIONAL WEATHER SERVICE now reports Hurricane Nancy is maintaining its Category Four strength with winds reaching 130 miles per hour. The eye is currently approaching the town of Homeland in northeast Florida and maintaining its track north-west at 25 miles per hour. The storm is expected to stay on this path for the next two hours and reenter the Atlantic just south of Brunswick, Georgia. Residents along the upper east coast of Florida and Georgia are again urged to evacuate if they have not already done so. Specifically, the cities of St. Augustine and Jacksonville on up the coast to Amelia Island, Jekyll Island, Kings Bay, and Brunswick. Again, if you reside in these cities, particularly the barrier island communities, you are urged to evacuate. This is a major storm that will result in high winds and massive flooding. Expected storm surge is augmenting the current high tide and causing massive beach erosion. All counties along the coast remain under a flash flood warning. This storm may also produce multiple tornados at any time with little warning.

Our computer models now predict the storm to travel north-east and then gradually turn north as this cold front and the jet stream push down from the north. The spaghetti models now take it north-east, making its way up the coast of Georgia and the Carolinas, before once again being shoved out over the Atlantic. This storm may weaken slightly with the combination of high-level wind shear and from being over land, but our model tells us this weakening will be slight, perhaps only enough to drop Nancy to a Category Three.

If you are currently in the village of Homeland, you will be inside the eye of the storm very soon. We urge you to stay in shelter and not venture out. The storm will return within minutes, and the winds will come from the opposite direction, creating new debris as well as returning what it has already created.

To repeat, the National Weather Service now reports Hurricane Nancy is back to Category Four strength with winds reaching 130 miles per hour ...

"HE'S YOUR FATHER?" Sydney repeated. "Why didn't he come here?" The question came out before she could stop herself.

They had been talking for several minutes, long enough for Sydney to introduce herself and get his medical history, and some feedback on his pain and mental status. Kyle seemed to be doing okay. She gave him a bit of water, just enough to cure his dry mouth, before sitting down in the chair.

"Yeah, well. Dad's always been a cop first. He and Connor are the only two between here and Jacksonville. When I left the Corps and came home because of Mom, we kind of had a falling out."

Sydney checked his bandages and the monitor before scribbling some numbers on the bedsheet. It was an old paramedic habit she had yet to break.

Kyle is a cop now, but his dad isn't anymore? Sydney thought. *Something was obviously missing.* She wanted to keep Kyle awake, and talking to him was the best way to do that. She decided to skate around the subject.

"What did you do in the Marines?"

"I was an MP. Parris Island and then Kings Bay

for a while, guarding submarines and stuff. And then they sent me to Iraq."

"Get shot at, did ya?"

"Yup. We mostly did convoy security and perimeter stuff, and every once in a while, they'd take a swing at us. I was down in the southern part with a lot of British soldiers. Most of the action was up north. I was supposed to be heading that way when I had to come home."

There it was again. She took the bait this time.

"Had to come home?"

"Mom got cancer. She'd been having some pain, but as usual didn't tell anybody. Then one day they were out somewhere, and it hit her hard. Dad took her into J-ville, and the doctors did their thing. She had a couple rounds of chemo, and then they went in after it. There ... it was a lot. Doc said he got it all out, but her guts were in a bad way. She had one of those ... what do you call 'em?" He gestured to his gut. "Bag things."

"Colostomy bag?" Sydney offered.

"Yeah. Anyway, they did more chemo, and she did okay for a while. At least that's what the docs said. She didn't look okay. She lost a ton of weight, and all her hair was gone. She couldn't walk far without getting tired, so we got her a wheelchair.

Dad didn't handle it too good. She had lots of friends, though, that helped him ..."

He trailed off and his eyes watered up. Sydney pretended not to notice and gathered some trash and carried it away to give him some time to get himself together.

"I'm sorry, Kyle. We don't need to talk about this."

"Nothin' else to do, is there? Not like we're going anywhere." He offered a smile.

"No, no, I guess we aren't. Up to you."

"Sorry. Guess I shouldn't be dumping all this on you, I just ... I never talked to anyone about it. Around here folks keep that stuff to themselves."

Sydney understood. She had seen and heard it before as a paramedic. Patients who thought they were dying would bare their souls to you as you raced them to the hospital. It was if they knew time was short and had to unload the burden before they couldn't do so anymore. It didn't matter to them if it was someone they had just met.

"Nothing like getting shot to put things in perspective," Sydney offered.

"Yeah, I guess so."

Sydney waited patiently for him to continue. As long as he was talking, she was content to let him.

"You got any more water? I'm so thirsty."

It was a risk, but one she thought she could allow. She'd located some bottled water in the office and had moved a few into the room. She cracked the seal on one and offered it.

"Small sips," she instructed.

She let him have five before taking it away. "Let's see how your belly tolerates that. Okay?"

Kyle knew a command voice when it was directed at him. "Yes, ma'am."

Sydney sat back down and watched the monitor for a second before asking a question.

"What was your mom like?"

"She was everybody's mom. I had to share her with all my friends. The house was never locked. They just walked in and out, same as me. They called her Mom, too. Dad was always a bit hardheaded, but she won him over pretty easily. I mean, he had rules and all—he was the sheriff—but he let a lot of stuff slide, too. She was definitely in charge at home. He always wanted to lock the door at night and Mom wouldn't let him. She knew that some of us kids would do stupid things and need a place to go. Sometimes, I'd get up for school and find one of my friends sleeping on the couch. They'd either gotten in a fight with their parents or maybe drank too much and couldn't go home without getting their ass beat. Mom never said anything. She just fixed breakfast, like it happened all the time, and then sent us on our way.

"Dad had to step in once or twice if things got bad. I remember once when one of Mom's friends showed up on our couch with nothing but her baby and a fresh black eye. Dad didn't say a thing; he just put on his uniform, got in the car, and drove off. By the time I was eating lunch at school, word was already out that Dad had thrown her husband in jail. Lemme tell ya, it's a long ride to the county jail from here, and Dad had plenty of time to talk on the way there. Her husband never came back. Mom drove her home to Kansas a few months later, I guess she had family there. I forget her name now, but she came back to visit when Mom passed away. A nice lady. Told me a bunch of stuff Mom did for her that nobody knew about."

"Your mom sounds like an amazing woman," Sydney said.

"Yeah. The whole town come out to see her off."

"How'd your dad handle it?"

"Not good. He was tired. Said his heart wasn't in the job anymore. I didn't believe that. I think it was just an excuse to get me to come home. He'd hired Connor and wanted me to go through the academy so he could hire me, too. I had to finish up with the Corps and then went straight to Panama City for the academy. Didn't see Dad again until it was time for me to graduate."

Kyle's voice got hard with the last sentence. Sydney waited.

"He shows up with Jerri, one of Mom's old friends. They weren't all cuddly and shit, but it wasn't hard to tell there was something going on. We went out to some fancy restaurant, and she keeps an eye on him all night. I kept my mouth shut. Not sure how, but I did. They left after dinner. I'm not sure if they stayed the night someplace in town or just drove back here, but as soon as they were gone, I called Connor."

"And they were seeing each other," Sydney finished.

"I cussed him up and down for not telling me, and he just took it. When I finally ran out of steam, he filled me in. I should have seen it, but I guess I wasn't looking." Kyle stopped for a deep breath before going on. "Dad had started drinking. The front door policy was still in effect, and I guess people were finding him passed out on the couch. He was late for work a few times and even missed a few days. Connor had to cover for him. I guess he tried to keep it quiet, but the town's too small for that. His friends tried to come over and keep his intake under control, but they couldn't be there all the time. And then I guess Jerri found out."

"Who's Jerri again?"

"Jerri Neilson. Her and her husband have been here since they were kids. Mom and her were pretty close. They go way back. Jerri was Dad's date to the prom. Anyway, she was a nurse and helped us take care of Mom a lot there toward the end. Her husband and my dad were good friends, too. Hunting buddies. Fishing. They had one daughter who joined the navy and got pregnant before her husband was killed in a training accident. I think they wanted more kids, but it never happened. Probably why I got Christmas presents from them every year. Jerri used to work at the clinic here in town, until everybody started leaving. Now we got a doc who lives in J-ville and comes around once a week, so she runs the store here in town and takes care of her grandson. Her husband died from a heart attack about five years back."

Sydney nodded. "How old is the grandson?"

"Aaron? Oh, I guess he's about eight or nine. He's ... what do you call it? Autistic?"

"Oh?"

"Kid's super smart, though. I mean like solve a

Rubik's cube in a couple of minutes smart. Reads a book in about an hour or two. Puts together a whole puzzle in about the same. He just doesn't talk and pretty much stays at home all the time. Guess he doesn't do crowds very well. She home-schools him. We ain't got any teachers for that around here."

"Does he like you?"

"Yeah. I mean he doesn't run away from me. I've played video games with him. He likes *HALO* and *Call of Duty*. He beats me every time and laughs when he does it. I think he likes knowing he beat a real soldier. He'll nod yes or no if you ask him something; he just won't talk."

"Did he use to?" Sydney asked.

"Yeah. Just up and quit one day. His mom thinks it's because his dad didn't come home. He understands everything. Jerri speaks French to him, and he understands her, so I don't think there's anything stopping him from talking. I guess he'll get there when he's ready."

"What's his name, again?"

"Aaron."

"Does Aaron like your dad?"

"I don't know. I think he does, but I haven't been over there since I got back."

Kyle seemed hesitant to go there, so Sydney let that subject drop. He surprised her though.

"Connor filled me in. Jerri ambushed Dad with a couple of his friends about the drinking. I guess they started spending a lot of time together after that. Connor said Dad quit drinking cold turkey and got back on the job. That, and he started seeing them around town together."

"And you have a problem with that."

"Yeah, I have a problem with that! My mother hasn't even been gone six months!"

"Calm down. You'll open that wound back up."

Kyle took a deep breath and set his head back down. Sydney took the pillow and folded it in half before putting it back behind his head.

"Thanks."

"What happened then?"

"I was back, and Dad put me on the force. Connor and I did most of the patrolling and paperwork and what not. The more I drove around, the more I saw his car over there. Less when her daughter was there, but still."

"And something happened?"

"I had a few too many beers one Saturday night and walked over there to his place. Found 'em snuggled up on the couch together. I ... I lost it —went off on them both and said a bunch a stuff.

Accused him of cheating on Mom while she was sick, called Jerri a home wrecker. She left crying, and Dad and I yelled a lot. I stormed out, went home and slept it off. I come in to work on Monday, and Connor's the new sheriff. Seems like Dad retired so him and I wouldn't have to work together. We ... we haven't spoken since."

Not knowing what to say, Sydney said nothing.

They both listened silently to the storm raging outside.

19

8.6 million people were without power following Hurricane Sandy.

S anford cussed the rain and wind and the vehicle in front of him. The tire was shredded and the holes punched in the side of the van were so obviously from a shotgun they couldn't be ignored. There was a jack inside and he pulled it out before slamming the doors and looking underneath for the spare.

Empty space.

There was no spare! What the hell were they going to do now?

He got back to his feet and flung the jack at the nearest gas pump. It bounced off and skidded away before coming to rest in a puddle.

"Screw this!" he yelled before planting himself into the wind and pushing his way to the door. Wallace flung it open and stepped back. He was keeping a distance between them at all times now.

"What's the problem?"

Sanford raked the water from his face and spit on the floor. "Dumbass got us a van with no spare. We're screwed!"

"Son of a ... Kobe!"

KOBE FOUND the jacket right where she had told him she had left it. Green, made of that fleece stuff. Looked like it was for a man more than a woman. Whatever. He checked the pockets. In the right side, he found a tube of Chapstick and a mint, in the left was a set of keys. They said FORD on them, just as she said they would, and had a little green plastic tab. He squinted at the small letters and made out the words "Clinic Four" on it.

The lady was telling the truth. He'd have to make it look good.

"Kobe!"

Wallace was calling him. Kobe stepped out of the bedroom. The clothes were dry, and he was warm for the first time in hours. The jeans were grease stained and worn, probably from their owner working out in the garage, and the boots matched. He didn't care. He clomped his way toward the front with the shoelaces untied, giving the slightest of nods to Jerri.

"Yeah?"

"You dumbass! You got—" Sanford started. Wallace cut him off with a wave of his gun.

"Van's got no spare. Need you to go find another one."

"Maybe not. Look what I found in this jacket." He held up the keys and handed them over.

Wallace read the tag, and the rage was evident on his face. He clenched the keys tight in his fist and stalked toward the back.

"You two stay here."

"Anything?"

Steve looked up from where he sat at the radio and shook his head.

"Nothing. No radio; the tower's definitely down. I can't even pick up the emergency channels or the Coast Guard. No cell service either. I had internet for a bit and fired an email off to the station in town, but either they aren't there and didn't see it, or the internet went out before they did. We're on our own, Mark."

"Damn it," Mark cursed and gazed out the window at the storm.

"Are we even sure somebody got shot? I mean —you can barely see fifty feet out there. Maybe they just think they saw it."

"They all tell the same story. I talked to both of them separately for a bit and they tell it the same. Sounds like Kyle, but it could be Connor, too. Even the little girl tells the same story."

"We're not exactly unarmed here, you know," Steve ventured.

Mark frowned at that. It was both true and untrue. While on duty, he and his men were forbidden by law from being armed. The thinking was that you couldn't be a fireman or paramedic *and* a cop at the same time, so the lawmakers had made the rule, and it had stuck. Mark didn't necessarily disagree, but then he didn't work in a big city. His guys were all good ol' country boys, and every one of their personal vehicles they had shoehorned inside the bay had at least one gun inside it. Mark was wondering if this fell into what some lawyer would no doubt call "special circumstances."

Then there was the damn tree. Mark had seen the cottonwood every time he drove past, and it was huge. The thought of cutting it in half had never entered his mind until today. A half hour ago, he had braved the storm long enough to venture out and take a look. The tree was about chin height on him and completely across the road. It would take a major effort to get it cut in half. Even if they managed that, the only thing they had to shove it aside was the pump truck. The truck was huge and had some serious horsepower, but he wondered if it was enough to budge a tree that big.

Cursing again he looked back out the window.

"Hey ... Does it look like it's getting lighter outside to you?"

Steve stood up and faced the glass.

"Yeah. Wind's died a little too."

"It's the eye!" He took another long look and made a decision. "Get your gear on."

"What?"

"Get your gear on! We're cutting that damn tree!"

He headed for the day room.

"Rich! Rob! Get it on! Get both trucks and the saws. We're cutting that damn tree!"

"DON'T LIE TO ME!" Wallace screamed, spit flying.

Jerri cowered on the floor with Aaron. The man had entered and without warning slapped her off her feet. Aaron had screamed and dove to the floor beside her and she now tried to shield him from any more attacks. Tyler had jerked awake and was watching wild-eyed, gun in hand, as Wallace screamed at the woman. Kobe watched from the doorway with Sanford behind him. The bigger man was obviously enjoying the show.

"Where is it!?"

"What? I don't—"

"The car! Where is it?" Wallace demanded again. "Look at me, bitch!"

Jerri pulled her arms from around her head and Aaron's to see him standing over her and dangling the keys in her face. Her eye was already blurry and starting to swell, but she could still make them out.

"Clinic four? What's clinic four?" he demanded.

"It's ... it's just a small doctor's office. About a mile away. I volunteer there."

"What kind of car is it? Is it there?"

"It's a van. I didn't know ... I didn't know I had the keys! I'm sorry, I didn't know. I didn't know!"

Wallace reined himself in and stood up straight. He noticed Sanford and barked, "Get yo ass back up front!"

Sanford left, but not before shooting Tyler a look. *You're dead*, it said.

"Not yet, asshole," Tyler muttered before turning back to Wallace. The boy he'd been whispering to in French for the past hour was cowering with his grandmother. Wallace paced a bit over them with the gun in his hand. Tyler had to calm him down. He glanced at Kobe, who was shocked into silence. No help there.

"C'mon, boss. She'd have told us if she knew. Why would she want us to stay here?"

Tyler watched Wallace chew on the words for a bit, and then he calmed down. He holstered the gun and then pulled it back out to stand over her again. Jerri chanced a look up, still in fear of another slap.

"What kind of van? New, or a piece of shit like the one outside?"

"It's ... it's a few years old, but good. In a garage on the side of the building. The doctor uses it to move his equipment around. It hardly ever moves. I haven't seen it in over a month."

Kobe found his voice. "I ... I might have seen it."

Wallace spun around. "You know where it's at?"

"Maybe. Hard to see anything out there."

"There's only one turn," Jerri added. "And then it's a straight shot all the way there."

Wallace stared at her, his eyes still on fire. Jerri forced herself to hold his gaze. He pointed the gun at her face.

"If you're lying to me ..."

Jerri summoned all her strength to put force into her reply. "I'm not."

Tyler fingered the gun in his hand. He slowly aimed the barrel at Wallace's back. Kobe's eyes went wide, but he remained frozen in the doorway, blocking Sanford's view.

"You better not be."

Wallace spun and stalked out.

"C'mere, Kobe!"

Tyler nodded at Kobe and then jerked his

head, telling him to go. Kobe swallowed and went. Tyler followed him with his eyes and saw the three of them having a discussion at the front door. He turned his attention to Jerri and Aaron.

"Bien, d'accord?" he asked.

Jerri smoothed Aaron's hair and hugged him close. "All right, okay," she answered.

Tyler gave her the slightest of smiles. This was one tough lady.

"Did it work?"

Tyler looked back at the small huddle.

"We'll soon find out."

"So, WHAT NOW?" Sydney asked.

"What do you mean?" Kyle said.

"Can't stay mad forever. What're you going to do? Drive past each other every day and pretend not to see each other? An adult version of the silent treatment? How old are you?"

"I don't remember asking your opinion," Kyle said, his eyes now on the ceiling.

"Really? Well, since I saved your fricking life, and you're unable to walk away from me at the moment, you're getting it anyway. Answer the question."

"I—I don't know."

"Are all Marines this thick?"

"Hey."

"You don't even realize."

"And what's that, Ms. Know-it-all? What makes you such an expert? I bet your parents are super proud of you. FBI agent. You probably never hear the end of it."

Sydney just shook her head. "What do I know? I know this: Yes, I'm an FBI agent. I have a degree and have worked some of the biggest cases we've had in the last few years. I've met the President, and several senators and congressman. I've been decorated and promoted and even teach other agents. I have a very interesting life."

"See! You—"

"And I'd give it all up in a second to have my dad back for one day."

Kyle deflated. His lips became a thin pale line.

Sydney softened her tone and went on. "You have no idea. Can't you see that your mom was your dad's world? She was the rock that he needed to keep himself grounded. Without her, he was lost. What did you expect him to do? Sit at home and stare at the walls for the rest of his days? Just give up on life all together? Just so you wouldn't get upset? What kind of a son wishes that on their own parent?"

Kyle had no reply to that. They sat in silence for a moment before the sound of the wind and rain abruptly ceased.

"Is it over?" Kyle said.

"No, it's just the eye passing through. We got a long way to go yet." She stood and donned the stethoscope again to take his blood pressure. Maybe she could hear it on the first try now.

"So, how we gonna get there?" Sanford asked. "The van's still got a flat with no spare."

"It'll make it," Kobe said.

Wallace looked at the boy with disgust. "How?"

Kobe didn't know much, but he knew about cars. He'd also had a little more time to think about it than these two.

"It's not the drive wheel. It's the other side. We only going a mile or so and doing it slow. We just get everybody on the passenger's side and keep the weight off the bad wheel as much as we can. It'll make it a mile."

"Yeah. Yeah, okay," Sanford said. "But then

what? What we gonna do with them? Leave 'em here or take 'em with us?"

"No," Wallace said. "Not with those cops still out there. We take them with us in case we need some bargaining power. If they can't travel then, we leave 'em." He shared a look with Sanford, who nodded agreement with the hidden statement.

Kobe wasn't sure what that meant, but he chose to keep his mouth shut. If these two wanted to leave him and Dom at the clinic with this lady, he was good with that. He felt a little better. He'd done what Dom had told him, and it had worked. Now they just had to do it.

Their conversation was interrupted by the sound of the wind dying. It had been so loud and constant for the last several hours that its sudden absence was shocking. Sanford spun and looked out the peephole.

"I can see the sky!"

"It's the center," Wallace said. "We must be right in the middle of the storm."

The banging of the metal roof, which had guided Kobe back to them, slowed and then became erratic. The wind was now a fraction of what it had been. Sunlight stabbed into the room through the peephole and the cracks between the plywood. Wallace yelled to the three in back.

"Let's go! We movin'!"

CONNOR IGNORED THE BUILDINGS' shelter and stayed in the ditch. The water was waist-deep and cold, but it offered slightly less resistance than the wind. Keeping his body low, the ditch did the rest, and he was at least able to breathe a little better. Twice, the mud threatened to take his boots off, but he wiggled them free without losing them. He came to the cross street and ruled out the tunnel underneath it. It was at least a foot underwater.

He worked his way to the bank and pulled himself out using the tall weeds until he lay on the gravel edge of the street. He could make out the shape of his cruiser just down the street. To his amazement, he found he could breathe a bit better. He examined the sky again.

It *was* getting lighter! Was this the eye of the storm? If so, it was supposed to be calmer. He watched for a minute to make sure.

"What the hell are you waiting for!" he yelled at himself.

He pushed himself up and made a dash for the cruiser. The wind had shifted and was now at his back, pushing him along faster than he intended.

The best he could do was remain on his feet and steer. The cruiser was coming up fast, and he threw out his arms before impacting the front fender.

The wind slammed him face down on the hood, and he managed to get his arms under him in time to save his face. Still, it took his breath, and he remained pinned until he had it back. The steel was not as forgiving as the grass had been, and he felt the beginning of some swelling over his right eye. He pulled himself off the hood and slid his way down the body of the car. Trying the door handle, he was relieved to find it unlocked.

Almost there, he thought. Just get inside and the rest is cake.

He pried the door open enough to get his arm and shoulder in, and then slowly worked the rest of his body forward. The wind did its best to pin him in place, but he was too close to his goal to let it defeat him now. As soon as he had a leg in, he applied greater leverage and yanked in the other. He sprawled across the front seat and the storm slammed the door behind him.

"Ha! Take that Nancy, you bitch!"

He pulled himself upright and got arranged in the driver's seat. Digging in his wet pants with cold and numb fingers proved to be a challenge, but after a minute and some cursing, he got the key out and into the ignition. He held his breath and turned the key.

The starter cranked. And cranked. And cranked some more.

"No, no, no. C'mon, baby! I need you!"

KOBE PUMPED gas while the others loaded up. He watched as Wallace helped Dom across the parking lot and then into the side doors. Jerri had already walked Aaron out and into the van. The boy had his earmuffs on, and Jerri kept shoving a handheld video game in front of him every time he looked up. She kept up a stream of words in his ear, and so far, it was working. She planted him behind the driver's seat on the floor and stroked his hair again.

"All right, okay."

The boy rocked and furiously pushed the buttons. She turned away and checked on Tyler. His face was set in stone as he fought the pain of being moved. She checked the tube she had clamped off and was relieved to see no fresh bleeding. The bottles of the makeshift suction unit were staying behind. They were just not portable enough, and

Jerri felt that the risk of them getting caught or dropped and yanking out the tube were far greater than him being without suction for the short trip. There were suction units at the clinic, and she prayed that they still had power there.

"One thing at a time," she told herself.

"What?" Tyler asked.

She gave him a smile of confidence. "Nothing. You okay?"

"No, I'm shot," he said. An attempt at humor. She replied with a crooked grin.

Wallace climbed in and closed the doors while Sanford got in the passenger seat. Wallace moved away from the wheel well over the flat tire and got as far forward as he could. Kobe jumped in and looked behind them.

"Let's move."

"A block right and then turn left," Jerri told him. "After that, just go straight."

"Do what the lady says."

Sanford scanned the streets in front of them before turning and holding out his hand.

"What you want?"

"My steel."

"Fuck you."

"What if we meet the cops? What am I supposed to use? My finger?"

Wallace considered that and then looked at the two guns he had on him. One was his six-shooter. It now held only five rounds after he'd spent one in the wall of the bedroom. The other was Sanford's automatic. It held about fourteen rounds, and he had the extra magazine as well. He spun the butt of the six-shooter around and handed it to Sanford, who frowned at his choice.

"Make 'em count," Wallace told him. "Just remember, I'm right behind you."

Sanford turned back to face out the front.

"Let's go, Kobe."

Kobe dropped the van in gear, and it swayed on its three good wheels as he guided it over the curb and onto the street.

Behind him, Tyler clenched his teeth against the bumps. It was getting hard to breathe again. Jerri saw this and bit her lip.

20

In August of 1992, Hurricane Andrew, a Category 5 storm, caused $26 billion in damages and killed 26 people.

Connor forced himself to wait a full minute before turning the key again. This time he held it down.

The engine caught but threatened to stall. He

carefully fed it gas and it rumbled back to life. He fed it more and kept the RPMs high for a full two minutes to blow whatever moisture was on the wires and battery away. With an ear cocked for any sound of it failing, he slowly let up.

The cruiser purred.

"Yes." He let his head fall forward to rest on the steering wheel. He vowed to never bad-mouth his secondhand cruiser again.

Straightening up, he cranked up the heat before turning on the wipers to their highest setting. Only then did he notice it.

The bridge was no longer standing. In its place was a twisted mass of steel barely attached to the concrete pilings. He craned his head to look across and saw that the supports that had prompted him to close the bridge had buckled and collapsed into the river.

"Holy shit," he whispered as he surveyed the damage.

He remembered worrying about stopping the traffic, afraid that he had done so for nothing and trapped all those people in the storm. Well, the guys with the guns would probably be somewhere in Georgia right now, but some of those families could be on the bottom of the river, too.

"You made the right call," he told himself.

It was warm now, and the windows were fogging up. He switched the defrosters on and warmed his hands for a moment on the dash vents. Outside, the wind was dropping in intensity, and he could see the hole in the clouds fast approaching. It was time for him to get moving toward the station, while he still could.

He'd just dropped the car in gear when motion caught his eye. Four blocks away, he saw a van moving across the intersection. He recognized it immediately. It was Jay's van, and it looked like it was leaning over a little. Why would Jay be out in the storm?

Then he realized. It wasn't Jay. His wife would have never let him go out in this, and he wasn't that stupid anyway. It had to be somebody else.

He waited until the van was out of sight around the corner building before feeding the car gas.

What should he do here?

He snatched up the radio but then remembered that the tower was down.

He wished Frank was there with him.

"Look!" Frank shouted.

Jack jumped so hard his knee hit the dash. He turned to find Frank pointing a finger down the alley, and Jack followed it to see a van driving across the intersection. It was mostly blue and rust-covered and vaguely familiar. It disappeared behind the houses to their left.

"Who was that?"

"It looked like Jay's van. But what the hell would he be doing out in this?"

"Anything important in that direction? He got any family over that way?"

"No. His wife is from J-ville, and he's got no other family here after his brother left town. She's one of those recluses, too, never comes out of the house."

Jack sat up. "Then I doubt it was Jay. You see the driver?"

"No, not really. Too far."

Jack looked back at the BMW. It wasn't going anywhere, and he didn't like the van out for no reason.

"Let's follow it. If it's your buddy Jay, we come back here."

Frank dropped the car in gear. "What if it's not?"

"I guess we find out when we get there. Catch

up, but don't get too close until we know where they're going."

"All right. Not like there's a lot of places to go."

"Where does this road go?"

"Straight until it hits a bend in the river, then it follows it for a bit and then loops back around to the main road."

"The one I came in on? The one that goes to the highway?"

"That's the one. But there's a tree down, remember? They can't get past it."

"They don't know that."

"True."

They reached the corner and gazed down the road. They could see the van in the distance.

"What's it going to be?" Frank asked.

"I'd rather catch them out of town than in. We don't need any stray bullets passing through houses and hitting anybody."

"Agree with that."

"Let's keep them in sight and then figure something out when they get out of town."

"We'll pass right by the clinic. Maybe pick up Connor?"

"There's an idea. Kill your lights first."

Frank did so as he pulled the cruiser out to follow.

"Looks like the eye is passing through," Sydney said as she reentered the exam room. "You can even see the sky."

But she was talking to herself. Kyle's eyes were closed, and his breathing was deep and regular. He was asleep. She glanced at the monitor and saw that his heart rate was up a bit.

It should be the other way.

She reached for the blood pressure cuff and stuck the stethoscope in her ears.

"Right there. That building on the right," Jerri called.

Kobe guided the van gently into the small parking lot and up to the front door before Wallace stopped him.

"No park it around the side. I don't want anybody to know we're here."

He moved the van just around the corner. A small garage greeted them, and they all perked up at the sight of it.

"The van in there?" Sanford demanded.

"Yes."

"Can you get in from the inside of the building?"

"You'll have to break into the building next door," she replied. "There's a door into the garage from there."

"Let's go."

Sanford piled out and walked to the front door without closing the van. He examined the door. Before kicking at it tried the knob.

It was open. Odd. Was there somebody inside?

He switched the gun to the opposite hand before turning the handle all the way and throwing his shoulder into it. The door gave without a fight, and he charged in.

SYDNEY WROTE Kyle's pressure on the sheet again and frowned at the numbers before pulling the scope from her ears.

She heard movement behind her. Someone walking across the floor. Jack?

She turned around to see and a fist flashed before her eyes before catching her full on the chin.

WALLACE OPENED the side door as Kobe ran around to the back. Jerri had Dom sitting up and the boy was clinging to her sleeve.

"Let's move!"

He checked behind him to see Sanford moving around to the front door. He let him go. He should have the door open by the time they got to it. He grabbed Dom's arm and pulled him up. Kobe got him on the other side, and they half-walked, half-carried him around the corner.

Two things immediately competed for their attention. The door to the clinic was wide open, and a police cruiser was speeding toward them.

"Get inside!" Wallace yelled before dropping Dom's arm and raising his pistol. Jerri grabbed for Dom and caught him as he fell. Aaron grabbed him, too, and the three of them made it to the door just as the police car swerved to a halt out in the street. Jerri saw the frightened face of Frank behind the wheel and another man beside him. They both bailed out the driver's side and reappeared over the hood.

Wallace's gun roared.

SANFORD LOOKED DOWN at the unconscious woman at his feet and then up at the man lying on the bed. With a start, he realized it was the cop he had shot earlier. He was about to turn and inform Wallace when he heard the roaring engine followed by the boom of Wallace's gun.

He bolted from the room to find Jerri, Kobe and Dom in a pile on the floor just inside the door. An incoming round chipped splinters from the doorframe as Wallace dove through it. Sanford kicked Kobe's legs aside and slammed the door shut.

"Cops outside. They drove right up on us!" Wallace told him. "Stay down!"

Sanford planted his back to the wall next to the door and slid down to the floor. Wallace crawled to the other side and put his back to the wall.

"They won't shoot," Wallace said. "They know we got people in here."

"There's two more back there." Sanford pointed. "That cop I shot and some woman that was taking care of him. I knocked her ass out."

Wallace looked in the indicated direction but saw only a hallway. Kobe got to his knees and bent over Dom on the floor. He was breathing hard and clutching his side. Jerri was applying pressure to the area around the tube she had stuck in him. The boy had crawled to the corner and was cowering there, rocking back and forth and humming.

They were in the way.

"Get them back there somewhere!" he ordered Kobe.

"That chair." Jerri pointed.

Kobe fetched the indicated wheelchair, and they struggled to get Dom into it. She quickly pushed him toward the back. Kobe made to follow, but Wallace stopped him.

"Whoever that bitch is back there, tie her ass up first. And then go find that door to the garage."

"But what about—?"

"Do it!"

Kobe left them behind.

Sanford stuck an eye to the crack in the plywood and examined the car with the two men behind it.

"There's just two of them. You see any more?"

"No, just two."

"Two to three," Sanford offered. "We could—"

"Shut up! Just shut up for a damn minute!"

JACK COULDN'T BELIEVE what had just happened. He and Frank had been following the van from a distance, letting the rusted hulk get out of town as planned and trying to stay out of sight. It looked like the driver's side rearview mirror was gone, so Frank was staying to the left as much as possible. The rear windows had been blacked out with what looked like spray paint. The tire on the driver's side was clearly flat, and Jack was trying to figure out what the men inside the van must be planning, when it suddenly left the road and pulled into a parking lot.

"Oh, no," Frank had said before punching the accelerator.

"What?"

"That's the clinic!"

The van pulled out of sight around the corner of the building, and a man appeared a second later. He was big and sporting a shaved head. Jack recognized him immediately. The man with the gun at the roadblock. He was inside before they got within a block, and Jack saw more people appear. A woman with a shock of blond hair blowing in the wind. She seemed to be helping another man inside with the help of a third. A kid was also with them, but it was the large black man leading the parade with the gun in his hand who drew Jack's attention.

"Jerri!" Frank gasped.

Jack concentrated on the man in front. He had a large handgun in his fist and was turning at the sound of their approach.

"Gun!" Jack yelled.

Frank snapped the wheel to the right and then back left. The rear tires broke loose of the wet pavement, and he held the cruiser into the controlled slide, which ended in the street in front of the building. The man with the gun had raised it, and Jack now saw it buck in his hand. He and Frank ducked down under the dash. The windshield shattered into a spider web. The round passed between them, shattering the Plexiglas partition and exiting out the back window.

"Out your side!" Jack ordered.

Frank was already moving. He popped the door open and slid out onto the asphalt with Jack right behind. They both instinctively took cover behind the engine block. Jack leveled the shotgun at the man, but he was already diving through the open door. Knowing Sydney was inside, Jack held his fire.

The door slammed shut, stopping him from seeing anything more.

Jack's eyes searched for any movement, but the plywood covering the windows prevented him from seeing any clue of what was happening inside.

"Is there a backdoor?" he shouted at Frank.

"Only if you go through to the other side."

"How the hell ...?" Didn't they have fire codes out here?

"It's an old building!" was Frank's explanation.

"So, can they get to it or not?"

"Since the vet clinic shut down, the backdoor's been locked. Maybe through the garage, though?"

"What's in the garage?"

His reply was cut off by the sound of a car rapidly approaching from their rear. Both of them swung around, and Jack leveled the shotgun at the oncoming vehicle.

"Wait! It's Connor!" Frank yelled.

Jack shifted his aim to the sky as the cruiser raced up and then pulled in on an angle next to them. The two cars now overlapped slightly with his hood next to their trunk. Connor slammed the car into park and bailed out his door.

"What's going on?"

Jack and Frank stared at him openmouthed for a moment, before Jack asked the obvious.

"Why are you not inside?"

"Sydney sent me out to the firehouse to get the medic and some stuff she needs. I'd just gotten to my car when I saw you take off after Jay's van!"

"It's not Jay's van anymore! Our visitors have it!" Jack yelled back. "They've got some other people with them!"

"Who?"

Frank answered, "It's Jerri and Aaron!"

A look of horror hit the young sheriff's face.

21

Out of respect for the lives lost, seventy-eight hurricane and cyclone names have been retired.

Muffled shouting woke her. Sydney rolled her head to the side and pain shot through it. She opened her eyes and listened but couldn't understand the words. Her view was of nothing but the cheap linoleum covering the floor. She tried to raise her head, and her face peeled away from the floor. She looked. Blood. Was it hers? She tried to raise a hand to feel her head and discovered it secured behind her back.

It came back. A big guy. Tattoos. A bald head and wild eyes. And then a fist. After that, nothing. How long had she been out?

She ran her tongue around her mouth and tasted blood. Her jaw was tender, and she carefully worked it before deciding it was intact. She carefully raised her head and looked around.

Her feet were wrapped in cloth tape, and she suspected the same was around her hands. She gave them a try. A little movement, but not much. Her feet were taped together over her shoes. That was an opening. She could probably slip her boots off if she tried hard enough. No tape at her knees or elbows. She'd been bound by an amateur.

Looking around the room, she saw the chair she had been sitting in and Kyle still on the bed. The beeping of the monitor told her he was still alive, but not much else.

People talking. She strained to hear them and soon figured out there were two conversations: one in the next room across the hall, and one out in the front. The closer one had a woman's voice, and Sydney listened intently for a moment before the sound of a suction unit drowned out the words. Footsteps. She quickly put her head back down and closed her eyes. The footsteps entered the room, and she cracked an eye open just enough to see a teenage kid with a gun in his hand snatch the roll of tape off the counter. He eyeballed her once and then left.

What the hell is going on?

Wallace was on his feet.

"Stay here," he ordered Sanford, before setting off down the hallway.

He stopped long enough to take in the first exam room with Sydney on the floor and the cop on the bed. Seeing her hands and feet taped up, he dismissed the two of them and moved on. Checking the empty office, and then the second exam room.

Jerri and Kobe were standing over Dom and a machine on the wall was making noise. The boy was in the corner, furiously punching the buttons on his video game. Dom was on the table, muttering in French and kicking his feet, while the woman did whatever she was doing. He dismissed them as well.

Working his way down the hallway he found the other exam rooms, the supply room and the closet. The door at the end was heavy and locked and he tried to shoulder it twice before giving up and heading back to the exam room.

———

JERRI STRIPPED off the bloody gloves and took a moment to gather herself. The last few minutes had been confusing and frightening, but she had somehow gotten through them. The sight of Frank's car barreling toward them had at first made her heart leap, only for that feeling to turn to horror when Wallace's gun had come up and put a round through the windshield. The sudden movement of Kobe had forced her to run with Tyler in her arms toward the door, and they had all tripped and fallen on entering the narrow door. Aaron had clung to her, maintaining a two-handed death grip on her jacket, and she had dragged him along with them while Tyler screamed in pain. She had rolled to her knees to find him clenching his abdomen, blood pouring from between his fingers.

Had the tube been ripped out?

Wallace had yelled and Kobe had responded.

They had dragged Tyler to the first exam room only to find it occupied by Kyle on the bed and a woman with a head wound on the floor. She had gaped at the sight, frozen for a moment until Kobe had jerked her away, and they propelled Tyler down the hall and into another room.

Aaron had broken away to cower in the corner, and Jerri was on autopilot. She stripped off the jacket and grabbed a pair of gloves while shouting at Tyler to move his hands. He didn't hear her or couldn't comply, so she forced them apart.

The tube was torn loose. Blood was coming from it and around it.

"Damn it!"

Tyler grimaced and grabbed at Kobe. The boy didn't know what to do. He stared at Tyler as the man kicked his feet in pain.

"Pull his hands away!"

Kobe just looked at her. Jerri slapped his arm, and he blinked.

"Put the damn gun down and grab his hands!"

Kobe came out of his shock and stuck the gun in his waistband, before grabbing Tyler's hands and pulling them back. Jerri could now see. She examined the damage and reached for the suction unit on the wall.

"The chest tube came out. I need to replace it."

Jerri saw that Tyler was struggling to remain still, but the pain was too great. That, and he couldn't breathe. She knew it was getting worse with every breath and the growing tightness in his chest had him near panic. His eyes pleaded with her to do something, and she grabbed for the suction unit on the wall and unwrapped a coil of plastic tubing. She threw it down on his chest before stepping to the small cabinet and going through the drawers. She pulled out what looked like a set of small scissors and slipped them on her finger before grabbing the tubing and sticking it in her mouth.

"Hold him!" she yelled.

Kobe's hands held him down just as she pulled the tube out. The pain was like a hot iron and Tyler bit his tongue till it bled. He gagged briefly and a crimson trickle ran from the corner of his mouth. She ignored it and inserted the scissor-like object to probe into his chest. Her free hand grabbed for the tube in her mouth, and she crammed it in the hole she had just made.

"Hold still!" she yelled. "Just hold still! I got you!"

She hesitated for a moment and saw Tyler summon what strength he had left to fight the pain. Kobe was leaning over him and his face was inches away, his face full of fear. Tyler still had a handful of Kobe's shirts, and he released him and grabbed onto the metal bed rail instead. Jerri turned knobs and cursed before realizing the unit wasn't plugged in. She snatched up the cord and snapped it into the outlet. A green light came on.

"C'mon, baby, work for me!" she commanded it.

She hit a button, and the machine let off a rattle that quickly settled into a steady rhythm. The plastic canister underneath splashed crimson red with his blood.

"Yes!" she cried, before slapping her hands down and around the tube where it emerged from his chest. She divided her gaze between the suction unit and the tube in his chest. The blood flow slowed to a trickle.

"I need ... I need an occlusive dressing," she muttered between ragged breaths.

"A what?" Kobe asked.

"Get me some tape! Check the other room!"

Kobe left and returned a few seconds later with a roll. She didn't ask; she just started taping off the site, making an airtight seal.

But then Wallace was there. Glaring at her. She ignored him and lightly slapped Tyler's face.

"You still with me?"

He opened his eyes and met hers.

"Can you breathe?"

She watched his face change as he realized that he could. He took a few breaths and then offered Jerri a brave smile before passing out.

"Kobe! C'mere."

"I need him!" Jerri protested.

"Get out here!" Wallace roared.

Jerri looked at the boy, hoping he would resist. Instead, Kobe dropped the tape he was holding and backed away from the bed. Wallace grabbed him by the collar and dragged him out before pushing him down the hall, leaving her alone with Tyler and Aaron. She decided the tube needed new sutures and began rummaging through the drawers.

"SEE THAT DOOR?" Wallace pointed with the gun as if Kobe needed further detail. "It's locked. Get it the hell open. Find the garage and this van she promised us. Do it fast!" He waved the gun at his face to punctuate the order before stalking back toward the front.

Kobe sized up the heavy door and then Wallace's retreating form. How did he expect him to do this?

Looking around, he spotted the open closet. On the floor was a toolbox. He yanked it out and flipped the lid open to find the usual household tools. Screwdrivers. Pliers. A few wrenches. He lifted the tray and looked underneath.

A claw hammer. It was small, but it might be enough.

He tossed the tray aside and kicked the toolbox away before setting his feet and taking a swing. The hammer dug into the wood and held. He pried it loose, and it took a chunk of the door with it.

Dom let out a yell of pain from down the hall, and he hesitated. He heard Jerri talking to him. She sounded calm. He pushed his concern aside and swung again. The door rattled with the impact.

"WHAT DO WE DO?"

Jack didn't have an answer to that.

"How many did you see?" Jack said.

"At least three. Jerri was holding one of them

up, looked like. Somebody opened the door first though."

"I saw him. A big guy. I think he's the one who was driving the car when they were at the bridge. I recognized the fat one and the kid, too. That's four, then. They're all here, and one of them is wounded."

"They must have broken into the store," Frank said.

"Why'd they come here?" Connor asked.

Frank answered that one. "Same reason you brought Kyle here. Because Jerri's a nurse and one of them is shot. And I'm an idiot."

"No way to know they were there, Frank," Jack said. "Let's think about what we're doing next. They have four hostages; we need to separate them."

"How do you propose to do that?"

Jack looked the building over again. It was boarded up the same as every other building in town, but he could see cracks through which the men inside could probably see. The van was just visible around the corner, with its flat tire and obvious resulting list.

"They came here for more than just the clinic. They need a car, too. What's in that garage?"

Frank eyeballed the garage and shook his

head. "If that's what they came for, they're in for a surprise."

Jack turned and looked at him. "Why is that?"

"WHAT THE HELL they doing back there?" Sanford asked.

"She's working on Dom," Wallace said, "and I got Kobe forcing a door open. What you see out there?"

"Its three to three now. That other cop showed up."

"You think they're all cops?"

"That first car is an old cop car. You can see where the stickers use to be. So, yeah, they may be. One of 'em's gotta shotgun."

"Shit."

"What we doing, man? That storm's coming back."

Wallace nostrils flared as he thought through their options. None of them were good. But they had hostages. They could use the woman and the kid and whoever that was on the floor back there as shields. Maybe trade them for safe passage out of here.

"Think they saw all of us?" Sanford asked.

"I dunno. Why?"

"I don't know, man! I'm just trying to find a way out of here!"

Sanford was rattled. Wallace knew that if he wasn't here the big man would be gearing up for a gun battle, trying to shoot his way out. That wasn't going to work. He'd have to find another way. The sound of Kobe beating on the door made him think.

"Kobe gets through that door, and we find this van, we can get out."

"How?"

"We put the two women and the kid up in the windows, see? Keep a gun on 'em where them cops can see it. We drive out and go to the car and get the stuff. Nothing they can do but watch."

Sanford turned it over in his head a few times.

"Yeah ... okay. What about Dom? Can't be dragging his ass with us everywhere."

"We leave him. Even if he lives, he won't talk."

"And the woman and the kid? They got our names and faces and shit. What about them?"

"We fix that as soon as we're out of this damn town," Wallace replied.

"How?"

"Permanently."

Kobe sank the claw hammer deep into the wood and pried away more of it. He could now see the lock mechanism in the hole. Picking up the biggest screwdriver, he set the end against the metal and hammered it. The metal bent but held. He moved the screwdriver to the wood and chiseled around it. Soon, he could see the deadbolt. He wedged the screwdriver in and hammered it sideways twice. It gave and the door sprung slightly.

He dropped the hammer and grabbed the knob. The door came open. He gaped at what he found on the other side.

Another door.

"Son of a ..."

He grabbed the knob of the second door. He turned it and applied pressure. It was unlocked, but stuck. He shouldered it and it burst open in a cloud of dust and paint chips. Kobe fell through onto the floor.

It was an exam room. Only bigger than the ones he'd seen already. There was a big light hanging from the ceiling, and instead of a bed there was a big stainless-steel table in the middle of the room. The cabinets were all glass and steel, too, and held a variety of jars and trays and other stuff he didn't recognize. On the walls were posters. Dog and cat skeletons, pictures of their insides. It was like something out of a horror movie.

He felt for a light switch and turned it on. The room lit up, but didn't get any less creepy. He spotted a door on the other side and headed through it.

Another hallway like the one next door. He hit another set of lights and then followed it down to what looked like a waiting room, before turning around and checking the rooms. The floors were tiled, and the first one held a variety of cages. Obviously for pets, they were of several sizes. It smelled like animals.

The other rooms were exam rooms. The only differences were the stainless tables in place of the beds. He dismissed them and searched on. The third door turned out to be an office. There were two other doors inside. One was a closet. The other had to lead outside.

Kobe tried the door and found it locked. He slammed a boot into it, but it held firm. He cursed it and was about to head back for the hammer and screwdriver when a thought hit him.

He walked to the desk and opened a drawer. Pens and pencils, and business cards, and markers, and candy, and napkins, and paperclips, and sticky notes, and staples and ... a set of keys. He snatched them up and examined them. Maybe this one.

He slid the key into the lock and twisted and the door responded. He opened it, half-expecting to see a sheet of plywood staring back, but instead he found the garage. He felt for a light switch next to the door and threw it.

It was a van. Wedged into the tight space with barely enough room left for a person to reach the driver's door. A layer of dust several months old coated it, and the tires on this side were both flat. The hood was up, and he could see that the battery was missing. This van wasn't going anywhere. The garage door rattled in the wind, and a shower of dust drifted down on him from the rafters.

Wallace was not going to be happy.

22

"Anyone who says they're not afraid at the time of a hurricane is either a fool or a liar, or a little bit of both."

—*Anderson Cooper*

"So, they need a car. That's good for us."

"How's that?" Connor asked. He saw nothing good about the situation. People he knew and cared about were being held hostage by men with guns. One of them had been shot already and was now at the mercy of the men who had done so. On top of that, they had a kid with them.

"Simple. We have something they want, and they have something we want. We offer a trade."

"They can find another car somewhere. They don't need ours," Connor pointed out.

"Oh, but they really want ours. Or they will in a minute. Keys, Frank?" He held out his hand.

"In the ignition."

Keeping low, Jack moved around Connor and crawled into the driver's seat. He removed the key he needed and then started the car again before slithering back out and to the back of the car. Glad that Connor had parked with his engine block between them and the back of Frank's car, he opened the trunk.

"How you going to do this?" he asked himself.

Grabbing three of the packages, he wormed his way to Connor's cruiser. He turned on the radio and cranked the volume high before selecting the loudspeaker option and then stretching the cord as far as it would go.

Now leaning across the hood of Connor's car he examined the front door again for movement. They were watching. Jack had no doubt about that. What he planned to do next would really get their attention.

He keyed the mic and got a blast of feedback. It was louder than he expected and certainly loud enough for the men inside to hear. He shot a look toward Frank and Connor, who were both watching him through the glass of Frank's cruiser. Frank looked determined. Connor looked a bit nervous but was nodding in approval about what Jack was doing. Obviously, Frank had filled him in on what was in the trunk.

"You inside! We want to make a deal!"

"Okay, you and Steve get on the other side, Rich and I will start here! Keep taking out wedges! If it starts complaining, sing out and get the hell out of the way! Got it?"

Mark watched the two of them move off in the direction of the base, loaded down with the heavy chainsaw and a couple of gas cans, their bunker gear flapping in the wind and their helmets cocked back on their heads. The tree was huge and the journey around the base would take them a few minutes.

He stared at the base that had once held the

giant in the ground. Its broken roots jutted into the sky and were still holding a good chunk of the earth in their grasp. It had been a hell of a fight, he saw, but the storm had finally won and pulled the massive tree free from the saturated ground. He examined the other trees in the area. A few of them were possible threats, but if the wind hadn't brought them down already, they were probably safe.

He thought "probably" because he knew better. It wasn't his first hurricane, and he knew that the storm would very soon be back as strong as before and blowing from the opposite direction. Just because the trees had stood up to the wind in one direction, it didn't mean they would handle it from the opposite. The only thing he had to help counter that was the retired engineer from Rhode Island now standing next to him. But the guy had not hesitated when he'd asked for his help, so he had to give him credit for that.

Mark examined the tree again. It was lying directly across the road and at a slightly upward angle. There was some space showing under one side and he was worried about it snapping and possibly rolling onto one or more of his guys. The tree had also brought down two of its neighbors on its way down, and they had to be cleared away before they could attack the main obstacle. That should only take a few minutes. The plan was to cut the trunk in two and then hopefully have enough horsepower to shove one end forward enough for the ambulance to fit through. It was the only choice that Mark could see.

"What do I do?" the man asked over the wind.

Mark looked him over. He looked out of place in the borrowed bunker gear and helmet, but his face was determined. Mark pointed to the heavy bumper of the truck.

"I need you to stand up there and watch those other trees! If you see one that might look like it's gonna come down on us, sound the alarm, okay? We'll be too busy with the saws to pay attention!"

The man looked left, right, and then up at the trees, before turning back to Mark and giving him a thumbs up. He climbed up on the bumper and grasped the air-horn in his hand before scanning the area.

"Well, okay then."

He turned to find Rich working the saw and clearing the smaller tree from their path. It was a little less than a foot in diameter, and the saw was making quick work of it under his expert attention. The first eight-foot section fell a few seconds later, and Mark spun the end around before kicking clear.

The second saw started up on the other side, and Mark saw chips flying up and over the trunk. He gazed up at the wall of clouds off to the west. It seemed to stretch forever, like they were inside a giant cylinder. They didn't have much time.

With another look at their borrowed engineer / new safety officer, he picked up a heavy pry bar and attacked the next log Rich cut free. Revving the saw, Rich turned and sized up the wall of wood in front of him.

Bracing his feet, he cleared sawdust from his face shield, raised the saw over his head, and dug the blade into the wood.

WALLACE STARED AT THE VAN. Its lifeless form and the thick layer of dust taunted him.

"The battery's over there, but there's no charger hooked up to it, so it's probably dead. Even then, we'd have to pump up the tires somehow."

Kobe offered the information from as far back in the room as he could get. He was waiting for Wallace's reaction and not looking forward to it.

"Bitch!"

His fist turned pale around the gun, he was gripping it so hard. He turned without another word and stormed back out. Kobe scrambled out of the way and then followed at a distance.

Jerri was keeping Dom alive, he thought. What if he ...? His own gun found its way into his hand. *What do I do?*

They were in the hallway now and Wallace had increased his pace. The gun came up and Kobe saw him cock the hammer back. His own became slippery with sweat. He grabbed it with both hands to keep from dropping it.

A loud squeal from outside sounded and Wallace stopped in his tracks just short of the door, the gun frozen in midair. Kobe was breathing very fast. They heard Sanford yell.

"Son of a bitch! Wallace! You better come see this!"

A voice through a speaker sounded from outside.

"You inside. We want to make a deal!"

Kobe raised the gun and pointed it at Wallace's back. It shook so bad he needed both hands.

Wallace lowered the gun and walked past the exam room with Dom and Jerri inside. Wallace joined Sanford at the door.

"Bastards got our blow, man!" Sanford yelled.

SYDNEY'S HEAD came up at the sound of Jack's voice.

She had feigned unconsciousness in favor of listening and learning as much as she could. There were four of them. One of them was the kid she had seen get the tape. The others had to be with him. One of them was the man she had seen shoot Kyle. Another was the fat man she had seen walk past with the boy a second ago.

Where was the fourth? He had to be the wounded man across the hall. The woman was a hostage. A doctor maybe? Connor hadn't mentioned any doctors in town. Maybe a nurse or a veterinarian? It didn't matter. Whoever she was, they were in this together.

She listened to the monitor and determined that Kyle was doing okay. But his IV bag was empty. If he was still bleeding, he wouldn't be stable for long.

But what could she do?

She took an inventory. Her gun and holster were under her coat on the chair and luckily still out of sight. If she could get her hands free and get to it, she could possibly end this. But the tape was holding. She had tried to work it a bit but was afraid of being caught.

She heard Jack's voice again from outside. She was about to roll to the cabinets and hopefully find something to cut the tape, when she saw motion in the doorway.

Jerri's face poked around the corner.

"You okay?" she whispered.

Sydney nodded. "What's going on?"

She wasn't listening; she was looking at Kyle.

"He's stable for now, but he needs a surgeon," Sydney told her. "What—"

Jerri cut her off. "Stay put." And then she was gone.

"Wait!" she hissed.

But there was nobody. She lay still and listened for Jack's words. She didn't like what she was hearing.

"THAT'S THE DEAL! The hostages for the car and the coke! What's it going to be!?"

Jack exchanged a look with Frank. There was no response yet. Should he give them a push? He'd wait one minute.

The wind gusted and drew his attention to the

sky. The eye was directly over them now. They were at the halfway point. Soon, the towering wall of clouds to the west would slam into them and the wind would switch to the north. Everything that had been blown or bent already would be sent back the way it had come. It would be worse than before. They had to do something quick.

"WHAT CHOICE WE GOT!"

"I don't like it. How we know those muthas won't come after us if we give up the women?"

"In the storm? How they gonna do that?"

"Same way we are, dumbass!"

"Okay, then we keep one. Keep the nurse, or the kid—I don't care."

Wallace thought it through. He knew they didn't have much time; he had to make a choice. The one he made in his head was not the one he shared with the others. He'd had enough. First chance he had he was either ditching or shooting every one of them, starting with this tattooed asshole next to him who had started this whole mess. He should have listened to Dom earlier. It would have been just the two of them, heading up the highway alone. Now Dom was dying in the next room, and he was stuck in here with this crazy asshole. Not for long, though.

"I'll take the nurse, and you use that chick on the floor back there. Kobe walks behind us until we get the car. Once we're there, he gets behind the wheel and drives it slow while we walk with it. We get a little bit away, and you shove yours aside while I keep mine, and we bail. They follow us, you put some rounds through their engine. Got it?"

"What about Dom?"

"Dom on his own."

Sanford was about to say something smart when the speaker outside screeched again. They both looked out the crack to see an object flying through the air. It landed in front of the door with a large puff of smoke.

Only it wasn't smoke.

The package of cocaine exploded apart on the hard concrete, and a cloud of powder burst forth to be carried away on the wind.

"What the hell he doing!"

Another bundle arced through the air to explode next to the first.

Wallace dove for the door and cracked it open.

"All right! All right! We'll take the deal!" he screamed out the narrow opening.

"Thirty seconds, or I keep throwing!" was the answer.

JACK SMILED at the response and turned to his two companions.

"Spread out and get ready!" he yelled.

Frank spoke and pointed, and Connor followed his direction. Running hunched over, he moved around Jack and took up a position over the trunk of his own cruiser.

"Frank, open the doors on the other side!"

Frank set the shotgun on the pavement and crawled into his cruiser to open both doors on the passenger side. Squirming backwards, he exited onto the wet pavement and returned to the hood.

"Ready, Connor?" he called.

"I'm ready."

Jack picked up the mic. "Ten seconds," he called before heaving another package aloft. He had the range and wind measured now and the snowy powder exploded right in front of the cracked door. Some of it even blew inside.

"We're coming!"

SYDNEY FELT for the edge of the bracket holding the wheels of the bed. Was it sharp enough? No way to know until you try. She rolled around and felt her way to the position needed. She had just planted the tape on the metal edge when a pair of boots stopped in front of her face.

"Awake now, pretty? Good, 'cause we have a date."

Sanford reached down and ripped the tape off her feet before roughly yanking her to her feet. He planted her face first into the wall and hissed into her ear.

"We're walking out to the car, you and me. You try anything and it's the last thing you'll do. Understand?" She felt the cold steel of a large revolver against her neck.

"I understand."

"Good girl. Now, move."

23

During Hurricane Katrina, buoys in the Gulf of Mexico recorded waves reaching heights of 51 feet.

Mark buried the blade into the tree again, and this time the wedge came loose. Rich attacked it from his perch on top of the trunk with the pry bar and the wedge fell free. A loud pop sounded from the trunk, and they all stepped back. Rich flexed his knees in preparation to jump, but the trunk stayed still.

"A little more!"

The saws revved higher as he and Steve attacked from opposite sides. They had refueled and switched off so many times he had lost count. Mark's arms were burning from the effort, and his legs were sore from bracing himself on the rough edges of his previous cuts. The tree was fighting them even in death, its hard wood resisting the saws and dulling their chains. It was getting harder to make a cut.

"Mark!"

He looked up and the rain and wind cleared his face shield enough for him to see Rich gesturing for the saw.

"What?"

"Give me the knife and get back!"

Mark measured the distance. Could Rich reach both sides of the cut from up there? He handed him the saw and then tried to see over the trunk. Steve's helmet could be seen on the other side. It was a lot closer than the last time he had looked. Rich revved the little engine and waved them back. Mark retreated to the bumper of the truck and joined the engineer up on it to get a better view.

"Not sure I'd let him do that!" the man said.

"I normally wouldn't, but he does this for a living and we're running out of time!"

Mark looked for Steve and Rob on the other side and saw they were well clear. He gave Rich the go ahead.

Rich wasted no time. He examined the ground around him, and then the cuts they had made so far in front of him, before selecting his spot and carefully setting the blade. It bit in through the last of the bark and sank straight down, connecting the two wedges they had chiseled into the massive trunk on both sides. Mark glanced at the man next to him only to find him watching the top of the tree rather than the action in front of them. He quickly figured out why and was about to say something when the end they were watching twitched.

"Get off! Get off!" the man yelled before triggering the air horn. Its blast cut through the wind like a knife.

Rich yanked the saw free and tossed it aside as he leaped away. The trunk split a second later and then slowly rotated, twisting itself apart with a shower of splintered wood and popping cracks. Rich scrambled to his feet, and, leaving the saw behind, ran to the relative safety of the truck. The last few connecting strands of wood parted, sounding like rapid-fire gunshots, and they all flinched in response. The upper section pulled away, finally separated, and came to rest only a few feet from its bottom half.

"Nice job." Mark slapped their new recruit on the shoulder before jumping down. Rich policed up the saw he had dropped and gave it a test while the other two scrambled through the narrow opening and moved clear. Mark pointed to a few rough spots, and Rich made short work of them. The trunk was soon as smooth as they could make it.

"Might be a little tall!" Rob said.

"If it wrinkles the truck a little, we can fix that later! Let's go!"

The men loaded up and the gear was soon back on board. Mark rounded the front of the truck to get in and found the engineer still outside staring at the trunk.

"Safer in the truck!" he yelled.

The man spun around and then followed him, piling in the back with Rich.

Mark revved the big engine and then slowly inched it up to the tree. He planted the bumper against it and held his breath.

"Here goes nothing."

The accelerator was slowly applied and the truck strained against the bulk of the tree. The tree responded with a groan but moved only a fraction of an inch. Mark increased the RPMs, and the engine roared, but the tree refused to budge.

He let off.

"C'mon, Mark! Don't take that!"

Mark planted the bumper against the tree again and increased the pressure faster. The tree slid a few inches and then stopped solid. The RPMs were in the red and the warning buzzer sounded. Mark quickly backed down.

"She hasn't got it in her, boys!"

"Let's get the other truck and push with both of them!"

"Where's it going to go? In the ditch? There's not enough room for both of them!"

"We got tow straps; let's try pulling it!"

"If we don't have the horses to push, we sure as hell don't have them to pull it. Get the saws. We got some more cutting to do!"

"Mark, look." Rich pointed.

While they had all been shouting ideas, the engineer had quietly left the truck and was now standing on the side of the road examining the top of the tree. It led off into the woods among a few smaller ones, and was resting on a bed of smaller branches it had stripped off on the way down. The man abruptly left the road, waded through the ditch, and walked off into the woods.

"Where the hell is he going?"

"You find out," Rich replied. "I'm getting the saws back out." He scrambled out and the other two followed.

Mark left the truck and walked after the man, who had stopped again next to another tree.

"You all right, sir?"

The man ignored him. He pointed to the fallen trunk, at a point many times thinner than where they had cut so far.

"Cut there!" he yelled before pivoting and pointing at a tree still standing right next to the fallen trunk. "And here! As low as you can!" He then walked up the fallen trunk to a tree still standing up against it. It had missed being crushed by inches. He pounded a fist on it and grinned.

Mark tried to follow, but he didn't see it.

"What for?"

The man turned his grin to Mark. "I'll explain."

A minute later, Mark was smiling, too.

"That just might work."

"You have to stay. Grandma will be right back, I promise. Just a couple of minutes. I'll be right back. All right, okay?"

Aaron was shifting his gaze from Jerri to Tyler to Wallace and back. He was clearly scared and barely holding it together. Tyler smiled at him and repeated the words.

"*Bien, d'accord? Reste avec moi, mon pote.*"

Wallace had had enough. "Let's go!"

Jerri backed out of the room and continued to smile and motion Aaron to stay in the corner. She glanced at Tyler, and he waved her out. Wallace grabbed her and propelled her down the hallway.

Aaron's wail could be heard outside.

Tyler let out a breath and tried to call the boy. He'd been sure Wallace would plant a bullet in both of them before he left.

He began speaking softly to the boy in French. After a minute, he calmed down and appeared to be listening.

But was he really? Tyler had no way to tell.

The yelling from the man outside continued.

Tyler pushed himself up to a sitting position and stifled a cry of pain. He took several deep breaths before raising his head and finding Aaron standing before him.

"All right, okay?" he asked.

"All right, okay," the boy answered.

A clamp. She used one of those clamp things last time. He needed one now and was checking the littered countertop for one when Aaron stiffened. Tyler turned to see Kobe standing in the door.

"What are you doing, Kobe? Get out of here."

"What are you going to do?"

"I'll be all right, the lady will take care of me. Now go!"

"But—"

"Go, Kobe. It's your only chance."

"All right ... All right."

Tyler waved him out again, and this time Kobe turned and bolted. Tyler dismissed him. The boy would no doubt be dead very soon. Why had he even tried?

He gave up looking for the clamp and grabbed the roll of tape. He bent the tubing double and taped it up. The suction unit protested, and he yanked the tube free on that end. Free of any resistance, the motor took off, and he fumbled with the switch to silence it.

He stopped to let the pain subside and gathered what strength he had left. If whatever was going down outside didn't work, his three colleagues might try to get back in. He had to find a way to prevent that.

He slid off the bed and to his feet. His head swam as his blood pressure tried to stabilize, and he held the edge until he could see straight. He shuffled slowly to the door and gazed out.

They were gathered by the door. Sanford and some woman he had never seen before in front. Her hands taped behind her back and Wallace's big .357 at her head. It had five rounds left, he remembered. Wallace had spent one in the bedroom of the store. Wallace had an automatic, too. No telling how many rounds it had left, but it had a lot. Wallace was gazing out the crack in the door.

"Move away from the car!" he yelled.

Whomever he was yelling at must have complied. The two of them got ready to move. Tyler moved a bit more into the hall, leaning heavily on the doorway for support. Movement caught his eye, and he gazed across the hall and into the other examination room to see the deputy who had stopped them lying on the bed. A blood-soaked bandage covered his entire abdomen. Was this the man who had shot him? He was looking at him now with a confused expression, barely conscious.

"Nice shot, ace," Tyler told him.

Kyle's face clouded. He didn't understand.

"It's okay," Tyler told him. "Not your fault. Okay? You hear me? Not your fault. Don't worry. I got this."

Kyle's eyes lost focus and he slipped back into unconsciousness. The monitor beeped a little faster.

Tyler turned back to the front room. The men were standing now, and the door was wide open. He could see a police cruiser outside and some men behind it. The sky was surprisingly bright. The concrete was coated in some white powdery stuff, which he realized was cocaine. He smiled. He got it now. A tradeoff. If it worked. He changed his position to the other side of the door and planted his back against it for a better angle. Only then did he turn his head to find Aaron.

The boy was standing just inside the door and watching him. Tyler held out a hand.

"Aaron, it's my turn again."

Aaron grinned the way only a small boy could and reached for his waist band to tug his shirt up.

Tucked in his belt was Tyler's pistol. He handed it back to him and then softly clapped.

"*Bon travail,*" Tyler told him. "*Très bien.*"

Tyler gazed back out the door and flicked off the safety.

"Bang bang, Aaron," he warned the boy.

"Bang bang," he echoed back from the corner. He knelt and covered his ears.

WALLACE KICKED the door farther open, and the changing wind held it there. The cars were about twenty yards away. The doors were open, and they were both running. He spotted three of them. Two behind the hood of the second car, and another, an old man with grey hair and a shotgun, behind the hood of the first.

"Get away from the car!" he yelled.

The three seemed to be talking and finally the old man moved. They all gathered at the back of the second car. Still too close.

"Farther!" he ordered.

"That's all you get!" the cop yelled back.

"Screw it, man. Let's go. They ain't gonna shoot if we keep the women close."

"Make sure you do," Wallace told them. "Kobe,

you driving. Stay behind us until we get to the car, and then get your ass in. Got it?"

"O ... Okay."

Wallace pulled his head back and eyeballed the boy. He had his gun in his hand and was squatted down behind them. He looked ready, but his eyes said something else.

"They ain't gonna shoot, you hear me? Don't even look at 'em. Just keep your eyes on the prize. You good?"

The boy licked his lips and swallowed before replying, "Yeah, I'm good."

Wallace turned his gaze to Sanford. "And everybody be cool."

Sanford paused from his fingering of the gun in his hand and met Wallace's gaze.

"I'm cool. I got this."

Wallace grabbed Jerri by the hair and hissed into her ear. "You walk in front of me and nowhere else. You keep your hands up. You try something, just know the first bullet is yours."

Sanford dug the barrel into Sydney's neck. He had a handful of her collar.

"You hear that? I got one for you if you try something."

The two women traded terrified looks before Sydney nodded.

"I understand."

Sanford dragged her to her feet and the tape rubbed her wrists, taking some skin.

"All right, let's do this."

Wallace planted the gun in Jerri's neck where everyone could see it and shoved her out the door and into the wind.

24

The storm surge ahead of Hurricane Isaac made the Mississippi River run backwards for 24 hours.

Jack was considering tossing another key of cocaine at them when the door opened.

"Get ready," he told the men on either side.

The men yelled for Frank to move as he had expected. It was to buy time. Jack wanted to see who they were up against before they came out. He could now see a woman with blond hair standing in the doorway. An arm was around her neck and a pistol dug into its side. Her hands were in the air.

On the other side of the door, he could see half of Sydney. She was on her knees with her hands behind her back. Her long black hair was blowing around, and Jack thought he saw a smaller figure kneeling behind them. The shape moved, and he saw the outline of the teenager. That put the big man behind Sydney. As he watched, she was grabbed by the collar and pulled to her feet. Her hands remained behind her back.

They must be tied, he thought. Damn.

A large automatic was planted in her neck before the blond woman was pushed out. The boy followed, and then the giant pushing Sydney came last. Jack divided his time between all three and the door, before he realized that they were it.

"Where's the fourth one?" Connor asked.

"He must be inside with Kyle and Aaron," Frank answered.

"Or dead," Jack added.

"Let's hope," Frank shot back.

They were closer now, and Jack could see Sydney's face. Fear was present first. Followed by desperation as her eyes darted about, measuring everything and looking for a way out. Her eyes found his and they pleaded for him to do something. Jack trained the sights of the Browning on the big man's head, but it was repeatedly blocked by Sydney's as the man hid behind her and switched from side to side. He glanced at Frank and saw his eyes following Jerri.

"On the car, Frank."

Frank was their contingency plan. If the men tried to take the woman with them, Frank's job would be to take out the right rear tire of the car, the drive wheel, and disable it. It would lead to another hostage situation, but that was better than them getting away with the two women.

Frank seemed not to hear him and continued to track the man and Jerri. They were now walking through one of the piles of cocaine stuck to the wet concrete and it was caking on their boots.

SANFORD WAS YANKING her around by her hair now, and Sydney was struggling to keep her balance with her hands tied. The wind had been whipping her hair into her face and that of the man holding her, and he cursed it in her ear before wrapping it around his fist. Now she felt something on her shoes, making them slippery. Sanford twisted her around and she slipped, almost falling, but he yanked her back up.

"Don't even think of pulling that," he growled at her before planting the gun firmly in her neck again. Her hair was now wrapped up in both of his hands.

A FEW FEET away Jerri was having the same experience. The man had her by the collar and was jerking her around to keep her in front of him. Wallace's head was on a swivel as he tried to watch everyone at once. And then they walked through the cocaine.

Her shoes were simple walking shoes with very little tread. She made it two steps before they failed her.

TYLER RAISED the gun again and struggled to hold it on target. His breathing was getting rapidly harder to perform and his aim was all over the place. His arm dropped to his side as he fought the dizziness and a wave of nausea.

"No! Stay on target!" he hissed at himself.

The gun came back up and his only target was Wallace. He had to get closer. Summoning his remaining strength, he pushed himself off the wall that was holding him up and took three staggering steps into the room before his legs failed him. Sinking to his knees, he gazed out the door again. He could see them all, now. He took careful aim and waited for an opportunity.

Behind him, Aaron's head slowly emerged from the doorway.

KOBE SIDESTEPPED toward the car behind the two other men, waiting for the bullets to tear into him. He could see the cops behind the cars. Their guns aimed at the three of them. The long, wet barrel of the shotgun was shining bright and drawing his attention. He wanted nothing more than to turn and run, to flee into the woods and go home. He'd happily walk back to Miami if he had to. He measured the distance to the car and then the distance back to the clinic. He wasn't sure which way was better. He needed Dom. Dom would know what to do.

Jack was also measuring the distances and didn't like what he saw. He raised the mic to his lips while keeping the Browning aimed at the big man.

"That's far enough!"

"Bullshit! We leave them at the car!" the fat man yelled back.

Jack stood up, exposing himself, but also drawing everyone's attention to him. He dropped the mic, wrapped the Browning in both hands, and used his voice.

"You're not leaving with them! Take the car and go!"

Wallace eyeballed the distance and yanked Jerri toward the car.

She wasn't ready.

Jerri's feet went out from under her and Wallace was pulled off balance as she went down. A yell went out from behind them, followed by a gunshot.

Blood spurted from Wallace leg, and he went down, losing his grip on Jerri.

SYDNEY HAD BEEN PRACTICING the move in her head for the last minute. It was a desperate move, but she felt she had no choice. At the sound of the gunshot, she twisted her head down and away from the gun as she turned her body in place. Her long hair, wrapped in Sanford's fist, pulled the gun in the opposite direction.

The gun roared inches from her head, rendering her deaf as the side of her head was flash burned.

She twisted violently as she fell and heard the man yell as she did so. He yanked on her hair, and her head snapped back hard as her knees hit the ground. Her aim was off a bit because of it, and as a result only one of her knees landed squarely on the man's foot.

She felt the crunch of bone before the sharp reports of pistols, and the boom of the shotgun cancelled out further thought. Her hair was released, and she rolled her body away, kicking at the man's legs as she did so.

JERRI HIT the concrete next to Wallace with a cry and immediately covered her face and head with her arms. Wallace cursed loudly and swung the gun at her. His finger tightened on the trigger and the gun fired just as a round of buckshot tore into his chest.

KOBE FROZE at the sound of the first gunshot, but the blood spurting from Wallace's leg and a pistol round cracking past his head kicked in his survival reflexes. He turned and ran, fleeing around the van with the flat tire to run behind the back of the building. Another round buried itself in the steel as he passed, and he sprinted away into the storm.

SANFORD ROARED in rage and pain as Sydney's knee snapped the bones in his foot. His first instinct was to stop her escape attempt, and he was bringing the gun back down to aim at her when the shotgun sent a round of buckshot past his face and into Wallace's leg. He fired one round at the woman on the ground before yanking her back up by the hair and clamping her head in the crook of his arm. A round sped past his ear, and he turned to see the black-haired man behind the pistol. He returned fire, and the big .357 punched a neat hole in the door of the cruiser, only to pass through and do the same on the opposite side. It was enough to force the man to take cover.

He frantically searched for something to get behind and the only thing was the cruiser. He lifted the woman off her feet by the neck, choking her out and stopping any resistance. He used the adrenaline coursing through his veins to leap the remaining few feet to reach it. The big handgun boomed repeatedly, as he threw her in the back and got behind the wheel. Without even a glance at Wallace, he floored the accelerator. The car leaped forward, its doors all shutting at once with the force of the acceleration. The shotgun boomed again, and he felt the impact in the trunk. But the car never slowed.

A block later, he caught sight of the fleeing shape of Kobe running down a cross street and cackled at his plight.

"Good luck, kid! You on your own!"

JACK CURSED the fleeing car and tracked it with his Browning. He couldn't see Sydney, so he was forced to hold his fire.

The boom of Frank's shotgun sounded, and he saw the round punch holes in the fleeing car's trunk.

"Hold your fire!" he yelled. "She's in there!"

He spun to see Frank holding the shotgun in one hand and his opposite arm with the other. Blood poured out between his fingers and his jaw was set against the pain.

Jack ignored him and ran over to Wallace. Jerri was crawling away from him, and Jack helped her up while keeping his gun on the fat man. He lay still, his chest and side covered in blood from the shotgun round Frank had dropped him with.

"Where's the kid?" Jack yelled.

"He took off around the building!" Connor pointed.

Jack turned to Frank and pointed at him. "You okay?"

Frank nodded. "Go!"

Jack shifted his finger to Connor. "Go after the kid!"

Without another word, Jack spun and dove into Connor's cruiser. A second later, he was spinning the tires, racing after the retreating car.

Jerri made it to Frank and wrapped herself around him, her fear coming out in sobs of relief. He dropped the shotgun and held her tight.

"Frank?"

Frank turned and saw Connor examining his bloody shoulder.

"I'm okay. Go get the kid before he kills somebody else."

Connor ran.

25

Hurricane Katrina caused 53 breaches to various flood protection structures in and around the greater New Orleans area, submerging 80% of the city.

Tyler looked out the door from his place on the floor. His breaths were now short and rapid, and the gun had fallen from his grip. He allowed himself the faintest of smiles before the darkness came.

Behind him, Aaron cried with his hands over his mouth. He stepped forward on wobbly legs and knelt next to Tyler. He shook the man gently and got no response. He gazed outside, attempting to locate his grandmother. What he saw was something worse.

"THE TIRES," Jack said with a smile as he pushed the police cruiser forward.

The fleeing car in front of him was having a hard time staying straight. It swerved around the flooded areas and the wheels lost their grip twice before the driver got it straightened out.

While they had been negotiating with the men inside, he'd had Connor let most of the air out of the tires on the side facing away from the building. In the event they ended up chasing them, Jack had wanted their car to be seriously hampered. It was a move that was now paying off. He was quickly gaining on the fleeing car.

But what to do when he did catch up? He still wasn't sure. What he did know was that he had to stop the car by any means. Sydney's life depended on it. If the man got away, he had no doubt she would be dead on the side of the road soon after. He vowed to not let that happen.

CONNOR RAN in the direction he had seen the boy go but was soon at a loss of where to go next.

He stood in the flooded intersection and spun in circles, examining every cross street and back yard he could see. Picking the one that headed directly away from the clinic, he took off.

Half a block later he stopped again. The rain and wind were picking up, and he raked the water from his face before spinning around and checking every direction.

There. Fresh footprints in the mud coming out of that puddle. They led off between two houses. He followed them as far as the corner of the house and peeked around the corner. Nothing. The yard was clear. Where had he gone? He moved to the house next door and repeated the process. Except for an old swing set, the yard was empty here as well. He checked the fence. It was taller here, an effort by the owner to block the noise of the sawmill occupying the next block. He jumped and pulled himself up for a one second look. The field was empty.

He dropped back down and examined the fence again. In the corner, he saw mud smeared on the wood. He moved closer. Boot prints. Fresh ones the rain had only started working to erase. He backed off and made a running start.

He was halfway over the top when he realized the folly of his move. The kid could be waiting for him on the other side, and he was a perfect target silhouetted against the clouded sky. He braced himself for the bullet's impact.

The round struck him full in the chest, knocking him back into the yard he had come from. He coughed and kicked against the pain. His breath was gone, and he struggled to breathe. Turning on his stomach, he about drowned himself in a muddy puddle. His hands found his chest and the wetness there jolted him into action. He crawled free of the puddle and flipped over on his back in the grass. The rain hit him full in the face as his breath slowly returned.

Not here, he thought, *not in this backyard where some kid would find him*. The pain reduced itself to a strong ache, and he recovered his breath.

Snaking a hand inside his vest, he felt for the bloody hole he was sure was there. He pulled his hand out and examined it.

Nothing.

The vest had saved him. The heavy garment he had donned every day for the last year with hate. The unyielding, uncomfortable, hot, and awkward object of his daily scorn had just saved his ass.

"You're okay," he told himself. "Get up."

First to his knees and then to his feet. He grabbed his gun from the wet grass and went back the fence. He stayed low this time and traveled its length until he found a large knothole. Taking a nervous breath, he put his eye to it.

There was an open field on the other side. The kid was running, skirting around rusting equipment, for the other end as fast as he could go. Connor knew the area. The fence on that side was even taller. Ten feet or more where the boy was headed. But it dropped down to eight off to the west.

A plan now in place, Connor sprinted for the end of the fence. If this was going to work, he had to hurry. He welcomed the pain of his bruised chest and used it to fuel his effort. Two backyards later the fence turned ninety degrees. Connor made the turn without slowing down.

The wall of the storm towered behind him, seeming to chase him as he ran. He ignored it and drove on.

"MY GOD, Frank. Are you okay? Can you move it?" Jerri immediately went into nurse mode and began pulling at Frank's jacket.

"Hold on, hold on." He winced.

"We've got to get you inside. Oh, my God, Tyler! I almost forgot!"

"Who's Tyler? And what about Kyle?"

"I'll explain inside."

"Wait a minute. Grab my shotgun."

"Leave it! You don't need it anymore. We have to get this bleeding stopped!"

She grabbed his collar and tucked his wounded arm inside his jacket before examining his face.

But he wasn't looking at her, he was looking over her shoulder. She was wondering what he was looking at when his eyes suddenly went wide.

THE COLD RAIN hitting his face made him stir, and Wallace opened his eyes to see the wall of the hurricane's eye towering over him. The sight of it and the roar of the wind made him forget the pain in his chest for a moment, and he watched in fascination as the wall seemed to flex and bend as it grew closer. It was as if it were advertising the pain it was about to bring.

The cars. They were both gone. Sanford had left him. Kobe, too. Once again, he cussed himself for having not listened to Dom. He tried to move, and fire burned across his shoulder. Shotgun, his brain reminded him. The old man had caught him on the shoulder and in the side of the chest. His leg also throbbed. Where that one had come from, he couldn't remember.

He flexed his hand and found it full. It still held something. Some more investigation told him it was a gun. He had somehow retained it all the way to the ground.

Hearing voices, he let his head roll to the left. The old man and the nurse. He had her wrapped up in one arm. His other had a tear in the fabric of the jacket, and puffs of cotton insulation were being plucked out by the wind to travel away like snow. Some of it was stained red, however, and gluing itself in place. The arm hung lifeless at his side. Had he gotten a piece of the old man first? He couldn't remember.

The clatter of the shotgun hitting the ground hit his ears, and he saw it tossed away by the nurse before she tugged at his jacket.

If he was going to get away, this was his chance. Clenching his jaw, he half-rolled and pushed himself up, bringing the gun up and centering it on the woman's back. With any luck, he would get them both with one shot.

His finger tightened on the trigger, and the old man saw him, but there was nowhere to run. Wallace grinned and squeezed harder, and it boomed surprisingly early.

———

KOBE REACHED the fence at high speed and bounced off its surface before staggering back a few feet. It was much taller than it had looked from a block away. He rested both hands on his knees and sucked in air as fast as he could while he sized it up. The muscles of his legs burned from the activity, but it was not what he was concerned about. What concerned him was the obstacle in front of him.

The sight of the cop coming over the fence was burned into his brain, and he glanced behind him just in case.

Nothing. Was he dead? Had he killed him?

He had jumped the fence and kept running without really looking, but after seeing the sawmill and the wide-open area on the other side, he had elected to go back over. He'd returned to it only to see the cop's head pop up and over for a look. The cop was looking out over the field and didn't see him. With nowhere to run, he'd hunkered down next to its hard surface and aimed his gun, praying for the man to not return.

But he did. Not more than ten yards away and startling him. Kobe panicked and fired when the cop's leg was over the top. The bullet caught the man full in the chest, and with a grunt he had toppled back over onto the other side.

Kobe stared at the spot where the cop had been. Despite his years of loud talk and carrying a piece everywhere he went, this was the first time he had actually shot anyone. He'd stood frozen except for his trembling hands, staring at the place on the fence, his heart threatening to leap out of his chest.

A falling branch landing behind him had jolted him into action. He fled across the field at a dead sprint, heading for the fence on the other side as fast as his legs could carry him, waiting for the bullet he thought was sure to come to enter his back.

But it never came, and now he had a new problem. Too exhausted to climb the wet fence, he looked for options. The fence got shorter off to his right, and he saw the roof of a two-story home on the other side a block away. It was his only option. He had to get out of this open field and back into the houses before he was seen again. That, and the damn storm was coming back. He had no doubt the other two cops were out looking for him too.

Still gasping for breath, he set off in that direction.

SYDNEY STRUGGLED to hold herself in place, but there was nothing for her to grab onto. The seat was devoid of seatbelts. No doubt they had been tucked down into the seat cushion, and she had no way to reach them. The doors lacked handles, and the wall between her and the front was thick Plexiglas, spider-webbed by impacting bullets, but otherwise intact. It was a police car, built for transporting prisoners, and as such offered nothing in the way of weapons or security or escape.

The car swerved again, and she rolled off the seat and onto the floor, the transmission hump bending her back uncomfortably, but she welcomed the new position. She could brace herself between the wall and the lower seat and not be thrown around so much. It would also keep her out of the line of fire should Jack find a clear shot.

C'mon, Jack! She screamed in her head. *Do something!*

As if Jack had heard her, the roar of a car's engine sounded right outside her door. She had time to raise her head slightly before the car impacted the side of the car she was in. This prompted a string of curses from the driver as the car fishtailed across the road. She felt the tires leave the road and rattle through gravel before pulling back onto the pavement. The boom of the driver's handgun followed, and the passenger side window exploded outward. Its glass rattled down the side of the car as it passed.

"C'mon, cop! You want some more!"

The engine roared again as the man punched the accelerator, and this time the car jerked right to hit the one chasing it. Sydney heard the squealing of tires and the sound of rocks being thrown up, as they once again fishtailed across the wet concrete.

She braced herself for impact but had little hold. She was sure it was coming; it was just a matter of time.

The roar of the pursuing car sounded again.

This time on the other side. She felt the door crumple with her feet as the car slammed into them, sending it spinning. The view out the windows was one of sky and trees and sky again as the car traveled at high speed off the road. Cracking branches and slapping limbs sounded as they mowed down several small pines. The car halted and lurched upright, threatening to tip over before coming to a rest at a forty-five-degree angle. She cowered on the floor, waiting for the shot, but instead she got more cursing and the sound of the driver's door opening.

A shot from outside zipped past the car and was answered by the boom of the hand cannon and the sound of running feet.

"Syd! You okay?"

Her heart began beating again, and she let out a breath she hadn't realized she had been holding. She looked up to see Jack's face against the window.

"I'm okay! I'm okay!"

Another shot. This one closer but aimed away. She recognized the crack of Jack's Browning. She struggled to get back up on the seat, but without her hands it was too much. She managed to sit up enough to see out the window.

The car was off the road on a curve and held

up by a medium-sized pine. It wasn't going anywhere without a tow truck. The swollen banks of
the river could be seen below her.

"Syd!"

She turned to see Jack's face back in the window. He yanked on the door handle, but it was either locked or jammed.

"You okay?"

"I'm all right!"

"I can't get you out!"

"I'm okay, Jack! Stay after him!"

"What?"

"Stay after him, or he'll find another hostage!"

Jack looked in the direction the man had run,
and then back at her. Clearly torn.

"I'm fine. Go get him!" she ordered.

"Be right back!" he told her.

And he was gone.

26

Typhoon Yolanda (Haiyun) struck the Philippines in November of 2013 claiming 6,300 lives.

P ain.

Pain such as he had never felt.

Instant and intense. All consuming. Like fire had entered his entire chest.

He lost sight of the couple in his sights, and the gun tumbled from his grasp. A cough sent a torrent of blood from his mouth and across his chest to mix with the rain. Wallace found himself looking at the sky again. The blue disc above them turned to a grey tunnel. It got rapidly darker. The last thing he saw was the face of the old man standing over him, and the business end of a shotgun.

Then blackness.

JERRI PICKED herself up off the concrete, where Frank had shoved her down, and saw him standing over the man. He kicked the handgun aside and aimed the shotgun at his face, only to lower it a moment later.

There was a fresh hole in the man's chest. She watched as it pumped blood for a few more seconds and then stopped. The shot had gone through one side and out the other. Both lungs. The heart. No man could survive that. But who had shot him?

She pushed herself up and walked toward the door, waving Frank back as she creeped up on it. Two sounds met her ears. A voice she had not heard much lately, and a rapid beeping.

She stuck her head around the corner to find

Aaron with the web of his hand in his mouth and the other one tugging repeatedly on Tyler's arm. The boy was crying and mumbling around his bleeding hand.

"All right, okay? All right, okay? All right, okay?"

Frank joined her in the doorway. He took in the man on the floor, the automatic laying just outside his grasp, and the wounded boy.

"What the hell?"

Jerri ran to the boy and gathered him in his arms. He tried to push away and pointed to the man on the floor.

"No, no, no, no, no!"

"Okay, okay, baby. We'll help Tyler. C'mon, let's help Tyler." She tugged at Tyler's clothes and rolled him over. His lips were turning blue.

"The suction! We need the suction!"

"Leave him, Jerri!" Frank stooped to pick up the gun.

She shot him a look. "He's a cop, Frank! He's undercover!"

Frank's eyes popped. "Seriously?"

"Yes!" she cried. "Now help me get him in the exam room!"

Jerri grabbed Tyler under the arms, while Frank and Aaron grabbed a leg apiece. As they got to the hallway, the beeping from Kyle's room reached Jerri's ringing ears.

"Oh, my god! Kyle!" She dropped Tyler on the bed, swiftly connected the suction unit, and then bolted from the room with Frank behind her.

Aaron stayed next to Tyler's bed and patted his chest. He picked up the cadence where he had left off.

"All right, okay. All right, okay. All right, okay."

Next to him, on the wall, the suction unit pulled air and blood from Tyler's chest cavity, allowing his lung to inflate. He coughed, and a small trickle of blood appeared from the corner of his mouth. It reminded Aaron of his own wound, and he examined the webbing between his thumb and finger. There were two cuts, not deep, but they stung. Aaron did what kids did and stuck the wound in his mouth. It didn't stop the cadence, though.

"All right, okay. All right, okay. All right, okay."

He mumbled the words around his fist and watched Tyler breathe. The color returned to his lips and Aaron smiled.

SYDNEY SQUIRMED and pushed until she was back up on the seat with her legs below her. The car was at a sharp angle, resting against a pine tree on the edge of the embankment. Someone had planted a dozen or so here, probably for erosion control. The river was only a dozen yards down the slope, and she could see a couple of trees already underwater.

Her view out the front and back was flawed by the spiderweb-like cracks from passing bullets. The thick Plexiglas divider between the front and back seats was designed and intended for protecting the officer up front from his prisoner in back. How this retired cop had gotten one with the divider still intact was a mystery to her. They were supposed to be removed before resale. Whatever the reason, it now trapped her in the back seat. The side windows were equally thick, tempered for impact, and miraculously still intact. She was not really surprised. She had seen crazed prisoners kick and punch and beat their heads against them without them budging an inch.

She had no choice except to try.

Squirming into position took a minute, and she frowned at the angle and its lack of leverage. Nonetheless ...

"Here goes nothing," she said.

Drawing both legs back, she kicked the window as hard as she could. It shivered but held. She squirmed back up the seat and tried again. This time she thought she felt some give and waited for the car to stop rocking to try again.

A third kick.

A fourth.

Outside, the tree holding the car up was gathering rainwater in its cracked trunk. With each rock of the car, the trunk split another inch, its green wood doing so quietly.

So quietly that Sydney never heard it. She continued her assault on the window.

Five.

Six.

Seven.

SANFORD RAN for a gap between the nearest houses. A quick scan of the windows and doors revealed them to be all boarded up solid. He glanced behind him and heard shouts coming from the car he had just abandoned. He ran around a corner and through a muddy back yard before cutting into some low pines.

He stopped and looked for options. The

thought of trying to force one of the boarded-up homes open didn't last long. Kobe's bloodied head, and the story of the shotgun-wielding cracker, made him dismiss the idea. Even if the people inside weren't armed, it would take him a few minutes and a lot of noise to get inside. And once in, he'd be trapped again.

He examined the yards again and picked his route to the next block. About to set off, he stopped and retreated when he heard a gunshot. It was at least a few blocks away in the other direction. It was hard to determine with the swirly wind. His arm was already up and pointing the .357 at it.

Deciding that the round had not been aimed at him, he dropped the arm and cursed Wallace for taking his gun away and giving him this one. Five shots. Five lousy shots were all that he had, and he'd already used four of them. He had one left and didn't know what to do with it.

He gazed in the direction of the shot he had heard and wondered whose it was. Was the clinic back that way? He wasn't sure. The road had turned, and he'd been too busy fighting the car and his pursuer to pay attention to what direction he was moving in.

Kobe? The boy had run at the first shot, fleeing

around the corner and leaving them. If the little bastard had just gotten in the car and drove like they had told him, he could have aimed his shots and maybe taken out the cop chasing him. Instead, he had put the damn thing in the ditch. The steering was bad; the car had fought him the whole way. They should be home free right now with a trunk full of product. Kobe. If he met him out here in the storm, he'd use the last round on him. This much, he knew.

A sound behind him made him look out through the trees. The cop. The bigger one with black hair. Sanford watched him check around the corner and then sprint for the cover of the house on the other side. The man moved like a soldier, scanning ahead, and using the cover of the houses to keep himself out of the danger zones.

Sanford stayed hidden and waited, watching for the woman. No one followed the man. He'd left the girl in the car! The cop was alone. It was just the two of them out here.

Sanford liked that game. He snuck off to his left to circle around in front of the man. He may have only one round, but maybe that was all he needed?

"Don't cut it all the way through! Just fall it right at the truck!"

Rich measured the distance and frowned. It was going to be close, but he sure as hell wasn't climbing the tree to top it off in this storm. He looked at the engineer. The man gave him a confident nod and a double thumbs up.

"Rhode Island," Rich muttered before slapping his shield down and attacking the tree.

He cut the smallest of wedges out of the side facing the truck and then worked the backside. Here, he had some help from the wind, and before he was a few inches in, the trunk started popping. He backed off and the tree fell rapidly, slammed into the ground by the storm. Rich smiled when the trunk landed exactly where he wanted it to and remained attached at the base. They had their ramp. He moved up the tree now and cut away everything on top until he reached the road.

Rob jumped into the gap with the tow straps, and with Mark's help they soon had one wrapped around the trunk. They followed the tree Rich had just cut all the way to the second truck they had pulled from the station. It sat idling on the road, aimed directly up their tree. Rich was just clearing away the last few branches. He stopped the saw and set it down.

"This had better work. My arms have had it."

"It will work," the man assured him.

Mark secured the strap with a clevis to the massive hook welded to the frame of the truck, then stepped back to examine their work.

The man from Rhode Island spoke.

"The weakness is in the strap, but as long as it holds, we should have the leverage we need."

"What if that tree's rotten inside?" Rob asked.

"Then we will find out very quickly," the man replied.

Mark examined everything one more time. They had cleared the trees around the fallen trunk which were in the way, all except the big one that was right up against the fallen trunk about halfway between their new cuts. The strap was tied off to the far end and then to the second truck. The first truck was still resting up against the trunk in the road.

The engineer's plan called for one of them to push with the truck on the road, while the other pulled with the truck in back. The fallen tree would then pivot around the standing tree, sliding up the trunk of the tree Rich had just cut, and moving the other end off the road.

That was the plan, anyway. Mark still wasn't sure.

The wind picked up and that made his decision for him.

"Me up front. Rich in truck two. Everybody else get the hell out of the way."

"I'll watch from over there with this." The man held up the air horn. "One means go, two means stop."

"Okay," Mark agreed before looking at Rich. "Keep your helmet on."

"You too."

Mark walked to the truck and climbed in. He revved the engine a few times and then checked his mirrors. The engineer was in the woods where he could see both trucks and still be out of the pivot area. He held up a thumb in Mark's direction. Mark eased the truck forward, until it was in contact with the tree and then sent a thumbs up of his own out the window. The man rotated and did the same with Rich. Mark watched him take up the slack in the strap until it was drum tight.

They were ready.

"Okay, Bessy. Let's get to work." He patted the truck's wheel and revved the engine higher, while he listened for the signal out his open window.

WAAAAAA.

Mark increased the RPMs and found the same amount of resistance as before. The trunk wasn't moving. He was about to let off when he felt it give. Rich had stretched the strap to its maximum, and it was now applying force in the opposite direction. The trunk jerked and then jumped forward a few inches.

"C'mon, you bastard! Move!"

He pushed the RPMs higher, and the trunk jerked forward some more and then kept moving. Inch by inch, it creeped across the wet road. His tires began crunching in the wood chips left by their chainsaws.

"Keep going, baby! Keep going!"

The RPM buzzer sounded, but this time he didn't let up. They were almost there. Just another foot it looked like. He was looking at the ragged end of the cut out his side window now.

C'mon! Just a little more!"

They were almost there, and Mark was about to use the horn to stop them when a rifle shot went off behind him. The tree stopped moving, and Mark backed off the RPMs.

WAAAAA ... WAAAA.

Mark craned his head out the window and saw the strap in two pieces. The engineer was waving him off as he ran forward.

The man ran around the front of the truck and eyeballed the gap.

"Is it enough?" he shouted to Mark.

Mark stood up in the seat and measured the gap with his eyes.

"Maybe." He hopped out, and they all gathered to see.

"Truck won't make it," Steve said, "but the bus might."

"Only one way to find out."

"I'm on it." Steve bolted toward the station.

Mark looked over his remaining three men.

"Let's park these two in the bay and exchange our toys."

"Transmission light came on," Rich told him.

"Leave it there, then. Just grab every gun we have and load up in the bus." He turned to the man from Rhode Island. "Thanks for the help, but you better sit this one out. Lock the doors after we leave and don't open them for anybody."

"I'll stay with my family. You guys be careful."

Five minutes later, the station was secured, the ambulance was loaded, and they all checked their guns as Rob pulled them out into the storm. The man and his family stood in the open bay door. The little girl was waving goodbye. Mark returned the wave before collapsing in his seat. He was exhausted. Steve was looking through his gear and plugging in his monitor as they eased through the narrow gap in the tree. They had just cleared their way through when he yelled.

"Hold on!"

The ambulance stopped, and he bailed out the back, sprinting for the station.

"Where the hell is he going?"

Steve ran past the family still braving the storm and vanished inside only to reappear with a small cooler. He tossed it onboard and scrambled in after it.

"What the hell is that?"

"Almost forgot the blood," he explained. "Let's go."

Rob dropped the truck in gear again before looking out the window ahead.

"Will you look at that?"

They all leaned in to see through the narrow gap. The wall of the eye of the storm was now almost over them. The clouds went straight up and ended higher than the tallest building any of them had ever seen. It was a sight that froze them in place.

"Right down the center, Rob," Mark ordered. "Fast as you can."

Rob slipped the brakes and followed the directions of his chief.

27

Hurricane Sandy is officially listed as the largest Atlantic hurricane ever, with a diameter of 1,000 miles.

"Yes, sir?"

"Deacon, I have some bad news."

It's always bad news when the Attorney General calls, he thought, but he managed to keep himself from saying it out loud.

The Director had a heart attack on the way back from Israel. They landed in Keflavik."

"Is he all right?"

"He's alive, but it was bad. Even if he recovers, the docs feel he'll need a few months off at least."

"I see." Deacon braced himself for what was next.

"I've spoken to the President, and we'd like you to take over, at least until we know how things turn out."

"I ... Of course, sir. I'd be honored to fill in."

"Good. One of my aides will over soon with some paper for you to sign. While I have you here, where are we with the Shepherds case? I thought Mr. Randall was going to brief us today?"

"Yes, sir, uh, we had to push the meeting due to some travel issues and some possible new leads. I'll have him there as soon as he arrives."

"Please do. The President is not a fan of waiting."

"I understand, sir."

"Some things have changed, Mark, for all of us. I know you'll do a good job."

"Thank you, sir."

The line went dead, and Deacon couldn't help but stare at the receiver. He slowly set it in its cradle and sat back in his chair. Margaret was standing in the door with her concerned look.

"Did you hear all that?"

"Congratulations?"

"Yeah," he sighed. "You, too."

His eyes found the TV screen again. They were covering the hurricane non-stop now.

Where the hell was Jack?

JACK EYEBALLED the path in front of him. The house he was next to was old, and from the looks of it had been added onto a couple of times. A set of wooden stairs snuck up one wall to reach a narrow balcony and a boarded-up door. An apartment maybe, or a mother-in-law suite? Whatever it was, it was forcing him to hug the wall as the water had filled the drainage ditch to overflowing between it and the house next door. The stairs looked to have a pile of discarded items stacked under it, a couple of old appliances, along with a few trash containers.

Stopping at the foot of the stairs, he checked the yard next door. The rusted hulks of old cars got his attention, as did the large doghouse next to them. Any of them were large enough to hide the big man. His eyes automatically traveled to the windows, looking for reflections he might use to help him, but he was defeated by the plywood covering them.

A careful listen brought him only the sound of the approaching wind. Like a train in the distance, it was making its approach known and telling the world there was no stopping its arrival. Jack glanced at the sky, but it only served to back up the sound. The storm was coming. Whatever he was going to do, he needed to do it quick. He had to find this guy. Now.

Raising the Browning, he edged around the corner. Keeping his head and eyes moving, he caught motion in one of the cars. Was that a person?

He had just determined the motion to be a ripped headliner flapping in the wind when the roar of a gunshot sounded only a few feet in front of him. Pain struck his hand, and the Browning went flying away into the water.

Jack had barely registered the sound when the solid mass of Sanford emerged from the pile of trash under the stairs and charged him, his face a mask of anger and his voice a scream of rage. Jack had no time to even shift his feet before the man was on him, and the smoking gun came down, chopping at his head. He rolled to the side and the gun caught him with a glancing blow that produced stars in his vision.

And then the man was on him, and they both tumbled into the water. Jack landed a sharp knee into Sanford's stomach, but it had little effect. They rolled, and kicked, and struggled to land a blow, before Jack lost his grip of the man's wet arm and Sanford gained his back. Two solid hits to the back of Jack's head threatened to put him out, before he snaked a hand down and grabbed Sanford's foot. A twist and roll later, they were once again face to face and fighting to get on top. A well-aimed elbow caught Sanford in the chin and rocked him back long enough for Jack to kick free, but before he could gain his feet, Sanford swept them from under him and wrapped his massive fist around Jack's throat.

Jack punched and kicked and gouged at the man's face, but he absorbed the punishment and squeezed harder. His vision began to tunnel, and he pried at the steel fingers around his throat.

Sanford's toothy grin was the last thing Jack saw before everything went black.

"C'mon!"

Sydney stopped kicking and ignored her feet and ankles while they burned in protest. The window was not giving up, and she wondered how much more abuse her feet could take before it did. Outside, the wind roared, and the car shuddered from its position on its side against the tree. Sydney sized up the other windows while she caught her breath.

The back window? Was that the better target? It already had a couple bullet holes in it and would probably be weaker as a result. But could she get her body in a position to even kick it? Maybe. Was it worth trying, or should she just keep working on the side window?

Deciding to see if it was an option, she snaked her body around on the vinyl seat. Water was now being blown into the bullet holes and served to make the interior more slippery. She eventually found a position that might work. She lay with her head against the partition, and her body angled across and up the backrest. She got herself wedged in as best she could and planted a two-footed kick into the glass.

A large crack appeared and connected the two bullet holes. She was at first ecstatic, but then realized the car was rocking a lot more than it had before. She waited for it to stop before planting another kick.

More cracks, but more rocking. The wind had picked up and was adding to it.

She waited.

Another kick.

This time the cracks spread out in a few directions.

"Yes! Keep going!" She urged the cracks on while the car rocked from her efforts.

Then a sound. A new sound. A popping noise. She listened hard and with horror labeled it.

The tree. The tree holding the car up was cracking!

She felt the car settle before more cracking was heard. The car dropped another foot, and she swiveled up to look out the window.

The tree was giving, and the river was right there.

"No, no," she pleaded with the tree not to give up.

But it did. Sydney found herself sliding sideways down the embankment as the pine relinquished its grip on the cruiser. The car bowled over two other trees before a third tried to grab on, spinning the car around and allowing it to travel straighter and faster into the water.

The car slowed as it hit, and the front eased its way into the muddy water up to the front doors. Water began pooling on the floor, flooding the small interior space before the front seats. Sydney gawked at it and then recoiled as it entered the back.

"No, you're not going to get me!"

She swiveled in place and once again planted her feet on the back window. She began raining two-footed kicks into it as fast as she could. The glass continued to crack, but it held.

"Jack? Where are you?"

Her only answer was a gunshot in the distance.

KOBE WORKED his way down the fence as fast as he could. The rain and wind were picking up faster now and driving him on. He wasn't yet sure what to do after getting around it. Should he find shelter and try to wait it out? Or maybe find a hostage of his own? A car, maybe? Or should he set off into the woods as soon as the storm let him? He didn't know, and it was scaring him. He needed someone to tell him what to do! Where was Dom! Or even Wallace? He didn't know.

He came to the eight-foot section and debated what to do. After a long look behind him, he chinned himself up to see what was on the other side. A house. Boarded up, but with lights showing in the cracks. The image of the man with the shotgun at the van entered his mind, so he dismissed the house. Across the street, he saw an abandoned building. Concrete block with big windows that were cracked and not boarded. A door hung open and slammed in the wind. Shelter. No people. He could wait out the storm there and think of something to do.

His vaulted over the fence and entered the yard. A deer appeared from behind a tree, and Kobe jerked back before realizing it was fake. Evidence of target practice decorated its chest and shoulder with holes. Arrows or guns? Had to be arrows or the fence would be full of holes, too, he realized. Kobe stared at them for a long time and then the deer itself. The deer stared back. It was like they knew each other.

"Drop it!"

Kobe stopped and slowly turned.

"Drop the gun!"

Connor Clancy stood at the corner of the house, holding his gun in both hands. He had it aimed right at Kobe's chest.

Kobe's breathing kicked into high gear as his eyes searched for an opening.

"There's nowhere to go!" the young sheriff shouted.

Kobe thought about the words. If he found Sanford, the man would no doubt shoot him for running. Wallace, too. If he were to somehow make it home to Miami, Jackson would make an example of him, and he'd be just as dead. The sheriff was right—he had no place to go. He tapped the gun against his leg and blinked rain from his eyes. He was so close. The woods were right there. If he made it to them, he vowed to never leave them.

"Don't do it!" Clancy yelled.

Kobe spun and brought the gun up. He managed to get one shot off, before the sheriff's gun boomed and Kobe was thrown to the ground. His round went into the storm, never coming close. He found himself on the ground staring up at the deer. It seemed to have a sympathetic face. They now had something in common.

The shock passed and the pain began. Like nothing he had ever felt. He jerked as it hit and kicked his legs. His hand was suddenly pinned to the ground by the sheriff's boot and the gun was pried from his fist.

It hurt. It hurt so bad. He felt the warmth spread over his chest. A cough sent a sharper wave of pain through him, and he groaned.

His eyes met those of the man standing over him. He watched his face and the man watched his. Kobe heard him say something.

"You chose the wrong friends, kid," the man said.

The truth of the statement rang loud. Kobe had no choice but to agree. He looked to the sky in time to see the last of the blue fade away. The wall of the hurricane hit with the roar of a thousand trains. It was the last thing he saw before everything went black.

THE COLD WATER reached Sydney's head, and she recoiled in horror. She managed two more kicks before it was at her mouth. Raising her head, she sucked in air before sticking it underwater and bracing herself for more kicks.

Two more.

A breath.

Another two kicks.

The water was too deep! She struggled to rotate her body and turn in the tight space. Kicking violently to twist herself around and reach air.

There! She sucked the humid air in with gulping breaths and then examined the window. It was cracked in several places, some of them reaching all the way across, but it still held. The window had been designed for such punishment and was working hard to defeat her efforts.

"Think, Sydney. Think."

She rotated again, and ignoring the cold water, which threatened to take her breath, she planted her back against the window. Flexing at the knees and ignoring the pain in her bound hands, she slammed herself back into the glass. She heard a crack and smiled. It was working.

The pooling water reached her knees, and its cold eased the pain in her feet a bit. She repeated the blows, even letting her head contribute to the impacts.

"C'mon, you stubborn piece of shit! Break!"

The glass held. The rising water urged her on and she landed blow after blow into her target while the water continued to climb.

"Damn it, Jack! Where are you?"

SANFORD RAN, losing his balance and falling, got back to his feet and struggled on while shaking the blood from his face. Whoever the cop was, he had put up more of a fight than Sanford was used to. He couldn't see out of his right eye, and his hand came away bloody with every swipe. There was blood in his mouth, and his ribs screamed from the knees the man had planted in them, now made worse with the exertion of running through the muddy soil. His nose was broken, and it was hard to breathe. He fell twice more before reaching the road.

But there it was. The cop's car. Left in the middle of the road with the door hanging open. He staggered toward it, his broken foot now complaining louder, and checked the street in both directions. Seeing nothing, he slid into the driver's seat.

He reached up for the mirror, half-afraid of what he would find.

His right eye was now a bloody open socket. Tissue hung down and provided a trail for the blood which steadily poured from the wound. He gaped at it in awe.

"Damn cop!"

He scanned the interior hoping for a weapon. Wallace's .357 was somewhere in that flooded ditch along with the cop's gun. He'd wasted a whole twenty seconds looking for it before the roar of the storm and the sound of a distant gunshot had urged him on.

"Time to get out of this damn town," he said.

He reached for the ignition. It was empty! Where were the damn keys! He checked the floor and the visor. Nothing.

With the cop! He pulled the door release and kicked it open. At least he knew right where the damn cop was.

"Stupid, mutha—" he began cursing himself, but he stopped after looking down the road.

The cop. He was standing in the road.

"How the hell?"

The man was holding something. Something shiny.

The keys. He dangled them in Sanford's direction. It was an invitation.

Sanford accepted.

28

In 2004, Hurricane Ivan spawned 117 tornados. The highest ever recorded.

Frank stared at his son's still body lying on the exam table. His face was pale, and his abdomen was a mottled color of dusky bruising. The wires stuck to his chest led to a nearby machine, which beeped loudly and rapidly. Jerri paused the alarm with a push of a button and then checked Kyle over. She found the stethoscope tucked under his leg and put it on.

"Is he okay?"

"Hold on."

Jerri pumped up the cuff and frowned at the result.

"His pressure is real low."

"What's that mean?"

Jerri spun and looked him in the eye. "It's bad, Frank. He was shot in the abdomen. That woman must be a medic or something; she kept his pressure up." She turned back and examined the empty bags hanging from the IV pole.

"I need more of this stuff. Can you go—?"

She turned to see Frank slumped against the doorway.

"Frank?"

"Dizzy," he said.

She got to him in time to catch him and lower him into the nearby chair. Once she was confident he was not going to fall out of it, she snatched a pair of scissors off the counter and attacked the jacket.

"My good jacket," he protested.

"Oh, shut the hell up, Frank."

She sliced her way up the sleeve to the shoulder and fully exposed the arm.

It was worse than she had initially thought. The upper arm was deformed just above the elbow where the round had passed through. She knelt and examined both sides without moving the arm. A ragged hole showed her where the round had left after breaking Frank's humerus. A steady flow of bright red blood poured forth. The jacket had soaked up a great deal of it and hidden it from her.

"Brachial artery," she muttered.

"What?"

"Your arm is broken and you're bleeding bad, you fool! Why did you not say something?"

"I'm okay. People were shooting and I—"

"Oh, just shut up. You're worse than Kyle."

She took his opposing hand and planted it on his upper arm, placing his thumb underneath to reach the artery.

"Squeeze here!" she ordered.

He did and made a face.

"Serves you right. Harder."

He did as he was told, and the blood slowed to an ooze.

"Hold that."

She began going through the drawers. She found nothing close to what she needed.

"Stay put."

She bolted from the room and down the hall to the supply room, running through the pile of splintered wood and the open door to the vet's office next door. It had been years since she had worked here, and she was now attacking her memory for where things were. She found a few triangle bandages and a box of 4x4 gauze pads, but when she checked the fluids box, she found it empty. She threw the empty cardboard across the room in frustration. Whoever the woman was, she had used everything the clinic had already.

"Think, Jerri. Think."

No solution came to mind, so she finally gave up and ran back to the exam room and Frank. She found him watching his son intently. Kyle stayed still.

"Sit up," she ordered.

Ripping the plastic off with her teeth, she opened the bandages and shook them out. The 4x4s infuriated her with their individual packaging, and she ripped three at a time open until she had a sizable pile. She stacked them up and held them against the exit wound.

"Hold on." She packed the wound with the small squares. They quickly turned red, and she added more and more until the wound was full, and then added more still. Once the pile protruded by an inch, she wrapped it with the triangle bandage and snugged it tight. She examined Frank's face. His jaw was set, and the pain was evident, but he gave her a nod that said he was okay.

"Keep that pressure on. We're not done yet."

Wadding up the last of the 4x4s, she folded them in half and placed them next to Frank's thumb.

"Raise your thumb," she instructed, "but don't let go."

The thumb came up and Jerri replaced it with the gauze. Grabbing the second triangle bandage from around her neck, she placed it over the wad of gauze and cinched it tight. Frank let out a yelp of pain as the bones shifted, and Jerri ignored it as she tightened the pressure dressing until the bleeding from the entrance wound stopped completely.

She had just cut off blood flow to the arm. He might lose it, but it was better than losing him. It was all she could do.

Fashioning a sling from her last bandage, she draped it over his head and snugged the arm into it. Frank was breathing deeply against the pain.

"I'm done. You okay?"

"Yeah ... I'm good."

"Be right back."

Jerri glanced in Tyler's room to find Aaron sitting with him. Tyler's color was okay, and he seemed to be breathing all right. His chest rose and fell evenly.

"Okay, Aaron?"

"Okay."

Jerri smiled. He was talking! But she had no time to speak. She gave him a thumbs up and got one back before turning and racing to the supply room again.

She found more gauze. 5x9 dressings. Kerlix. ACE bandages. Betadine. Alcohol. Drug sample packs. Urinals. IV supplies. But no fluids.

"No," she quietly wailed. She buried her head in her hands. The beeping of Kyle's monitor sounded from down the hall. Taunting her.

"There has to be ..." She stood up. Maybe.

She ran from the room and down the hallway to the splintered door. Pushing it open, she found the vet's operating room. She crossed the room and threw the light switch.

The table looked so small. Everything was dusty. The vet had closed the office a year ago. He had performed spay and neuter procedures here, with the occasional broken leg or hog cut repair. She remembered bringing in the Barrets' dog after it got mauled by a coon. It had been a lot of stitching, but the dog had survived. The vet had a lot of equipment, most of it older models which nobody wanted any more. His son was in medical equipment sales and no doubt had found the man good deals on a variety of stuff.

But were there any supplies left?

She tore into the cabinets. Surgical supplies. Sealed trays for simple procedures. IV supplies! She looked further. They were in the bottom drawer.

Fluids. She yanked them out and threw them on the table where she could read them. Saline ... saline ... Ringers! She held the bag up and read the date. It had expired a month ago.

"Too bad—I'm using it anyway!"

Elated at her discovery, she ran back to Kyle's room. His heart rate was still rapid, a sign of low blood volume. She replaced the empty bag with the new one and opened the valve wide. Once she was confident it was flowing, she stepped back.

Only then did she notice the oxygen. The gauge read empty.

This was temporary at best. She could keep hanging fluids, but fluids were not a replacement for blood. Fluids didn't carry oxygen. If Kyle was still bleeding out, it wouldn't matter if she had a whole case to use. Without oxygen, the tissues would begin to die, and Kyle soon after. He would go into shock, and there was nothing she could do to stop it.

"Jerri?"

Jerri looked at Frank and read his silent question.

"I ... I don't know, honey. He's lost a lot of blood. I just don't know how long he can hang on."

Frank reached out and grasped his son's hand. It was cold.

JACK HAD COME to lying in the water, the rain filling his open mouth and triggering a coughing fit. He rolled over and spent precious seconds clearing the water from his lungs. His cracked ribs sent waves of pain through his body with each expulsion. His hand automatically searched for his weapon while he struggled to breathe.

Finally gaining enough air, he looked around. The man was gone.

Jack wiped the rain from his face and his hand came away sticky. He spat out a mouthful of blood and ran his tongue along his lip to find it laid open and bleeding. One eye was already swelling and would be closed soon. His left hand ached where he had planted it into the big man's head, and on his right side he found his trigger finger crooked.

He was damaged, but not out of the fight yet.

He gave himself a few more seconds to search the water for the Browning but doubted it would even be functional if he did find it. The gun had saved his life. He'd raised it up to his chest just as the big man had fired, and the round had torn into the pistol, sending it flying away from his grasp and breaking his finger in the process.

His hand found something hard, and he wrapped it up and pulled the object from the water.

A .357 magnum. Stainless steel, its frame glistening in the rain.

Was this why the guy hadn't finished him?

He released the cylinder and emptied the shells into his hand. They were all spent. The gun was empty. He considered taking it with him anyway but tossed it back into the puddle.

Jack pushed himself to his feet and looked back at the house. He saw it now: a gap between a pair of discarded appliances and a tarp. The man had hidden between them and had fired at Jack right through the steps of the stairs. He cursed himself for making such a mistake. He examined the trash, looking for anything he might use as a weapon, but nothing presented.

Where had he gone?

The car. He needed the car. Jack saw heavy footprints in the muddy grass heading back the way he had come. He searched his pockets before remembering.

Allowing himself a slight grin, he followed the man's trail.

This wasn't over yet.

29

The eye of Typhoon Carmen was measured at over 200 miles across.

"Look at that tree!"

Rob glanced to where Mark was pointing long enough to see a large oak down in the front yard of a home, but he quickly pulled his attention back to the road in front of him.

"Did it miss the house?"

"Looks like it. Man, we got a lot of cleaning up to do when this is over."

"Where the hell am I going?" Rob asked as he maneuvered around another fallen branch in the road.

"Last time I talked to Connor, he and Kyle were at the bridge. Let's go there first."

Rob took his instruction without comment and continued to weave through the debris. Mark sat next to him with a pistol in his hand, and he nervously tapped it against his leg as they drove.

"I can't believe the streetlights are still on."

"I guess burying the cables was a good idea after all," Mark answered before leaning forward and gaping out the windshield. "Is that the bridge?"

"Holy ... Guys, look at this!"

The men in the back all leaned into the narrow gap between the seats to look out the front. What they saw shocked them silent.

"Pull up here."

Rob stopped the truck at the entrance to the bridge. Connor's barricade now lay on its side, but it was no longer needed. They all scrambled out the back to see it closer.

The river had swollen to twice its normal size,

and the water turned white as it flowed around the pilings. The steel structure which had once been on top of them was no more. The pilings on the far side had collapsed and the steel had fallen, twisting itself into a modern art sculpture before wedging itself in place. The road had buckled in several places, and now pieces of it broke off to fall the twenty feet and splash into the raging water below.

"Check out the pipes," Steve said.

One side of the bridge supported two large pipes under the frame that had been installed the year before. They were on the opposite side of the collapsed portion, and both possessed a slight twist. Mark saw the beginning of a buckle at a joint on the other end. If it was leaking or not, he couldn't tell.

"The blue one is wastewater, but the yellow is the powerlines," he stated. "If it goes, we lose our lights."

"I imagine we'll know pretty quick—when that wind comes back—whether it'll hold or not."

They stared silently for a moment before Steve spoke.

"Good thing we cut the tree. It's the only way in or out now."

Mark frowned. They had left the family all

alone at the station. What if whoever had shot Kyle was on their way there right now? They had to find Connor and find out what was going on.

"Back in the truck, we need to find Connor."

"The station?"

Mark shook his head. What served as a police station here was nothing more than a small office with an open garage in the back. The county was building them a new one in a couple of months, one which was up to hurricane codes, and he doubted they would take shelter there. They were supposed to be at the school with everybody else. But if Kyle had been shot ...

"Either the school or the clinic, maybe. Let's head there first, it's closer. After that, we swing by Frank's house and then go check the school."

Nobody had a better plan, so they piled back in the truck and set off. They had only gone two blocks when Rob stopped the truck again.

"Look at that!"

Mark followed his finger and saw the BMW up over the curb and planted into the side of the building. Its doors hung open and the body was full of holes.

"Are those ... bullet holes?" Rob asked.

Mark's answer was to raise his gun and jack a shell into the chamber.

"The clinic. Now."

Before Rob could comply, the sharp crack of a gunshot could be heard off to their left.

"That way but be ready to bolt out of here if somebody starts shooting."

Rob swallowed, but didn't hesitate. He followed Mark's directions.

Mark turned to look behind him and saw all of them with their guns ready. Steve knelt by the side door with a .45, and Rich stared out the back with his shotgun at the ready. It was all they could do.

"Let's go."

Rob stepped on the gas and took another look at the sky. The wall of the eye was close. It would hit them in a couple of minutes and was already rocking the ambulance from side to side. If they were going to find the young sheriff, they would have to do it quickly.

JACK SIZED the man up as he emerged from the car. He looked even bigger, and the wet clothes accentuated his bulging muscles. His face was damaged, covered in blood, and dominated now by the glaring pit of his empty eye socket. Jack's hand had found its target, but the man's rage had overpowered his survival instincts. He now flexed his hands as he walked forward to meet Jack.

Jack slipped the keys back into his pocket and waited, letting the man come to him and looking for weaknesses. The eye was a big one. If Jack could get to the remaining one, the battle would be over. Knees. Ribs. Throat. If he could sufficiently damage any of them, the fight would also be over. The man had strength that countered Jack's speed. But did he have experience or training? Jack did. But was it enough for him to prevail?

"Gimme the keys and I'll leave!" the man called.

Jack said nothing. The man got closer.

"I'll finish you this time, cop! Don't think I won't!"

Jack let him waste his breath. He circled left and Sanford matched him. The wind chose that moment to pick up and howled around them, blowing rain horizontally into their faces. Jack felt himself ease into a controlled calm, his hands and feet positioned just so, his body coiling up for the coming action, his every sense hyperaware of what was around him. He waited for opportunity to come.

Sanford pawed at the blood flowing from his eye with the back of his fist, and Jack used the distraction to rush in, launching himself across the gap and leading with both a knee and an elbow. Both connected with a satisfying *thwack*, and blood was launched through the air from Sanford's mouth as Jack's knee drove the air from his lungs, and his elbow snapped Sanford's head back. He followed through and body-slammed the bigger man to the pavement, before rolling right and grasping for his wrist. Sanford rolled away, jerking his wet arm from Jack's hands and throwing a backhanded punch as he rode the momentum to his feet. The fist grazed Jack's head as he ducked it before scrambling back to his own feet. Sanford stopped his own rush short as Jack regained his footing and squared off with him again.

"Should have just stayed back at that house, little man," Sanford taunted him. "This is gonna hurt. You ready?"

Jack kept his face impassive, and Sanford's own face clouded for a second at the lack of response. He'd never had a silent adversary, and it was rattling him a bit.

Sanford flexed his arms and rotated his neck before stepping in. Jack let him advance and push him back until they were near the car before circling again. He couldn't let him pin him against the machine. The rubber soles of his tennis shoes squeaked as he dug them into the wet concrete.

Jack took a quick inventory. He'd inflicted little damage; the man had a healthy layer of muscle over his stomach and had regained his breath quickly. The elbow had been too low and missed the remaining good eye. His own eye was still swelling, and in a few minutes, he would be a cyclops like his opponent. But he'd also learned something: the man was slow. Whether it was from the injuries Jack had inflicted, or the post-adrenaline rush of their previous fight, he didn't know. All he knew was that he had the upper hand in that department. But how best to use it?

He examined Sanford's face as they circled one another. He was dividing his time between Jack and the area behind him. The loss of his eye had rattled him, and for all his tough talk, he was just as interested in getting away. That was to Jack's advantage.

He wasn't going anywhere.

Circling until the rain and wind were in Sanford's face, he paused. Sanford did too and looked for the reason, a wish for more time to figure things out. As a result, he wasn't ready.

Jack launched himself across the narrow gap.

Sanford reacted from reflex and reached for his gun.

This time Jack's elbow slipped under Sanford's forearm and struck him full in the neck. Jack went for the man's wrist with his other hand but was defeated when Sanford rolled with the impact. They both went down on the wet pavement and rolled twice before stopping.

Jack found himself on top and pushed away to try another elbow, but Sanford grabbed him and pulled him close, cancelling out any room for cocking an arm back. Jack found his arm pinned and his legs fighting for purchase on the wet road. A vicious head-butt knocked Jack back, and his grip on the man loosened.

With a roar, Sanford flung Jack aside and scrambled back to his feet. Jack rolled twice and then kept rolling until he was clear before doing the same.

They returned to circling.

Sanford was mad now, his thoughts less focused. He launched himself at Jack, closing the gap fast. This time Jack held his ground and let him come.

Ducking Sanford's hand going for his neck, Jack grabbed his wet shirt and dropped to the concrete, pulling them both down while planting both knees in the bigger man's chest and letting his momentum take him over Jack and off his feet to land flat on the ground. Jack rolled to his feet and launched himself into the air, both feet coming down on Sanford's chest with all of his weight behind them.

Sanford rolled left at the last second, and Jack's feet found only the hard pavement. He stepped back only to have Sanford sweep his legs and take him down, his giant paws dragging him under him and raining blows down.

Jack took two shots before he managed to grab a wrist and plant a foot in his attacker's neck. Stretching the arm to its fully extended position, he worked to pop it out at the shoulder.

But Sanford would have none of that. He twisted in the opposite direction and flipped Jack hard onto his face. A blow to the back of the head dazed Jack long enough for him to get an arm around his throat. Jack kicked for leverage and clawed at the arm and the face behind it, but Sanford protected his remaining eye and kept his head snugged in tight next to Jack's.

Jack struggled as the light faded. He needed something else. Anything.

SANFORD GRINNED when Jack's hands stopped tearing at his arm and face. A little more pressure. Just a little more. He felt Jack's hands reaching down his body and tightened the pressure. He had him. He opened his good eye and turned his head just in time to see it coming.

The knife sliced through the rain and into his one remaining eye before his startled mind could register it. There was a brief moment of light and pain, and then nothing.

30

In October 1998, the Fanthome, a 282-foot four-masted sailing ship based in Miami Beach, sank near Honduras in Hurricane Mitch, killing all 31 crew members onboard.

J ack tugged on the blade twice before giving up and leaving it there. He pushed the man's lifeless weight off him and rolled away, gasping for breath as the rain tried to fill his mouth with water. He coughed twice and then rolled to his feet to examine his adversary.

Sanford lay spread-eagled in the road. One eye was a gaping maw of raw flesh, the other held the fighting knife, its blade buried to the hilt through the man's brain. The grin was now frozen on his face.

Jack groaned and held his ribs as he forced himself up. He staggered a few steps and used the car to keep himself upright. The storm raged around him. Rain entered his boot where the knife had been, and he spat out a mouthful of blood only to see it instantly erased by the rain. He glanced up to see the blue disc of sky now gone, its light replaced by deep grey clouds and driving rain. Spinning in place, he fought to orient himself.

The clinic was back that way. But ... Sydney.

Shoving a hand down the front of his pants, he felt for the ignition key. He'd waved the others at Sanford to keep him here, but there was no way he was going to give him the key to the ignition.

Rounding the car, he quickly started it. And with one eye open, Jack navigated into the storm.

"DAD?"

Frank's head snapped up and he found his son looking at him, a concerned look on his face.

"Hey, son. How you doing?"

"Are you ... are you shot?"

"Yeah."

"Me too. What happened?"

"Nothing. They're gone now. It's all over. I'm okay."

"Where's Sydney?"

"She's ... she's out in the storm with her partner."

"Oh ... what's going on? Who were those guys?"

"Drug runners, it looks like. We're lucky those two FBI agents were behind them."

Kyle lay his head back down and sighed.

"I'm sorry, Dad."

"Don't be sorry. They got the drop on you, is all. Could've happened to—"

"No. No, not that. I'm sorry for ... everything. I've been an ass."

"It's okay, son."

"No. No, it's not. I was just ... I don't know. It seemed so soon, and I guess I didn't look at it from your point of view."

Frank bit his lip and glanced at the monitor.

Kyle's heartrate was climbing again, something Jerri had warned him to watch for.

"It's all right. We can talk about it later. You need to rest."

Voices sounded from the next room, and someone could be heard moving around.

"Who's here?"

"Jerri and Aaron. The druggies were at the store—tried to hold them hostage and then exchange them for one of our cars. Turns out one of them is an undercover DEA agent. He took a bullet to the chest. She's working on him across the hall." Frank left out who put the bullet there and hoped Kyle wouldn't ask. He tried to change the subject before Kyle could put it together.

"Aaron's talking again."

"He is? That's great."

"Seems this agent speaks French and got him going somehow."

Kyle dwelled on this for a moment.

"Dad, tell her I'm sorry."

"You tell her."

"Tell her I'm sorry and ... and I'm glad you and her ..."

Kyle slipped back out and the number on the monitor ticked up a couple more notches until it hit the alarm point. The beeping started.

"Kyle? Kyle?"

Frank reached out and shook his son but got no reply.

"Jerri!"

JACK PULLED up to the curve and examined the side of the road over the river. The car was gone! He cruised slowly until the white heartwood of the broken pines gleamed at him through the rain. He grabbed Frank's extra-large flashlight and bailed out.

Playing the beam down the bank, he saw the light reflected off the chrome of the cruiser's bumper. The river seemed to be sucking it in. He shone it across the windows and heard a high-pitched scream.

"Jack!"

"Syd!"

Jack threw himself down the muddy slope and quickly lost his footing. Giving up, he turned on his butt and let himself be taken to the car by gravity. Impacting the door, he grasped its handle and pulled himself up.

"Syd!"

"I'm still in here! The water's rising! Hurry!"

Jack flinched as her hand struck the glass on the other side and wiped away some of the fog. Her terrified face looked back at him from inches away with water up to her neck. He yanked on the locked door in vain before stepping back and raising the flashlight.

"Get back!"

Sydney took a breath and ducked under the water. The storm was strangely muted, but the roar of the river and its passing water took its place. She pulled her head under as far as she could just as the flashlight hit the window. The sound beat on her ears in the small space.

Again.

Her lungs began to burn, and she stuck her head up for a breath. The space was narrow now. She had to turn her face to get it in the remaining air.

"Get down!" she heard Jack yell. Her head was barely back under water when the flashlight struck again.

And again.

And again.

She heard air escaping through the holes in the glass, and then it stopped.

Again.

She looked up to see the shadow of Jack and

the raining blows of the flashlight cracking the window. The image tunneled and she felt the car settle further. The light began to fade. Gray, and then black.

Hands. A hand grabbing her hair. Her shirt tightened around her neck as it was pulled tight from behind. Yelling.

Air. Cold air on her face. She coughed and spit as she was dragged through the window, its jagged edge slicing her arms and ripping her clothes. She gagged on the water as she was wrapped in a bloody arm and pulled toward the shore, she turned in time to see the car just as its shiny chrome bumper disappeared beneath the brown swirling water.

Her foot struck something solid, and she pushed. Mud. The river's bank. The collar tightened again as Jack dragged her up the slope and clear of the water before collapsing himself. They both retched on muddy river water until they could breathe and then rolled over to escape the rain.

Sydney opened her eyes to see Jack's face inches away. A cut on his cheek, the split lip, and the swollen eye reminded her of where he had been.

"Are you ... okay?"

"Am I ...?" Jack forced a laugh. "Yeah. Yeah, I'm okay."

"Is he gone?"

"For good."

Sydney relaxed a fraction. They both rested for a moment until she couldn't take it anymore.

"Can you cut this tape off my hands now?"

"You have a knife?"

"No. Where's that sword you were carrying?"

"I ... I left it somewhere."

Jack sat up and rolled over to work on the tape. Finding the end, he scraped it free with a finger-nail and unwound the multiple layers until she was free.

"You've got some cuts that need attention. Let's go. Can you walk?'

"I'll sure as hell walk out of here."

They crawled up the muddy embankment until they could stand on firm ground. She took a second to catch her breath again and check him out.

"You sure you're okay?"

"The eye works. It's just swollen shut. Ribs are cracked. Finger's broke. I'll live."

She nodded, too exhausted to speak. The wind was picking up, and it was getting harder to stand. She turned them into it, and they saw the darkness approaching over the town. It served to jar her memory.

"Kyle! We have to go!"

They held each other up as they struggled to the car.

31

In July 1715, a hurricane struck the east coast of Central Florida and sank 10 Spanish galleons, killing almost 1,000 sailors and sending tons of gold and silver coins to the bottom of the ocean.

Connor was tired. It was a fatigue that he had not felt in all his years. The shots fired at the clinic. The chase through the streets. The bullet knocking him off the fence. His confrontation with the boy. It had drained the strength from him. Not even the rapidly approaching wall of the storm was enough to prompt him to move any faster. It was all he could do to put one wet boot in front of the other.

The image of the kid was still fresh in his mind. He was just a teenager, a few years younger than Connor himself. Running scared. Why didn't he drop the gun? Connor didn't want to shoot him. He really should have dropped the gun.

He rubbed the vest where the boy's bullet had hit. He could feel the round buried in it. His own gun fired the same size and shape. He had the boy's gun tucked into his belt. His own was now hanging in his hand and bouncing off his leg as he walked.

He really should have dropped the gun.

A replay of the boy spinning and firing played again in his head and Connor's gut tightened as he relived it. The crack of his own gun echoed and echoed in his mind.

Without warning, Connor bent and emptied his stomach onto the wet pavement. He retched, and then retched some more until every drop was out, and then dry heaved twice more.

Connor straightened and turned into the rain, wiping his mouth on his saturated sleeve. The cold hit him and he shivered. A couple of deep breaths later, he was walking again.

He really should have dropped the gun.

A block later, he came to an intersection and turned left. Had he really run all this way? The clinic seemed like it was miles away. How had he covered all that ground so fast?

He trudged on, the water in his boots squeezing between his toes with each step. The wind was in his face and making the slicker flap behind him. He was too tired to button it up. Putting his head down, he traveled on.

WHOOP-WHOOP!

Connor lifted his head at the sound and turned around. What he saw brought a smile. The red square shape of the ambulance advanced out of the deluge. A figure left the vehicle and ran toward him. It was Mark.

"Connor! You okay?"

Connor took in the dirty bunker gear and the handgun clenched in his fist. How did he know?

"Yeah. I'm okay. You gimme a ride?"

Mark was confused by the odd request. He saw the hole in Connor's slicker and reached out to pull it open. The hole was now a sizable dent in Connor's vest. What the hell was going on?

"You sure you're okay? Want me to get Steve to check you out?"

Connor waved the vest away. "I'm fine. Steve's with you?"

"Yeah. All of us are here. Some guy and his family showed up at the station and said somebody was shooting at the bridge. We cut through the tree I told you about and got here as fast as we could."

Connor's brain absorbed the information, and it jarred him into action. He looked at Mark as if waking from a dream.

"We need to get to the clinic, now!"

"Okay, come on, then." Mark tugged at his sleeve, and Connor allowed himself to be led to the back. Mark stuffed him inside, and Steve took over. Rounding the truck, Mark jumped back in the passenger seat.

"To the clinic, Rob, as fast as this tub will go."

Rob dropped the truck into gear and floored the accelerator.

"What's going on?"

"I don't know yet, but I bet we'll find out when we get there."

JERRI LISTENED to Tyler's breathing and stifled her frown.

Tyler was worse. The suction unit was pulling blood and air from his chest cavity at a steady rate, but the lung was damaged, and the constant loss and recovery of the suction had made whatever was bleeding start again. Still, as long as he had suction, he seemed to be hanging in there. Maybe if he just stayed still, the bleed would slow enough for him to make it through this.

"Okay?"

"Better. Real tired. Thirsty."

She took note of the short sentences. Something people did when short of breath. He needed blood, but so did Kyle, and they had none. She considered auto transfusion, but she didn't have the equipment.

"What's your blood type?"

"O-negative."

Jerri grimaced at the news. O-negative people could only accept O-negative blood. It was the same problem she had with Kyle. Not even Frank could donate to him. Jerri was A-positive and so was Aaron. There was nobody else.

She caught Tyler watching her face. Were her thoughts evident?

"Sucks to be me right now, I take it?"

Tyler knew what his blood type meant, she realized, so she didn't try to hide it.

"There's nobody here. Maybe the agents, if they come back, or Connor."

"It's okay," he assured her. "I can wait."

She smiled at his show of false bravery before arranging the pillow under his head again.

"Just stay as still as possible. You have to give whatever is bleeding in there a chance to clot off."

"Oui, m'dame."

Jerri had just straightened up when a beeping sounded. Her face clouded and then turned to panic as Frank yelled.

"Jerri!"

JACK PULLED the cruiser into the lot and parked it close to the door. Rather than fight the wind on her side, Sydney slid across the seat and followed him the three steps to the door. Jack shouldered it open, and they tumbled inside. Jack raked his hair back to see a gun pointed at him from the nearest exam room.

"It's Jack, Frank! Jack and Sydney!"

"In here," he replied.

Sydney entered first and saw Jerri checking on

Kyle. He was pale and unconscious and the rate on the monitor was rapid.

"How is he?" Sydney asked her.

"He's alive, thanks to you," she answered.

"What happened?" Frank asked Jack, taking in their injuries along with their bloody and muddy clothes.

"I got my guy. He won't be back. Where's Connor?"

"I don't know. He took off after the kid."

"Will you two take it out there?" Sydney barked. She and Jerri were hovering over Kyle and the room was crowded.

The two men beat a hasty retreat.

"If he's not back yet, maybe we better go look for him?"

"Storm's going to hit again in just a few minutes. If he doesn't make it back before it does, he'll have to hunker down somewhere. If that kid's out there with a gun, we could walk right into an ambush and never see it coming. Let's give him a little time to get back here first, otherwise we'll have three of us wandering around out there instead of one."

Frank didn't like the idea, but he had to agree.

"So, what do we do while we wait?"

The answer came from Sydney. She entered

the room and walked up them, close enough to keep their words among the three of them.

"Both of them need blood."

"I can donate," Frank immediately answered.

"No, I'm sorry, but Jerri says you're the wrong blood type."

"I'm his father!"

"That's not how it works, I'm afraid. Jack, you can't either. We need someone who's O-neg ... or we need the blood they have at the fire station. It's why I sent Connor back out into the storm. To go get it."

Jack shared a look with Frank. "How far is that?"

"About twelve miles back toward the highway."

As if to punctuate her statement, the wind gusted higher and rattled the building. Debris could be heard hitting the roof of the building.

"If that's what it takes," Jack said.

The wind roared and the lights flickered.

"Better get a generator, too."

"There's one at Jerri's garage. We can grab it on the way back."

"We? Frank, your arm is near shot in two. You're not going anywhere."

"The hell I'm not! That's my son in there!"

"And who watches the door in case that kid comes back?" Jack countered.

"We can board it up and—"

"Will you two shut up! Jack, get going! Frank, you're on the door." Sydney's tone brooked no argument, and the two men fell silent as Jerri joined them.

"Are you going?" she asked Jack.

"Yes."

"Please hurry. We need a miracle."

JACK SHOULDERED the door of the clinic and pushed, using all the power he had in both legs to get it open before wedging his body into the gap and forcing his way through. The door slammed shut behind him, and he gripped the shotgun tight as he put his head down and crawled toward the cruiser. It served to block the raging wind and rain enough for him to get inside. Jack's ribs screamed at him as he yanked the door shut. He lay on the seat and gazed up at the rain pounding the glass above him. He'd only gone a few feet, and he was already exhausted. How was he supposed to make it twelve miles in this?

Pushing himself across the seat with his legs,

he twisted into the driver's seat and started the car. Dropping it in gear, he glanced in the rear view out of habit.

"What the ...?"

Lights. From a vehicle.

His hand reached for the shotgun on the seat next to him.

Was it the kid? Had he found another car and come back for his buddies? Jack slid down in the seat and watched the lights approach in the driver's side mirror.

A big truck, it looked like.

The truck left the road and lit up the rear window with its headlights, blinding Jack. He squinted as he grabbed the door handle. The wind would whip it open for him. All he had to do was release it and then roll out onto the pavement. He could have the shotgun on the driver the second he stepped out of the cab. He clicked the safety off and took a deep breath as the truck stopped right behind the cruiser.

"One ... two ..."

The ambulance scene lights lit up the face of the clinic. The passenger side's door opened, and Jack heard several voices.

"Jack!?"

Jack sat up and lowered the shotgun. A face appeared in the passenger side window.

"Connor?"

The door opened to reveal Connor's smiling face.

"Jack! What are you doing?"

"I was going to the station to ... never mind," he screamed back. "Who you with?"

"The cavalry!"

32

Hurricane Patricia had an estimated wind speed of 200 miles per hour, the highest ever recorded worldwide.

S ydney and Jerri were in the supply room. They had left Aaron with Tyler, and Frank with Kyle, and then found a place to speak in private.

"You're a medic?" Jerri asked.

"Yes, and a little more. I was part of the body

farm at Vanderbilt. I have mostly a forensic background. Post-mortem analysis. Gunshot wounds mostly. It's what got me into the FBI."

"Autopsies?"

"A ton."

"So, you know surgery?"

"I wouldn't say that. The patients were already dead."

Jerri was looking through a cabinet for more fluids but quickly gave up and faced her.

"Listen, I was a surgical first-assist in my younger days. Mostly general surgeries below the diaphragm. I'd assist the surgeon and close when we were done."

"Okay? Where are you going here?"

"Follow me."

Sydney followed her out of the room and down the hall to the splintered door. She glanced down the hall to see Frank seated in a chair between the two exam rooms, his eyes on the front door and his back to them. He held the one remaining pistol they had in his good hand.

Jerri led her through the door and into the room, before closing it behind her. She flicked on the lights, and Sydney saw where the conversation was going.

"It's an old vet's surgery room. There are some

sealed trays in the cabinets, and the equipment still works."

Sydney gazed about the room. It was not like any operating room she had ever seen—not even in Africa—but it seemed to have the basics.

"Are you suggesting we ... do surgery on them here?"

"I don't see any other options for Kyle. He's bleeding into his gut and unless we stop it ..." Her eyes welled up with tears. "I ... I don't know what else to do. Tell me what to do."

"We ... we've got no anesthesia," Sydney protested. "No blood. This room is far from being sterile. I don't ..." Sydney broke down.

"I see no other option. We can locate the bullet with the ultrasound machine. That will help tell us where to look for the bleeder. We just go in, follow the clotting to the bleeder, and clamp it. Nothing else."

Sydney examined the woman's face. She was clearly desperate, willing to try anything.

"Still, Jerri. You know without blood—"

"He'll likely bleed out," she finished. "But we have to try!"

Sydney wanted to believe, too, but her experience told her it was a fool's errand.

"Jerri, I—"

She was cut off by a shout from Frank. They both bolted to the door, and Sydney had to throw out an arm to stop Jerri from jumping out into any incoming bullets. It couldn't be Jack. He had just left. Connor, maybe? Or that kid? She peered cautiously around the corner and exhaled with relief to see Jack standing in the doorway.

He wasn't alone.

INTRODUCTIONS WERE QUICK. Sydney swiftly took charge.

She zeroed in on Steve, the only man with a paramedic patch on his sleeve. He was standing in the hallway between the two exam rooms.

"We've got a chest in there, and a belly in there. Both with massive blood loss. What do you have?"

"Uh, I've got Ringers and saline. At least four of each. And two units of packed red blood cells."

"You have blood?"

"Just PRBCs. They're talking about giving us some O-neg, but the protocol hasn't been approved yet, and—"

Sydney cut him off. "Get it all in here! We need your stretcher, your monitor, all your intubation equipment, and all your drugs! Move."

The men knew that tone of voice from training and jumped. Jack and Frank scrambled out of the way as the firemen pushed themselves back out into the storm.

"What are you two doing here, Syd?"

The two women shared a look.

"A Hail Mary."

SYDNEY WATCHED from the hallway with Jerri as the fireman moved Kyle over to their gurney. The technology had changed since her day. The stretcher was very high tech. She marveled at the flexibility of the equipment, as Steve adjusted it to the exact height of the bed Kyle was on with a push of a button. The ancient Lifepack was replaced with a brand-new Phillips monitor, and a fresh tank of oxygen once again fed the much-needed gas to Kyle's nose. She stepped back farther as they threw the straps across him. They would need the space to get him out of the tight quarters.

"Sydney?"

Sydney turned to see Jerri examining the contents of the cooler. Her face was clouded.

"What is it?"

"There's only two units."

"And?"

"I don't think it's enough." She lowered her voice. "I don't think it's enough for both." She glanced at the room holding Tyler and saw him lying still with his eyes closed. Was he asleep? She couldn't tell.

"How is he doing?"

"Stable. But for how long?"

"We have Ringers and Saline. If his bleed stays slow—"

"I'm not sure it is. He's already lost a lot of blood. If you'd seen the floor at my store, you'd be worried, too. How much did he lose before that? And then more here when he ... I just don't know what we should do here."

"And none of the crew can donate?"

"Three A's and a B positive."

"Somebody else?"

"There's no time to find anybody else. Even if we did, by the time they got here Kyle would be gone. We have to move now."

"So, we give him a unit before we go in and hope it's enough."

"If that's not enough—"

"Give him both units," Tyler said.

"Oh my God, Tyler. I'm sorry, we just—"

"It's okay. He's worse off than me. Give him the blood. I'll be okay."

"Tyler? I'm Sydney. I ... I can't ask you to do this. I think the best—"

"The best thing is for you to give him the blood and do what you have to do. I'm breathing okay. Give him the blood. I can hang."

Sydney and Jerri shared a look. Did he understand what he was saying?

"Tyler, you understand that ... well ..."

"Comes with the job. I've been undercover with this crew for almost a year. I could have died any one of those days up till now. Why should today be any different? Go do what you need to do. I'll be right here with my man Aaron. Okay, Aaron?"

"All right, okay," Aaron answered.

Sydney examined his face, and Tyler offered her a smile and a thumbs-up. She had no answer ready.

"Okay. Steve stays here with Tyler and Frank. You and I are in the O.R. with two of the fire crew. Jack and Frank and Connor can watch the doors. Let's go."

Jerri moved, and the crew with Kyle followed her down the hallway. Sydney stopped Steve and pulled him into an empty exam room.

"Jerri and I are going in after the bleed. I need you to stay here with Tyler and Frank. Keep Frank still, but busy, and watch Tyler's pressure closely."

"All right. You handle the tube?"

"I think I can still pull that off." He handed her the intubation bag and a smaller one that rattled. His drug kit.

"What do you have here?"

"Etomidate and Sucs. A couple of Diprivan. It's all we carry. We just tube traumas or full arrests out here, maybe a diff-breather once in a while. This stuff isn't meant for surgery."

"Well, today it is. We'll make do. You got this?"

Steve recalled his brief look at Tyler on the exam table.

"GSW to the upper chest. Chest tube with suction. No exit and an internal bleed. That's what Jerri told me. Anything else?"

"Let's hope not."

"Okay. Yell if you need me. And good luck."

"You too."

They left in opposite directions, and Sydney found the crew had already offloaded Kyle onto the stainless-steel table. Jerri now had them wiping down every surface of the room, and the smell of bleach was heavy in the air.

"It's bathroom cleaner with bleach. All I could find. Don't open the cabinets until we're done."

"The ultrasound?"

"In the supply room."

"I'll get it," Mark said. He got to the door before turning. "What does it look like?"

Jerri described it and off he raced. Sydney policed up the bleach and paper towels and picked up where he'd left off.

The monitor began beeping, urging them all to move faster.

33

The highest documented storm surge in the U.S. occurred in 2005 during Hurricane Katrina, when Pass Christian, MS, recorded a 27.8-foot storm surge above mean sea level.

"You okay, Connor?"

Jack had just returned from a bathroom down the hall. He now had a few Steri-Strips holding the cut over his eye closed, and a wad of Kerlix in his mouth to stop the bleeding from his lip. A chemical icepack was held to his eye with one hand, while his other now sported a pair of tongue depressors taped around his broken trigger finger.

Connor turned from the crack in the board he'd been gazing through. The storm was raging outside. He'd stripped off his wet clothes and donned one of the doctor's dress shirts. A few damp towels lay in a pile on the floor. Jack was likewise stripped to the waist, and the bruising over his ribs was very apparent.

"Yeah, I ... You look like shit!"

"I feel like shit," Jack answered. "Help me out here, will ya?"

Connor took the offered ACE bandage Jack had scrounged and wrapped Jack's ribs as tightly as he could handle. After a few deep breaths, he nodded that he was okay.

Jack repeated his question. "You okay, Connor?"

"Yeah ... I guess. Never shot anybody before."

Jack glanced at Frank. He was sitting in a chair and staring at the floor, his thoughts obviously with Kyle next door.

"He had a gun. He shot you. You didn't have any choice, Connor."

"Yeah ... I guess so." He rubbed the spot on his chest where the bullet had struck. There was a small bruise that would soon grow larger.

"Don't beat yourself up. The man made his choice."

"He was just a kid. Stupid. I gave him a chance to give up, but he took another shot at me. Why didn't he give up? I had him dead to rights and he *still* tried to shoot me again. Stupid."

"It's an incredible waste, one you'll never understand. Trying to do so will just make you crazy."

"Yeah ... I guess."

A repeated answer. Jack took a good look at him. He was young, inexperienced, and yet he'd performed well, considering.

"Connor. You did your job. You protected the town and the people in it. It's not your fault those men decided to come here. It's not your fault they shot Kyle. You'll need to remember that and understand it to be true in the next few weeks. None of this comes back to you."

"Yeah, guess so."

"Connor." Jack waited until the man looked at him. "Remember this: You did *not* make the decision to kill those men. Those men, and especially that kid, made that decision *for you*. You had no say in the matter. You understand what I'm telling you here?"

Connor gave it some thought, and Jack saw his face soften. Had he gotten through? It would take a few days to really know for sure. Maybe Frank could help him with that. He stuck the icepack back over his eye and watched Connor straighten up and return to the window. He was standing straighter, his shoulders no longer slumped in defeat. Maybe he did understand what Jack was saying.

Jack turned and saw the medic—what was his name? Steve?—talking softly with Tyler. Jack was about to find a chair and join Frank when the medic left the room and walked toward him.

"Sir?"

"Jack."

"I'm Steve. You're FBI?"

"That's right."

"He wants to talk to you."

Jack entered the room with Steve and found Tyler on the table with oxygen tubing in his nose. His color was poor, but his eyes were bright.

"Agent Turner?"

"Mr. Randall. Forgive me for not standing."

"Quite all right."

Tyler motioned to Jack's face. "Sanford?"

"I'm sorry?"

"The big guy with the tattoos?"

"Oh. Yes, he, uh ... he won't be a problem anymore."

"I see." He smiled and motioned to Steve, who pulled out his phone and aimed it at the two of them.

"What's this?" Jack asked.

"I'm gonna talk for a bit, and I need someone to witness it. Get this to a guy named Lyle Smith at the DEA. He'll know what to do with it."

Jack exchanged a look with Steve, who just shrugged and held up the camera until he had both men in the shot.

"Go."

Tyler took a deep breath, looked straight into the camera, and started talking.

SYDNEY DIDN'T LIKE IT.

The smell of bleach was in her nose from the firemen scrubbing every surface, but they were quickly running out of the cleaner. She had halted the stretcher holding Kyle from entering until one of them cleaned the dust from the overhead light, and they had taped a plastic bag over the vents to prevent any more from entering the room. A bottle of laundry bleach had been discovered with an inch of fluid still in the bottom, and they had saved it for the floor. The fumes were so strong that her eyes were watering, but they had no choice but to work through them while the floor dried.

Jerri was using the ultrasound machine to search for the bullet, while Sydney got her equipment ready. The screen gave off a mottled picture as she played it across Kyle's belly. They had cut the wraps to reveal the discolored skin, and Jerri had fought back tears as they rapidly shaved him.

"A lot of blood in there," she said. "It looks like it bounced off his pelvis here ... and tracked up ... There it is!"

Sydney stopped her preparation to look at the screen. The deformed shape of a 9mm round could be seen in the upper left quadrant. She measured the distance with her eyes and frowned.

"Close to the spleen. Lucky in a way."

"Aorta looks intact. Missed the liver and kidneys. If it hit nothing but bowel and omentum ... we may be okay. But I can't rule out a small artery in there somewhere." She placed an X over the spot and then shoved the machine aside.

Mark moved it away. "What do I do?"

Sydney said, "I'm going to intubate him. Once I

have that done, I'll need you to bag him and watch the monitor for us. That and keep an eye on the drips and make sure they stay running."

"Okay."

An IV pole had been scrounged from a room down the hall and now held a bag of saline and one of the precious bags of red blood cells. Jerri had voted in favor of starting the infusion now, before they got started, so they would be ahead a bit before they went in after the bleed. Jerri watched out of the corner of her eye, as Sydney laid out the various drugs and filled syringes. The Diprivan hung on the IV pole as well, ready to flow into the second IV she had installed in Kyle's other arm.

"You've done this before?" Jerri asked.

"Intubate? I can't begin to count how many tubes I've dropped. It's an everyday thing for medics. We do it inside wrecked cars and on flights of stairs, sometimes while it's raining on us. A nice well-lit operating room is a welcome vacation. I'll use the Etomidate to make sure he's out and then the Succinylcholine to paralyze him before tubing him. Once it's secure, I'll start the drip to keep him out. The Sucs will only work short-term, though. After ten minutes or so you may get some reflex muscle contractions, so we better be quick."

"I'll be quick as I can."

Jerri cleaned the ultrasound gel off Kyle's stomach before swabbing it down with Betadine. She scrubbed while Sydney arranged her equipment. She watched as she bent the tube into the shape of a hockey stick and set it on Kyle's chest. Once she was happy, she picked up the first syringe.

"Etomidate in," she announced.

The process was quicker than Jerri had ever seen it done. Sydney pushed one drug and then the other while Mark bagged Kyle with the oxygen attached. Sydney checked the monitor twice before nodding her head for Mark to move. She had the laryngoscope in and the tube in place within seconds and held in a vise grip until Mark attached the bag.

"Hold on," she warned him as she donned her stethoscope with one hand. She listened to the belly.

"Squeeze."

Jerri held her breath as Sydney checked her tube.

"We're good. Give me one more minute."

Jerri probed for landmarks while Sydney secured the tube and then checked it again.

"We're ready here," she announced before moving to the table across from Jerri. Mark took his place at Kyle's head and bagged him. Sydney donned a fresh pair of gloves and took a deep breath.

Out of habit, Jerri looked up at the clock. It was several hours off. A reminder of the desperate measures they were taking.

She picked up the scalpel and held it over Kyle's abdomen. Before she could start, her hands began to tremble. Sydney slowly reached out and held Jerri's hands in hers.

"Okay?"

Jerri took another deep breath. The shaking stopped.

"Yes."

"He needs you to do this, Jerri."

"I ... I know."

Sydney let go and Jerri once again moved in, her hands now rock steady. The skin parted and she traced the mid-line incision down, around the umbilicus, and on for a few inches before returning and going deeper.

"Geez," Mark commented.

Sydney looked up at him. "You okay? Don't pass out on me!"

"I'm okay. Just never seen a surgery before."

"Don't watch us, watch the monitors. That's your job here."

"I got it. Sorry."

With Sydney retracting and Jerri working the blade, they were soon through the layers. The sight that greeted them made them recoil.

The loops of bowel were surrounded by dark patches of clotted blood and threatened to push out of the opening. Jerri dropped the scalpel and began digging the clots out with her fingers, tossing them into a bowl she had scrounged from a cabinet.

"We're going to shift everything left," she told Sydney.

Working together, they moved the loops left and followed the trail of clotted blood deeper into Kyle's abdomen.

"Heartrate's up a bit," Mark warned.

"Squeeze the bag," Sydney replied without looking up.

Mark pumped up the blood pressure cuff she had wrapped around the saline bag, forcing the flow to speed up.

"Suction!"

Sydney handed her the catheter, while Mark powered on the device. She sucked blood free of the area around her probing fingers, and Sydney had no choice but to keep her own head back and not block her light. The suction container was filling fast, and the blood was bright red. An arterial bleed? It was coming out faster than it was going in.

"Jerri?"

"Hold on ..."

The monitor started beeping. Kyle's heart was speeding up in response to the blood loss. His pulse-ox was also crashing.

"Jerri!"

"Almost there ..." The suction tube went dark again with fresh blood.

"I got it!" Jerri called out.

"The bullet?"

"No, the bleed. It's uh ... a lesser gastric, I think. I need a clamp! A Kelly or a stat!" She held out her hand and shook it impatiently, flicking blood across the table.

Sydney grabbed the instrument and slapped it into her hand. The monitor screamed, but she couldn't touch it without contaminating her gloves. Mark was bagging with one hand while he increased the pressure on the saline. It was a race, and there was no time to stop the noise.

"C'mon, you little ... Got it. It's clamped! How we doing?"

They all checked the monitor and held their breath. The numbers paused their upward climb but refused to drop. Sydney checked the IV pole only to see that the blood had run dry.

"I'm out!"

She pulled her hands from Kyle's abdomen and stripped off the bloody gloves and flung them into the corner. She opened the cooler at Mark's feet and snatched out the second bag, hurriedly hanging it next to the empty one. A few seconds later, she re-opened the clamps, and the blood flowed. She stripped the B/P cuff from its position around the bag of saline and wrapped it around Kyle's arm instead.

"Eighty-four over forty-two," she informed them.

"Squeeze it in?" Jerri asked, her hands frozen inside Kyle's gut.

"Do it," she told Mark as she wrapped the cuff back around the bag. She donned another pair of gloves. She returned to her position on the other side of the table and pulled retraction for Jerri.

"What's next?"

"I don't see any other arterial bleeds," Jerri replied. "The omentum is oozing a bit and, there's some perforations of course ... but ..."

"But what?"

"Do I go after the bullet? Do I just tie off this bleed and close him up? Do I close the perforations? I'm not a surgeon, Sydney! I don't know what's best to do."

Sydney didn't either, but she had a plan, one that she used before when no other option presented.

"A smart guy once told me: 'When it all goes to shit, just do one thing at a time.' So, what's next, Jerri?"

Jerri nodded twice, forcing herself to calm down. "Tie off the bleed."

"Okay, then. And after that?"

"Close the perforations."

"Okay, then. Let's get to work."

DOWN THE HALL and a world away, Tyler finished his report. Steve had had to restart his camera a few times, but the narrative was captured. Jack had listened for the first minutes and then stopped him long enough to find something to write on, before allowing him to continue.

"That GPS unit, it's still in the car?" Jack asked.

"Yeah, I mounted it under the mirror, right where we could both reach it, so he'd be tempted to use it. Should be out of the rain even with the doors open. Wallace, the fat dude, he punched in a few addresses and checked a few routes. I didn't have a chance to check it since I was in the back seat, but I know one was in DC and another one was in Baltimore. He checked out Boston, too, I think. He wasn't very familiar with using it, so I'm sure the addresses are still in the memory. If you can get it, and it still works, I bet it will lead you right to where we were going."

"And Jackson?"

"We were shorthanded when we brought it all out from the freezer. He helped us load the product. If any of it is salvageable from the car, or the packages you were throwing, his prints will be on it. You said you left the stuff wrapped up?"

Jack thought hard. He and Frank had been out in the storm and in a hurry.

"I don't think I opened the last box. The plastic was clear, and I just verified what it was through it. If it was sealed tight, it should still be dry."

"Then you have him."

Tyler let out a breath and squirmed on the bed. The interrogation had exhausted him. He closed his eyes.

"That was some good work, Agent Turner," Jack told him.

"You too."

"You okay?"

"Think I might pass out now, if that's okay."

A small whimper opened his eyes, and he saw Aaron standing next to him.

"Hey, little man. You did good. Really good. You take care of your grandma. She needs you. I'll be all right, okay."

Aaron sniffed before reaching out. Tears filled his eyes. He patted Tyler's arm.

"All right, okay?" Tyler asked him.

"All right, okay," the boy answered.

Tyler smiled and closed his eyes.

"Sydney, I ... I can't see. Does it go all the way through?"

"Hold on." She angled the flashlight to the left while retracting with the other hand. The overhead light had proven to be inadequate, so Mark had yelled for Rich. He'd delivered a large Mag

Light, and they were using to find whatever damage the bullet had made. So far, Jerri had sutured and had stapled a few bleeds closed, but they were past time to be done. Sydney couldn't help but glance up every few seconds at the last unit of blood as it emptied from the bag. That and the clock, which mocked her with its frozen hands.

"It's not, looks like it just tore down the side. It looks like a run in a stocking. What do you do for that?"

"Well—"

Jerri's reply was cut off by a hard gust hitting the building. The lights flickered and then died.

"No! We're so close! Not now!"

"Jack!"

END

I welcome any comments, feedback, or questions at randall.wood@scribecount.

I also welcome any input pertaining to mistakes I may have missed, not necessarily typos or grammar, as they are self-explanatory, but mistakes about procedures or content. Mistakes of this nature tend to pull the reader out of the story and make it less enjoyable. If you should find such an error, please fire off an email in my direction. The beauty of e-books and print-on-demand books is that they can always be updated to fix such things.

I also welcome any and all reviews, with one small request. With the controversy over fake reviews garnering so much attention, it gives your review greater credibility if you do so in your real name and with the verified purchase icon. Doing so helps readers call honest attention to their favorite writers and keeps the integrity of the online review process intact.

Who knows? Your review may end up on the back of the next book.

You can find links to purchase all the Jack Randall Thrillers, including links to purchase directly from me at a discount, at http://randall woodauthor.com/universal-link.

What happens to Jack?

Jack and his crew venture on in the subsequent books in the series. The best place to find out more, and get those books at a discount, is by visiting my website at https://randallwoodauthor. com/books/. There you will find the complete library of my works, bonus content such as short stories and character bios, cool swag, books that are unavailable anywhere else, and an inside look at how I create these stories.

What happens to Danny?

Sign up for my email list at https://randallwoodau thor.com/newsletter/ and you'll get a free novel with Danny's latest adventure plus additional content, previews of coming books, discount offers, and a whole lot more.

Want the latest book the minute it's ready?

We can do that too. Just opt-in to the subscription option at https://randallwoodauthor.com/subscrip tion/ and get the latest book automatically delivered to you the day it comes out, months before it hits the shelves anywhere else.

Want to know even more?

You can also learn about the places, organizations, government workings, weapons, gear, and law enforcement tactics used in the books, by visiting my Facebook page at Randall Wood Author.

Stay in touch!

Sign up for my email newsletter at https://randall woodauthor.com/newsletter/

Subscribe at https://randallwoodauthor.com/subscription/

Follow me on Facebook at Randall Wood Author.

I welcome any comments, feedback, or questions at randall.wood@scribecount.com.

Want a sneak peak at Jack's next adventure?

Read on!

A SNEAK PEEK AT BOOK 9: RENAISSANCE

"Fantastic gripping drama just what you always get from this author."—*Alan Kent*

RENAISSANCE: CHAPTER 1

"Let us remember we are all part of one American family. We are united in common values, and that includes belief in equality under the law, basic respect for public order, and the right of peaceful protest."

—*Barack Obama*

The cab let them out in front of the building, and Jack grumbled a little when

Sydney grabbed his arm as he got out. The stitches over his eye and the splint on his arm, combined with the bruising, made him a bit of a sight. A few passing agents eyeballed him curiously as they made their way inside. Jack and Sydney crossed the lobby and walked over the seal on the floor to the front desk. Karen looked up and her mouth fell open.

"My god, Jack. Are you okay?"

"I'm fine, Karen. Had a little run in with some bad guys down in Florida."

"We heard. But I ... Are you sure you don't need a few days off?"

Jack gave her his best disarming smile. Karen had been at the front desk of the building for many years and couldn't help regarding the agents as her own children.

"No, it looks worse than it is; the doc says I'm fine," he lied. "And duty calls."

"Okay. I'd maybe get a second opinion if I were you. How are you, Sydney?"

"A little beat up, but Jack got the worst of it. Is Deacon in his office?"

"Yes, and I was told to inform him of your arrival. Are you heading straight up?"

"Yes."

"Okay. Good luck."

They passed through the security gate and headed for the elevators, both of them still exhausted from their ordeal in Florida. Sydney reluctantly punched the button for the top floor and then let herself fall back against the wall with a sigh.

"A massage, at an all-day spa. Someplace with no phones."

"I said all right the first dozen times," Jack replied.

"Someplace with wine."

"Okay." Jack had promised her a day off at a spa after she'd pointed out repeatedly that their injuries were all his fault for choosing to drive through a hurricane. Jack had quickly given in just to placate her. He was hurting himself, but he knew there was not going to be any time for a spa day. They had come straight from the airport to the Hoover building to report in. Luckily, Debra had gone to the beach house to batten down the hatches in case Hurricane Nancy decided to work its way up the coast. He'd called her on the way into town, and she was already on her way. He'd have that do deal with after they met with Deacon.

It was going to be an ass chewing. Like a disobedient teenager, Jack had refused to come home when told to and instead gone off to Florida to pursue the latest Twelve Shepherds' target. The encounter with the drug traffickers could not have been predicted, but he doubted that was going to lessen their boss's wrath any. Maybe his injuries would help a little? Either way, they would soon find out.

He turned his head to check on his partner. She was leaning against the wall with her eyes closed, grabbing whatever rest she could before the doors opened. He didn't blame her. They had been through two days of hell in Homeland, and the flight from Jacksonville to DC had been too short and bumpy to get any real rest. The hurricane was out to sea now, but its reach was still sufficient to make their flight a miserable one. The hours of inactivity had done nothing but allow their battered muscles to cramp and stiffen, and they both now made noises when they sat or got up. It was like they had each aged twenty years.

"You okay?"

Sydney opened her eyes. "Yeah, a little stiff, but—"

"No, I mean ... are you okay?"

She turned and looked at him. It wasn't just a casual question. In the last few days she had survived getting shot at, beaten up, held hostage, and then almost drown in a sinking car. It was a lot for anyone, even a seasoned agent, to take.

"I ... I'll know in a couple of days if I'm not, I guess." She shrugged.

"Where's Lenny?" Jack asked. Sydney's current boyfriend was an Interpol agent based in France. The two of them had been trying hard to make a long-distance relationship work.

"I sent him a text. He's flying in on Sunday."

"Good."

Before any more could be said, the doors opened.

"Let's get this over with." Jack said as he led her off the elevator and down the hall. A passing secretary glanced at Jack's face and then smiled a nervous apology before quickly moving off on her way.

"Is my face really that bad?" he asked Sydney.

"Compared to what?"

Before Jack could answer they arrived at the office and were met by Margaret's shocked face.

"Jack, my god. You look worse than Greg! What the hell is going on down there?"

"I ... you know, Margaret. I'm fine, really, and also a little tired of explaining that. Can you be a dear and just accept that, so we can move on to the next thing? I'll be happy to tell everyone the whole story later."

He got a sour look for that, but she quickly nodded. "He's inside. They're expecting you."

"Thanks." Jack moved past her, and Margaret used the moment to shoot Sydney a questioning look. She gave her a nod of reassurance and another when Margaret pointed at her. They would catch up later, her look said.

Jack walked in to find Deacon standing behind his desk with Larry and Greg sat in the corner. Greg had a bandage on his head, and another on his neck, but other than that, he was dressed in a clean suit and sporting a fresh haircut. Larry looked his usual disheveled self, and he stood at the sight of the two of them entering.

"Jack, you two okay?"

Jack waved to Sydney. "Your turn."

"We're fine, guys. Jack got in a fight, and I almost drown, but other than that, it's just come cuts and bruises. We'll live. How're you doing, Greg?"

"I still gotta headache, but I'm good."

"Laurie?"

"At home with her ankle up. You two just can't stay out of trouble, can you?"

"It wasn't anything we planned; the guys opened up on a cop right in front of us. It became a running shoot-out and then just got worse from there. I'm sorry for the delay, sir, but it just couldn't be helped."

Deacon rounded the desk and walked over until he was standing in front of them both. He'd read the hasty one-page report Jack had sent from the plane, as well as the report filed by the local police, and now looked them both over from head to toe. Seeing now that Jack had sugar-coated their injuries, he couldn't help but shake his head as he addressed them.

"I had a royal ass-chewing all prepared and ready to let fly, but Margaret tells me this room has heard enough cursing in the last twenty-four hours to last a year. You two okay? Seriously?"

"Yes, sir."

"How's that local sheriff doing?"

Sydney answered that one. "He's stable. He coded on us once, after we got him closed up, but we got him back. Tyler deteriorated on the ride to Jacksonville. They're both still in critical condition, but the doctor there was optimistic."

"Good. Some things happened while you were gone."

Deacon pointed to the TV in the corner. It was on mute, but that didn't stop them from seeing that Jack and Sydney were the top story of the day.

Scenes from the streets of Homeland traded spots with footage of Jack and Sydney leaving the hospital. Pictures of them in New York and again in Niagara Falls soon followed.

"You're getting a lot of airtime. Fortunately, it may be just the thing you need right now."

Jack traded a questioning look with Sydney and then another with Larry, who frowned. Whatever his boss's remark meant, it was something Jack wasn't going to like.

"You have any clean clothes here?" Deacon asked.

"Uh ... yeah. I have a spare suit in my office. Syd?"

"I have some downstairs. Are we going somewhere?"

Deacon turned back toward his desk and answered the question on the way.

"The White House. Go get dressed and meet me downstairs. The president wants to see you."

"I ... " Jack glanced at Greg, who waved his question off. Don't question, just go, his gesture said.

"Okay. Ten minutes?"

"Make it less. The man's waiting."

He and Sydney turned to leave.

"I'll walk you." Larry said, jumping up to follow.

The three of them walked in silence until they were back on the elevator. Once again, Sydney pushed the button and then collapsed against the wall as the doors closed.

"Okay, what's going on?" Jack asked.

"Remember that whole 'face of the investigation' thing you said I wouldn't have to do?"

"Yeah?"

"You were right."

CARTER WOKE when the rocking of the railcar diminished. The train was slowing down. He gazed out the window to see them entering the edge of the city, and then examined the GPS's tiny screen to confirm it was indeed Denver. They had passed through Pueblo and Colorado Springs without stopping, and both he and Tye had relaxed after, confident that their car was going to make it all the way. Tye's enjoyment of the modern car and its luxurious leather interior was short-lived, as the mild rocking and warm seat soon had him nodding off. It had given Carter time to think.

There was a Shepherd's cache in Denver. One that any of them could access if needed. It was small and held no vehicles; just the necessities to assist one of them if they were on the run. It was monitored by William, just like all the others, so if used, he would immediately know. Carter had been thinking about the cache and weighing the risks of visiting it for the entire trip up from El Paso. If Dayton's intent had been to take him out, he could be waiting for him there, but Carter doubted it. The things happening in the paper had him wondering about the General and the mission. Was it time? Had Rubicon been activated? He didn't know. He needed information, and for that there was only one place to go.

The flashing lights and ringing bells of a major road crossing flashed through the interior and across Tye's face. It was enough to make him stir.

"Where we at?"

"Denver. Should we be thinking about getting ready to get off?"

Tye rubbed his eyes and took a good look at the passing scenery before replying.

"Got about ... fifteen minutes, I'd say. Thas if they goin' to the yard they did last time. I was on a box then, so not sure."

Carter slid down in the seat as they passed another busy intersection. It wouldn't do good to be seen riding in the car right now. Someone could call it in and have the cops waiting when the train stopped. There was really nothing to see but the lights of city's suburbs passing by anyway. He watched their progress on the tiny map instead. He had dimmed its brightness to its lowest setting hours ago.

"So, we get off in the yard," Carter said. "Then what?"

"Food would be good. There's a kitchen not too far from there. Be open in a few hours."

"After that?"

"Hell, I dunno. I take it one problem at a time, ya know?" Tye laughed.

Carter rubbed his growing beard. It was still in the itchy phase, and he was dealing with it. He thought about how he might separate himself from Tye—at least long enough for him to visit the cache.

"Is there somewhere you hang out around here?"

"Stayed a few times at a mission when the snow was bad and the trains weren't running. It wasn't a bad place, just not my thing. Likes to keep moving, but the snow don't care about that, I guess. Why?"

"I got an old friend, here. He may have a few spare dollars. Thought I might stop by."

"Hmmm. You sure? In my experience, it's a good way to lose the friend."

"Old Marine Corps buddy."

"Oh, well, thas different. At least for a few visits. I s'pose I could hang around a bit."

Carter turned to the GPS and played with the buttons. Tye watched for a minute before losing interest and taking in the passing buildings. Carter found the yard they were travelling to and then explored the area around it. Like in most cities, it was a mixture of things. The railroad had been built early, and the town had grown around it. The yard was now surrounded by three major highways in what would now be called an industrial section. He saw a lumber yard and distribution complex for the Coors Brewing Company nearby. Several warehouses. After that, it was a short walk to the suburbs in one direction, and downtown in the other.

"You see that Pepsi place, you know we getting close." Tye said.

Carter saw the Pepsi Center on the map and nodded. "Got ya."

He kept scanning the downtown area until he found it. It was another ten blocks or so, but that was nothing to Carter. Just south of the park, he found the library. Moving the map around, he memorized the route and the major landmarks before moving on and locating the storage facility. It would be another schlep from there and even farther back to the yard after. Could he do all that in one afternoon? Was it best to keep traveling with Tye? He'd have options after the cache. Maybe best to think about them once he was in and out safely.

"Where this mission at?" Carter was adopting Tye's poor English without realizing it.

"Oh, about a half mile towards town. Just past the stadium and then south a few blocks."

On the way, Carter thought. *Good*. He'd drop Tye off there and then continue on. He checked the clock in the corner of the dashboard. Three hours until sunrise. He wanted to be through the city and waiting when the place opened. If the distances were easy to navigate, he should have no problem.

"There she is." Tye pointed.

Carter looked up in time to see the stadium appear on their right, its rust-colored façade lit up by several lights even at this early morning hour. It faded away behind them as the train slowed and then passed under a major road.

"We best be gittin' out," Tye said.

"Right."

They both popped the doors and slipped out onto the railcar itself. The cold night air found its way inside their clothes, and they both shivered as they hunkered down behind the Lexus. Carter reached up and returned the keys to their previous hiding place, before huddling on the steel next to Tye.

"Gonna have to remember that key trick; this'a been a bad ride without 'em," Tye remarked.

"Yeah, I guess so. Didn't think it'd be this cold."

"We been going uphill for the past four hours," Tye said.

"You can tell."

They sat in silence as the train slowed further and finally stopped. Tye hopped off with a practiced motion and immediately set off in the direction of the downtown high rises. Carter followed with only one look back toward the engine. Nobody emerged to challenge them, so he kept walking. Soon they were across the yard and through a convenient hole in the fence. It seemed like the buildings were right in front of them.

"I'll meet up with you at the mission."

"Okay." Tye shrugged.

Carter left his friend at the first street corner

they came to and broke away to the south. Once he was out of sight, he quickened his pace to the mile-eating stride of the infantry soldier. He kept to the shadows and moved with purpose, following the map in his head until he came upon his destination.

The Denver Public Library. He walked its perimeter and finally decided on a dark corner belonging to the art museum next door to wait in. He checked his watch before settling back. A few hours. He made sure the rising sun wouldn't reveal his location too soon and then looked for any company which might find him interesting. He ruled out both, before closing his eyes and letting himself relax a bit.

He was about to take a major risk, one that could end in disaster—or something else. Something he wasn't sure of yet.

RENAISSANCE: CHAPTER 2

"There may be times when we are powerless to prevent injustice, but there must never be a time when we fail to protest."

—*Elie Wiesel*

J ack left Sydney on the elevator to go to her office in the basement while he and Larry walked off in the direction of his. They both

kept their mouths shut until they got to it, and Jack quickly opened the door before motioning Larry inside.

"Okay, what's going on?" Larry said.

Larry walked to Jack's desk and planted his butt on its edge. Jack noticed a pile of mail on its surface and forced himself to look away. It was not unusual. If the box on the wall outside his door got too full, the night security team would move it inside. As much as he wanted to paw through it right now, he had to wait. For a moment, he considered telling Larry about the message but discarded the idea quickly. He didn't know enough yet.

"You mean with your meeting?"

"Yes, with the meeting. It's more than just to brief them on what happened, isn't it? Why's Deacon being cagey?"

"I'm guessing he made you the same deal he made me, and now he has to go back on it."

Jack walked to the closet while stripping off his shirt. Inside, he found two still in the plastic from the dry cleaner and breathed a sigh of relief. He couldn't remember if he had restocked the closet or not. Maybe Margaret had conspired with Debra? It wouldn't be the first time.

"It's become a popularity contest—at least that's what they think. They've decided that

Deacon is too much of an official face. With the Director in the hospital and unlikely to return, he's no longer the face of the investigation. I mean, the people expect him to be in charge. Nobody is surprised or ... intrigued, I guess, when they see him on TV giving a briefing. That, and, well, you know."

"What?"

"He looks too ... bureaucratic. Another old white guy in a suit. One that looks like he should be behind a desk. They want someone less, I don't know, rigid? Is that the word I'm looking for?"

Jack worked on getting the suit on over his fractured ribs and sore muscles. He grimaced while he pulled a new shirt on and crunched this new information. He tugged too hard and a button popped off. Cursing himself, he stripped off the shirt and reached for the second.

"What you're telling me is that I'm the new face of the investigation?"

"Pretty much. Like Sydney said, you're already famous."

Jack slipped a tie over his head and snugged it down.

"How's my hair?"

Larry gave him a grin. "You're asking me for hair advice?"

Jack eyeballed Larry's head and his perpetually mussed mop of hair. "Good point."

"If you really want to know, I think the style goes well with the bandages and sutures. It's a defined look."

Jack finished with the tie and put on the jacket before standing in front of the mirror on the inside of the closet door. He tried to smooth the hair into place, but the bandages only allowed him so much. A few strands still stuck up no matter how hard he tried. The bruises on his jaw, combined with the sutures and bandage over his eye, seemed to nullify the hair anyway. Screw it. He gave up.

"Why Sydney?"

"What do you mean?"

"Deacon said both of us. Why her?"

Larry shrugged. "She's famous, too. Maybe not at your level, but they want her standing next to you just the same, I imagine."

"Show the public we're taking it seriously, that kind of thing?"

"I imagine you'll get all this from Deacon on the ride in."

"Yeah ... all right. Let's you and I have another drink real soon. Okay?"

"Sure."

With that, Jack filled his pockets with his keys,

his wallet, and a small notebook, before they both filed out of the room. Jack's gaze landed on the pile of mail sitting on the desk as he pulled the door shut. He'd be back here soon to examine it.

Larry waked him to the elevator. The doors quickly parted, and Jack hopped on.

"Any advice?" Jack said.

"Keep your mouth as shut as possible. Write everything down the minute you leave."

The doors started to close.

"Will do."

RENAISSANCE: CHAPTER 3

"To sin by silence, when we should protest, Makes cowards out of men."

—Ella Wheeler Wilcox

The clang of the trashcan lid hitting the sidewalk woke him, and he flinched before seeing the man attending to it. The

sun was up, and a sliver of it stabbed its way between the two buildings and warmed his feet. He
shook the cobwebs from his mind and scanned his
surroundings. It was still quiet, Carter noticed, and
he wondered why. This was still the downtown
area, and it should have been busy with people on
their way to work. Odd. He got to his feet and
checked the watch.

Saturday. He had lost track. 8:12 am. The place
should be open. He looked up to see the man
finish with his trash duties. He nodded a polite
greeting in Carter's direction, before climbing the
steps and disappearing inside. Carter moved to
follow.

Inside, he found an open lobby with several
signs and an empty desk surrounded by a low
wall. As he gazed about, a middle-aged woman
appeared with a stack of books piled high. She attempted to get through the narrow opening to the
desk and the books fell. Carter leaped forward in
time to save most of them, but some made it all the
way to the ground. The woman stepped back on
seeing his size and attire, but Carter ignored her
look and offered the books with a friendly smile.

"Here you go."

"I ... Thank you." She took the books and

stepped back. She smiled nervously as she rounded the desk, and Carter wondered how bad he looked.

"Ma'am, I was just hoping to check my email, real quick?" he told her. "Just that, and I'll be on my way."

The woman relaxed a bit at his politeness and pleasant tone. She pointed to a room off to the left.

"You can use one of the computers in there. The password and rules are on the wall."

"Okay, thanks. I won't be long."

She just smiled and nodded before glancing across the lobby. Carter turned and saw the trash man watching from the hallway. He gave him a nod and smile, before moving off to the computers' room. He chose a seat from which he could look out through a window at the lobby and through the front door. The woman returned to her stack of books, and the man began sweeping the lobby after a few words with her. Nobody reached for a phone.

Good.

After a few tries, he managed to get online and input the password. The message was waiting, just as he expected. He read it twice before sitting back and giving it some thought.

The message urged him to make contact. It also gave updates on the FBI and their pursuit of him. Nothing about the rail lines was mentioned. Jack Randall was being called back to DC. Were they removing him from the case? Carter rubbed his knuckles, still sore from when he had knocked the man out back at his storage area and thought about the agent who had interrogated him in the jail cell. The man was smart, Carter had to give him that, and he had treated Carter with respect, despite the fact that he was his prisoner. In the end, Carter had had no choice but to respect the man. He was a formidable enemy; of that, he had no doubt.

But what of the Shepherds? Were they his enemy, too, now? Carter's days with them were over. His face was known, and like an undercover cop who had been exposed, he was no longer any good for missions. So why were they calling him in? Did Dayton merely wish to keep him out of the hands of the FBI? Or was it to permanently remove him, as he was now too great a risk? Or did they have other jobs he would be good for? Could he still contribute to the mission? Perhaps. How, he wasn't sure, but it was a possibility.

What were his alternatives? A life on the run? Where would he go? Africa came to mind first, for the simple fact that he would be able to blend in easier. Maybe find an ex-pat community to join while he learned the local language? South Africa, maybe. Or Namibia.

He shook his head at the thoughts. There was no way he was going to Africa, and he knew it. It just ... wasn't in his nature. Besides, he wanted answers, on his own terms, and there was only one way to get them.

He left the email site behind and punched up a map of the pacific northwest. After dragging and zooming around for ten minutes, he finally turned on the satellite view. He explored the area for several minutes, writing down names and landmarks on a piece of copy paper. He then expanded the search, looking for railway lines. The closest yard was a town called West Glacier. He wrote it down and underlined it. It was his new destination.

A couple of students walked in and gave him a look before settling in behind a pair of monitors across the room. Carter kept an eye in that direction and tried to get caught up on the news. Protests were happening. A lot of them. What that meant, he couldn't be sure. Was it Rubicon? Had the Shepherds launched it? Or were they just spontaneous gatherings prompted by the issues the Shepherds were uncovering? He had no way of knowing.

He caught the first student looking his way again, and determined it was time to go. He pocketed the paper and logged off, before rising and heading for the nearest exit. He caught the man, in the reflection of the glass, aiming a phone his way. Or was he just holding it? Carter couldn't tell. He kept his back turned and walked out, past the now empty desk and on out the door into the morning sun.

He would find Tye. But only after he made a run to the storage unit. He rounded the building and moved in the opposite direction of his destination for a few blocks, before circling back and changing course. Nobody followed him, but he found the students in the computer room a bit worrisome. Had he been recognized? There was no way to be sure. He increased his pace just the same.

A block later, he heard a siren. He stopped and listened closer before determining that it was headed his way.

"Shit."

DEACON'S DRIVER stood next to the running limo with the door to the rear open. Inside, Deacon was sat in the back with a file in his hand. Sydney waited in the seat opposite him with a nervous look on her face. Jack wasted no time and slide in next to him.

"What's on the agenda?" Jack asked his boss.

"Larry filled you in, did he?"

"A little."

Deacon flipped the file shut and tossed it on the seat next to him in disgust.

"They're reneging on the deal. Evidently, now that I'm the acting Director, I'm no longer pretty enough to be in charge of the investigation. At least the public side of it. They want you. I wouldn't be surprised if they have you booked on the morning shows, come Sunday."

"Larry suspected."

"This was not my idea, Jack; they came up with this all on their own. It stinks of Parker, but it could have been Cook, too."

The car pulled out onto the streets of DC and began weaving through traffic. Protestors soon appeared, and they all examined them as they walked the streets in groups of two and three, silently holding their signs as they circled the area. A few shouted at their car as it zipped by. The driver was good, keeping the car away from the curb and out of range of any attack. They hardly felt the application of the brakes as he weaved through the traffic. After two turns, they were almost at their destination. Jack forced his attention back inside the car.

"What's the difference?"

"I'm ... not sure. But something is off. Parker is a political animal through and through. Cook is ... something else. Let's be very careful in there, Jack. I'm not sure what their real motivation is here. We, or you, may be getting set up to take the fall. If so, I'm not going to just roll over and take it."

Jack thought about it as he exchanged a look with Sydney. It was what she had predicted back in California.

Deacon spoke rapidly as they pulled up to the gate. "If they suggest anything that's out of bounds —anything at all—I'm ready to hand over my resignation. Just so you know. You'll have to make your own decision; I'm just letting you know where I stand."

"Yes, sir."

"Yes, sir." Sydney echoed.

"Okay. Let's go see the man."

HE QUICKLY SCANNED THE AREA, but the options were few. Between a pair of dumpsters, an ally led off a short distance away, and he ducked there. Gazing up at the building, he saw that the windows had all been bricked in some time ago. Encouraged by that, he ducked down behind the dumpster and opened his backpack.

Colors. He was switching every one he could. The black coat was wadded up and replaced by the fat man's blue shirt. The red ball cap landed on his head, and he tucked the shirt in and smoothed the wrinkles best he could. The backpack was moved from his back to his hand. Color of clothes were the first thing cops and people describing others used.

He waited.

Less than a minute later, the police unit roared past the mouth of the ally. Carter immediately picked up the backpack and walked to the ally entrance. The car had disappeared around the corner leading to the library, and Carter moved out quickly, walking with purpose while still being as casual as he could. He caught up to a threesome of young males with backpacks of their own heading in the same direction, and he got as close as he could to them without rousing their suspicion. They were all dividing their time between the phones in their hands and the sidewalk in front of them, and Carter used that to help him blend in.

Another police car came down the street. Carter closed ranks on the three men in front of him and tried not to look in the officers' direction. He saw the officers gaze pass over the group and held his breath when he left his line of sight. After a half block, he couldn't stand it any longer and glanced behind him, only to see that the cop had continued on without slowing.

"E and E," he mumbled. At the next intersection, he stood with the group at the light and then crossed with them before breaking away and heading north.

The storage unit was several blocks away. If he could make it there, he would have a number of options. He was contemplating them, when the police car appeared at the next intersection in front of him.

The cop was looking right at him.

Want to know what happens next?
Get your copy of *RENAISSANCE* direct from

the author at https://randallwoodauthor.com/prod
uct/renaissance-a-jack-randall-thriller/!

RENAISSANCE is also available on all major
online retailers; you'll find links at http://randall
woodauthor.com/universal-links.

(Did I mention the books are discounted if you
buy directly from me?)

ABOUT THE AUTHOR

Randall Wood is the author of the bestselling Jack Randall series of thrillers and the Half a World Post-Apocalyptic series. He is also the founder and CEO of ScribeCount, a data aggregation company that provides sales dashboards, marketing analytics, and a variety of other services to the author community.

When he's not penning stories or crunching numbers, he and his wife divide their time between the beaches of south Florida and the mountains of western North Carolina. Whether they are hiking or swimming they are usually accompanied by Henry their giant of a Great Dane.

Randall welcomes readers to his website at www.randallwoodauthor.com and his fellow writers to ScribeCount at www.scribecount.com, where he tries hard to not refer to himself in the third person.